THE D'ARTHEZ CASE

translated from the German by
MICHAEL LEBECK

FARRAR, STRAUS & GIROUX
New York

The D'Arthez Case

by Hans Erich Nossack

*Creating a clown like that
is no laughing matter, due to
his exaggerated reality.*
          Max Beckmann

THE D'ARTHEZ CASE

one

Asked if he were in the habit of making notes or keeping a journal, d'Arthez replied, "Now, I ask you, wouldn't that be rather indiscreet for one of us?"

Of course Chief Inspector Glatschke was too experienced an official to register even faint surprise at such an answer; that is, surprise detectable by the author of this report, who was only indirectly present at this encounter. In fact, the author was sitting with earphones on his head next door in a dark cubbyhole where interrogations were taped, and fully expected Dr. Glatschke to counter d'Arthez's surprising reply immediately with a further question. It would have been enough if he had raised an eyebrow, so to speak, and with irony quipped, "Indiscreet?" But this did not occur. Apart from Dr. Glatschke's total lack of humor, his seeming irritation with another aspect of d'Arthez's answer and attitude made him prefer to drop this particular line of inquiry.

What had irritated Glatschke became clear soon afterward. It was not the astonishing word "indiscreet"—which one might have suspected—but the phrase "one of us." As soon as d'Arthez had left, Dr. Glatschke played the tape repeatedly. Because it disturbed him so, the following day he listened to it twice more. Several colleagues were asked to comment on the tape, as was an expert from the regular police, who had a reputation for his technique in interrogations. Obviously Dr. Glatschke felt it was of the utmost importance to ascertain whether or not the phrase "one of us" presupposed the existence of a secret society or a subversive group. For a microphone often picks up nuances that escape the human ear in direct confrontation.

The tape, however, betrayed not the slightest variation in tone or dynamics. The suspicious phrase received no unconscious emphasis. The only thing the microphone had caught was a hint of a Saxon accent. Its effect was in no way comic. And besides, there was documentary evidence that d'Arthez had grown up and gone to school in Dresden. According to his papers, he had been born there as well, early in 1911, a few months after the return of his parents from their honeymoon in New York. For his father the trip to the United States had another purpose besides pleasure. He wanted to gather information about the state of the synthetic-fiber industry and to find a New York bank to help him finance the modernization of his Dresden plant. His mother too is said to have enjoyed excellent connections with foreign financial circles, particularly American. She had been born into a family of well-to-do industrialists. It is quite possible that this had some bearing on the satisfactory conclusion of these negotiations.

Strangely enough, in the archives both place and date of birth had been queried. In the opinion of the Secret Service, this indicated the possibility of an old and incredibly cunning forgery. But due to the many intervening wars during which cities and archives vanished and to the continual flux of governmental ideology—an even more important factor—this could no longer be demonstrated. D'Arthez himself claimed that such questions were irrelevant. In an interview on the occasion of his fiftieth birthday, he expressed himself as follows: "One's date of birth is fixed by totally indifferent chance. Instead, far more important is one's date of death. Most of us have been mistaken about that. Nor can I, gentlemen, provide you with reliable information." As always, d'Arthez makes it difficult for us to decide whether he was merely trying to avoid a reporter's embarrassing questions. Or did he mean what he said? This question will be dealt with later.

For the present let it be mentioned that the very day on which he interrogated d'Arthez, Dr. Glatschke also celebrated a birthday—his forty-sixth, as documented by the icing on a cake that the entire staff contributed to. On this occasion he had invited several of his colleagues and subordinates to his official residence, one of a row of houses with a minuscule garden in a suburb north of Frankfurt. For a glass of wine after supper, as he put it in the invitation. Among the guests was the author of this report, who in the remaining pages shall be termed "the narrator." Being a junior subordinate, of course, he could not think of declining. The whole department was aware of Frau Glatschke's having a cousin in the Foreign Office and of how she had worked with female tenacity for her husband's transfer to Bonn and the advancement it meant. It was she who had asked the narrator in the small foyer where they were dancing—yet another duty of the junior subordinate—if there

5

hadn't been some unpleasantness at the office that day. But when the narrator replied, according to the protocol he had been taught, "Not that I know of, madame—the usual routine," she tapped him on the shoulder coquettishly and exclaimed, "Oh, all this pussyfooting!" Nevertheless, even before dinner a hint of what had caused the head of the family's ill humor seemed to have filtered down, since his daughter too had noticed something. She was a good-humored girl of eighteen with whom it was considerably more pleasant to dance. She never bothered her head about her mother's ambitious plans. "What sort of Saxon did you have in today?" she asked. Her father had reacted to her calling him away from the day's mail to dinner by slamming his hand on his desk and hissing, "That blasted Saxon!" His exclamation was all the stranger since Dr. Glatschke came from Merseburg in Saxony, and only the end of the war had brought him to the West. In fact, the name Glatschke betrays his Slavic origins. Where his wife was born has slipped the narrator's mind, but that she was named Sieglinde was no secret, for the staff whispered this name often when gossiping about the boss. Such given names are determined by the generation to which one belongs. Her parents must have been wild about Wagner, the Nibelungen and very probably the Nazis.

In much the same way, their daughter's name was Irmgard. She went right on talking. "Papa was terribly insulted. As we entered the dining room he said, 'Small wonder the Nazis chucked the bugger in a concentration camp. I'd have done the same. Well, skip it. We'll be on to him soon.'—Now, that must be one dangerous Saxon. Too bad you weren't there. But then luckily we had *crème russe*—that's Papa's favorite dessert." At a quarter to twelve the narrator felt he could leave. He expressed his gratitude for a pleasant evening—and the honor.

The only excuse for including all this is the emotional element it contributed to the narrator's decision to make these notes. Although this report is not concerned with the narrator but only with d'Arthez, it might still be fitting if it began with the statement that the day of this interrogation and the evening at Glatschke's constituted a turning point in the narrator's life. Everything the narrator knows—or believes he knows—about d'Arthez he owes to the files of Security or other departments, or to tapes, TV shows, interviews with the press, picture biographies and similar publications about this phenomenon called d'Arthez. In other words, his information is all second- or third-hand at best. That is why, and not for reasons of false modesty, the compiler of this report appears here as "the narrator." Moreover, by calling himself the narrator, he is sticking to his trade, so to speak; for it was as a *referendar* that he worked with Security for a time; and where "reporter" would suggest a journalist, this title is more accurately translated as "narrator."

Documents, of course, were of dubious value for this study. Much more important were the firsthand impressions that the narrator received from the information conveyed to him by persons who are or once were close to d'Arthez. Not even the fact that their testimony was emotionally colored lessens its value. Here two persons in particular deserve mention, persons with whom the narrator came into contact in Frankfurt during the preliminary stage of the compilation of this report: Edith Nasemann, d'Arthez's daughter, and his friend Lambert. The narrator will not pass over in silence the debt of gratitude he owes these two for the readiness and candor with which they discussed father and friend. And thus the narrator requests that his attempt to reproduce their testimony as near to verbatim as possible not be considered an indiscretion.

Lambert in particular did everything in his power to hinder the progress of this report once he learned of the narrator's plan. He heaped abuse and cynical remarks upon the narrator in the expectation that this would turn him from his purpose or discourage him. But this very defensiveness brought much fresh material to light. Lambert's reaction, undertaken not to protect himself but solely in the interest of his friend, is part of the problem itself. For instance, he reproached the narrator with cowardice because he chose to appear in this report under the designation of narrator. "What arrogance!" he cried. "You haven't the least right to anonymity. For that something more is required. What do *you* have either to conceal or to forget? Why can't you say *I*? Saying *I* is an excellent way to disguise your own emptiness!"

The ego as pseudonym? Those were bitter words from an embittered man who had fled into the role of a rather odd outsider. But bitter for the narrator as well, for Lambert had mercilessly laid bare his motive in compiling this report.

"Narrator? What's it to you? How can you expect to narrate something that you neither saw nor participated in? A past that doesn't belong to you, and won't be spoken of by those whose past it is. Why don't you write the narrative of your own lack of a past? Now *that* would be something. A tale in the telling of which you would see that nothing had happened worth telling. A mirror in which nothing shows but the historical silvering with which your epoch festoons itself, but no face, no person, nothing one could care for or wish to save. Or, if you please, why not write about this waiting room?"

As a matter of record, this conversation took place in the waiting room of the Central Station in Frankfurt. "Describe the hustle and bustle of people who no longer know how to despair. There's a theme for you. There's a timetable, isn't there? A loudspeaker announces the trains. So why despair? That would be old-fashioned. That woman over there is off to visit her children, you can tell from the presents she's dragging along. And the children? They are waiting in the station of some little town. They have had to make a few changes in their arrangements so that Mother will have a room and a bed of her own. They don't have much space themselves. It's a nuisance. Oh well, two weeks of it won't kill them. Did you buy a round-trip ticket, Mama? It's cheaper. Back where? Home? Home hasn't existed now for ages, but there is the timetable and one can depend on that. Why, even rail accidents are a thing of the past. Everything is that safe! Why don't you write about the security agency you work for? National security and still no nation . . . Now *that* would be a theme! Do you at least have the first sentence?"

Now, twenty or thirty years previously Lambert had written a couple of best sellers. He called them trash, and no history of contemporary literature so much as mentions them. His question alluded to a hypothesis—which perhaps he no longer seriously entertained—that in the success of a book everything depends on the first sentence. If you have the opening sentence, you have the whole book—something to that effect. Before the narrator finished assuring him that he did not intend writing a *novel*, Lambert had obviously stopped listening.

"Yes, here's a great way to begin: 'Yesterday evening I met an old writer seeking in vain for the first sentence of what would be his last book.' Describe how he fidgets in an attempt to camouflage his superfluity. If you caricature him a bit, it's nothing to me. And the end? How do you see the end, Mr. Narrator? Heart attack? Cancer of the lungs? How do you expect to write about someone without a clear notion of his end?"

By "end" Lambert quite obviously meant something other than death and burial. These he considered a mere convention to surmount an embarrassing situation that in no way concerns the principal character. "An end is something one earns no less than anonymity," he sneered. As for the burial itself, everything had been agreed on in advance between d'Arthez and Lambert. An announcement should not appear in the papers until after the burial, so that people would be spared wreaths and stale eulogies. "And above all to prevent anyone's catching cold in the cemetery. You can't be considerate enough." Edith Nasemann too was aware of this arrangement and not a little shocked. "Some day I'll be thinking about my father, certain he's still around, and suddenly I'll hear he's already buried. No, that will not do."

As already stated, Lambert meant something altogether different by "end." He seems to have seriously thought the matter through in conversation with his friend d'Arthez. With inexorable logic he had conceived an end for d'Arthez and cast it as a stage sketch. In recounting this scene, Lambert revealed something new which does not appear to be common knowledge; namely, that the ideas on which many of d'Arthez's best-known pantomimes are based originated with Lambert. D'Arthez is said to have remarked that, although short on imagination, he could perform anything imaginable. And Lambert snapped scornfully, "Ideas are cheap." Yet the end that Lambert suggested did not meet with d'Arthez's approval. He declined it with the objection, "That would be just one more theatrical end, not a real one."

These allusions and snippets of conversation of a much later date the narrator feels justified in recording at this early stage —in his preface, as it were—if for no other reason than to characterize the defense mechanisms and attempts at evasion indulged in by his informants. Or was it just insecurity? Typical of the almost indeterminable value of such testimony, purely fortuitous as most of it was, would be the remark with which a woman reacted to a question by Edith Nasemann. This woman had been an actress and is one of d'Arthez's oldest acquaintances. She lives in Berlin, at the corner of Rankestrasse and Augsburgerstrasse, where she dabbles in palmistry, Tarot and the like. She was spoken of by all interested parties as the "Woman in the Window"—her sobriquet.

When Edith Nasemann asked her if she had read her father's future, she shook her head and replied, "I'd have known better. There's nothing there to read, dear."

What did the woman mean? Was she simply chiding a daughter's curiosity?

two

The interrogation mentioned earlier took place in either February or March 1965. One could easily check the exact date, since the death and burial of old lady Nasemann, d'Arthez's mother, occurred at the same time. Thus all one need do is leaf through the appropriate pages of the *Frankfurter Allgemeine* or one of the other large dailies. For such an occasion, of course, was not passed over in silence by either the Nasemann family or NANY Inc. They didn't skimp on eye-catching announcements.

Since then, right up to the time of writing, little has changed. Mere peripheral changes, as Lambert used to say. "Just peripheral phenomena with which your Dr. Glatschke can be depended on to deal unaided." The stock-market average has suffered, of course. Strangely enough, Lambert always followed developments in the market with the closest attention, although he could scarcely have owned a single share. He said that it was only by the financial pages that one could tell whether the headline announcing a new crisis was serious, not just cooked up to catch readers. "And besides, what else is there in this city of banks and dividends for the man who wants to be up to date?" he said with a concerned wrinkling of his brows. He hoped that any chance hearers at the table would take him seriously. This conversation took place one night over supper in a little beer hall in the Rothofstrasse. And his audience did take Lambert's pronouncements for the gospel truth, nodding their heads in worried agreement.

It is not likely that much has changed for d'Arthez in the meantime. The narrator cannot say whether the same holds true for Edith Nasemann. It is only for himself, that much, if not everything, has changed. Suffice it to say that at the moment of writing he sits on board a ship bound for Nigeria, where he will be under contract for three years. He considers the case closed. Be that as it may, the narrator has now laid down his role of narrator. But one is not to assume on the basis of this that he already considers himself worthy of saying "I"— if that is the point after all. How he will feel about these notes in three years—if he ever does return—or about that portion of his life when it seemed necessary to write them down, is at least temporarily of no consequence. Around him in his cabin lie handbooks on native dialects. There are phonograph records and tapes as well. For the accent. Was it not the microphone which brought d'Arthez's Saxon accent to light?

Now, the interrogation was no interrogation in the legal or criminal sense of the word. On the contrary, it had been expressly ordered that everything should be avoided which might give what was taking place the semblance of an interrogation. For this reason Dr. Glatschke had to be on his toes; he had to do without the routine police questions. This was extraordinarily difficult for him and certainly contributed to his bad humor.

It was far from a summons to an interrogation that d'Arthez received from the Frankfurt division of the Security police. An older colleague of the narrator was sent with a note to the Hotel Intercontinental, politely asking d'Arthez if he would mind dropping by the department to assist the police in solving a problem that they could not hope to solve alone. "We would be extraordinarily grateful . . . It is only natural that in all this we are completely at your disposal . . . and if you prefer, this short conversation could just as easily be arranged in your hotel or at the home of your mother . . . nor will the undersigned miss this opportunity of assuring you, in the name of his department, of heartfelt sympathy in this painful loss which you have suffered . . ." and so forth.

The beautiful rhetoric notwithstanding, the narrator was sent into the archives for anything he could unearth about d'Arthez. Dr. Glatschke went over the file most thoroughly. Since the material in Frankfurt was incomplete, the chief considered it necessary to phone Berlin long-distance. He talked for some time. The narrator, however, knows nothing more about this call; at the time it was placed, he was having lunch in the canteen. This is only worth recording since Lambert had asked, "What did you have for lunch?" when the narrator mentioned the fact. As it happened, the narrator did remember that this was the day they served stuffed cabbage. "That is most important," said Lambert. "Trivial detail can never be invented. And it is only therein we find truth."

There was a good reason for all this courtesy on d'Arthez's account. It has nothing to do with constitutional rights. Besides, one can scarcely conceive of d'Arthez calling on the protection of the constitution. At the time, however, neither Dr. Glatschke nor the narrator could have guessed this. The case in question was one in which an official could easily get his fingers burned; indeed, could even lose his job. And it was this that forced on Dr. Glatschke those tortured courtesies which he performed with so little grace. A carbon of his letter was scrupulously committed to the registry office. In Security, loyalty was unheard of. Someone always lurked just waiting for an error (or for some action that later on might be construed as such), for no other purpose than to chase the culprit from his desk and to take over his still-warm chair. For this reason the files were absolutely crawling with carbons. Even the most insignificant proceedings were carefully documented. There was no other way of preventing future recriminations, of protecting oneself against intrigues, and of creating the possibility of blaming any oversight on a colleague.

Of course, the government was only too aware that the personality known to the public under the pseudonym or *nom d'artiste* of d'Arthez in reality bore the name Ernst Nasemann and was related to Nasemann Nylon Incorporated, NANY for short. D'Arthez's relatives, who owned it, had removed their whole operation to the West after the destruction of Dresden. Everyone knows the factory's imposing silhouette on the western edge of Frankfurt. A few years before, people complained about the unmoving clouds of waste gas that hung over the Taunus hills. Housewives in that part of town had gone so far as to claim that the fumes were a danger to health, but this was an exaggeration. The department responsible for public health was able to prove only that in this district a film of dirt settled on balconies and windows in the course of a single day, and that curtains there had to be cleaned more often than elsewhere. Such criticism, however, was not intended to prejudice

Frankfurt's citizens against such an important contributor to their standard of living—not to mention the tax receipts involved.

For a long time now NANY Inc. had been a household word, yet few people were aware that behind it stood the name Nasemann. Innumerable neon tubes spelled NANY Inc. out in blue-green all over the world. In every streetcar or bus people read it. In films and television commercials beautiful models praised the durability and gentleness of NANY products. In the daily papers eye-catching NANY-clad legs, by coming within a hair's breadth of the limits of good taste, successfully distracted readers from the vexing events of the day. Curiously enough, Edith Nasemann did not wear NANY hosiery. Her refusal, however, was not intended as an insult to her relatives. Her reasons were of a purely practical nature. She claimed that her feet were just too small for the sizes NANY produced and that their hosiery tended to stretch and wrinkle over her calves.

In short, the watchword was deference if one did not want to tangle with a worldwide business empire. But it was not the name Nasemann alone that necessitated such great tact in dealing with d'Arthez. His pseudonym too had attained something like fame. Even *Who's Who* contained this entry: "D'ARTHEZ (*né* Ernst Nasemann) celebrated German actor." I government archives and in his passport too, his profession was alternately given as "actor" or "cabaret artist." If one were to ask d'Arthez himself, he would always call himself a comic. This designation, however, although it obviously had d'Arthez's approval, had never found its way into official documents. In other words, both names—d'Arthez and Nasemann—had achieved international notoriety. Perhaps by terming his offerings brief pantomimes, the narrator can indicate why they were suitable for export, that is, for foreign tours. Even in Warsaw, Prague and Budapest, as well as in other capitals where Marxism flourished, d'Arthez was welcome. Naturally, in such places his sketches were greeted with one-sided enthusiasm—as if they were aimed only at conditions in the West. The responsible people in Bonn were perfectly aware of this, but not wanting to be accused of undemocratic narrowness of mind, they suppressed their chagrin and informed the appropriate organizations that the famous mime was a useful item for the cultural-exchange program. Television was responsible for d'Arthez's becoming a favorite of millions. An illustrated paperback about d'Arthez came out in the mid-fifties and is long since out of print. One assumes it made money for the publishers. Perhaps it would not be too much to say that d'Arthez, whose picture could also be seen in all the illustrated magazines quite regularly, represented something of a model to a certain segment of society in our time of restoration, especially to the sons and daughters of the industrialists. His impeccable correctness, even if only put on, or perhaps precisely for that reason, obviously impressed them. The narrator must confess that, although he never belonged to this class, he too was fascinated by this phenomenon in his earlier years. Thus it scarcely need be added that d'Arthez's income-tax forms filed with Internal Revenue revealed that he made a lot of money as an actor and did not have to fall back on NANY Inc.

From all this it should be obvious that Dr. Glatschke found himself in no easy position. Even the slightest indiscretion might raise the specter of "police invasions of privacy" from a sensation-hungry press. One even had to be prepared for demonstrations by the actor's younger admirers. Thus, from the very beginning Dr. Glatschke felt that his hands were tied, and this perhaps explains his irritability. Added to this was the fact that as an actor d'Arthez had command of his most trivial gesture and grimace—or rather of his almost total absence of expression, since this was actually what emanated from him. No matter what part he played, d'Arthez always left a spectator in doubt as to whether he should laugh or shiver. Only when

17

other people burst out in nervous laughter did one dare laugh. Reviewing one of his pantomimes, a critic had speculated as to what sort of face d'Arthez put on when he woke up in the morning or what face he went to bed with at night. And precisely what, our critic says with perhaps excessive earnestness, does this face betray when a girl sitting opposite arouses desire?

The journalist's indiscreet question is not completely inappropriate. As Lambert said much later, d'Arthez had asked him when he arrived in Frankfurt on the occasion of his mother's death, "What sort of face *do* you wear to stand at the foot of your mother's bier?" That sounds cynical, as one writes it down baldly or reads it out of context, unaware of how seriously these two friends discussed such matters.

"*You* can ask such a question?" Lambert replied.

"Oh, when the others are standing around, of course it's no problem. But when I'm standing alone with the casket, what then?"

At this point the manner in which this scene came off in reality might as well be inserted. D'Arthez had described it to his friend.

"Well, the housekeeper let me in. She's a widow who wears a wig, a tough old customer. Even my mother was afraid of her —and that's saying something, I can tell you. Now this Frau Schorn pulled a long sympathetic face, as well she might have, and led me into the salon where the bier stood. Naturally there was the odor of flowers and wreaths. Not even potted palms were left out. There were candelabra too—they hadn't pinched pennies. And of course Frau Schorn left me standing there alone. For the son to pay his last respects to his mother, you know. She played her part with tact, absolutely irreproachable. At that point, though, between the potted laurels, or whatever, I noticed that a gap had been left, and in it was hung a little painting I remembered. Why this gap? Could it have been mere chance? No, it did not conceal a microphone. They probably didn't feel one would be necessary. Just in case, I checked anyway so we would have no unpleasantness later. The painting, though, I remembered from Dresden—and I'd never given it another thought. Even then it hung in the salon. When we had visitors and they began to bore me, I used to study it. A tiny picture, a seascape. The dark silhouette of a schooner against a red and yellow evening sky. Absolutely peaceful, although, as I said, dark. The heavy gold frame was almost twice the size of the canvas, and tacked on at the bottom was a label, just like a museum's. Melbye, a Danish painter of the last century. When you have a chance, look him up in the university library—if you want. I believe his first name was Anton. Perhaps the painting has gone up in value again. In any event, they dragged it along when they fled Dresden. It seemed perfectly natural that it should be there and that I could gaze at it now just as I had as a child. But then I heard a car drive up and very probably a door slammed recklessly. Someone must have been in a big hurry, so I left the painting quickly. Anyone catching me in front of it would have taken for granted that it meant something to me and I wanted to inherit it. And naturally that would have made its value skyrocket. So I walked out into the foyer. Frau Schorn had already opened the door and my sister Lotte tumbled in to throw herself into my arms. 'Isn't it horrible?' she cried. An admirable scene; Frau Schorn looked pleased as punch. What a pity no camera was present to preserve it for posterity. My sister with inflamed cheeks, her eyes teary. Why, she got my shoulder wet! She let me hold her up as though she were in a faint. Since she had begun putting on weight, this took some doing. Her voice broke with sorrow. How did she do it? She had come all the way from Basel and must have been on the road four hours, if not five. Her husband, a vice-president in a bank, has always been a careful driver. Now, no one can cry their eyes out for four or five hours, it isn't humanly possible. And, moreover, one couldn't also keep an eye on the traffic (my sister is a backseat driver of long standing). How did she bring it off? She must have chosen just the right moment to collapse and burst into tears as they pulled up before the house of mourning. Truly admirable. And there he was, the Herr Direktor from the Swiss Union Bank, walking up the steps from the garden with two suitcases, just a bit out of breath, but very serious and dependable. And of course full of the expected sympathy."

Thus far Lambert's description. But there is also another scene, which Edith Nasemann communicated to the narrator. She was present. This time the whole family was assembled to meet with the pastor of Bad Königstein, who wanted to collect important dates in the life of the deceased and anecdotes about her for the funeral sermon he was expected to preach. "Aunt Lotte behaved like a fool," Edith Nasemann said. "She burst into loud tears repeatedly. Once she even had to leave the room shouting, 'I just can't stand it!' Her husband had to run out and bring her back."

Edith Nasemann certainly would not consent to her remarks being preserved in writing. The narrator considers it his duty to point out that she derived no joy from gossiping about relations whom she scarcely ever saw or from blackening their reputations. If she discussed her family at all, it was only at the narrator's request, and primarily because she was astonished at her father's behavior. Throughout his sister's hysterical outbursts he sat there without even frowning; he even appeared to approve. He said no more to his daughter than "She lacks training. That's why she exaggerates so."

Dr. Glatschke's difficulties proceeded from the fact that d'Arthez was no ordinary suspect from whom he might extract a maximum of information thanks to his refined technique of interrogation. On the contrary, d'Arthez was that well-known exemplary type of suspect whom no one could expect to break or catch out in anything. And the matter was further complicated by d'Arthez's totally opaque past. The times through which they had lived made this a common feature of his generation. In d'Arthez's case, however, tangible grounds existed for suspicion after, rather than during or before, the war. This the records made clear, and not so much the German records but those of American Intelligence in Berlin. What had moved them, toward the end of the fifties, to investigate d'Arthez was still unknown; but they even went so far as to search his apartment. Exceptionally, the American authorities failed to communicate their reasons for this investigation to their German counterpart, although the Americans demanded the support of their German colleagues in most cases. On the other hand, nothing to do with East Berlin or the like had aroused American suspicion. Otherwise the German authorities would almost certainly have been informed. Thus the affair must have concerned the Americans alone, and been of a nature that they thought best to conceal even from the information bureau of an ally. In any event, at the time his apartment was being searched, d'Arthez was not in Berlin. He was in Paris making a film for French television.

All the same, no matter how long ago it had taken place, the search had left a trace: the Frankfurt branch had a photocopy of the American report, which was rather short and written in English. Dr. Glatschke had studied it thoroughly. He handed it to the narrator for perusal with the question, "What do you make of it? Don't you notice something fishy?" Instinctively, one was prejudiced against anyone whose house had been searched; even when the search turned up nothing, one tended to attribute this to the cunning of the suspect, rather than to accept it as proof of his innocence. And, actually, something about this report did strike the reader. In spite of the customary jargon in which such documents are invariably couched, the astonishment which d'Arthez's apartment had inspired in the investigator could not be overlooked. Unconsciously his suspicions increased the more he saw of this apartment; so did Dr. Glatschke's once he had studied this report.

The apartment was on the Karlsruherstrasse. D'Arthez lived there—he still does—as a boarder in a single furnished room. The owner of the apartment, Frau von Konnsdorf, quite old already, seemed to have the greatest respect for her tenant. Probably he embodied for her some sort of ideal from more elegant days. He never failed to ask after her health, and afternoons he always sat with her for a quarter of an hour. This had almost become a ritual. "I've never understood why Papa does it," Edith Nasemann told the narrator. "It must bore him to tears. I have to drink tea with the old lady, too, whenever I visit my father in Berlin. You hardly had a chance to sit down before she would pull out an old leather album to show you photographs of the estate in Pomerania or West Prussia where she grew up. Papa acted as if he were fascinated, even though he must have seen these pictures many times before. He even asked about the material of the dresses worn by the girls in this or that picture—down to the hair ribbons. The old lady would describe them in detail. Cloth like that isn't to be found anywhere nowadays, my child, she'd explain. I was suddenly afraid that she would have samples stored away in a drawer or a chest somewhere and she'd send Marie, her old housemaid, up to the attic to look for the stuff. Now Marie came from the same village—as you might have guessed from her accent. She was cross as a bear. Whenever her mistress mused, 'Marie, do you remember . . .' Marie brought her down to earth with 'We left that in the hands of the Russians.' Unfortunately, there were always more albums that had to be trotted out. This old lady at some time or other had devoted her life to the arts, or at least to those artists whom she could receive. The women had fantastic hairdos, the men wore high collars. All of them great celebrities no one has ever heard of. Poets and painters and actors. And of course every photograph was inscribed. 'For my unforgettable, highly admired Helene,' and the like. Not one signature was legible. I always think of this in restaurants when I see *poire Hélène* on the menu. Papa acted as though he had met each person whose photo he held in his hand. But once Marie looked over his shoulder as she poured the tea and snorted contemptuously at the picture of a big-bosomed lady. 'She's the one who had an affair with X and Y,' said Marie. The old lady looked up and fixed me with her eyes; she was so shocked she put her hand on my arm and sighed, 'Oh, that was a Great Love, my child. Things like that simply no longer happen.'" Now, all this has little enough to do with d'Arthez, but it may possibly serve to give one a notion of the life-style that he considered suitable to himself. He seems never to have entertained a change.

On the Karlsruherstrasse many old buildings survived the destruction of Berlin. Due to the lack of money, few have been restored. In cities that have never been saturation-bombed, Paris or London, for instance, these old-fashioned buildings are a familiar part of the vista. In Germany, on the other hand, anything still standing from before looks unnatural. One cannot help feeling unsure of himself as soon as he turns the corner into such a street. And discomfort only increases inside such buildings if one meets with superficial modernization—indirect lighting, which doesn't go with the pompous staircase, or heat registers instead of the immense tiled stoves in use when the building was constructed.

D'Arthez was already living here by the summer of 1945. That is, he moved in after he was liberated from a concentration camp, and as soon as he had spent a short time in a hospital. Probably he was assigned these quarters as a person who had suffered at the hands of the regime, a *Nazi Geschädigten* as they were then termed. Of what had once been an eight-room apartment, he occupied those portions in which guests would have been received—the former salon and boudoir. The American report reads as follows: "Living room 30' × 16'. Ceilings higher than 10', stuccoed. Three floor-to-ceiling windows and a door leading to a narrow balcony. Furnishings Louis XV. Worn pink carpet in the same style. Large crystal chandelier. Paintings of the school of Defregger, Kaulbach, Thoma, etc." Where the American agent who wrote this report had learned to identify these painters, one could only guess. Possibly he was an emigrant whose knowledge of both languages made him useful to the Americans.

The narrator, however, was unable to visualize this room until he ran across an illustration in the picture biography of d'Arthez. Since the photograph was of a high, narrow, baroque mirror reaching almost from floor to ceiling, the shot was most artful. The mirror reflected d'Arthez dressed up, straightening his tie; behind him could be seen some of the furnishings mentioned in the report. And the mirror appeared to be *real*, that is to say, antique, clouded here and there and cracked along one edge. The condition of the glass lent the photograph an attractive vagueness and magnified one's sense of the size of the room.

But Lambert and Edith Nasemann have touched on this room as well. All Lambert had to say was "What's the difference? How a man lives in this sense is irrelevant." This he accompanied with a shrug of his shoulders. Edith Nasemann, on the other hand, did her best to defend her father. "It's just that he wants to avoid owning anything," she said. "Papa needs the space and the mirror to rehearse his pantomimes. At least, I suppose so. I've never seen him and I've never asked. Of course he has to rehearse, don't all actors?" This last she'd added a bit peevishly. But she made no bones about finding this room's total lack of warmth extremely vexing. "And the furnishings aren't even real antiques, only reproductions that must have

24

cost a fortune when they were bought. Chairs and a sofa up-
holstered in pale green silk. And how uncomfortable they were!
The carving always made my elbows black and blue, and once
I got a run in my stocking from some fool brass fittings. It
made Papa laugh. He said something to the effect that I was
increasing the turnover of NANY Inc."

Besides the larger room there was another, smaller one that
d'Arthez used as a bedroom. He had paid for the installation of
a modern bathroom. Even the soberest of hotel rooms would
have given a more personal impression than the style he had
chosen. "It not only looked but even smelled as though it had
never been used," Edith Nasemann said. "Every time you
walked in from the dark hall you wanted to say, 'Oh, excuse
me! I must have gotten the wrong room.' I couldn't talk to Papa
about this. He was far too accustomed to it all."

This absence of any personal touch had struck the agent who
put together the search report. For this reason he had taken
special notice of the single living spot of color among all the
stage properties—a paperback in a gaudy jacket lying parallel
to the edge of a desk, on which there was nothing except a
gigantic marble inkwell, a leather writing kit stamped with a
gold crest and an absolute horror of a reading lamp, a big
bronze frog whose long arms and thin fingers held up a bronze
dome slightly askew. The dome was pierced around its diame-
ter with ovals of a greenish glass which looked like translucent
soap, and to cap this off, the dome sported a silk fringe to
dampen the light. "Papa always flicked the lamp in passing. It
gave out a faint, broken-bell tone," Edith Nasemann added.
The "gaudy paperback" particularly had aroused the agent's
suspicions, since it was an American murder mystery, not in
translation. But what would he have said if he had known
about an old newspaper interview that Security had clipped
out, in which d'Arthez confessed that he had a weakness for
American murder mysteries. "The English ones must be written

by faggots. No one commits murder that way any more," he had remarked to a reporter. Even the title of the book occurred in the report—*Red Harvest*. Dr. Glatschke, a man who followed up every conceivable clue with pedantic dispatch, directed the narrator to investigate this novel immediately. The woman who sells paperbacks in a little shop in the Goethe-Passage consulted a fat index and came up with the author's name, Dashiell Hammett. Later, when the narrator mentioned the name and the novel, Lambert knew them. "A famous book. André Gide wanted to translate it," he replied. That no other books were lying around struck the American agent. A bookmark at page 114 increased his suspicions. Why page 114? Different experts read this page through several times without being able to formulate a plausible explanation. And then there was the bookmark itself. It was a piece of heavy green paper, torn from a boarding pass, the sort issued at airports all over the world. On the front was 407 written with a felt-tipped pen; on the back, the memorable slogan of a worldwide auto rental firm: "HERTZ is on hand wherever you land." Naturally this too had been investigated. The number designated the Tempelhof-Orly flight, or the return flight, but that scarcely explained the bookmark itself and the number 407 least of all. What relation did this number bear to that of the page, 114? Why had d'Arthez kept this scrap of paper and used it as a bookmark? Could it possibly be the badge of a secret society? A token by which members of some secret organization recognized one another? Of course, these figures would have engaged the attention of any secret service and set them to work; but the experts in Cryptography were unable to solve this riddle.

Now, it might have been too that on discovery of this scrap of paper in his breast pocket d'Arthez had realized what a fine bookmark it would make. And for the fact of only this one paperback lying around, Edith Nasemann offered an even simpler explanation. Her father always passed them on to Frau von Konnsdorf as soon as he finished them. The old lady spoke perfect English. Her husband had once held a diplomatic post in an English-speaking country. The colorful paperbacks rising in piles in her rooms must have escaped the attention of the people who searched the house. Edith Nasemann was surprised that the old lady read "such stuff." Her father she excused, of course. "He needs it for relaxation." She even recalled the picture on the cover of one of these books lying face up on Frau von Konnsdorf's tea table. "A man with the face of a gangster, lying in bed. One of his arms bandaged, in a sling; in the other hand he holds a gun. At the foot of the bed sits a girl in a transparent negligee, painting her toenails. In order to do so, she has one of her legs up on the bed, naturally displaying a great deal of thigh. At first I took it for pornography."

The report of this investigation also contained mention of a potted palm, since the agent had not dared spare himself the pains of tipping over the pot to search the earth for documents or arms. The palm stood on a dais, or rather on the openwork railing that partly fenced it in. Since there was no hint of this dais in the photo reproduced in the book about d'Arthez, we must assume that it stood somewhere to the side and near the windows. As was only natural, there was a sofa on it and a small table with rococo legs. "I asked Papa what people used to have a dais for and he showed me. Papa was always extremely patient when anyone asked him questions like that. I had to pose up there as artistically as I could, with my elbows on the balustrade, while Papa stood below and recited 'It is the nightingale and not the lark . . .' I couldn't help laughing, but he looked so serious it embarrassed me. And then he added that such raised platforms taught a girl how to walk downstairs without tripping over her long dress. I didn't even own a long dress though." In neither bedroom nor bath had the agent noticed anything suspicious. We can assume that all the pockets and linings of d'Arthez's suits were carefully examined. That is part of the routine. Nor would the agent have overlooked the toilet tank or the hot-water heater. Usually the man assigned to such an investigation comes in the guise of a mechanic sent by Gas and Electricity to check out the equipment.

Since no papers had been turned up by this search, the investigator wondered where they were kept; because it was almost certain that insurance policies, contracts and bank statements had to exist, possibly even a will. None of these was discovered in the apartment—indeed, not even personal letters; for instance, no letters from his daughter, who wrote her father at least once a month and received answers. The narrator once heard Lambert remark, under completely different circumstances, that "for God's sake" one should never keep letters. They only "lead to complications." Whether d'Arthez felt the same and thus destroyed all letters as soon as they were read, it is impossible to say. But the question about other documents is easy to answer. D'Arthez had a theater agent who kept his contracts and business correspondence. Everything else was in the hands of a lawyer. American Intelligence would not have dared search the premises of these men to whom d'Arthez had given powers of attorney. That would have required more complicated diplomatic and legal groundwork than the Americans seemed willing to undertake, and it might have given them unwelcome publicity. In the apartment itself only two papers came to light, and these in the leather folder stamped with a gold crest. Obviously it had been the crest of the Konnsdorf family (this identification was made by means of a handbook on heraldry) that had tempted d'Arthez to sketch out a crest for the family Nasemann, or possibly for NANY Inc. He had made several handsome attempts on a large sheet of paper, perhaps only for the fun of it or for relaxation. He had imitated the Konnsdorf crest rather closely in the outline. Above, a helmet with plumes; around the shield, drapery like a raised curtain; and below, cannons, halberds and the rest of the usual symbols; four rows of barbed wire (to quote the report) and above them a woman's stocking fluttering like a pennant in the form of a question mark lying on its side, having an airplane at the toe. In a crescent d'Arthez had lettered a motto: *Ad Aspera.* Another attempt represented striped prison- or concentration-camp garb hanging on a coat hanger. Beneath it stood an open grave or an open coffin from which a corpse with an oversized nose—*Nase* in German, as the agent pointed out—stretched in vain toward the striped uniform. The motto attached to this crest read *In Hoc Signo Vinces.* But doubt seems to have overcome d'Arthez in this case, for below it, in his usual handwriting, he had noted, "Or perhaps *Non Olet,* so as to avoid the imputation of blasphemy?" One scarcely need remark that in the report these Latin citations were conscientiously run to earth in the hopes of gleaning from them some secret double meaning. When Dr. Glatschke came across this passage, he simply said, "The fellow's nuts." Though one could scarcely expect the Americans to keep abreast of economic developments at NANY Inc., Dr. Glatschke should certainly have understood the allusions. But, for him, investigating an industry of this magnitude was simply taboo.

The other paper that had turned up in the same leather folder, hidden or perhaps forgotten among the blotting paper, was reproduced photographically in the report. The paper and ink had been subjected to chemical analysis and a graphological appraisal had been made. Its composition and mode of production indicated that the paper was incontestably one hundred to one hundred and twenty years old. Since it was not a large sheet and had been recently cut along one side, one could not avoid the conclusion that its source was the end papers of an old book. The ink, on the other hand, despite its faded appearance, was of recent manufacture. Apparently, to further his deception, d'Arthez thinned the ink with water before use. Equally incontestable was the identification of the handwriting by a graphologist as that of "the individual known under the pseudonym of d'Arthez," in spite of a naïve attempt to reverse the angle of his hand and to imitate "old-fashioned flourishes." All this was suspicious enough, but in addition there was the following text:

> The bearer is entitled to make use of my name in the maintenance of our interests. Should he, due to the numerous wars and other perturbations of spirit from which our continent suffers, grow fatigued and consider himself unable to meet the demands of this task, then he is also authorized to pass this mandate along, without further inquiry, to the person whom he considers most suitable.
>
> Any misuse of my name to effect a mere shock will be ruthlessly unmasked. More is at stake here than ephemeral happiness resulting from work well done. True genius is a gift for crossing deserts without complaint.
>
> We have absolute confidence in you.
>
> d'Arthez
>
> Paris, 18 August 1850

What the Americans made of this text could not be gathered from the report. Dr. Glatschke naturally stressed the importance of the recurring "we" and "our" throughout the text. He took this as corroboration of his hypothesis that the document indicated the existence of a secret society, very likely professing pacifist tendencies. That d'Arthez had issued his own authorization was taken to prove how refined were the deceptions this alleged organization practiced. "Nor should you overlook that phrase 'ruthlessly unmask.' We must entertain the possibility of assassinations . . ." said Dr. Glatschke. For his part, the narrator copied out this text. He has read it often. A certain reticence, however, always prevented his mentioning it to Lambert, who certainly could have offered some explanation. Nor did the narrator mention this text to Edith Nasemann.

Could this letter have been a mere trifle, no different, really, from the sketched crests? How could the presence of this document be explained—there in an apartment where d'Arthez had otherwise left nothing written or personal? How was the page seemingly forgotten among the blotting paper in the writing kit? Why didn't d'Arthez carry this power of attorney on his person? Was it perhaps his intention to make the discovery and the transmission of this authorization dependent on chance?

But to be done with this report filed so many years ago, let it be mentioned, if only in passing, that the rest of the suspect's daily life also underwent a routine investigation. D'Arthez used to spend part of every morning over two espressos and the morning papers in the café Old Vienna on the Kurfürstendamm. Mostly he sat alone. He was joined occasionally by acquaintances who spotted him from the street, but only for a short time. If he wasn't filming a television show (which happened quite often), he lunched regularly in the Paris Bar, and here too he mostly sat alone, or at least that is what the headwaiter said; naturally d'Arthez knew many other regulars and sometimes he talked to them. Less frequently—only when he had foreign guests to entertain—he ate in the Maison de France, to which he had access thanks to his connections in French television. Afternoons d'Arthez generally spent in his apartment. Whatever else he may have done there, he was known to give no more than half an hour of his time to Frau von Konnsdorf. "The old lady's whole life would fall to pieces if I once failed to observe that rule," he once explained to his daughter, and he added, "The afternoon hours are critical and there's no getting around it." Evenings he ate in the Fasanen Stübchen, a family beerhouse where a few younger writers met regularly. D'Arthez knew them all and sat with them on occasion. The report added that he did not take part in their literary arguments; he just listened. No one could say whether he was on a more intimate footing with one or another of these writers. And finally, the agent mentioned that late at night, on his way home from a performance, he dropped by a bar called Die Volle Pulle on the Steinplatz to consume an oxtail soup at the circular bar. He conversed with Charlie, the celebrated barman, about the daily events and the talk of the town. Apparently the American agent passed many evenings next to d'Arthez at that bar. His report even contained scraps of conversation. Charlie had remarked that X was already on page 276 of his new book and Y was in Taormina. D'Arthez hadn't said anything. X and Y were both well-known men of letters. Most of his customers used the familiar *du* with Charlie, but not d'Arthez. That was not his style. From everything Lambert later told the narrator, it seemed quite possible that d'Arthez had spotted the American agent.

This report also observed that d'Arthez did not own a car and probably didn't even have a driver's license. He walked a great deal and made use of taxis only for longer stretches or in bad weather.

An uneventful life, one might say, setting aside his work in television and his travels and tours. Indeed, it was precisely this uneventfulness that increased Security's suspicions. It seemed positively unthinkable that a man could so completely abstain from diversions without having some clandestine purpose. It struck the agent entrusted with this investigation as enigmatic, unnatural, that no woman or women could be found with whom d'Arthez was intimately involved. No men either, as the report pointed out, so that there were no grounds for suspicions of homosexuality.

Now the Frankfurt bureau knew a bit more than the Americans could have gleaned from a report already out-of-date by almost a decade. For instance, it was now known that every three months d'Arthez flew to Frankfurt to see his mother, who owned a house in nearby Bad Königstein that her late husband, the former head of NANY Inc., had providentially purchased as long ago as 1941. It was an old house but solidly built, in the style of a Swiss chalet, much too spacious for old lady Nasemann, who lived there alone except for her companion and a cook-and-chauffeur couple. Most of the old furnishings had been removed from Dresden in time to avoid destruction in the great air raid. The house was overcrowded and the furniture didn't suit the new decor. But the old lady wouldn't hear of parting with anything. She still held what she called "family days," but d'Arthez never put in an appearance at them. Each time he pleaded a tour or some other previous engagement. His father had died long before, in Dresden in 1943, and was buried there. Before the end of the war or the destruction of the city, the migration to the West had been planned and later implemented by his second son and successor, Otto Nasemann, the present chairman of the board of NANY Inc. Since NANY Inc. was a "war-essential industry," both the Party and the Army had cooperated with NANY Inc. in acquiring land in the West in case events should necessitate rebuilding. NANY Inc. had excellent connections.

D'Arthez always made this quarterly visit to his mother unannounced. It piqued his mother greatly, since it prevented her from making preparations or inviting other members of the family. Long emotional outbursts were occasioned by the fact that her son would not spend the night under her roof but preferred the Hotel Intercontinental in Frankfurt, if he didn't return directly to Berlin by the late plane. "You're just throwing money away," she would complain—but in reality she was impressed. Still, she could never persuade d'Arthez to change his plans. He came out unannounced on the early afternoon bus from Frankfurt and appeared on her doorstep with flowers or candy. He listened politely to the usual lamentations: she hadn't been able to bake him a cake, he had chosen her cleaning day, etc. He stayed for about two and a half hours, then glanced at his watch, excused himself to go to a previous engagement or an interview, and jumped on the bus back to Frankfurt. That left his mother with something to talk about for the next few weeks; for instance, how well her son looked, how devoted he was in spite of his tiring profession, and so on. It had always been her way to play one member of the family off against another.

The other relatives, particularly his brother, he never visited and seldom ran into. His brother had an honorary doctorate and was an overseer of a university that he had endowed munificently with an Institute for the Natural Sciences. As far as the authorities knew, the brothers had met only twice in recent years, and both times by accident—once in a hotel in Milan.

Hastily drawn conclusions are apt to be mistaken. There was no tension in their relations, much less a family feud. On birthdays and other occasions they punctiliously exchanged greetings. D'Arthez always spoke of his brother as "der Herr Generaldirektor," but he did so without irony, merely stating a fact. The Generaldirektor for his part spoke of d'Arthez—when he could not avoid the topic altogether—as "my brother, the celebrated artist." That he declined to use the expression "actor" or "comedian" is understandable. Regard for his wife and children demanded it. Of course, they frequently met with someone who exclaimed, "What, you're related to d'Arthez? Why, how exciting!"

The above-mentioned greetings were the usual cards. It is worth pointing out that d'Arthez advised his daughter to send them without fail. He went so far as to write her out a list of all the family birthdays. This quite annoyed Edith Nasemann, who would have preferred to forget the family altogether. "I'm merely tolerated by them. Because my name happens to be Nasemann they feel they have to behave this way," she said.

34

"Why should I send them picture postcards? They'll only twist them into a hint that I want something from them."

"They think that already," d'Arthez is said to have replied. "They cannot help but think that. Why can't you help them out a little?"

Edith Nasemann couldn't agree with this point of view. She considered such tactics a sign of cowardice. Nor was Lambert in agreement with d'Arthez, as it turned out one day when Edith complained about the cards. This subject seems to have caused more than one argument between father and daughter. That he gave her this advice was all the odder, since, as far as the narrator can judge, d'Arthez shied away from giving anyone advice on how to behave, his daughter least of all. And in this Lambert concurred heartily. "We have lost any right we ever had to advise others," he said when the narrator came to him very much in need of advice. Lambert, however, did not always live up to his ideals. His temper occasionally ran away with him.

In the end Edith Nasemann followed her father's advice, but without ever being convinced that his point of view was right. She did it more out of love than anything else; she believed it might some day help him if she remembered her relations' stupid birthdays. It was touching, the way she always supported her father, even when his actions were incomprehensible. One might even say that this had to happen before she really rushed to his defense.

About birthdays he had these words for her. "Because they have nothing else to talk about, they will always have something to say about us. For this reason we must provide them with subjects. Otherwise, we won't know what they are saying. In this way one protects oneself from them. All they ask is to be kept busy. Can't you see them handing your card around! If the reproduction happens to be an abstract painting, they'll say, 'Oh, she's playing at being modern . . .' If you send an icon, they'll ask, 'Has she suddenly got religion?' Those are topics that can be chatted about easily. You must speak to them in their own language. Remember how a foreigner sometimes speaks German with better grammar than we do . . ."

His daughter always knew of d'Arthez's visits to Frankfurt in advance. His friend Lambert heard when d'Arthez rang him up from the hotel to lay plans for the coming night. All this, in outline at least, the authorities were acquainted with, but thus far they had seen no particular reason to pursue the matter further.

This changed overnight when the French authorities appealed quite urgently for information about persons living in Germany by the name of d'Arthez. Yes, they used the plural, as though more than one man bore this name. Bonn relayed this request by way of Berlin to Frankfurt, where the death of his mother had detained d'Arthez for more than a week.

three

Old lady Nasemann's burial took place in the cemetery in Bad Königstein, "in the bosom of her family," as the expression goes—which of course was far from true, since business associates refused to be deprived of their right to follow the casket and shake hands with the bereaved beside the grave. The announcements requested that no flowers be sent; instead, a memorial contribution to the Red Cross would be appreciated. D'Arthez is said to have remarked that the affair was staged to appear reverent and unpretentious to any who might read about it in the newspapers.

Not only the local press covered the casket's lying in state in the main hangar of the NANY Inc. factory. This event also supplied the illustrated magazines and the newsreels with magnificent footage. The casket was obscured by flowers, wreaths whose broad ribbons had been smoothed out so the legends showed: "Our unforgettable chief," "The stalwart defender of our undertaking" and other mottoes designed to indicate cordial relations between employer and employee. Add to this the great machines and assembly lines as a backdrop, the whole rank and file marching past the casket, the women and girls bearing touching small bouquets that they deposited at the foot of the bier. Everyone in work clothes, it goes without saying. In other words, their distress found completely spontaneous expression. The whole work force got half a day off.

One might have known VIPs would not be lacking. A member of the cabinet, a few mayors with wives, all of them looking very sad . . . Nor could a general's uniform pass unnoticed in the photographs. "Well, look at that," d'Arthez is said to have exclaimed when he saw these pictures. "They really do think of everything."

"Imposture on such a scale I've never seen!" Lambert supposedly cried in anger. Edith Nasemann later described the event to the narrator. The whole time, flashbulbs flashed, spotlights lighted the scene. For journalists and camera crews there was a cafeteria offering a copious free lunch.

Edith Nasemann, too, considered it an imposture. She had never pretended to feel anything for her grandmother. "She always called me Little Edith. It was enough to make you scream." Lambert accomplished nothing by explaining that the old lady meant no harm. In Saxony it was customary to use the diminutive of every noun to make it more familiar. A provincial point of view and nothing more. Besides, Edith Nasemann had only met her grandmother recently and had begun to see more of her just two years before the old lady's death. This contributed to her feeling of being a stranger in the family circle, a tolerated outsider.

"Before, they didn't even know I existed," she said once when the old lady was still alive, "and now I'm suddenly a member of the family. And at Christmas she sends her chauffeur around to drop off a package where I live. As if I can't feed myself! What does that woman think? I give it away to my landlady and the girls at work. And sometimes I even send some of it home—back home they can always use things like that . . ." But clearly she had never converted her father to her way of thinking. "Papa believes I should be glad she sends nothing more than a basket of delicacies. Just think, he'd say, think what it would be like if she had imagination and sent you something personal! That would be the end. But as it is, you are merely a name on the list of People Who Receive a Basket of Goodies, so you can do or not do whatever you please." Edith Nasemann was convinced that they patronized her like a poor relation.

Of course, Lambert was quite right in calling the whole funeral a public-relations campaign. Though the old lady was the principal stockholder, she had never taken the least interest in the business. She only marched on the scene when a new cafeteria was opened or a lying-in hospital dedicated. On the letterheads of church fund-raising campaigns her name headed the list. Yet Lambert's criticism could not change d'Arthez's attitude. He is said to have answered, "Precisely because it *is* theater, I find it easy to play along. It is even fun to be able to play their kind of melodrama better than they. It confuses them. If you don't play along, they take it for protest, and then one has given them the advantage of having taken oneself seriously, of having enjoyed one's spotless conscience. Protest! As though there were nothing more important in life than protesting against their bad theater and the red splotches on my sister Lotte's cheeks! But as long as you play along, they feel unsure of themselves and don't dare become vicious. Just wait until the will is read."

The narrator believes he has rather detailed information about the reading of this will. To the astonishment of everyone concerned, d'Arthez brought Edith into the picture as nothing less than the key figure. Edith Nasemann was outraged. "What does Papa think he's doing? I couldn't care less! Let them be happy with all their money if they can." Lambert too was outraged, feeling that d'Arthez had cast his daughter in a role still far beyond her powers. The narrator was asked his opinion only because he had studied law and Lambert assumed he might know more than they. But fundamentally there was no legal problem at all.

It was the reading of this will that kept d'Arthez in Frankfurt a few days after the burial. The reading occurred on neutral ground, so to speak, off the Rathenauplatz in the chambers of Wiedemann, Ihle & Krantz, counsel for NANY Inc. Present were Generaldirektor Otto Nasemann with his wife Amelie, née Biltz, from Schwartau near Lübeck; Frau Charlotte Fischer, née Nasemann, with her husband, Direktor Urs Fischer of Basel; and Ernst Nasemann, alias d'Arthez.

The narrator considers it unnecessary to put down here the text of a will that, all in all, seems just and unambiguous. Despite the coolness that d'Arthez had maintained in regard to NANY Inc. over the past three decades, the will did not slight him. Indeed, there was even this phrase, "My son Ernst, who never enjoyed the privileges of the other children, shall . . ." This sentence sounded like out-and-out favoritism, but to the satisfaction of the other heirs, such favoritism found no material expression.

After the will had been read, as a matter of form d'Arthez, as the oldest son, was asked if he accepted all its clauses. (The other heirs appeared to be acquainted with the will before the reading.) All those present, particularly the Herr Generaldirektor and his sister Charlotte, seemed to take his acceptance as a foregone conclusion. In their opinion their brother should have been pleasantly surprised, considering the indifference with which he had always treated NANY Inc.'s affairs, to find himself so unexpectedly (if not undeservedly) and handsomely remembered. Of course, there were stipulations to prevent the sale of shares, for this might result in a take-over of the company by foreign capital; and the actual voting of the shares that would fall to d'Arthez remained unconditionally in the hands of the management. But this in no way affected the large dividends that his equity would produce. Thus, his words were all the more surprising when he replied in his polite, soft voice, "I must request that you allow me time for reflection."

All eyes turned to him. The splotches of red on his sister Lotte's cheeks grew deeper. She poked her husband the banker in the ribs as if to say, What did I tell you? But Dr. Wiedemann, an experienced master of ceremonies, still had the reins firmly in hand.

"Time for reflection? May I inquire about what?"

"Because the decision does not rest with me."

"Oh, I see. And with whom, if I may ask, does the decision rest?"

"With Edith Nasemann."

At that the storm broke out.

"Edith?" shrieked Frau Charlotte Nasemann Fischer.

D'Arthez gave her a friendly nod.

"What does Edith have to do with it?" And since d'Arthez did not answer but merely continued to look amicably in her direction, she scanned the assembled family for assistance. Finally she settled on her husband. "What do you say, Urs?"

In answer Urs Fischer, the Basel banker, only grunted.

"But Edith doesn't even enter into consideration," continued Frau Charlotte Nasemann. The splotches on her cheeks could not have been redder.

41

"Nor are your children mentioned in the will, if I understood it correctly. What do you say, Urs?" d'Arthez in turn asked the Basel banker, who only replied with, "Well, well . . ."

Dr. Wiedemann tried to put an end to this discussion, but with Frau Charlotte Nasemann speaking, he could not get a word in edgewise.

"Edith is still too young to bother her head with such things," she said superciliously.

"Precisely," answered d'Arthez without losing an ounce of his courtesy.

"I don't understand you, Ernst."

"Did anyone ask you to, Lotte?"

At last Dr. Wiedemann was able to get a hearing. He wished to point out that in fact the presumptive assigns of the designated heirs had no say in the acceptance or rejection of the will. Frau Charlotte Nasemann commented approvingly with a "Didn't I tell you so? Didn't I tell you so?" as well as with a "What do you say, Urs?" Dr. Wiedemann was not to be diverted by these interjections. He turned to d'Arthez and asked if the closing paragraph had escaped his attention. This stipulated that any heir who did not accept all the clauses of the will or attempted to delay its execution should be given his legal portion and nothing more. "I cannot believe for a minute that you could consider it in your interest to create difficulties that would make us resort to that final paragraph . . ."

"Difficulties?" d'Arthez replied, and raised one eyebrow in a sign of astonishment most effective in his pantomimes. "May I request, Dr. Wiedemann, that in the minutes of this negotiation it be specifically noted that this word 'difficulties' was used first not by me but by you!"

This remark put even the lawyer off balance. Fortunately for him, the noisy interventions of Frau Charlotte Nasemann relieved him of the labor of taking a stand.

"But you *are* making difficulties," she squealed.

"I?"

"Well, your Edith then."

"It could be as little in my Edith's interest as in your children's to create what Dr. Wiedemann calls difficulties. In the end a heap of money is at stake. What do you say, Urs?"

By remaining casual and calmly addressing the peaceable Swiss banker, thus robbing Frau Charlotte Nasemann of her customary strategy of appealing to her husband for help, d'Arthez brought the situation to the boiling point. Proof of this could be read in the flaming cheeks of the lady in question. For a moment it looked as though she might pounce upon her husband; he never had a chance to grunt in reply to d'Arthez's question. But before she had gotten as far as making a scene, she glanced around the circle and hit on a stronger ally.

"What do you say, Otto?" she called to her brother across the table. "Wasn't Ernst always making difficulties?"

Until this moment, the gentleman she addressed had merely listened and even seemed somewhat indifferent to the whole discussion. Doubtless he had experienced many such conferences and knew that the best strategy was to let arguing associates fight it out without interfering. Once they had vented their fury, one got what one wanted easily enough.

"I too take exception to the word 'difficulties,' Dr. Wiedemann," he said. "But why should grown men and women quarrel over a misused word? All of us here are aware that more important matters are at stake."

"Well, well!" This time the banker meant to express his approval.

"Money," said d'Arthez cordially, perhaps as if lost in thought.

"The family business," his brother corrected him, not without a certain unction.

But d'Arthez overtrumped his brother's emotion with sentimentality. "No, I believe that our immediate concern here is

43

the last will and testament of our dearly beloved mother. Unless I misinterpret that closing paragraph, something that Dr. Wiedemann will certainly keep me from doing, it signifies her all-consuming desire to assure continuing peaceful relationships among her family. Our dearly beloved mother, as we all know—and you best of all, Lotte dear—was always for peace at any price."

"You see? You see?" said Frau Charlotte Nasemann. These words about peace and their dearly beloved mother had touched her deeply. At last she was able to make a show of tears.

"And for that very reason," continued d'Arthez, "assuming I interpret the closing paragraph correctly, which is something only Dr. Wiedemann can say, I see that our only guideline is to keep this peace so fervently desired by our dear departed mother."

"Then why are you making difficulties?" wailed Charlotte Nasemann.

"Now we are not going to use that word again." Herr Generaldirektor Nasemann's tone was somewhat sharp. "Forgive us, Ernst. Let's get to the point. I too am a bit puzzled by your demand for time to think. Do you still insist?"

"Yes, Otto, I do, and even more strongly now, if I am to adequately fulfill the wishes of our dear mother. I am admittedly a bit less certain of them than I was at the beginning of our discussion. I must think conscientiously about her intentions if I am to reach a decision that would satisfy her."

"I thought you needed to speak with Edith—although Dr. Wiedemann has explained that neither Edith nor Lotte's children nor my own have anything to do with the acceptance of this will, at least not legally speaking, since they do not figure in it as assigns. I hope I have expressed myself correctly, doctor."

"You misunderstood me, Otto," d'Arthez replied. "I am not concerned here with anything legal. There's no problem there, or if there is, it's one so simple that we can confidently leave it in Dr. Wiedemann's hands. No, what concerns me is that aspect of our dear departed mother's intention that is quite possibly beyond the grasp of the legal mind, although it must have been this intention that inspired the legally precise wording of the will. *You* will say that her underlying intention is expressed by the word NANY Inc. I couldn't agree more. As Generaldirektor you cannot say anything else. That point of view suits you perfectly. But, if you will allow me to say so, this point of view does not satisfy *me*. It is too abstract. Mind you, I'm not trying to convert anyone to my point of view. For, as I have already remarked, a heap of money is at stake."

"Yes, of course. What do you really want?" asked Otto Nasemann.

"Perhaps it would simplify my task considerably if you would explain to me what you meant by difficulties."

"But we didn't want to use that word!"

"Forgive me, but I must use it, you see. And I would scarcely have repeated it if Lotte hadn't let it slip out involuntarily when she remarked that I'd always caused difficulties."

"Yes, involuntarily, as you yourself just said."

"But nevertheless, Otto, I have to know more in order to reach my decision. How else am I to find out whether these so-called 'difficulties' and the 'always' that slipped out at the same time in reference to me are a part of some sort of family legend about which my long absences prevented my learning. If our dear mother had also encouraged these ideas, this fact would be of the greatest importance in correctly interpreting her will."

"She made a point of referring to you at some length! I simply cannot understand what more you want. Could you read the passage in question once more?" The Generaldirektor

45

turned to Dr. Wiedemann, who obliged him with the following sentence: "My son Ernst, who never enjoyed the privileges of the other children, shall—"

"Thank you, that will do. See, Ernst? Can't you be satisfied with that?"

"I should think so!" Frau Charlotte Nasemann had to make her agreement heard. "Of all things, privileges!"

"Please, Lotte, allow us . . ." began Otto Nasemann in an attempt to head off his sister.

"Just what privileges, I'd like to know! I never noticed any. And now we're reproached with them? It certainly wasn't our fault that Ernst was always making difficulties!"

"Please, Lotte, that has nothing to do with it!"

"But it's *so*, Otto. And always was. Even in the old days. But I was little more than a child then and didn't pay much attention to such matters. But even then when Ernst first became interested in politics . . ."

"Please, Lotte, there's no reason to bring that up."

"No, Ernst is absolutely right. Mama was always afraid that he would get into mischief again. How embarrassing it always was! What worries Papa had over the factory when we feared the Nazis might connect us with Ernst. You know this as well as I do, Otto. So suddenly all of this is *our* fault? What do you say, Urs?"

"This isn't getting us anywhere . . ." Otto Nasemann sounded resigned.

"On the contrary, Otto," said d'Arthez, finally reentering the fray. "We have already gotten quite far. And I think Lotte is perfectly right. The sentence in question, then, can be interpreted as proposing reparations, a sort of indemnification."

"Indemnification!"

"Please, Otto, don't take exception to the word just because our reparations to Israel have given it a certain notoriety. The

46

only point at issue is a correct understanding of our dear mother's last will. And in this respect I am wholeheartedly in agreement with you, Lotte. I cannot see any reason why a certain Ernst Nasemann should be paid reparations at your expense."

"Indemnification!" the Herr Generaldirektor Otto Nasemann howled again. Despite all his experience in handling difficult colleagues, he had finally lost his patience.

"Neither indemnifications nor claims to them can be considered by NANY Inc. or by this family. Indeed, I am deeply hurt that such a word has come up. It needn't have. I would like to point out that it was not *I* who first used it here. Just let me remind you, Ernst, how intolerably embarrassing it was for us under the former regime, and in wartime too, to learn that a person who bore our name had been arrested and chucked in a concentration camp. The way things were, it could easily have spelled the end for NANY Inc."

"Why, Papa even lost his appetite! Remember, Otto?" Frau Charlotte Nasemann interjected.

"Please, Lotte, don't interrupt. I'm afraid I know quite a bit more than you about these unpleasant facts. All the same, Ernst, let me assure you, we never left you in the lurch. Despite the ticklish situation our owning NANY Inc. put us in, we immediately did all we could. We had a few connections, of course, and Papa had . . ."

"Mama swallowed her pride and actually paid a call on that unspeakable woman, that district leader's wife, or whatever they used to call them. Good lord, how embarrassing it all was," Frau Charlotte Nasemann once again butted in.

"Now, Ernst, of course what we did we are proud of. It was our duty, wasn't it? I only bring it up because you're contesting the will and demanding—astonishingly enough—time to think. And now you've brought up the notion of reparations! Forgive me, Ernst, but the case could be argued from the opposite angle. Presumably you would have received much worse treatment if it hadn't been for the influence of NANY Inc. One might even suggest that our connections are responsible for saving your life—always assuming that what has been printed about the concentration camps is true. No matter, that is all over and done with now. I only want you to think about it because this will concern our business and nothing else; otherwise we wouldn't need to waste words about all that."

"Thank you, Otto," said d'Arthez in a friendly voice. "Now that I have heard your argument, I need time for reflection all the more—and to discuss this affair with Edith."

"What can Edith have to do with all this?" sister Lotte cried, up in arms again.

"Oh, a great deal. After hearing Otto's case, I must interpret the will of our dear mother as requiring me to pay reparations to NANY Inc. and to all of you."

"Who said anything of the kind?" cried Otto Nasemann.

"I do. And you must realize, Otto, that if I must commit myself to the payment of reparations, I should have the approval of my probable heir."

"Who ever heard of such rot!" cried the Herr Generaldirektor in a passion.

"Now which of us is making a fuss?" d'Arthez asked with a friendly smile, turning toward his sister Lotte.

"Me?" she cried. "Certainly not me! No one wants money from you. What a silly notion. Money doesn't enter into it."

"Oh, then I have been on the wrong track all this time. Now, Dr. Wiedemann, in that case we must depend on your qualifications as a jurist. Couldn't we say . . ."

There is no purpose served in transcribing verbatim any more of the discussion. D'Arthez asked for four weeks to reflect, but the family beat him down to fourteen days, and even that against the better judgment of Frau Charlotte Fischer, née Nasemann. "Otherwise we'll all of us have to come here again," she complained, "just because of you and your reflections. What do you say, Urs?"

But this objection was disposed of by Dr. Wiedemann's assurance that a written acceptance, once notarized, would suffice. Moreover, a document was drawn up and signed to the effect that during these two weeks the management of NANY Inc. should remain in the hands of the Generaldirektor (as it would once the will was accepted) and that the other heirs would refrain from interference.

With that the negotiations came to an end. Nothing remained but a few common courtesies. For instance, Frau Amelie Nasemann, after keeping silent throughout the argument, now told d'Arthez how sorry she was that he wouldn't be staying with them; he parried this by pleading the number of telephone calls he received, a source of annoyance in a well-run household. Frau Charlotte Fischer couldn't refrain from remarking, as she was saying goodbye, "I simply can't understand you, Ernst."

Although he was apprised of the problem only much later, the narrator feels that the decision that d'Arthez reached after his period of reflection should be dealt with now, despite the original plan, which was quite different. Since the vicissitudes of the affair have already been narrated, the outcome might just as well be appended.

As for the discussion quoted above, since d'Arthez had not informed Edith Nasemann of it, it was communicated to the narrator by Lambert. It would appear from Lambert's version that d'Arthez's intentions were far from clear. Only after long acquaintance with the matter does the narrator feel that he now understands what d'Arthez had in mind. As in his pantomimes, he merely frayed the nerve ends of his audience ever so slightly and tried to make them feel unsure of themselves by exaggerating their conventions.

In other words, he had already decided to refuse the inheritance. That much is now clear, and that he could have had anything else in mind would be greatly disappointing. But for his daughter's sake he hesitated to come right out with a refusal that for himself alone would have been a matter of course.

The two friends must have discussed this at great length. Of course Lambert supported his refusal. He expressed himself rather bluntly about both NANY Inc. and the Nasemann family. Nor was there any real doubt that Edith too would applaud her father's decision. But above all, d'Arthez wanted to avoid her deciding anything merely to please him and perhaps regretting it later. This alone occasioned his breaking a rule that these two friends otherwise observed—namely, never to discuss purely personal matters. D'Arthez is reported to have remarked, "We are meddling with another generation, and this is forbidden us." Lambert then suggested that d'Arthez should settle for a lump sum. That would scarcely affect a concern the size of NANY Inc. In so doing, he would be drawing a line between the business and family on one side and himself and Edith on the other. "And if you and Edith don't want the money," he mused, "you can parcel it out to persons persecuted by the Nazis or to relatives of former inmates of concentration camps."

This d'Arthez rejected out of hand. "Even if I believed in such half measures, this one would be of advantage only to NANY Inc. Let them advertise with the most beautiful female legs they can find, but I won't have them making use of sham philanthropies."

And finally there was one point d'Arthez discussed with his daughter quite unwillingly and with the most extraordinary caution, to avoid swaying her or wounding her feelings. The narrator refers to Edith Nasemann's own family, consisting of her mother, d'Arthez's former wife, her stepfather and their children. "There is her mother, after all," said d'Arthez to Lambert, "and her second husband and their children, who are, strictly speaking, Edith's real family. All in all, she spent nearly twenty years with them and grew up in their home." Lambert made no bones about his utter detestation of this so-called "family," although aside from Edith's mother he had met none of them. Later he even attempted to convert the narrator to his views, hoping thereby to win Edith over too. "She must be talked out of feeling false gratitude," he said. "Gratitude! This idiotic taboo has strangled so many already. And I'll wager that this so-called family of hers has been living off Edith." Lambert told d'Arthez that he was for Edith "buying herself free of them" once and for all with a lump sum. And what would it cost actually? he mused. Give them fifty thousand marks and they'd jump for joy. But d'Arthez objected that after a year or two they would crawl to Edith complaining that fifty wasn't enough, why not one hundred thousand; that was the way things were. "No, money isn't the answer. It won't accomplish a thing. Luckily this problem each of us must solve for himself—and risk going down the drain in the process. Yes, one can help someone who feels lonely after having deserted the human ant heap and hasn't yet grown accustomed to the fresh air that blows outside the family circle. But this decision each person must reach for himself." Probably d'Arthez would have expressed himself differently. His words as given here smell suspiciously of Lambert's vocabulary. But no matter, d'Arthez absolutely refused to make any attempt to sway his daughter. He reduced his friend to silence with the objection, "Just how do you propose to demonstrate the correctness of *our* choice?"

Edith Nasemann was offended that her father felt he had to ask her about the will at all. "I know for a fact that Papa wants to refuse the inheritance. Can he really believe I'm greedy for money? What do I care about those Nasemanns? I've only known them two years. I see them only because Papa considers it proper I should. Let them try to be happy with all their money! What nonsense! Papa actually believes I might regret it later when I have children of my own. Well, I had rather not have children than have them depend on money from NANY Inc., as I told Papa."

All this came out much later. To return to the will: before the fourteen days were out, Dr. Wiedmann received a notarized letter of renunciation not only signed by d'Arthez but bearing Edith Nasemann's approval of her father's act as well. This letter gave no reasons for their renunciation nor suggested what should be done with the inheritance thereby renounced. How the Nasemann family reached agreement in this matter, and whether the "peace so fervently desired by our dear departed mother" was kept, does not belong in this report. All the same, a sort of epilogue was played out. Only a few who saw the pantomime on television, doubtless inspired by the reading of this will, would have been aware of this epilogue.

It begins with a stage empty except for a casket, which is empty too and open, lying on the floor, the cover nearby. A little to one side stands a dressmaker's dummy, buxom, with swelling hips. It is short, covered with black calico, without a head, and instead of legs stands on a tripod having small rubber wheels. As we shall presently see, this dressmaker's dummy plays an important role in Lambert's thoughts—and in his pantomimes. One could go so far as to claim that this dummy was d'Arthez's sole stage partner. Lambert even kept the dummy in his room. He assured the narrator, as the latter recoiled in horror at his first sight of the monstrosity, that he even carried on conversations with her from time to time. He explained that this was one way of keeping one's feet on the ground. Edith Nasemann loathed the dummy. She no longer said anything about it, since quite enough had already been said, but every time she entered Lambert's room she grimaced to find the dummy still there. And, as a matter of fact, the narrator too felt that by its mere presence this dummy influenced or inhibited conversation. Moreover, this superannuated female form had two jointed wire arms. Whether for the purpose of tailoring sleeves, as Edith believed, the narrator cannot say. Lambert often tossed his scarf over these arms. "All night long this poor woman has to hold my shirt and underwear," he reported with a grin. "And she's glad to, don't you think?" As he said this, he slapped the dummy on the back.

Later, it will become clear that this dummy, which at the time the narrator took for nothing more than the whim of an eccentric, played a more important role in Lambert's life than the narrator could have guessed. In her instinctive loathing of it, Edith Nasemann was on the right track. But how did d'Arthez himself feel about the dummy? It would be instructive if we knew. His daughter insisted that he simply no longer noticed it, any more than he would any other piece of furniture. "For Papa the dummy is simply a prop. Papa must feel differently about women," she said defensively.

In the pantomime inspired by the reading of his mother's will, d'Arthez enters in his usual costume—the correct dark jacket and discreetly striped trousers, the black homburg, gloves and cane, and of course the small English mustache he always affected on stage. As soon as he notices the open casket, he is startled and immediately takes off his hat as is the custom. Then he notices the dummy and walks over to express his sympathy with an earnest expression.

There is no way to describe this without robbing the act of its effect. But every viewer knows immediately that d'Arthez isn't simply expressing his condolences to a mourner. Only too obviously, he believes the casket is intended for the dummy, and this is why he is consoling her. One can almost hear him saying, If you look at it the right way, my dear, it's perhaps all for the best—without the pain of a long-drawn-out illness, which merely costs the bereaved a fortune, and with as little fuss as possible. In truth, a lovely death.

But d'Arthez is mistaken. The casket wasn't ordered for the dummy; it's for him. The dummy evinces a certain indignation in informing him of this. D'Arthez creates this impression by stepping back half a pace, not as though he were frightened or surprised but as if to say, Oh, for *me*? As he steps back, he points an index finger at his breast.

Then he turns around—once more, he is obviously reacting to something the dummy has brought to his attention—and gazes toward the casket; indeed, there at the foot an oval silver plaque reads "D'ARTHEZ."

He walks over and stoops to make certain he isn't mistaken, straightens up, shrugs ever so slightly and makes a scarcely perceptible gesture, as if to say, Oh well, there's nothing to be done. Then he lays down hat, gloves and cane before returning to the casket to examine its interior; he even feels whether the cushions are soft enough. All this seems to have satisfied him, for he smiles at the dummy amicably. In the meantime, she hasn't moved an inch.

"Isn't that the spitting image of Aunt Lotte?" crowed Edith Nasemann, seeing this on television in the narrator's company. D'Arthez pulls a piece of paper out of his breast pocket and motions the dummy over. And the dummy does turn ever so slightly in his direction—by means of ropes or wires invisible to the audience, the dummy could be wheeled about.

D'Arthez unfolds the paper so everyone can read "My Will." He lets the dummy see this too. Smiling benignly, he nods encouragement. Finally he hands it to her—that is, he sticks it in the mesh of one of her outstretched wire arms. As soon as he's done this, the dummy turns away quickly. The will obviously interests her more than anything else. This doesn't seem to offend d'Arthez.

He returns to the casket and picks up his things—gloves, cane and the black homburg. Why, he even puts his hat on. But no sooner has he done so than he takes it off again as if to say, Dear me, no! It isn't done, lying down with one's hat on . . . Then he climbs into the casket and lies down. He tugs a bit at trousers and jacket until everything is just right. He folds his hands, holding hat and gloves on his stomach. At last everything seems proper enough for him to close his eyes. As he does so, a harmonium strikes up Handel's "Largo," pianissimo at first.

The dummy has not taken notice of any of this. She stands with her back to the casket, or rather her full-bottomed rear. She is busy with the will. This is indicated by her jerky movements to the left and to the right and toward the audience. The contents of the will appear to please her very much. The viewer cannot help imagining what she is thinking about: the pleasant life she will lead thanks to this inherited money. What a piece of luck his opportune death is. What good would it have done if I had come into this too late? In the meantime, d'Arthez rests peacefully in his casket and the harmonium grows gradually louder. But then it stops. Suddenly d'Arthez raises his head and notices that the dummy isn't standing next to the casket mourning; she's still poring over the will. So he climbs out of the casket. As he does so, the music stops, but the dummy doesn't notice.

He puts on his hat, hangs the cane over his left arm and walks over to the dummy. She is startled and can't move for fright. Without changing his expression, d'Arthez takes the will and walks back to the casket. The dummy seems to skip after him in short spurts like a hen. The viewer can't help feeling that she is gesticulating wildly, although in reality she is not. But d'Arthez isn't paying any attention.

Without haste, he tears the will into small pieces—eight times, if the narrator observed accurately—and lets the snippets flutter into the casket. Then he pulls on one of his gloves, waves his hat once or twice in the direction of the casket and departs.

Now mourning disconsolately, the bereaved dummy stands beside the casket and looks into it. A saxophone imitates a woman's unrestrained sobbing. Curtain.

The narrator apologizes for this all-too-detailed and, at the same time, so imperfect rendering of this scene. Millions of viewers will have seen it for themselves on television and formed their own mental approximations of it. For the narrator this scene matters only because it might allow one to draw some conclusions as to the extent to which d'Arthez's offerings were influenced by everyday events and circumstances—in spite of his aloof behavior.

To return one last time to the burial of old lady Nasemann: in one respect this real-life theater seemed to gratify Edith Nasemann. This became clear when she showed the narrator her photographs and clippings. She exhaustively examined pictures in which she figured; they seemed to meet with her approval.

Admittedly, she and her father stood out somehow, catching the eye immediately. Quite unintentionally, they contrasted sharply with other bystanders who held quite similar poses. Someone who didn't recognize them would have wanted to know who they were. Two pictures in particular pleased Edith. In one of them the mourners had been snapped from behind, diagonally, as they followed the casket from the chapel to the grave. D'Arthez had stepped aside to allow his brother the Generaldirektor and his wife to lead the group, but he followed immediately behind with Edith, whose arm he gently held. The other photograph showed the whole family again, but this time gathered about the bier in the main hangar of the factory. Around them stood all the prominent people present at the funeral—ministers, lord mayors, union presidents and so on. The uniformed general was also visible.

D'Arthez was usually taken, as in his pantomimes, for a celebrated diplomat or a British prime minister—that is to say, the sort of man one imagines to be a British prime minister, since in reality the type has long since vanished. His daughter looked much taller in the photographs, not even a head shorter than her father. This was not merely the result of her wearing black or of her standing up particularly straight. There was another reason.

"I was wearing high heels," Edith told the narrator. "Papa thought it best, so we bought them the previous day. Then I stayed up half the night walking around my room getting used to them so the damned things wouldn't pinch. Papa feels that shoes you aren't accustomed to make the task of putting in a formal appearance easier: they require the person wearing them to follow *their* directions. Well, he has more experience in such matters, and anyway I could wear them on other formal occasions later."

D'Arthez also looked after the rest of his daughter's funeral outfit—the right sort of dress, coat and handbag. He went with her to the shops and helped her select these things. Edith was astonished at how much experience he showed. "He knew much more about it than I did, and even when I didn't want something because I felt it didn't suit me, or cost too much, I had to agree with him later. Papa sat there and watched while I tried things on before a mirror, and I had to parade before him like a mannequin. He had patience. At the milliner's, for instance, I must have tried on at least thirty hats and was already so tired of the ordeal I would have settled for the next one that came along, just to get home. But Papa stuck to his guns. How do you like this droll little hat with the black veil? Don't you find it much too sophisticated for me? I felt positively foolish when the saleslady put it on my head. I thought everyone would laugh. But Papa said, 'At last you've found the right one!' And of course the saleslady agreed with him. You can't imagine how expensive it was, but no one laughed, that's true. And the coat was far too expensive; Papa shouldn't have spent so much money for this single occasion. How often do I attend a funeral? And when do I go to formal parties? Papa thought, you see, that I could use this coat for other things. But of course I wanted Papa to be proud of me. I mean because of that stuck-up family of his. And I think I brought it all off pretty well, don't you?" Edith turned critically to the pictures once more. "That fellow even kissed my hand. He thought I was a star. I was absolutely dumfounded, but I didn't let it show because stupid Aunt Lotte was giving me a nasty look just then. Papa praised me to the skies afterward. He said I might have made even the most experienced actor lose his head. People aren't in the habit of kissing hands at funerals, you know. He was the son of a French industrialist, I think. Some sort of playboy.

"Yes, and would you believe it, Papa even made me buy new lingerie? Imagine that. As though one's underthings matter at a funeral. And as if the lingerie I already had weren't perfectly decent! I said as much to Papa, but he explained that one feels entirely different with brand-new cloth next to one's skin; one feels confident that nothing will split or start sliding down. To think that Papa knows a thing like that. He even bought me a nightgown . . . A nightgown for a funeral! It just happened to be hanging there in the shop. They had it draped over a stand as though wafted gently by the wind. That's the way you'll see them now in almost any shopwindow. All enormously expensive and made of see-through material. It must have taken Papa's fancy, because he was always looking over while we selected the other things, and finally he asked me, 'What about that?' I told him to stop this nonsense—I must have been a bit short with him. But when I came out of the booth where I had been trying something on, there he stood next to this silly nightgown, talking to the woman who owned the shop and feeling the material and the seams. Then he just went ahead and bought it. I found it when I was unwrapping the other things."

In any case, her entrance seems to have produced the desired effect. And the black dress and coat acquired for this event were used again, unfortunately much sooner than anyone could have expected. It was in these later circumstances that the narrator gained firsthand knowledge of the black dress, the expensive coat and that little hat with the tiny bit of veil.

This occurred at Lambert's interment. He unexpectedly suffered a heart attack in the library and died two days later in the hospital. But perhaps he had been sick a long time, refusing to take proper care of himself and never mentioning his condition. D'Arthez happened to be on tour in America at the time, so Edith had to decide what was to be done; the narrator did his best to assist her. That Lambert's body should be transported to Wiesbaden, where his wife had died in '49 or '50, was easily decided. But should an announcement be placed in the papers after the interment? And if so, what should it say? Most important, under what name should the announcement be placed? For Lambert wasn't really named Lambert. His real name was Ludwig Lembke. But Edith was right when she exclaimed, "What do we care about the people who knew him as Lembke? Lambert would be annoyed. Papa, too." And so the following brief notice appeared in the *Frankfurter Allgemeine*:

1911–1966
LOUIS LAMBERT

The bereaved:
 d'Arthez
 Edith Nasemann
 (the narrator's name)

Edith insisted on the narrator's signing. She invoked her father and Lambert himself and paid no attention to the narrator's objections. Whether anyone noticed this announcement, of course, it is impossible to say. Who would have known who Louis Lambert was? Most of those who could have known were dead or had vanished in the war or had become indifferent.

Edith and the narrator left Frankfurt for Wiesbaden in the morning. The narrator apologized that his clothes were unstylish compared with Edith's outfit. Naturally, he was wearing a dark suit; he had even bought a black tie for the occasion. But that scarcely added up to suitable attire. And since it looked like rain, he had cautiously taken his raincoat, which was light-colored. Edith had a black umbrella with a long curved handle.

She and the narrator were the only persons to follow the bier. That too was fitting (except, of course, that d'Arthez was missing). Edith and the narrator could not bring themselves to hunt up a man of the cloth. Not even Edith knew whether Lambert had been brought up as a Catholic or a Lutheran. And besides, Ludwig Lembke wasn't being buried; it was Lambert. Edith cried for a long time beside the grave— that should not be forgotten. And the narrator too felt tears in his eyes because he had never before seen Edith cry. People who claim that it is only mourning for one's own mortality that provokes one to carry on so, don't know what they're talking about.

Lambert always claimed we were fortunate not to have a past. But now suddenly Edith and the narrator did have a past because they had stood beside a grave together and couldn't help crying. And, also, it was a kind of farewell.

four

The narrator cannot conceive of Dr. Glatschke's knowing about any of these things—either the burial of old lady Nasemann or the reading of the will and what was said on that occasion. At any rate, at the time of the so-called interrogation, he did not know.

Of course Dr. Glatschke was compelled to explain his reason for requesting that d'Arthez drop by. He did so most unwillingly and repeatedly slipped in the entreaty that this be considered highly confidential, although in point of fact it was a commonplace affair and secrecy was not in order. Any French newspaper reader could have read about it two days before, but it was nothing sensational, since the facts would not lend themselves to such treatment. *Le Figaro* carried nothing more than a line or two under the heading "Tribunaux." However, hindsight leads one to wonder at this, for in a certain sense the press had slipped up here. Evidently the affair looked so routine that the city desk sent their most inexperienced reporter to the scene. The curiosity of a relatively seasoned journalist, even one with no intellectual pretensions, would have been whetted immediately on hearing the victim's name, or at least one would assume so. However, in this case Police or Security had been more alert than the press.

And Dr. Glatschke may have been doing no more than employing one of the oldest tricks in the detective's bag. A request for discretion often catches a person off guard, making him spill things he would otherwise have kept to himself. By thus calculating on the vanity of his visitor, Dr. Glatschke certainly did not pick the winning number, particularly since the visitor was a man of d'Arthez's caliber. But how could Glatschke have known about this? Equally ignorant was the narrator, who lacked any personal interest since the subject of d'Arthez was then something quite novel to him. At the time, the narrator was cooped up in a stale cubbyhole where, for the moment, nothing concerned him more than the functioning of his tape recorder. At first, it did not strike him how clumsy Dr. Glatschke's method was. Only as the recorded interrogation began to fascinate him did he start to lose patience. But anyone who listens carefully to the recording would have realized at once that d'Arthez was only playing along with Dr. Glatschke's method with simulated ingenuousness and in so doing proved himself Glatschke's superior from the very start. It must have been this which enraged Dr. Glatschke so, and as might have been predicted of a man of his type, he worked off his rage by convincing himself that d'Arthez was a dangerous malefactor with something to hide. Otherwise, the steps that Dr. Glatschke took immediately after the interrogation, which were absolutely ridiculous and of considerable expense to the state, make no sense at all.

The narrator would give a great deal to have been in the room during this interrogation. As it is, he can only reconstruct the scene acoustically or by following the transcripts based on the tape, copies of which, naturally enough, were forwarded to the Central Bureau. But just listening to the tape already provided him with a fair notion of the scene itself. No hint of irony could be inferred from d'Arthez's tone of voice. (One would have assumed his tone was ironic if one merely read the transcript.) The concentration which d'Arthez brought to bear on Dr. Glatschke's statements and inquiries must have been infuriating. He tried to answer each question with a courteous and slightly apologetic conversational tone as if to say, How could a mere layman like me provide *you* with information? Yet each time he managed to shy away from the heart of the matter into such generalities that Dr. Glatschke was hard-pressed not to have the rug pulled out from under him.

D'Arthez must have known the conversation was being taped. The narrator is now convinced of this. And not just because Lambert insisted that all of them were aware that anything they said might be taped—that could simply be another of Lambert's whims. But at the time a seemingly trivial incident occurred that does reinforce this assumption.

When this so-called interrogation had come to an end, which one deduced from the phrases used and the scraping of chairs as the gentlemen stood up, the narrator turned the tape recorder off and put his ear to the door that separated the taping room from the small anteroom in which his desk was. The two men would have to pass by this room. Naturally Dr. Glatschke saw his visitor to the door, thanking him for his kindness all the way. After they had passed, the narrator opened his door and watched them enter one of the outer offices, where a secretary sat typing at her desk.

Their backs were turned to him. D'Arthez gave the girl a friendly nod while Dr. Glatschke continued his effusions. At the hall door, however, something happened. The narrator has to admit that his curiosity got the better of him. Herr Dr. Glatschke had just opened the door for d'Arthez. Before parting, they had to shake hands and this required that d'Arthez turn around. The narrator cannot be certain, but at that moment d'Arthez seemed to wink at him over Dr. Glatschke's shoulder.

When Edith Nasemann heard this anecdote from the narrator, she said, "That sounds just like Papa. He notices everything, even the trivial details."

And Dr. Glatschke, too, seems to have noticed something. He stormed back into the room and chewed the narrator out. "Now you've ruined everything! Bring that tape in immediately! Hurry up! Hurry up!"

Here follows a transcript of the interrogation. Omitted are only the introductory phrases with which Dr. Glatschke greeted d'Arthez and apologized for having caused him the trouble of paying him a visit. It hardly needs mentioning that, throughout, Dr. Glatschke addressed d'Arthez as "Herr Nasemann."

GLATSCHKE: Presumably this request from the Paris police is purely routine and the case doesn't really concern us. But a few days ago, four to be exact, a corpse was found in the rue Lauriston.

D'ARTHEZ: Rue Lauriston? And where might that be?

GLATSCHKE: A relatively quiet side street running from the Avenue Victor Hugo to the Avenue Kléber, a scant five minutes from the Étoile. [Shortly before this meeting, Dr. Glatschke had asked for a map of Paris to orient himself in this neighborhood.] As I said, a quiet street. Just a few shops, a single modern office building, a small hotel, if I'm not mistaken, and the rest old-fashioned Parisian apartment houses. You'd take it for a dead-end street although it really isn't. It only gives that impression because it is set up higher than the avenues. From the Avenue Victor Hugo, for example, you have to climb a few steps. But why should I go into such detail, excuse me. All this must be only too familiar to you.

[D'Arthez simply takes no notice of this cheap trick. Obviously he is just sitting there looking at Dr. Glatschke inquisitively; the latter continues after a short pause.]

GLATSCHKE: No?

D'ARTHEZ: I almost never visit that part of town. Perhaps once or twice I've passed by in a taxi.

GLATSCHKE: Oh, I see. And besides, that isn't really what concerns us, is it? To make a long story short, in the lower section of the street, two or three doors past the rue Valéry, there's an empty lot where construction has been held up for quite a time now. In Paris some union or other is always on strike, you know. Behind the fence a body was discovered. A woman who lives on the fourth floor saw him lying there when she went to the window in the morning to shake out her dustcloth.

D'ARTHEZ: A dustcloth? Was it really a dustcloth?

GLATSCHKE: Yes, why not?

D'ARTHEZ: Wasn't it perhaps one of those other cleaning things, I think you call them dust *mops*?"

GLATSCHKE [astonished, as one might conclude from his tone of voice; for a moment he is weighing the possibility that d'Arthez has given himself away and knows more about this case than he has let on]: Does that really matter?

D'ARTHEZ [with great courtesy]: For a mere layman like myself it is fabulously important if he is to gain an accurate picture of the circumstances. Was it an old or a young lady?

GLATSCHKE: She was no lady.

D'ARTHEZ: Oh, forgive me.

GLATSCHKE [One can hear him riffling through his papers]: Madame Untel, wife of a clerk in the Finance Ministry.

D'ARTHEZ [feigning astonishment]: Aha! Finance . . . Isn't that a clue?

GLATSCHKE [expressing first consternation, then rage, at this questioning of the competence of the Paris police]: Let us drop the lady. You can rest assured, Herr Nasemann, that her particulars have been thoroughly investigated. Our confreres in Paris are conscientious to a fault and have the most exhaustive documentation at their fingertips. This is demonstrated by their having come straight to us in this case. [Since d'Arthez does not react, he continues.] Well, then, to make a long story short, this lady, or woman rather, took the murdered man for a drunk sleeping it off. For this reason, it was noon before she called the police, after noticing that the fellow was still lying there. As I said, it was murder. He had been slain with one of the many bricks that were lying around.

D'ARTHEZ: With a brick?

GLATSCHKE: Yes, indeed. No, wait a minute. Perhaps "cinder block" would be the more accurate translation. It was found, with traces of skin and hair on it.

D'ARTHEZ [almost inaudibly]: Impossible . . .

GLATSCHKE: Excuse me?

D'ARTHEZ: An impossible death. Forgive me, Herr Oberregierungsrat.

GLATSCHKE: Well, the case itself demonstrates just how possible such a death is.

D'ARTHEZ: It will take me time to accustom myself to the idea. Once again, you must forgive me.

GLATSCHKE: The murder weapon doesn't concern us here. Triv-

66

ial details we can leave to Paris. The reason for their turning to us, and our turning to you, Herr Nasemann, is entirely different. The murdered man was carrying papers, a *carte d'identité* to be precise, which turned out to be a damned clever forgery; by the way, under the name—and it was under this name, let me add, that the murdered man was also known to his associates—in short, under the name d'Arthez.

[And here the tape was silent for such a long time that the narrator, hearing it for the first time, feared that his machine had malfunctioned. Now he considers the pause highly significant. What happened seems to have been this: Obviously counting on some exclamation from d'Arthez at this piece of news, Dr. Glatschke was watching his visitor's face expectantly to ascertain whether his surprise was real or assumed. Yet, the expected exclamation failed to materialize. No sound on the tape hinted that d'Arthez had so much as shifted in his chair. Presumably he looked at Dr. Glatschke courteously, patiently awaiting further information, and thus Dr. Glatschke was robbed of his carefully calculated effect. Finally the detective lost his patience.]

GLATSCHKE [rather brusquely]: You have nothing to say?

D'ARTHEZ: A forgery?

GLATSCHKE: Yes, indeed, and quite an old one too. And Paris believes it's nailed down the source but doesn't say anything further. Forgery or not, that doesn't matter here. It's the name.

D'ARTHEZ: To be sure.

GLATSCHKE: Aren't you even a trifle surprised?

D'ARTHEZ: Why should it surprise me?

GLATSCHKE: Then you were aware that other people were making use of this name?

D'ARTHEZ: Aware is going too far, but I can't say that I'm surprised. Untold numbers have been on the loose since 1945 under names assumed to hide a past. Many of them have respectable occupations, a wife and children, and appear to be pillars of the community. But you know more about this than I, Herr Oberregierungsrat.

GLATSCHKE: But under such an unusual name . . .

D'ARTHEZ: What is so unusual about it? Anyone is welcome to it. But then he must prove that he is entitled to use it and that isn't always easy. Was the man stripped?

GLATSCHKE: Stripped?

D'ARTHEZ: The corpse, of course. Stripped and mutilated?

GLATSCHKE: Mutilated?

D'ARTHEZ: Things like that go right on happening, even though they are unimaginable. I couldn't believe my eyes either when I saw such things some years ago, but unfortunately we must always reckon with their recurrence.

GLATSCHKE [looking through the dossier, to judge from the rustling of papers]: Paris doesn't report anything of the kind. Why do you ask?

D'ARTHEZ: Because I would like to be of assistance to you and your French confreres. For instance, didn't you mention earlier that a street nearby is named Paul Valéry? That street name must be relatively new . . .

GLATSCHKE: So you know the street?

D'ARTHEZ: Not at all, but I knew the man after whom the street is named. He died only about twenty years ago. Someone will have to look up the exact date; I have no memory for figures, I'm sorry to say.

GLATSCHKE: And what does this have to do with our d'Arthez?

D'ARTHEZ: It should enable you to draw certain conclusions. But again you must forgive me, Herr Oberregierungsrat, I am no detective. My unprofessional conclusions would strike you as ridiculous. It could be too that the victim did not

68

stumble on this name in the process of his education. You were speaking a while ago of "his associates." Did you mean drugs?

GLATSCHKE: How do you know?

D'ARTHEZ: I read detective stories. Drugs are the latest thing.

GLATSCHKE: Oh, I see.

D'ARTHEZ: Perhaps he was a former Nazi? Or perhaps a collaborator?

GLATSCHKE: Indeed, it is astonishing how accurate your information is, Herr Nasemann.

D'ARTHEZ: No, no, nothing of the kind. Why flatter me? I only asked because it might explain the brick. Some old accounts are often squared so late that one would think they might have been amnestied by some statute of limitations. But the desire for revenge is extraordinarily long-lived, I'm sorry to say.

GLATSCHKE: Our d'Arthez was something of a tout up on Montmartre. He wasn't strictly a pimp and he kept on the right side of the law, but he was always ready to make a deal with the tourists. No particular specialty. Hundreds must eke out their existence in this manner . . . They are all known to the police and used as the occasion demands.

D'ARTHEZ: Then it could very well be that this man spotted the name on a theater marquee or in a program guide and found "d'Arthez" suitable just at the moment when he needed protective coloration. It won't be easy for me to assist you here. I am not at home in Montmartre, really. But of course I will begin inquiries immediately.

GLATSCHKE: Begin inquiries?

D'ARTHEZ: Why not? The name in question happens to be the one which I am known by. Even though I have nothing against touts personally, no theatrical agency is going to stand idly by if some columnist connects my name with this

69

regrettable affair involving a brick. Why, I will write to Paris this very day and ask that the business be looked into.

GLATSCHKE: And you believe your friends can get somewhere?

D'ARTHEZ: Friends! Forgive me, but that word is far too grand . . . And of course we scarcely have at our disposal an instrument so refined as the police; yet it is a sort of secret service and it can function with as much accuracy and rapidity. You see, for us anything you might consider mere gossip, even scandal is *real* and forms a reality that we must deal with effectively. And, moreover, this reality will be communicated with the speed of light—if one has the proper antennae.

GLATSCHKE: Well now, isn't that interesting. I really cannot express enough gratitude at your setting your organization to work.

D'ARTHEZ: Organization? Oh, Herr Oberregierungsrat, we manage quite well without organization. Now, please do not take that for criticism! But to return to the case that brings us together: we are not quite up to date on Right Bank practices. We are more at home on the Left Bank. Certainly this might be termed one-sided, and as time goes by, we hope to change this. I once tried to acquaint myself with the other bank. That was two years ago and had nothing whatever to do with your brick. Before that date I had always chosen hotels on the Left Bank, but this once I tried one on the Île Saint-Louis, Quai d'Anjou, I believe, overlooking the Right Bank and next to a bridge. My French colleagues were astonished at my staying there. I never betrayed my reasons since they were purely professional. Otherwise, they might have taken me for a sentimentalist or a romantic. Beside the entrance to the hotel—Hôtel de la Paix, it just occurs to me, and what else could it have been called?—there was a sign on which, among other things, appeared the words *Confort moderne.* The sign was pre-World War I and so were the comforts. Not the sort you find in the Frankfurt Intercontinental. My professional experiment was to test the role of a twenty-one-year-old student who might have boarded there, say, thirty years ago. *"Confort moderne"* and the view across the Seine much facilitated the task of putting oneself in such a young man's place. Seriously, Herr Oberregierungsrat, this is merely professional cunning. What I really wanted to know was what the world might have been like if this young man had enjoyed the good fortune of living there thirty years ago. Very well, not to bore you with shop talk but to give you a few facts for your dossier: the role is such that nobody can do a thing with it. At most it causes a few sour reflections on history. And in my opinion this is an aspect of modern comfort we cannot afford. This is a fact which you can confidently pass on to your Parisian colleagues. Put it in the minutes. For, you see, in this area I consider myself an expert.

GLATSCHKE: Yes, of course, Herr Nasemann. No one doubts it. But as I said, this isn't what we are here for. We are here . . .

D'ARTHEZ [interrupting him]: On the contrary, Herr Oberregierungsrat. That brick is the most reprehensible kind of romanticism. The police should consider it beneath their dignity to waste a thought on that brick.

GLATSCHKE: But you fail to understand what I'm driving at: the brick is none of *our* business, just the name d'Arthez. And then there is the political angle. That is the sole reason why the Paris police sent inquiries our way. And that's our sole purpose in troubling you. It seems the man in question had an American passport in his room in the name of Zahorski; no, Sulkowski. Does that name ring a bell?

D'ARTHEZ: Sulkowski, I believe, is old Polish nobility.

GLATSCHKE: Aha! Are you acquainted with any of them?

D'ARTHEZ: Oh yes, out of history books. I believe there was a general by that name.

GLATSCHKE: Aha! The police, you see, have reason to believe that the man was some sort of agent . . .

D'ARTHEZ: Marxist?

GLATSCHKE: Oh no, the opposite. A group of the extreme right, perhaps even monarchists. In Paris they would like to know who's putting up the money.

D'ARTHEZ: Now why would I be financing a bunch of monarchists? That is quite outside my line.

GLATSCHKE: Please try to understand what I am saying, Herr Nasemann. No one has ever entertained such a preposterous notion. It is only the name d'Arthez! Can you be astonished that the occurrence of this uncommon name should make Paris think of you at once? All we want to know, all we ask of you, is, yes or no, do you know or did you know that others were using this name?

D'ARTHEZ: The only d'Arthez I know . . .

GLATSCHKE [interrupting him]: So you do know one other?

D'ARTHEZ: But of course. Would I have taken the name otherwise?

[There is a silence here. The only thing to be heard is a quick intake of breath. Obviously Dr. Glatschke was flabbergasted—there's no other word for it. He had to collect his wits.]

GLATSCHKE: Now we're geting somewhere. I am most grateful to you for this information. And what can you tell us about *this* d'Arthez?

D'ARTHEZ: He has dropped out of sight. That explains why I took his name. I hoped I could lure him out of his seclusion. Can you suggest any better way? A better method than the one I've chosen? The name can be heard on the radio, read everywhere on theater marquees and so on. It strikes me as a tremendous manhunt. Every time I go on stage I expect someone in the audience to hoot me off, shouting, "You aren't the one!"

GLATSCHKE: But so far he hasn't stepped forward?

D'ARTHEZ: I am still waiting. Patience is necessary, Herr Oberregierungsrat. Just as in your profession. There is doubtless some perfectly good reason for my friend's remaining hidden.

GLATSCHKE: And you have never exchanged letters?

D'ARTHEZ: But, Herr Oberregierungsrat, the first rule is: *Nothing in writing!* I scarcely need remind you of that. All the more when the business is strictly confidential.

GLATSCHKE: Yes, of course, that goes without saying. Thank you.

D'ARTHEZ [getting up, to judge from the noise]: Will that be all?

GLATSCHKE: Oh no, excuse me! Just another minute or two, Herr Nasemann. I know how valuable your time is, and also what a painful occasion it is that brings you to Frankfurt, but there is one more question. Could you divulge the date of the last information you have had about your friend d'Arthez?

D'ARTHEZ: I am afraid I cannot recall the precise date. As I have already said, numbers are not my strong suit. One of us will always stick to facts. Let me see, the last news of d'Arthez that reached me was not from the man himself, of course, but rather by way of the grapevine; this last news was to the effect that he had been snared by the Duchess de Maufrigneuse.

GLATSCHKE: The Duchess de Maufrigneuse?

D'ARTHEZ: Your colleagues in Paris will have heard of her. She is a young lady one might describe as *amoureuse*, and she has an astonishing instinct for which men are on the way up, whether monarchist or republican. The lady herself, although a monarchist by nature (what else could she be?), never allowed such fine points to interfere with the exercise of her charms. In this respect she was above politics. Your Parisian colleagues will surely vouch for this. The duchess made no bones about her affairs.

GLATSCHKE: Would this d'Arthez of yours be a member of the nobility?

D'ARTHEZ: Possibly. He might come from the impoverished gentry. That is of no importance among intellectuals. One's origins do not matter to us. But it may very well be that Balzac ennobled him. Balzac, you see, ennobled himself. He was obsessed with this slightly unfashionable weakness for the nobility. In a mighty bourgeois epoch it was quite useful for one's career.

GLATSCHKE: How did Balzac get into the act?

D'ARTHEZ: But it was Balzac who passed on the last news I've had of d'Arthez! Naturally, in the middle of an affair with a duchess, d'Arthez could scarcely be expected to let his own voice be heard. Wouldn't you do the same? And what difference does it make? In any case, for us d'Arthez is still the ideal of the patient, clandestine, intellectual opposition. An ideal because he will not be diverted from his goal by trumped-up momentary crises—that is, topicality. And his goal is revolution.

GLATSCHKE [frightened]: Revolution?

D'ARTHEZ [sighs]: Yes, in those days revolution was still a reality; men believed in it even though a few revolutions had proved to be mere trumped-up topicality. But why discuss this, Herr Oberregierungsrat? We are merely wasting each other's time. And in Paris they know more about this than we ever shall. Unfortunately, Balzac is dead, or I would surely learn more about the later course of d'Arthez's life. Balzac was one of our most reliable narrators. In any case, the affair with the little duchess was not a trumped-up

74

topicality, we can be certain of that. An amusing story. It gladdens the heart, to use an archaic expression. But simply because this story has no end, everything must remain up in the air. Hence I lost sight of my friend in his duchess's bed. Since then, not a word. Singular! What could have possessed the man to vanish completely to this very day? Is it our fault? My fault, forgive me! I am quite perturbed by this question. And what became of the Duchess de Maufrigneuse? Now there is something the police in Paris should look into! The last I heard of her, she was engaged in a fine piece of feminine cunning. She was playing the little innocent whom no one would dare even to touch; then, with a rustle of silks, out went the light. It would work on stage.

[Since Dr. Glatschke had nothing to say to all this, or perhaps quite pointedly refused to say anything so as not to interrupt d'Arthez, who was at last speaking freely, d'Arthez got up—as one could deduce from the noise of a chair—and continued his monologue standing.]

Naturally one musters all sorts of rationalizations to try to exculpate oneself. For instance, it's possible that d'Arthez sent a message which has gone astray. He may even have asked for help, but I haven't heard. How many wars, trenches, Maginot Lines and innumerable dead separate him from us! It's easy enough for the mail to go astray in such circumstances; even secret messages are torn to shreds by grenades. One waits in vain. On other hand, d'Arthez may have thought, "My people don't seem to expect news of me at the moment. Very well, every man for himself." That would be like him. So-called contemporary history has upset a great deal more than the archives; personal relationships too have suffered. And yet we wait for news. You can count on one thing, Herr Oberregierungsrat, and pass it on to your colleagues in France: no man of d'Arthez's caliber could end his days in the arms of a woman of fashion, no matter how charming. For this reason, his friends all over the world would, as the old saying goes, put their hand in the fire. That wouldn't suit us at all and we won't settle for it under any circumstances. Yes, and let me add that we were almost sure d'Arthez would pop up during the last war in the Resistance. You must have better access than I to any documentation, since I was in confinement at the time. Now, who can say whether d'Arthez considered the German occupation of too little consequence, or whether he felt that the time was not yet ripe for active intervention? His friends can only respect his silence and accept his aloofness as binding on us as well. And again, I can only advise you to make inquiries chez madame la duchesse. Surely she will be able to give you information about the end of the affair. Naturally she will lie a bit to save face, but a polished detective will find lies as rich in clues as the truth. And into such a situation as this, you suddenly charge with the news that a man calling himself d'Arthez without any right whatsoever has been slain in the rue—forgive me, I've forgotten the name of the street—with a brick! This is the first bit of news about d'Arthez since that love affair! Why, it's staggering. The forged *carte d'identité*, his contact with prostitutes, the drugs—all of this may interest the police, but none of it strikes us as uncommon. Just that brick, can you imagine? What a prosaic century! Really, one might almost think that the true d'Arthez had slain this petit-bourgeois individual who misused his name, and in fact chose a brick just to make an example of him. As his present representative, I would have done the same in these circumstances. Yes, search for the true d'Arthez, Herr Oberregierungsrat. That would doubtless contribute to the solution of this case. And in searching for him, you would do me a personal favor. But I must depart for Bad Königstein! Forgive me. We are having a sort of family reunion. The bus leaves in a quarter of an hour and I can just make it.

Here ends the tape and its transcript. Asking around in the department about Balzac was the first measure Dr. Glatschke took, but since no one could satisfy him completely there, he telephoned a journalist who was rated "reliable." Since this did not produce the desired result either, the narrator was assigned the task of locating his novels and combing them for references to d'Arthez. In his short paper on the subject, the narrator merely established that d'Arthez was a character in Balzac's *La Comédie humaine,* and scarcely a major one, rather a subordinate figure on the sidelines, mentioned only at junctures where the author felt compelled to offset France's political, commercial and literary frenzy with the nation's intellectual conscience, so to speak: one man who refused to board the bandwagon of fashion, however attractive, to engage in the wheeling and dealing of the epoch. Today no one would hesitate to term such men nihilists, if for no other reason than that they denigrate and question whatever current trend guarantees success—all the catchwords and clichés—even when they do so just by standing aloof. Formulated by the narrator naïvely, but to the best of his knowledge and within the bounds set by conscience, this evaluation was later seized on, as we shall see, by Dr. Glatschke and used out of context, twisted into a proof of the hypothesis that d'Arthez had espoused the cause of nihilism and thus represented a threat to national security. You could have knocked the narrator down with a feather; he had meant no harm. His sole purpose had been to deliver as accurate a report as possible. But Lambert, too, interpreted the sentence exactly as Dr. Glatschke had, and mused, "You really delivered the goods!" When he wrote his report, the narrator still lacked an insight into the reality of what, with more experience, he would easily have thrust aside as merely novelistic, as of interest only to a historian of literature. In his paper he noted in passing that even if, in portraying d'Arthez, Balzac had drawn from life a figure known to many readers, the fact of this model's having lived more than one hundred and twenty years ago meant that he was long since dead and thus beyond the reach of the usual methods of police surveillance. This remark, although intended to serve a purely official purpose, also aroused Lambert's applause. "Long since dead! Oh, bravo! We can use that in a pantomime." At that time the narrator was still apt to feel insulted by applause of this sort.

Yet, fundamentally, neither the transcript of the interrogation nor the carbon of this report seemed to please Lambert. "You still have the thought patterns of Security," he scolded. "As a result, your presentation has an ironic effect. It is easy to see that your Dr. Glatschke is a fool, and an easily fooled fool at that. But precisely because he *is* a fool, this type of man is mortally dangerous. These things strike me as far too serious for irony. And they should be serious to you too, if you will allow me to say so."

Nonetheless, two important questions still remained unanswered. Why had the actor Ernst Nasemann taken the pseudonym d'Arthez? Why had an obscure individual whose papers were forged in the same name been slain in Paris? In reply to the first of these questions, Dr. Glatschke had a ready answer: "This name d'Arthez is nothing other than the password of a secret society. An old, old trick. And these people think they're so sophisticated . . ." It is probable that he passed this on to his superiors in Bonn and that they passed it on to their colleagues in Paris. The correspondence touching on this matter did not come to the narrator's eyes because in the meantime he had given up his job with Security.

Odd as this may sound, the reading of the novels of Balzac shook the very foundations of the narrator's world—much against his will, of course, without his having the prerequisites for such an event, so to speak. In the course of reading these novels, he had also stumbled on the name Lambert, which he considered it his duty to mention in this report. For this Dr.

Glatschke praised him—something quite unusual. "Now we're getting somewhere!" he commented. "Bring me Lambert's file."

For Lambert too had a dossier. Not that Security had anything on him; it was simply that anyone who, after using a pseudonym for years, suddenly and for no obvious reason returns to his former legal name quite naturally excites suspicion. Also, this Lambert/Lembke's being born in Dresden and being, apparently, still a close friend of d'Arthez had not escaped the authorities.

Thus, the narrator combed the novels of Balzac in the employ of the state. He had been assigned this reading, and if he were praised by Dr. Glatschke, it could under certain circumstances be of great importance to his advancement. Furthermore, the novels of Balzac amply supplied the narrator with something to talk about, during evenings spent with colleagues and acquaintances, without breaking the oath of silence that the authorities laid upon him. Naturally these acquaintances were astonished and asked, "Since when do you read novels?" Some of them did not like the idea. One person in particular, who at the time seemed quite intimate with the narrator, expressed her surprise and made no bones about disapproving of this, "for his own good and perhaps for hers too."

In short, while the narrator deluded himself into thinking that he was dealing with a world of novels that he had to be aware of only in his capacity as a Security employee—a dreamworld which existed for him only when he came home late at night from a party or as he fell asleep, but vanished into thin air when he shaved or was on the way to the office—it was his very occupation which propelled him into this world even before he had learned its language.

In other words, he received from Dr. Glatschke the task, the *honorable* task, as they say, of approaching Lambert and, after establishing a personal relationship with him, drawing him out. In itself, such an assignment has always been accepted as part of a younger official's training. The authorities felt that a young man had to prove himself at least once by doing pure detective work even if he was slated to advance to the higher echelons of the ministry some day. So the assignment could not be regarded as something completely shameful; but it made the narrator feel intolerably ashamed. Today he would like to believe that he can trace this sense of shame—or whatever it is to be called—right back to d'Arthez's interrogation.

Be that as it may, Dr. Glatschke said, "This can hardly give you trouble. You want to make the grade of Assessor. For that you need books. And books will naturally bring you in contact with librarians. This is child's play. The authorities will make good your expenses. Of course you will have to itemize them. It's perfectly all right if you invite the man for dinner in a restaurant once. It doesn't have to be deluxe. And if you feel that conversation will flow easier, by all means take your fiancée along. We won't object to that. Women often notice trivial details which in a certain light can be most revealing. So, old boy, don't worry about a thing! You understand that I will assign another agent of ours to the case to keep an eye on this individual. We must do everything in our power to expose this secret society, even if it seems quite harmless *now*. We can ill afford anything of the kind."

That was a year and a half ago. The fiancée to whom Dr. Glatschke could not forbear referring ceased being a fiancée as soon as the narrator had resigned his position. The sense of shame remains. Not even the notes he made, which form the basis of this report, helped him dispel his sense of unease. Or is it only a sense of insecurity, this lightness in the region of the stomach, and shame at this insecurity that other people do not appear to feel?

five

Two months later another murder took place, in Frankfurt this time. D'Arthez happened to be abroad, so he could not be implicated. This murder, moreover, was such a run-of-the-mill crime of passion, it offered the police no riddles. They solved it overnight. And yet two elements did call d'Arthez to mind.

The murdered man happened to be the police spy, or "agent," whom Dr. Glatschke had assigned to keep an eye on Lambert; a former policeman, he had been dismissed years before for some misdemeanor or other, and now Security used this dubious individual for its meanest spying. The murderer was an Italian who lived in the neighborhood near the station and engaged in various illicit activities.

Of Dr. Glatschke's reaction to this crime the narrator has no firsthand information, as by then he had left the agency. The investigation of the case lay entirely with the regular police. Presumably the connection with Security was hushed up; there was no mention of it in the press.

The second element calling d'Arthez to mind made Dr. Glatschke even more thoughtful. The crime was discovered by Lambert himself, who, as witness of a sort, called in the police. And as though this were not enough, the narrator happened to be present too; or rather, at the time the murder took place, he had been in Lambert's room for more than an hour. This fact and the alibis of both men were quite naturally checked out by the police. Since the murderer was very quickly apprehended, the police lost interest. As for Lambert, he just shrugged his shoulders and mused, "Lately we seem to have developed a certain power of attraction for these tedious killings . . ."

Nevertheless, much remained puzzling—and not just for Dr. Glatschke, whose very livelihood, so to speak, depended on such puzzles, but for the narrator as well, who happened to be one of the parties concerned. To this day he does not understand how Lambert could have observed the killing, simply from an optical standpoint. Lambert himself said, "Why not? I reckoned with it, that's why." But that only makes the business all the more difficult to explain.

As already stated, the narrator was visiting Lambert in the Goethestrasse. They had been talking about Lambert himself, about Edith Nasemann, but most of all about certain problems that concerned the narrator alone. The room was on the seventh floor, with an excellent view over the rooftops of Frankfurt. Lambert had the habit of standing—often half the night—at the window. This fact was mentioned from the very first reports, ones which the narrator, then still a Security employee, had a chance to read. These reports added that he frequently conversed with another party, presumably female, about whom nothing so far had been ascertained. How did this person enter the apartment house to reach Lambert's room? Inquiries in the other apartments yielded no information.

The party in question was none other than the above-mentioned dressmaker's dummy, which Lambert usually stood beside him at the window, frequently leaving her there when he left the room. She was not really the person to whom he addressed himself, although he did claim that she loosened his tongue. It more truthfully could have been said that Lambert was addressing the whole of sleeping Frankfurt. Moreover, both he and the narrator realized that the room was being watched; and Lambert discovered that it was bugged. He learned to neutralize the microphone whenever he had a mind to. His room was under observation from the attic window of a building in the Kleine Bockenheimerstrasse. Security, under the alias of a firm of certified public accountants, had rented the attic supposedly for the storage of old documents but in reality just to plant an agent armed with night glasses to keep an eye on Lambert's room from late afternoon till early morning. The narrator had not needed to warn Lambert of this measure; unassisted, he spotted it remarkably fast. Being for years in the habit of standing at this window, Lambert could not fail to register the slightest change in his surroundings. First, there were those two little circles; sometimes they sparkled like eyes. The lenses of the night glasses reflected blue light from a neon sign. "What bunglers your Dr. Glatschke uses!" Lambert sneered. That was the night he discovered that the man up in the attic had a chrome-plated thermos. Every time he poured himself a drink, it flashed. As for the neon sign, it also bathed Lambert's face in waves of bright red and green as he stood at the window. Most of the time he stood there without moving, even when he spoke. As his posture was poor, he looked much stockier and older than he was. Nor did he hold up his head; thus the bags under his eyes added an impression of listlessness. Anyone who ran into him on the street would have taken him for an old man on a pension who no longer knows what to make of himself or the world. But the reflected light playing across his face and across what he said and thought as he stood at the window for hours gave him a mysterious vitality. "Like a portrait by some Expressionist," Edith Nasemann once remarked.

On the evening in question, Lambert suddenly said, "There it is. Now the idiot has gone and got himself stabbed. And by a professional, at that! I guess it is our duty as citizens to report this to the police."

But let us drop this murder, which is altogether uninteresting and not to be distinguished from other murders that occur now and then in Frankfurt. The murderer was found the next day in the bed of a prostitute, who had been the cause of the slaying.

Now, none of that has anything to do with d'Arthez, although "the d'Arthez case" was far from being solved, at least not where Dr. Glatschke was concerned. That, too, the narrator only discovered when he ran into Dr. Glatschke's daughter several months later on the Bockenheimer Landstrasse. She had passed her examinations and was now studying German literature and theater in Munich, so the university must have been closed for vacation. Her father had not yet wangled that transfer to Bonn. When the narrator said in parting, "Remember me to your honored Herr Vater," she laughed and commented, "My honored father won't be particularly honored by your greeting. Even now he sometimes sighs, 'Too bad about the young man. He fell for that damned Saxon's line. Botched his whole future.'" The girl was wide-awake, as already noted.

Unlike d'Arthez, Lambert had laid aside his pseudonym fifteen years before. D'Arthez was the only person left who called

84

him Lambert, except for Edith Nasemann, who addressed him as Uncle Lambert. And thus it came to be, if only after the passage of time, that the narrator too felt he could call him Lambert. "But please, never *Herr* Lambert. That sounds far too cynical."

Officially Lambert had been going by his legal name, Ludwig Lembke, ever since his wife's death. Under this name, he was employed part-time in the university library—part-time only because he had failed to complete the required studies.

The narrator never met anyone in Frankfurt who had an inkling that this Ludwig Lembke for more than a decade had been quite a celebrity under the name Louis Lambert. Lambert had done everything in his power to bury this fact. But he could not prevent—or perhaps for financial reasons did not sincerely attempt to prevent—his nom de plume, Louis Lambert, from appearing on the spines of two paperbacks, although no one outside the publisher's office realized that this Louis Lambert was identical with the part-time librarian Ludwig Lembke. This writer of former best sellers was generally thought to be dead. Naturally, all this was known to Security, but thus far no one had taken an interest in the case.

As a matter of fact, the death of his wife must have been a turning point for Lambert. That may sound romantic, but monstrous would be more like it—as will be clear if the narrator succeeds in telling what he has learned. This will be no easy task. A possibility always exists that one misunderstands, particularly when one takes into account that the narrator felt quite helpless in the face of such a totally alien past. Little enough could be pried from Lambert himself. As soon as he realized where the conversation was headed, he would caustically object, "These matters are no longer accessible to Security."

Most of what the narrator learned he owes to Edith Nasemann. She, too, wondered about Uncle Lambert and also

85

about her father. As a woman, she was naturally astonished that evidently no woman had played a part in either of their lives. She seriously sought an explanation, if for no other reason than to defend her father. "Uncle Lambert's marriage must have been unspeakably miserable," she told the narrator when, as sometimes happened, he was seeing her home. "Papa's marriage too was quite miserable. Not that Mama was entirely to blame, not at all. But I believe this used to be true of all marriages. Most couples simply didn't notice; they thought this was the way things had to be and even considered themselves lucky. But Papa and Uncle Lambert knew better."

This conversation, as the narrator well remembers, took place on the corner of the Elkenbachstrasse, where Edith Nasemann lived. One must not forget that Edith was not yet twenty-two. She had studied two or three semesters of sociology and then one day dropped out and found a job in a bookstore. She had a very stern face as she stood there discussing her father's marriage and Lambert's marriage. Between her eyebrows, the skin furrowed in concentration. Moments like these make the narrator regret that he is not a painter or that he does not possess at least the ability to fix accurately in words that face and the totality of that nocturnal scene in the empty street.

Now, whether these two marriages were really as miserable as Edith suspected, the narrator quite frankly isn't even interested in knowing. What he, as a younger man, found incomprehensible and what Edith too failed to comprehend was Lambert's present behavior. It mystified both of them. How could a man go on living after throwing away such a highly successful past like a worn-out suit of clothes? Was this wisdom? Was this a model worthy of emulation? His standard of living was no higher than one would have assumed for a part-time librarian with a claim to a pension—and with a dressmaker's dummy to boot. Previously, he had at least been the author of best sellers, even if the books weren't worth much and no one would read them nowadays. Was Lambert waiting as inconspicuously as possible for death? But how can a man do nothing but that? Of course no one could ask him, it might have hurt his feelings. And probably he would not have answered or would have answered evasively. "What's it to your generation?" he once remarked. All this was confusing to Edith too, although she was not puzzled primarily for Lambert's sake, no matter how much he meant to her, but rather because one ended with her father when one began thinking about Lambert. If she were irritated, she sometimes thought their behavior was very close to pussyfooting. "They won't concede that we might be ready for their deepest convictions," she would say, and feel insulted. But she so admired her father that she would take the words back as soon as she said them. For Lambert's behavior she had arrived at a simple psychological explanation. "He is ashamed of having written those bad books and now he would like to write a good one but can't." But when she told this to her father, he laughed before answering, "Lambert long ago crossed that limit beyond which one no longer needs literature." Is that the truth? Was that really what d'Arthez thought?

Both of these pseudonyms were arrived at in the simplest possible way—"nothing but teen-age pranks," as Edith put it. "Who likes his own name? I could never stand being called Edith. Marlene is a much nicer name. When I told the other girls, they laughed and said my legs weren't long enough! Of course they meant the actress, but I hadn't even thought of her. I had been thinking of the fairy tale with the refrain about a girl named Marlene who gathers together her brother's bones. As a child I was awfully sentimental. Fairy tales made me cry."

Ernst Nasemann and Ludwig Lembke had been classmates. They were educated in the same gymnasium in Dresden—the Kreuzschule, if the narrator, who has never been in Dresden, is not mistaken. Since both their families lived in the suburb known as the Weisser Hirsch, the boys took the same streetcar and struck up a friendship. At fourteen or fifteen they happened to read one or two novels by Balzac, where they discovered the characters d'Arthez and Louis Lambert. They identified with them, as have innumerable adolescents all over the world, just as Edith was later to identify with the Marlene of the fairy tale. Nor is it out of the ordinary that, in order to isolate themselves from their environment, their parents, their school and the other students, they addressed each other by the names of their heroes. Nor did it present any great riddle that they should have simply retained these names as pseudonyms for their forays into public life. Why should they have looked elsewhere for pseudonyms when they already had ones to which they were accustomed? Here Dr. Glatschke would interrupt: "Why a pseudonym in the first place?" He has a point.

But for this there is an explanation so simple, one blushes not to have hit on it oneself. Imagine what would have happened had Lambert published his first novel—which was a great success—under a name like Ludwig Lembke! It would have sounded like a bad joke. One can get nowhere in literature with a name like that, not even in the light-reading division—perhaps there least of all. Thus, purely practical considerations counseled a pseudonym. The average reader, confronted with this author's name, assumed that he had bought a translation from the French.

Lambert himself (for of course the narrator is not going to stop calling him that now) was well aware of his misuse of the name and chided himself angrily. "An unheard-of fraud scarcely to be atoned for by vegetating for the rest of my days as Ludwig Lembke. To become a Louis Lambert takes something more than the student's wretched life that children have suffered daily for a thousand years and will still be suffering a thousand years from now. Look at him standing there beside the fireplace as though talking to himself and saying, 'I have no heaven in common with this man.' Or another quotation: 'I feel no affection whatsoever for the two syllables Lam and bert.' I should have noted those two passages somewhat earlier, oh yes." And another time—Edith was present—Lambert almost admonished the narrator with the following allusion: "One will have to justify such a misuse to one's wife as well. And what a wife! At first she tried to collaborate in the writing of her husband's books, but then she stopped because she thought it improper to turn words like his into literature. That is exemplary, but fool that I was, I attached no importance to it." And when Edith asked, "But what became of her?" all Lambert had to say was, "Is that the point, my child?" But at another time, when talking to the narrator, he returned to the subject. "His wife was a Jewess. Or half Jewish, as they would say nowadays. An ugly expression." He spoke facing the window, the dressmaker's dummy beside him. "Half Jewish indeed. That was the only thing we had in common. Well? *Well?*" he shouted furiously into the night. This was the first time the narrator saw him lose his self-control. But he quickly got a grip on himself. He slapped the dummy on the back. "Imagine, we have an innocent here who still believes he has to make a woman happy! As though you had to depend on that, eh?"

Edith loathed this dummy more than anything else. And Lambert was considerate enough never to carry on his little game with the dummy in her presence. But when Edith suggested he throw away this stupid thing, "which only gathers dust" as she put it, he did not agree. "You poor innocents!" he would sigh, and the word he used, Waisenkinder, never failed to rile Edith. Literally, it means "orphan children." He used it often.

D'Arthez too had held on to his pseudonym from his boyhood, for rather similar reasons, when he began his career as an actor. Just imagine this in a review: "Ernst Nasemann, the young romantic lead." No, that would be impossible. This was the way d'Arthez explained it in an interview quoted in a brief biography. And besides this purely practical motivation, which he shared with Lambert, there was something more in d'Arthez's retaining his pseudonym. He wished thereby to isolate himself from his family, if for no other reason than to keep them from meddling with him. And also to spare them the possibility of scandal. "One should not ask too much of NANY Inc., and surely not such a dubious experiment as this," he is reported to have remarked. And Edith couldn't help adding, by way of emphasis, that her father was always the very soul of consideration, which, by the way, provided Lambert with the opportunity for getting off one of his more cynical lines: "The only possible method to keep the family off your back is to treat its members with the greatest consideration. In this way, you sterilize the vermin." The narrator is of two minds as to whether such chance remarks don't gain an exaggerated importance by the very fact of being noted down.

This isolation must have begun long before the two young men left home to study in Berlin. That must have been the winter semester of 1930–31; perhaps the university archives could be checked—if they were not destroyed along with most of Berlin. The two friends shared a room there, at least for the first two or three years. Possibly Ernst Nasemann paid more than his share of the rent and in this way made the education of the young Ludwig Lembke less expensive. Lembke's father had not risen very high in the state educational system and consequently his family was rather constricted and frugal. There were two other children to be fed and clothed as well, but of them nothing more is known. Perhaps they vanished in the war. The Lembkes lived in a small, somewhat dilapidated house that their mother contributed as her dowry. She was the daughter of a small merchant in the New Town. The difference in the social status of the two families—to think in outmoded terms—was unimaginably great in those far-off times; naturally they would never have met socially. Today that all sounds downright comical. The Nasemanns lived in a pretentious villa behind a colonnaded portico with a view out over a steeply terraced garden to the Elbe, Loschwitz and Blasewitz, and to the bridge that was referred to as the Blue Wonder. Their synthetic-fiber plant was already doing well, even though it was not until the late twenties that they invented NANY Inc. as an advertising gimmick. What bound these two young men together more than anything else must have been their efforts to liberate themselves from the stereotypes imposed by their families. It is difficult to imagine Lambert as a young man in the grandiose rooms of the Nasemann villa. He never spoke of his youth or of Dresden or of his feelings for his parents, or of whether it embarrassed him to say good morning to old Frau Nasemann when he was dressed in a cheap suit. Did young Lambert help his friend with homework and were those hours of extra tutoring paid for? Lambert was an excellent scholar, while d'Arthez just barely got his diploma. Even while at school, he infuriated his teachers because he always slightly exaggerated the good behavior that they demanded of him, so that they felt he was not showing them the proper respect. Nor does the narrator know anything about young d'Arthez except the occasional anecdote his daughter happened to tell. "Papa and Uncle Lambert used to crawl under the enormous grand piano in the salon when Grandmother was pouring tea for her friends in the next room. From their hiding place the two boys could hear the ladies discussing their servants and bragging about their children. 'It was pure fraud,' Papa said, 'since we knew those children better than their mothers did.'"

Whether her father was destined to study law or chemistry, Edith did not know. Nor does it matter. In any event, whatever he studied, it was with the aim of going into his father's factory. Ludwig Lembke, on the other hand, studied literature and the rest with the profession of librarian in view from the very beginning. He also took a few preliminary examinations, which made it easier for him to gain the post of a part-time librarian at the university in Frankfurt. After the war, librarians were in short supply.

Naturally, everyone will immediately ask what the political orientation of these two youngsters was, particularly since they belonged to the very generation from whom the National Socialists recruited so many. Just knowing today that they were opponents of the regime is not good enough. Precisely how did d'Arthez and Lambert behave as twenty-year-olds in that epoch of German hysteria? The archives are laconic on the subject. About Lambert there is nothing at all. Yet he must at least have belonged to the Nazi Writers' Union if he was to go on publishing in the thirties. Did they know him as Ludwig Lembke? Did they make an exception in his case because of his "non-Aryan" wife? And concerning d'Arthez there was simply the dossier which the Occupation forces had put together when he popped up in Berlin again after his escape from the concentration camp. One would like to believe that this canceled out the entire past. And yet, in the case of so carefully documented a celebrity as d'Arthez, it was odd that not one curious reporter had ever sniffed out a *faux pas*. And to anticipate another question: Ludwig Lembke was judged unfit for military service due to a minor childhood operation for rupture, while d'Arthez served a year in Kiel in the navy. Saxons are known to prefer the navy.

Here the narrator must expressly ask to be excused for his feeling that it is necessary to cite all this long-winded material that relates directly to the history of our time. The narrator does not even seek to write a factually perfect biography. Once

Lambert observed, "We would have turned out the same without the Nazis or the war. We don't even have that excuse." Now that is an exaggeration, but Lambert hated anyone's blaming history for the turn his life had taken.

But above all, none of this contemporary history can explain how those two young men turned into the present d'Arthez and Lambert. How are we to explain their leaving so suddenly the careers traced out for them? For what reason, after two years at the university, did Ludwig Lembke sit down one night and in a matter of weeks write a historical novel? And what caused Ernst Nasemann to enter a school of acting and undertake that sort of training?

Do questions like these have any meaning at all? If anyone thirty years from now asked the narrator, "What made you suddenly break off what you call the career traced out for you? Was it because a career as a judge seemed too dull that you applied for a job in Security as soon as you had passed the legal exams? And now suddenly you turn up on a ship bound for Africa, where you intend to offer your services in the so-called evolution of a so-called underdeveloped nation. Is it idealism? You wouldn't have us believe that the content of an interrogation that you merely know from tape, that the voice of a man whom you have never met and who only missed becoming the object of a compulsive psychosis because you met a friend of his and his daughter, you wouldn't have us believe, would you, that this is the real cause of your—if you will pardon the expression—quixotic act? Can you pretend that this explanation will satisfy *you* when you finally come to regret this act?"

If anyone were to ask this thirty years from now, no satisfactory answer would be forthcoming. Obviously, motives too change with the years, no matter how unambiguous they may have seemed at the time. This observation would hardly satisfy a jurist. Out of a mistake, if it was a mistake, a truly positive

93

decision develops, and vice versa. Perhaps with such inexplicable upheavals as these, what Lambert means by the word "past" begins.

Now, as for Lambert, he claims he wanted to make some money as fast as possible in order not to be a burden to his father any longer. And since the library had supplied him with a superfluity of history books, the writing of a historical novel —"trash," as he called it himself—was so easy that he just kept at it. That he kept at it after striking it rich with his first book is no surprise, but that scarcely touches on the real issue—his beginning at all. There are many other ways of making money and that epoch offered many possibilities which vanished with it. All Lambert need have done was sell his soul to the Nazis. And for d'Arthez, too, every explanation using hindsight remains even more unsatisfactory. It simply won't do to assume that he became an actor out of spite, just to annoy his family. He could have done this without becoming an actor. Nor had Edith anything to tell the narrator about this period of her father's life. This is scarcely surprising when one recalls that she learned of his existence only after the war, when she was still a young girl. This rather catty remark of Edith's mother is perhaps significant: "Your father was *already* an actor, at home as well. Even when we were alone, he invented. I should never have married him." Edith repeated this remark unwillingly, and to free it from any gravity, she added, "Papa must have fallen for some actress. That does happen." As a matter of fact, there was a woman, as we shall see, who had gone to acting school with d'Arthez when she was a girl. The narrator has even spoken with her. She laughed in his face when he asked her if she had occasioned this remark. "There was nothing about him anyone could seduce" was her comment.

In a much later interview, long after he had become the celebrated d'Arthez, he expressed himself as follows (if we can trust the reporter): "No one could possibly take all those hyperthyroid roles like Laertes, Marquis Posa or Orestes seriously. For God's sake, it's even hard in everyday life to get people to take you seriously enough to believe what you say." That is quoted verbatim from the interview. Even if we are skeptical about such material, this passage still offers an explanation of the almost spooky comedy of the pantomimes in which d'Arthez appeared. The audience never knew for certain whether they should laugh or cry; hence they felt somewhat insulted. Dr. Glatschke's reaction is proof of this, even though an interrogation scarcely qualifies as a piece of theater.

It might even be that back in the early thirties, at a rehearsal for a showcase performance of *Hamlet* or *Iphigenia,* an experienced director noticed a young actor who played the part of Laertes or Orestes with such exaggerated earnestness that the part had an oddly comic effect. One can hear the exclamation, "Good lord! Even *you* can't believe what you're doing!" and see the young d'Arthez in the appropriate costume walk to the footlights and ask with an innocent face, "What did I do wrong?"

At that moment the true d'Arthez was discovered, or perhaps he had already discovered himself. The manner in which he appears on stage today—or in real life, for that matter—had always been in his blood and was not merely an attempt to defend himself against his family and the mortal dangers of his time, as the epilogue in the picture biography claims. The author of that epilogue prides himself far too much on his passing acquaintance with psychology. Admittedly, one should not forget that people in those hysterical times got a thrill out of playing parts that were absolutely out of date, intoxicating themselves with shrill lines that had lost all validity a hundred years or more before. To do this was nothing other than to tempt catastrophe and self-destruction. But there is also a possibility that the young d'Arthez realized how badly his contemporaries and their idols played these parts for which they were so ill-

95

suited—mere dilettantes, one would like to call them—and that he thus made up his mind to play the roles which fell to him as perfectly as he knew how. And if, as Edith believed, he actually did fall in love with a girl who studied acting, which would be nothing out of the ordinary and thus not worth our contesting, he must have said to himself something like "Very well, I've fallen for this fetching girl. There's nothing to be done. I must play the part so that no one can doubt it." Edith was outraged when the narrator suggested this explanation. She brought the conversation to a halt with the objection that, in any event, it hadn't been her mother, since her mother had never gone to acting school and had lived in Kiel. She seemed totally oblivious of the fact that this affair with an actress, if there was such an affair, would have taken place long before d'Arthez met Edith's mother. It would have happened while he was doing his year in the navy.

And suddenly another scene characteristic of d'Arthez occurs to the narrator. This happened much later, just a couple of years ago. When one deals with d'Arthez, the attempt to arrange the narrative in chronological order will get nowhere. It would merely be a reworking of the picture, and everything would look so simplified, one couldn't help saying, "No, it couldn't have been like this. Somewhere the principal point has been lost sight of." Not even Lambert knew about the scene in question. He certainly would have been amused, but he was dead before the narrator had a chance to pass it on. Actually, the telegram announcing his death arrived only a few hours after the scene first came to the narrator's own ears. This is all so strange. Edith and the narrator were compelled to return that very night to Frankfurt, although they had originally planned to spend a few days in Berlin. D'Arthez, as already remarked, was abroad. Thus Edith could sleep in his room, leaving the other room for the narrator, so the trip to Berlin was inexpensive.

Contrary to expectation, the telegram was addressed to the narrator rather than to Edith. Lambert had collapsed in the university library. It must have been one of those sweltering days that sometimes dawn in Frankfurt. He sank down to the platform on which his desk stood in the reading room, but so slowly that he knocked nothing over. Naturally, he was hurried to the hospital, where he lay for two days. He had taken special pains to write down the address at which the narrator could be reached and he gave the slip of paper to a nurse or doctor in case of the worst. There was even a will, although of doubtful legal validity. It consisted of a few lines in Lambert's hand and read: "Dear————, with the stuff that you will find at my place you can do as you please. Relations, God be praised, I have none! Yours, Louis Lambert."

This was the first time that Lambert ever used the familiar *du* in addressing the narrator. Lambert's estate was scarcely worthy of the name. The cost of the burial, including transportation to Wiesbaden, was just met. The receipts are at Edith Nasemann's, in case anyone with a right to the inheritance should turn up during the narrator's absence.

All the same, one cannot help wondering why Lambert had entrusted the narrator with his papers rather than his friend d'Arthez or Edith Nasemann, whom he had known much longer. Edith found nothing strange in this. "He didn't want to bother Papa with them; and besides, he had grown accustomed to you in that one year." Edith and the narrator were already using the familiar *du*.

But to return to the former actress, because it was she who communicated to Edith and the narrator the scene in question —she had been cast in a supporting role, one might say. Edith knew the woman from a previous visit to Berlin; her father had taken her along. This trip, it was only at the narrator's entreaty that she visited her again, and only because, in so doing, the narrator believed he could learn more about d'Arthez. In point of fact, Edith distrusted the woman deeply. Left to herself, she would never have visited her again. The woman was aware of this and cracked jokes about it. "Never fear, love," she said. "I won't take your Papa away from you. Life has taught me just enough not to try that. Well, and just look at me! Your father's well preserved, but me . . . Unhappiness keeps people young, I've often observed. If only you accept the worst, in time it can't hurt you any longer, while the rest of us who are always straining after happiness are always in a frenzy. So don't worry."

This woman must have been in her mid-fifties, but she looked much older—"ravaged," as Edith put it. Her name was Sybille Wuster. That must have been her maiden name, which she had taken again. Perhaps it wasn't even her maiden name but her mother's maiden name.

Lambert knew her from before the war, of course; and we can assume that, after the war as well, he saw her once or twice, on those rare occasions when d'Arthez persuaded him to visit Berlin. Lambert hated to travel. Be that as it may, it must have been on one of these occasions that Lambert thought of the sobriquet the "Woman in the Window"; for d'Arthez, although he accepted this nickname, never would have hit on it alone. Moreover, the woman had only begun sitting in the window of her room on the mezzanine of a building at the corner of the Rankestrasse and the Augsburgerstrasse one or two years after the war. During the troubled time toward the end of the war, she had been evacuated to Freilassing. Around the corner in the Rankestrasse—it might have been in the same building— there was a cellar cabaret where d'Arthez occasionally appeared, although seldom, and then more as a favor to help out old friends. It was too political for him. "Or too topical," as Edith said. "The audience laughs at the jokes, but nothing changes. Papa didn't want to participate. It just makes for melancholy, he says. And that's how it always is with topicality, as he calls it. All one is doing is beating around the bush, and such talk only makes it easier for others to do the same."

Nor had Lambert hit upon this designation, the "Woman in the Window," unaided; by chance he recalled a treatise in the annals of some learned society. He even brought the faded pamphlet home to show to the narrator. Under the main title in Greek letters stood a subtitle, "An Essay concerning the Woman in the Window." So this designation does not stem, as one would have assumed it did, from his own habit of standing in the window with that dressmaker's dummy beside him.

In his treatise, the author dealt with Near Eastern statuettes of the first millennium B.C., and more particularly with what they might have signified. There was a wealth of learned footnotes. Even the story of Jezebel was dragged in from the Bible, in an effort to illuminate the mythological background.

The archaeologist was seeking the origin of an ancient tale that had lived on, although under various guises, into late Roman times. Despite the dry scientific approach, the facts that must have led to the creation of the tale managed to shine through with unabated vitality. Lambert even jokingly turned to Edith to say, "That ought to interest you. Didn't you study sociology?"

This tale is told of a young man of humble birth (or, as the scholar suggested, from a tribe that had wandered into the region and remained there on sufferance) who falls in love with the daughter of a person of substance (that is, a girl from the aristocracy, which is composed of the city's original inhabitants). The girl rejects all his advances and the young man dies of a broken heart. In other words, a common enough love story, not wholly free from sentimentality and socially pointed moral. But what follows is much more revealing. As the funeral procession passes the girl's house, she leans out the window to watch the proceedings. Her behavior so outrages the Love Goddess that she changes the girl to stone. Later, prostitutes made this woman in the window their symbol, as the learned author demonstrates. Occasionally the figure is represented with doves or pigeons. Now, it is well known that Frankfurt does not lack for prostitutes, and also that the city suffers from a superfluity of pigeons, so almost anyone would have drawn an analogy with that dressmaker's dummy. But, as already pointed out, she does not enter into this at all.

Edith took exception to this tale. It was, in her opinion, the girl's right to reject the young man. To which Lambert replied that, even so, one did not have to enjoy oneself at the poor girl's expense after he'd done himself in. But Edith was mistaken if she assumed that Lambert was using this tale to criticize her behavior. (A few months before meeting the narrator, she had broken off her engagement to a young engineer. None of this was known to the narrator at that time.)

Moreover, she found this whole historical or archaeological explication of *their* Woman in the Window nonsensical. "Uncle Lambert always hopes he can impress us with his learning." It seems she had discovered on an earlier visit that the woman had a little mirror outside her window—the kind that used to be called a "spy"—in which she could observe the goings-on down in the street, the Augsburgerstrasse in particular. "The girls who ply their trade there would have noticed this ages ago and would have started calling her the Woman in the Window." And at least this much was true, that quite a few of these women did visit her from time to time to have her read the cards for them. The Woman in the Window actually told this to Edith and the narrator. "With Mimi, that redhead over there —oh, of course, she must be sleeping now—I have a grand time. She would like to marry this man out in Tegel who owns a grocery, but it won't work, he's still married—although his wife does have cancer. Mimi wants me to tell her how much longer the woman will live with that cancer. I believe she may even think I could hurry things along—sticking pins in the woman's picture, or something like that. But, for the love of God, that's a case where magic can't help, only patience. That's hard to learn."

Despite the natural antipathy that Edith felt for this woman, she struck the narrator as an important figure nonetheless, since his subject was d'Arthez. Oh, not because of some former love affair that rankled Edith, but for another reason which the narrator, due to his lack of experience in this realm, finds he has no words for. Perhaps it can be paraphrased as follows: If it were possible to imagine a partner d'Arthez's equal—not for love, and God knows not for bed—then it would have to be such a woman. Edith asked in a fury, "What can you see in that person?" but perhaps what outraged her so was not being able to prevent herself from being impressed by the woman—and not wanting to admit this.

But to turn at last to the scene: it took place at a party a well-known Berlin industrialist threw in his garden. In Dahlem, or perhaps not in Dahlem—the narrator does not know Berlin very well. "A party in his garden—a 'garden party,' in other words. Something new," she said, "for which they have borrowed another foreign word . . . With a swimming pool, of course, so that at least one of the girls can fall in and come out with her clothes sticking to her fanny while the other silly geese shriek. You can't have a garden party without an incident like that. And what energy they expend disgracing themselves! They could manage it all much cheaper at home, but they have to have witnesses. You can imagine the sausage booths and tents where drinks were served, all of it as real as a Hollywood film. It must have cost a packet just straightening out the garden afterwards, but perhaps it comes off his taxable income, how would I know? Anyway, they had to have a fortune-teller too, so that no possible source of pleasure would be lacking. One of the ladies must have gotten the idea in her head, enough of them bring me their childish nonsense. Previously, before the Wall went up, I even had clients in the East, where such stuff is strictly forbidden. Capitalist humbug, they call it. Humbug, fair enough! But humbug is one of those things Marxism won't change, that's why they're so outraged. Or can your old Hegel do something about it after all, love? Now don't get excited. Your father told me you were reading Hegel, that's all. We'll have to talk about it some time when he isn't around. Perhaps you can collect a few phrases out of Hegel that I can let drop when I have certain clients. Something that sounds modern. Oh, there's time, don't get angry. And perhaps there's something more up to date . . . Where was I? Oh, yes, that garden party . . . Well, why not? I did pretty well there, a fine fee besides what the guests paid me. You see, you have to let people pay; otherwise, they don't take you seriously. I even went to the hairdresser and got a wild hairdo with comical little curls and so on. And an old dress with sequins and lace and such junk. And my lips more blue than red and my eyes made up to look mysterious. Precisely the way they imagine a fortune-teller has to look. Besides all this, there's my enormous ring that looks Egyptian. I can show it to you later. It pinches, so I don't wear it unless I have to. Very well, there I was, but this big industrialist had dreamed up another treat for his guests. There always has to be *something else,* extra, or nothing counts. He wanted to have a proper clown there, so with all his money, why not engage the world-famous Wuz? You both know who I mean, the one who did himself in last year with sleeping pills in his villa in Grasse or somewhere down there where the air smells of lavender . . . Because of a detached retina, they say. He was always terribly nearsighted and had protruding eyes. He was rich, you know, and world-famous, but that didn't help. For a clown it must be harder to bear than for one of us, I believe. Anyway, he was here in Berlin at the time, maybe with the Pappenheim Circus? But how would I know. So he could afford to take on this extra engagement for an afternoon. Naturally, they counted on his appearing in his usual costume, with his violin and that comical bag of his he can play like a concertina—what they used to call a Gladstone bag. But hold on, children! The host said to himself: Why just one clown? Why not two? No one has ever seen the like . . . That will really be a helluva lot of fun. The man calculated the way he had been taught: two is twice the fun of one. Any adding machine would agree. How could anyone suggest to the man that in this case the result would be zero? Absolutely zero. *Absolute* zero, you might say! Two clowns—why, they cancel each other out. That's simply the way it is. Perhaps you would have a better way of putting it, love—or perhaps your young man there would. You've both studied. To make a long story short, your father was engaged too. Now don't make another face that soon, you'll just get wrinkles before your time. All right, so your father isn't what most people consider a clown, not a man who continually stumbles over his own feet and who always has bad luck and consoles himself with his violin so well that everyone else cries for him—and all the rest that's expected of him. Your papa isn't the right size. He was always too slender and tall and elegant, and that's why he has become a sort of Lord Chamberlain. I know more about that than you, love—you weren't even born. He had thought this all out quite carefully. He said to himself: There are plenty of clowns already, better ones than I'll ever be; there's Chaplin, for instance—no use trying to imitate him. And, besides, it couldn't be done. That's why he glued on that little mustache and turned into an Englishman. Oh, not all at once! That's not the sort of thing one does right off the bat, for heaven's sake! But he is a clown after all, love, and I can't imagine why you won't admit it. After all, it's the highest praise a girl has for a man. All right, of course you're annoyed with him at first, because you can't get your hands on him the way you do with all the others

—but that's the very reason why you don't try the same old tricks, and that's already something! You let him stay the way he is, and hats off! You, there, with your unwrinkled forehead, some day you'll see it my way, love. You can't knock a clown off his feet, you'd only fall flat on your face. Your papa has been trying for ages to arrange a comeback for me; he's always trying to persuade me. But I never really wanted to; the theater I have here does just fine. He imagined a sort of female d'Arthez —oh, not on the same stage with him, for heaven's sake! An old woman who flaps about the stage and comes to grips with life in an elegant manner—and, don't let's forget, without saying a word. Exactly what he does in his pantomimes. But he made a mistake, if you will allow me to say so. I explained what I meant to him, and apparently he saw it my way. A man will be believed without saying a word; perhaps it's even easier for him if he doesn't open his mouth. But a woman deals with things differently and she has to talk or she's no woman. Well, I can talk to my heart's content here, so I don't need the stage. You can't imagine how much I talk here! Always the same thing, always the same, and that's the way it should be. Even if I should read the cards for you some day, or look into that little palm of yours, I would only say the same things I've said hundreds of times before. There's no more to it than that. Now I don't believe that your father knew Wuz. Possibly they had been introduced on stage or under the big top, but they were not personally acquainted. This fellow Wuz was really named Charles Meier—can you believe it, Meier—although it may have been spelled with "ai" or "y"; how would I know? Sounds like a joke, doesn't it? With these boys, everything turns into a joke even when they can't have wanted it to. Anyway, it all ended with a detached retina. Naturally the hosts couldn't keep their mouths shut and rumors were flying: something extra-special was being mounted for that garden party. Two clowns and so on: people were already licking their lips. It's the same, love, whether I use the word clown or another. Do you have a better word? I thought not. It's the same with the word 'angel.' Yes, young man, I said angel! Don't look so astonished. Naturally there's nothing about them in the books you read, but they exist all the same. You can believe an old woman. They may not be running around out there on the Kurfürstendamm, and they surely don't have wings, and they didn't originate in the Bible—that's all nonsense. But they do exist, even at home in Frankfurt. And if you haven't already noticed as much, then I think I have a right to feel sorry for you . . . I also happen to feel sorry for angels. But as I was saying, that's another name that isn't quite right—but at least it's a beautiful word, and why should we look for another? Whether your father knew that this Wuz was also of the party, I can't say. Or whether Wuz knew, either. Would they have accepted, anyway? Or would they have avoided that somehow? If we only knew . . . Of course, curious old girl that I am, I did ask him afterward: 'Tell me, Ernst, did the two of you arrange it all in advance?' Now, don't try to make anything of my calling him Ernst. It means nothing, so put that out of your pretty little head once and for all. In the theater everyone calls everyone else by their first name, it's the custom. Should I call him d'Arthez? It would make a cat laugh . . . Well, he certainly gave me the run-around, the so-and-so. Anyway, I never give straightforward answers either—why the hell should I? What good are straight-forward answers to the people who come here and sit across from me almost wetting their pants from fear? So, your father said, 'Things like that don't have to be prearranged. As soon as both parties notice what's happened, they do their best to help each other over the embarrassment.' Well, all the same, it was terribly disappointing. I was sitting there, all curls and sequins. They had constructed a sort of lair for me, papered with con-stellations and the rest of the bag of tricks. The women were already lining up. 'But, madame, there's something I can't possibly tell you here in public'—and I'd make a concerned face. That always puts them in a tizzy. You should have seen the way they tripped to the buffet and gulped down the champagne. And then suddenly, in a short hush, who do I see but dear old Ernst—excuse me, love—with the host rushing up to greet him. Then he takes him over to the lady of the house, whose hand he kisses as proper as you please. Naturally he was not in uniform, by which I mean that silly mustache. No, the rest was as always: striped trousers and dark jacket, gray silk tie, I believe. Just the fact that he appeared without his mustache might have told them that he considered himself off duty, but people are dense. Now, I don't know either if perhaps this hadn't been agreed on, since the lady of the house and those around her acted as though they expected something—why, there was even a reporter, to make sure it didn't miss the papers—and the whole gang of them moving in my direction as if by chance, and your father behaving as though he hadn't noticed me, just chatting with the lady of the house and the others: 'What a divine party! Isn't it lucky the weather has held. Now tell me, dear lady, where did you get that enchanting dress? Certainly you didn't find it here in Berlin.' Your papa knows how to behave. Well then, as they were just level with my booth, the lady of the house asked as if out of the blue, 'Wouldn't you like to have your fortune told too?' Everyone held their breath, and I thought I had better do something to earn my pay, so I looked terrified and threw up my hands as if to ward off some evil—with people like this, you have to lay it on thick or they don't notice. And I said, 'This gentleman can more readily read my future than I his!' You should have seen them hesitate a second before they got their faces ready for the expected outcome. The reporter quoted me accurately. Of course your papa returned the serve. I held out my hand; he took it in his and studied it carefully. Then he turned to the lady of the house and said, 'Do you see this line here? Nothing cuts it short. The future will not be cut short for a few blunders. What an honor it is, milady, to have met with a happy person here at your garden party. How can I adequately express my gratitude?' People were standing around openmouthed, soaking up this revelation. But the second act had already begun. The host brought over a little man in a blue suit. A bit dumpy, you'd say, and perhaps his hair was already thinning. He walks with quick little steps and wears goldrimmed glasses. You would have taken him for the general agent of some foreign concern, a cunning businessman. Our host introduced him to his wife and the other ladies and then to your papa. 'Herr Nasemann! Herr Meier! Sehr angenehm. Enchanté de vous voir!' Herr Meier spoke decent German but he had an accent. 'Ah, von den NANY-Werken, monsieur? Quel hasard! I have always wanted to visit your truly admirable installations. In the interests of my own business in Paris, you see. Ah, and your stock! I was fortunate enough to acquire a few shares back in the old days, if you understand me, more than twelve years ago, even fifteen, when they were, how shall I say, still within a person's means . . . Today, yes, today, where do they stand today?' But your papa didn't know the price they were bringing in, and said, 'Why, let's ask the Herr Generaldirektor.' But not even he knew. There was a banker standing there who did know and he quoted the price. 'Ah, c'est étonnant!' It was almost a shriek. 'What do you advise, monsieur, shall I sell, or, or . . . ?' And your papa said, 'Those shares are as good as gold, Herr Meier. Excuse me, but as a Nasemann I can say nothing else. But perhaps you aren't interested in gold. If, on the other hand, you happen to be interested in a low price-earnings ratio . . .' How brilliantly your papa can run on about securities and the like! Even that banker turned red in the face with excitement and kept interrupting. I believe he had his heart set on doing Herr Meier out of those shares. Of course Herr Meier didn't own any. But the ladies were growing bored—they understood as little of what was said as I did. Finally there was no one standing there but those two gentlemen discussing their investments, the only two people at that party who showed any sense. All the others could do was squeal. Yes, it was at this point that one of the ladies fell in the pool. Perhaps someone bumped into her on purpose to bring a little life into the party. And Herr Meier shrieked, 'Quel malheur! Cette pauvre fille!' But your father held him back and explained that the weather was too fine for this to rank as a malheur. And then they returned to their securities. Well, young man, did you follow me? Look at him, love, as if he were taking it all down."

six

Establishing contact with Lambert, following Dr. Gatschke's assignment, was unexpectedly simple. Only today does it seem surprising just how natural the process was, almost as though Lambert had expected it all along. For, on the basis of everything said about him so far, it would be more likely for him to ward off anything that might disturb his solitude. This became clear to the narrator only recently; at the time, he was too caught up in what he considered a disagreeable task. How on earth was he to become acquainted with Lambert, much less cross-examine him about his friend d'Arthez? And then every evening compose a report on the success of his mission for Dr. Glatschke.

So the narrator spent many afternoons in the reading room of the library, quite pointedly choosing the hour before closing time for his arrival. He sat at a table and thumbed volumes that he either removed from the shelves himself or ordered from the stacks. He took notes. In this way he had an opportunity to become familiar with his surroundings, to observe the habits of the staff, and to become recognized as a regular user of the library. But what is most peculiar is how the subject of his research, which had been chosen as mere camouflage, began to fascinate the narrator. Footnotes and bibliographical references in the first volumes he selected led him to demand more and more books.

Lambert sat in a very small office just off the reading room, but it was advantageous for the narrator that Lambert often took the place of the supervisor late in the afternoon: as Lambert later explained, to allow the man to get home earlier. "He has a wife and children and a little garden, and what's the difference to me, after all?"

From the card index, Lambert knew what the narrator feigned an interest in. For, if Dr. Glatschke's plan was to succeed, it had to appear as if the narrator really intended to write a scholarly treatise for which he was gathering material. Need it be added that at the library Lambert was known only as the part-time librarian Ludwig Lembke? Apparently none of his colleagues had an inkling of his former pseudonym.

But what subject should occupy the narrator at the library had not been prescribed by Dr. Glatschke, and inasmuch as this was the case, the narrator was in error when, a few sentences back, he wrote that he merely feigned an interest. "Natural law"—and not only as a jurisprudential concept, but in its effect on present-day legal practice and on political and inter-

national decisions as well—had interested the narrator deeply
for a long time. In his doctoral dissertation he had analyzed the
presuppositions that had led to an improper popularization and
misuse of "the law of nature," so called, by the Nazis, for instance in such slogans as *gesundes Volksempfinden*, the
"people's healthy natural instincts," where the words "healthy"
and "people" are used as unassailable norms of the law of nature.

Still, that was nothing more than a doctoral dissertation; to
mention it today, after so much water has flowed under the
bridge, smacks of pretentiousness. But now—that is to say,
then—during his more or less enforced visits to the university
library, his interest in this historical, yet very pressing, contemporary problem began to increase. More precisely, he was interested in the change in concept natural law had undergone
from the time of the Council of Trent until our own days, when
John XXIII called the Second Vatican Council. Such research
not only led one to ancient and scarcely answerable questions
concerning the individual's freedom within society and within
an institution, but almost immediately to birth control and similar issues about which the daily press was in turmoil. So it
happened that the narrator did not stick to the purely legalistic
literature. He also sent in slips for treatises on canon law and
theology. That seems to have come to Lambert's attention. Beyond what one would expect of a part-time librarian, he was in
the habit of forming an impression of the users of the reading
room on the basis of the books requested and his card index.
The initial picture he formed of the narrator was false.
Strangely enough, it was this false picture that led to their making contact.

The fourth or fifth evening the narrator was the last person
to return the books and periodicals he had been working on,
Lambert asked him: "You're a theologian?"

"No, indeed. I'm a lawyer."

"Oh, I assumed you were, on the basis of the Council of Trent. I beg your pardon."

"I'm working on natural law."

"On what?"

"Natural law."

"What's that? Oh, I beg your pardon. I had no idea there was such a thing. Good night."

That was his first conversation with Lambert. Dr. Glatschke rubbed his hands when he read this the following afternoon. "Good! Excellent! I can see you're getting somewhere." Natural law and the Council of Trent meant nothing to Dr. Glatschke, but he considered the subjects a most sophisticated camouflage under which to find a point of contact and praised the narrator to the skies for the idea.

Next evening, as once again the narrator was returning his books, Lambert asked: "Is the theft of food part of the natural law?"

"No, that is fully covered in the civil code."

"Aha, the civil code. And what, may I ask, is natural? Does anyone know? I mean, in legal terms?"

The narrator had no answer. For that he apologized by remarking that this was a philosophical question rather than a legal one.

"Aha, a convention then. Thank you. Good night."

The narrator felt confused all the way home. In his report to Dr. Glatschke he repeated this short dialogue exactly as it had occurred, as was his duty, but he felt like kicking himself for doing so. It would have been easy enough to have invented a substitute, since what he reported amused Glatschke. "Nature only a convention? That fellow has *some nerve*." It was all the narrator could do to keep from showing his annoyance with him.

Nonetheless, and again out of his stupid sense of duty, he quoted the dialogue that took place the next evening.

Lambert asked: "Could you tell me, is suicide part of natural law?"

When Dr. Glatschke read this question, he laughed. "Does the fellow want to do himself in? Then you'd better hurry and worm all he knows about d'Arthez out of him." Sometimes it was difficult not to feel sorry for Dr. Glatschke. It didn't even make sense to be irritated with him.

For his part, the narrator was actually ashamed of not having raised the question himself. With one short question, Lambert had advanced to the heart of the problem. What was the use of explaining that in some countries suicide was considered a felony and suicides taken to court? Amusingly, the real issue was avoided by means of totally unworkable precautions that no one respected even in countries where it was part of the legal code.

Their conversation was no longer than on the previous evenings. Lambert apologized for asking questions. He saw very well that he had made the narrator ill at ease. But this time something else happened. As the narrator came out of the men's room to put on his coat in the checkroom, he saw Lambert waiting for him in the hall.

"I might as well admit that I read your dissertation," Lambert explained. "Excuse me for being curious. A man wants to know at least approximately what sort of people he's dealing with. And if I am not mistaken, you wanted to speak to me."

That assertion was so unexpected that the narrator could scarcely conceal his astonishment. Did I behave so ineptly that Lambert noticed, he asked himself. He did not include Lambert's remark in his report for Dr. Glatschke, who would only have reprimanded him.

But Lambert made things easy for the narrator by not continuing in this vein. "Oh well, you know what dissertations are like . . . I understood not a word of it and wasn't interested in what I did understand. Neither the Council nor the Enlightenment—which was no better than theological hair-splitting, anyway. What in God's name has that to do with your so-called nature? Or with *me,* if you prefer? And what does nature need a law for anyway, as though you could magnanimously enact one for her? And if, for example, suicide comes under natural law—I mean, of course, proper premeditated suicide, and not suicide committed in a state of hysteria or in a pout—how can the prevention of suicide be, as you say, your legal duty? Wouldn't that be presumptuous, or even a little over-self-confident? Excuse me if I do not express myself in the terms of the profession. You see, these are things that one can spend half a lifetime mulling over. It's all very well inventing a law or a prohibition or a system of morality or what you will. I, for one, have nothing against it; it brings a little order into the pigsty, at least temporarily, and I even act in accordance with it myself. But that simply isn't enough—not for one of us. You see, that's nothing more than a suit I put on so as not to stand out or get in trouble with the police and risk losing my right to a pension. And anyway, it doesn't pay to stand out. But what has any of this to do with nature? Is there any natural law in you late at night when you stand at the window and gaze out over the rooftops of this comical city of Frankfurt? Your dissertation? Very well, thanks to that dissertation you received your doctorate and reached your goal. Forgive me. Yes, the goal has been reached, what now? Where is the next goal? No, I don't mean *your* next goal, that is your private business, I mean goal in the abstract. For when the so-called goal is reached, there is nothing left to do but set a new goal as soon as possible—or the goal one has reached will do one in. By this I only wish to suggest that if you expect to talk about nature you will have to approach the concept from a totally different direction. You cannot begin with the goal, since goals soon grow boring. You must begin with the question: Why *haven't* these blasted goals been able to do us all in? And why, in spite of everything, haven't we done ourselves in? There you will find your natural law. But forgive me. That is more than a dissertation, that is a whole life. And it would be better if we had a bite to eat."

And the upshot of all this was that Lambert and the narrator left the library together, took the streetcar as far as the Opernplatz and then walked from there to the Milano in the Rothofstrasse. Lambert seldom ate there, despite the fact that it was just around the corner from his room in the Goethestrasse. He saved the Milano for special occasions, as he put it. "I have a young lady for company tonight and I couldn't expect her to face my regular tavern. Otherwise, she scolds me for neglecting myself. Come on. Perhaps you and she can discuss natural law. She spent a few semesters at the university."

The young lady was Edith Nasemann. She was already sitting at a table studying the menu. Naturally, when she was introduced, the narrator, like anyone else, missed her name. Could this have been sheer chance, or had Lambert arranged it? It almost appears that, from the very first, Lambert had seen through the narrator's shameful disguise as a police spy. Both he and d'Arthez in this respect possessed an astonishing shrewdness. Or, more precisely, watchfulness. For instance, many times after that night the narrator saw Lambert as he walked into a room lift a lamp or push a picture aside to check on the presence of a microphone. The gesture had become a habit. The narrator once pointed out that there simply could not be that many microphones. And Lambert apologized, but added, "There is always someone listening. Better keep that in mind."

That was something he said much later on, long after it had become unnecessary for the narrator to note down such remarks for Dr. Glatschke, who would only have concluded that

Lambert had something to hide. But to return to this evening in the Milano: while Edith Nasemann ate nothing more than a fruit salad, Lambert and the narrator both downed the daily special, with lots of macaroni. Edith spoke of her father having left for Berlin by plane on the previous evening, and for the moment only matters were discussed that concerned the two of them exclusively. Nothing made much sense to the narrator. There was talk about a burial and so on; also mention of a will, and Edith said that her father had demanded time to think it over. "I can't understand why, or what possible scruples Papa has."

"The young man is a lawyer," said Lambert. "Perhaps he can advise you."

"I need no advice," said Edith, and then begged the narrator's pardon. "I don't mean that the way it sounds, just that this is Papa's affair and I have nothing to do with it." And it was at this moment that the narrator realized whom they were talking about and who the young lady was, for then Lambert said to him, "You see, she is d'Arthez's daughter."

"Oh."

And then, to the narrator's amazement, Lambert explained that in Paris someone named d'Arthez had been murdered and that this explained the interrogation.

"What does Papa have to do with it?" Edith asked in astonishment.

"That is something you must ask the young man. That's why I brought him along."

Edith looked inquisitively at the narrator, who stuttered out something about "usual routine investigation" and scarcely knew what to do next.

"Let him finish eating first, my child. We discussed suicide the whole way here. Such romanticizing gives one a hearty appetite."

Not that Lambert's hearing of the murder in Paris was astonishing—d'Arthez could have mentioned that to him—but rather that he was aware, and that he took for granted that the *narrator* knew about both the murder and the interrogation. That was simply inexplicable. D'Arthez had merely winked at the narrator as he made a premature exit from the taping room, and even that could have been an optical illusion. It was unthinkable that on the basis of this he could have described the narrator so accurately that Lambert would have recognized him at once. For this the trifling scene in the corridor was all too short.

And how was any of this to be gotten across to Dr. Glatschke in the daily report? For it was scarcely something that could be kept back. Dr. Glatschke wouldn't stop at jumping all over the narrator for his presumed mishandling of this particular situation; he would also suspect the narrator of other *faux pas*—indeed, that he couldn't keep his mouth shut. And of course this would confirm his suspicions of the existence of a secret society dangerous to the security of the state, which moreover was now proven to possess an information service that functioned only too well. Did they have their own spies? Was there a weak link in his own organization? In point of fact, Dr. Glatschke did take steps in this direction, as we shall see, and these steps forced the narrator to take steps of his own.

They did not remain together much longer in the Milano. Edith said she was tired, and Lambert too wished to retire. They accompanied him to the apartment house in the Goethestrasse, only a few steps away, and then the narrator accompanied Edith to the Rathenauplatz, where she caught her streetcar. "Have you known Uncle Lambert long?" she asked.

"No, only a few days. We got to know each other at the library. Actually, we only really met today."

"And Papa?"

"I have never had the honor."

Edith wanted to ask something further but decided not to.

117

Thus they walked on in silence, and the upshot of all this was that they involuntarily wandered past the streetcar stop and over to a bookstore called the Frankfurter Bücherstube, where Edith stopped to examine the display attentively.

"How could you bring up suicide in Uncle Lambert's presence?" she asked suddenly in a reproachful tone.

"I didn't bring it up," the narrator said by way of defense, and then explained to her that he was doing research but not about suicide, the subject was natural law; and that Herr Lembke had asked about suicide on the basis of the books he saw being ordered.

"What sort of research?"

"For the examination for the grade of assessor, but perhaps a book could be made out of it which would do for a dissertation."

"You want to become a professor?"

"Frankly, I don't know for sure."

"You see, I work here," Edith said, pointing to the bookstore. "I haven't very long, just for half a year. Previous to that, I studied sociology for three semesters. Uncle Lambert still teases me about it. 'As a sociologist you must know . . . ,' he says. It's pure nonsense."

"And why did you . . . ?"

"It's a long story. Perhaps I simply wasn't suited to it. And you? What do you do in the meantime—I mean, while you wait until you've decided what you want to do?"

"At the moment I am a *referendar* with the Security Police." There was no longer any point in keeping this from Edith.

"Is it interesting?"

"No, not particularly. Only outsiders would think so. It is nothing but routine and red tape. And between you and me, often enough quite silly."

"And that's where you met Papa?"

"No, as I said, I haven't had the honor . . ."

"But then how is it . . . ?"

"I don't know myself. Between us—actually, I shouldn't be discussing this, but you are his daughter—I do know the text of the interrogation, it was taped."

"Why was it taped?"

"That's the routine procedure."

"What nonsense! What does Papa have to do with that murder in Paris? He was right here at the time for Grandmother's funeral."

"It was just because the name d'Arthez happened to be the same. We received a request. As I said, routine procedure. Why, a blind man would see that your father has nothing to do with it, but the police are like that . . . If you don't mind my saying so, I think your father takes the whole thing as a joke."

"Of course he does. It *is* a joke. But all the same, never mention suicide in front of Uncle Lambert again. You see, his wife killed herself."

They walked on a few minutes more in the direction of Zeil, then Edith stopped in front of a boutique and told the narrator that he didn't have to see her home. But it seemed natural for them to stay together, since Edith had begun to talk about Lambert to keep the narrator from making any other blunders, and thus they sat down in a small café and ordered two cups of coffee.

All that follows here about Lambert the narrator could scarcely have learned that first evening with Edith. After all, she also spoke of other things, about the Nasemann will, for instance—as has already been recounted—and that her father wanted to renounce it, and in Edith's opinion really ought to in any case. "He doesn't have to worry about me," she said. However, this much is certain: the narrator noticed that first evening that she referred to her father as Papa, but when she had

119

to speak of her mother she always said something like "My mother thinks . . ." or "My mother told me . . ." She did not seem to be aware of this herself.

"I never read Uncle Lambert's novels," said Edith. "I believe there are five of them, perhaps even six. You will never find them in any history of literature. You don't need to read them, Papa says. They really are trash, and not just because Uncle Lambert says so. But of course you can't decently talk to him about them, it's too embarrassing. I've only known Uncle Lambert myself for two or three years, but from the way he looks today, who could imagine that he, of all people, wrote trashy novels? I hear one of them takes place in Paris, another in Vienna and another in Warsaw. Or Venice. All of them take place in the sixteenth and seventeenth centuries. It must have been terrifically easy for him, he read so many history books and memoirs, all he had to do was sit down and write a book. One a year. The weekly magazines fought for them. Papa explained how the Nazis were at the bottom of this. In those days no one could just write as he pleased, and the truth was already strictly forbidden. So people read this historical fiction, it was safe and the Nazis considered it literature. Lambert was actually famous. He belonged to the Nazi Writers' Union, as they used to call it. In spite of his wife's being half Jewish, or even just a quarter Jewish—what's the difference? I'm only telling you all this so you'll be more careful in speaking to Uncle Lambert. One must be very careful, you see. I often get furious at him. I'd like to tell him a thing or two, about that idiotic dummy of his and his dumb chatter about how happy we ought to be that we have no past, but then suddenly I feel sorry for him and I hold my tongue. But he is clever enough to have noticed already. Perhaps it's all a result of calling himself Louis Lambert, after the character in Balzac, I mean. The original Louis Lambert goes mad like Hölderlin in his tower in Tübingen. I even went there once on an outing with the whole class.

That sounds romantic, but don't laugh, I'm not at all romantic. All the same, you do think about it afterwards and try to find an explanation. Perhaps Uncle Lambert was afraid that he too would go mad if he went on calling himself Louis Lambert, and that's why he would rather not talk about it and prefers to substitute that nonsense he feeds us, along with the dressmaker's dummy. Who can you discuss it all with? Even with Papa, I have the feeling he isn't happy to discuss certain things, although he makes an effort and I have his permission to ask anything I please. It's something you notice, you'll notice it too once you get to know us. You have to be careful, very careful. My mother believes it was all a matter of pull; by the time Uncle Lambert married, it was technically forbidden by the Nuremberg Laws, or whatever they were called. He just married her for her money, my mother thinks, and the party turned its head the other way to keep capital from fleeing the country. Things like that are said to have happened. But on the other hand, Uncle Lambert earned a good deal himself with those novels. He even had his own house in Zehlendorf or somewhere, not a large house, I believe, but all the same. The Americans confiscated it when they came in, and that's when Uncle Lambert moved to Wiesbaden—where his wife killed herself. Yes, he's even supposed to have had a car of his own in those days back in Berlin—it's hard to imagine. Papa has described to me how in those days he even helped support his family. He paid for repairs on the old house in the Weisser Hirsch—a new roof or central heating. His father couldn't afford it. Uncle Lambert is also supposed to have paid for one of his sister's education. He must have been making a lot of money, so that wasn't the cause. He had much more money than Papa, who wasn't at all well off then, since he wouldn't accept a penny from the Nasemanns. That explains my mother's fury whenever Uncle Lambert is mentioned. I can't believe he ever did anything to her. I've never seen a picture of his wife; all their photographs must have gotten lost in Berlin, and after that, in Wiesbaden, they didn't have anyone take pictures. Nor will you find photographs of Papa from the old days. And my mother too had to leave everything behind when we fled from the East. Certainly she would never have saved a picture of Lambert's wife, she couldn't stand her. 'Hysterical old cow,' she called her, so I can't ask *her* any questions on that subject. As a matter of fact, all I need do is mention Uncle Lambert and immediately she snaps, 'He is *not* your uncle,' so I've dropped the subject. She simply hates him, that's all. She comes from Kiel, she's the daughter of a professor. Her father was an authority on genetics. As soon as the war was over, they retired him. Toward the end he seems to have become very religious. In his study hung a gigantic cross, almost from floor to ceiling, solid wood. My mother took me with her when she went to wind up his estate. I was just ten or eleven, possibly thirteen. We could use the furniture, since we didn't have anything decent of our own. What became of that cross I can't imagine. Anyway, it would have been too big for the quarters my stepfather was allotted in Aalen. My mother must have sold it along with the books and all the other things we didn't need. I was too young to be able to pass judgment on what she did. And besides, I didn't know Papa then. Nevertheless, you do wonder, and I wondered about my father. He must have visited this house of Grandfather's and somehow it couldn't have suited him. Naturally my mother had fallen for him, that's easy to see. He must have been enchanting, and in a sailor suit besides! He still looks quite handsome. You notice it as soon as you walk down the street with him, the way the women turn around. And when they notice me beside him, they think: What does he want with a little girl like that? Don't laugh, it's the truth. Just imagine what it was like, when he was a young man serving there in Kiel! And perhaps Papa, too, believed he'd fallen in love, since in Kiel he knew no one but the soldiers he went around with. But they never should have married. And of course my mother had imagined a very different sort of life. Now don't think I'm finding fault with her. How could she have possibly understood? She had never once been outside Kiel. Probably she believed everything would be fine automatically—wasn't he one of those rich Nasemanns? That's why she was so horribly disappointed when they got to Berlin. And she never got used to it. She must have been terribly unhappy all those years. Papa wasn't famous as he is now—that was a very gradual process. And until he was, they lived in two rooms— I've forgotten the name of the street. And this explains why she despised all of Papa's friends and acquaintances. She believed they had a bad influence on Papa and were responsible for everything. As though *anyone* could influence Papa! You only imagine you have because he refuses to argue, but afterward you notice that nothing has changed. But perhaps he really was different in those days—it was before I was born. Oh, and now suddenly it comes to me, they were living in the Steinrückweg when I was born, and the whole year before. It must have been a sort of artists' colony where actors could live cheaply. I've never been there, and as a baby I was taken elsewhere. And that's another important point, I believe. They had already been married four or five years. How could anyone possibly be unhappy with Papa? It's incomprehensible. As soon as you've met him, you'll agree. Yet my mother wanted to have children as fast as possible and Papa didn't. He wanted to get somewhere first. I've talked with Uncle Lambert about this, it's only natural for a person to want to know the truth, but Uncle Lambert is prejudiced against my mother, so he can't be trusted. And anyway, how can he be so sure he knows the answer? Papa never would have discussed this with him, that's not like him, and at the time Uncle Lambert was living in Zehlendorf with his wife. They didn't see as much of each other as they had as students. And moreover, since those days Uncle Lambert has changed and now sees those things all wrong. Yes, he really is prejudiced and blames everything on my mother. Once he was so mean that I left in a rage, but later I felt sorry for him. He said it was just an old trick. Bring a child into the world as quickly as possible and the trap springs shut around a man, he'll never get away. Of course there are women like that, but my mother . . . Finally Papa did give in, though, but it was already too late. By the time I was born, he was under arrest. He was shut up in Spandau and came close to being executed. My mother got a divorce immediately. In those days it was easy in such cases because the Nazis were quick to grant permission. I almost missed being called Nasemann, since I was born after the divorce. My stepfather could have adopted me, nothing stood in the way. But a certain lawyer, some friend of Papa's, lodged a protest, without Papa's knowledge. Papa didn't even know if I had been born, he was denied visitors. Yes, the lawyer raised some legal objection—you would understand this better than I—so my mother was powerless to prevent my being named Nasemann after all. And perhaps later she was glad she had been unable to do anything about it. I only met Papa long after the war, when I was fourteen or fifteen. Naturally I was very proud of Papa, but I was already that, long before. When it was that they first told me he was my father, I can't recall. One day they must have had to tell me why I didn't have the same name as my mother and half brothers and half sisters. Because of school and the like. Yes, and it was thanks to the other school children that I discovered that my father was the celebrated d'Arthez whom they often saw on TV and in magazines. At home we had no TV, but the other girls would show me the pictures. So naturally I was very proud, it was something special, even if all I knew about my father was what I read in the papers. At home it was clear that I had better not let this new knowledge show, but nonetheless I managed to think of myself as something special. Only much later did I discover that all those years since the end of the war Papa had been sending my mother money for my upbringing. Even those CARE packages that came during the hungry years right after the war, he sent. At home we heard they came from a relative abroad and that didn't interest me—I was a child, just four or five. For a long time I thought we owed my stepfather everything because my mother made such a fuss to that effect. The first few years after the war were hard times for my stepfather. The new government didn't want to give him back his position in the school system because he had been a Nazi; my mother too. He didn't receive a salary, just unemployment compensation, and he had to tutor students to eke out a living. Now he has a good position again and they are better off. All his back pay was given him, my mother was relentless and she finally got her way. My mother should have told me all this much earlier, don't you think? But perhaps she found it embarrassing, or she had some silly principles about how children should be brought up. Papa, too, could have concerned himself with me sooner, I mean personally. Do you think he had the right to take me away from my mother? On the other hand, what would he have done with a small child? Probably that explains why he waited ten years. In this respect, too, Uncle Lambert is prejudiced. You see, as soon as he was liberated, Papa made inquiries about me through the Red Cross and the authorities. So he quickly learned that we had fled Posen at the end of the war and lived in Aalen in southwestern Germany. Papa never directly corresponded with my mother or I would know about it, but through connections in Berlin or through a Berlin lawyer he contacted old Grieshuber, the solicitor, and he doled out a monthly check to my mother to support me. Uncle Lambert claims, you see, that the whole family lived off that check, but that merely shows how prejudiced he is. And why not? Why should I have been better off than the rest of the family? That wouldn't do, and even Uncle Lambert should realize as much. Moreover, money means nothing to Papa. Another proof of that is this Nasemann will. Periodically, my mother had to take me to old Grieshuber's—quarterly, I believe it was—to fulfill some stipulation, or whatever lawyers call them. I never understood why we went. I always thought my mother was just going shopping and then stopped by the solicitor's and I just happened to be along. And as for the old man, he never said more than 'Well, if it isn't our little Edith!' And that was that. My mother received the money in an envelope and we went on our way. Yes, and it was in this old solicitor's office that I finally met Papa when the time came. How exciting it was, you simply cannot imagine. It had all been worked out in advance, certainly, but no one hinted a thing to me. They wanted it all to look like mere chance. Papa just laughed when I asked later, 'Why all that stupid secrecy?' 'Perhaps you might not have taken to me, then we could have dropped the whole thing,' he said. Yes, that's how he is, and perhaps he might not have taken to me . . . But I had to put on a new dress and my mother actually combed my hair herself and hurt me in the bargain and scolded the whole time about how poor my posture was and that I ought to be old enough to look after myself and that it was a crime that she still had to attend to everything. None of that was new, and all mothers go on like that, but I did wonder what all the excitement was, and anyway the arrangements didn't suit me, I had plans of my own. You could say they just threw me out. My mother simply said old Grieshuber had to speak to me about my future and which career I'd decided on. She was furious and I couldn't imagine why. Moreover, I was only in untersekunde and a diploma was a long way off. I had nothing against old Grieshuber, though. I actually liked the old fellow, with his white hair. Friendly, and so dignified. Sometimes I ran into him on the street and he never failed to tip his hat and ask me how I was. He had to check up, I suppose, and in a city that size you run into the same people often. He had an old woman who helped in his office whom I didn't care for at all, she was always so hearty. Like an old-maid schoolteacher with her old-fashioned glasses, and her clothes smelled as though they could do with an airing. How I loathed it when she threw her arms around me and fluted: 'Oh, darling, how is our little dear today?' But of course I had to behave myself all the same. This time she even had tears in her eyes as she led me into the office. 'Our little Edith is here,' she told the old solicitor—as if he didn't know what my name was. What a lot of silly carrying-on! She had her heart set on a touching scene, I realize today. Father and daughter, seeing each other for the first time, fall into each other's arms—something like that. But I still hadn't guessed. All I knew was that the old solicitor wanted to speak with me again, and that was a nuisance, other girls didn't have to go through this, but it never lasted long. I thought no more about it. The old bag imagined that I must have always longed for a real father, as if life were a novel, and that I would burst into tears. But I would have suppressed my tears out of stubbornness, something I had learned long ago, and besides, there was no cause for tears. I had worries of my own. You see, I was wearing stockings of my mother's because my own were full of runs. Her stockings were too big for me, so I'd tucked them under my toes to make them stay a little better, but that made lumps in my shoes that hurt, and they kept on wrinkling all the same, and this annoyed me. So as soon as I was seated across from the solicitor, who couldn't see from behind his desk what I was up to, I tried to pull them straight. But what do you think? Papa saw it. Papa sees everything. You believe he isn't paying attention and doesn't hear, but he *sees*. Why, he even notices things you don't yet know, then suddenly you *know,* and he hasn't said a word. I could almost believe this is what it was that made my mother so nervous and explains why she divorced him. Uncle Lambert doesn't have the proper perspective and it would be better if you didn't ask him about any of this, he would just distort the picture. At first I too was a bit nervous with my father. It's true, when you're with him you feel he loves you and everything's fine; you can even *prove* he loves you. But when you return home or drop him at the station or the airport, all sorts of doubts besiege you; you think you dreamed it all, or he was only acting. But you get used to this, and anyway that isn't even what I wanted to tell you about, it was those silly stockings. When we all stood up at the end of this conference or whatever it was, Papa suddenly asked, 'Is there a store here in Aalen where one can find a decent pair of stockings?' That's characteristic. Naturally, I turned red. My mother carried on something awful when I came home with new stockings—four pairs. 'As if we couldn't afford to buy them ourselves! What can your father be thinking?' She screamed on until my stepfather finally quieted her down. But I'm getting ahead of myself. My mother carries on like that quite often, it's the result of all she's gone through: the flight from the Russians, when she had to leave everything behind. And then those first difficult years in Aalen. We really didn't live very well at all, I realize that now; as a child, I simply took it all for granted. The street where we lived I didn't find so dreary, but my mother called it Suicide Alley. You know, the sort of street you'll find in small towns everywhere, most often on the outskirts. Brick houses, all of them alike—in those days they didn't go to much trouble, fifty years ago or whenever. One story high and an attic. We three children slept in the attic, and it was a tight fit. Yes, and here and there a little shop, grocery, dairy or a cobbler. Half a mile long, or perhaps it only seemed that long. Everyone knew everyone else. My mother always looked furious when she walked down the street in the hopes that the other women wouldn't speak, but of course they always did. How are you? Fine weather today! and so on. They were all simple people, and of course the difference of dialect . . . You can imagine.

My mother was always complaining to my stepfather that he was to blame. I felt sorry for him, finally. You know, we children didn't think it was so awful. And after all, it *wasn't* his fault that we lost the war. And actually he was such a peaceful man, and he really was afraid of my mother losing her temper. For some time now they've been better off and have every right to feel contented, but by then my mother was a discontented woman for good. Actually, even back then, when I first met Papa, they had the house where they live to this day. I had no idea that it was Papa when the old woman led me into the office. Of course he didn't have that mustache he always claps on before he goes on stage, but probably I'd have recognized him anyway if I had bothered to look at him closely. But I didn't, I just nodded in his direction and sat down opposite the solicitor. I took it for granted he was another client and that I was being squeezed in, since I'd only take a minute. The room smelled of cigars, it had always smelled of cigars. At home no one smoked, my stepfather had managed to break the habit. Then the old man cleared his throat and said, 'Well, my dear child, now as to why I have summoned you here . . . The matter does not require haste, we still have a couple of years of course. Still, we can begin with a discussion of the subject right now. Have you made plans for your future? I mean, do you know what you want to be?' As if I would have told the old man my plans! At home, too, they sometimes asked me, and I always answered that I wanted to study. I had accustomed myself to this because it was so simple and seemed to satisfy them too. That's why I said the same to him. 'Oh, study?' said the old man and cleared his throat again. 'Study? Why, that's fine . . . And what do you plan to study?' I turned to the old bag, who stood pressing her stomach against one edge of the desk. Her eyes never left me for an instant. She got on my nerves, and just to do the same to her, I said, 'Perhaps I won't study, after all. Perhaps I'll become a nurse. Or maybe a ballerina.' That just slipped out involuntarily. As a matter of fact, sometimes I did imagine that I wanted to be a dancer, but only when I was alone with other girls my age. At home they'd have laughed in my face, then scolded me. 'Ah, a ballerina!' said the old gentleman on the point of clearing his throat again. His bronchial tubes gave him trouble, what with all the cigars he smoked. But then the man in the corner by the window—whom I had lost sight of, since he didn't concern me—interrupted, 'But, Herr Doktor, you surely cannot expect anyone to discuss this when there are other persons present!' You see, that's the way Papa is—he notices everything, just like I said. I turned and looked in his direction, and what do you think? He raised one eyebrow, as if somehow we were already in cahoots. So the old bag was asked to leave. Naturally, the solicitor did this like a gentleman. 'I will call you,' he said, but of course she was furious at being hustled off, and made as much noise with her typewriter as she could. That cheered me up, but I didn't let this show, as I wanted to behave like a lady for the man in the corner. He was on my side, I felt that at once, and for this reason I wouldn't have to take just anything the old folks felt like dishing out. The solicitor was clearing his throat again, I believe he was embarrassed and didn't know what to do next. His forehead filled with wrinkles and he pretended to be terrifically concerned, although this was really no concern of his. 'Ah, a ballerina, then. An interesting career, as a matter of fact . . . And how do you propose to go about it?' So I really told him where to get off. If that unknown gentleman hadn't been sitting there behind me, I might not have done so, but as it was, I just let myself go. 'Look, I was just talking. Gabrielle Konradi, the daughter of the manufacturer, has a pair of ballet slippers. She practices in front of a mirror. She calls them positions, and I've tried a few myself. Of course a child would know that you can't become a ballerina here in Aalen, you have to go to the academy in Stuttgart.' For a moment the idea that all this had slipped out positively terrified me. What a nuisance for me if they ever found out about it at home. The old solicitor, too, was completely out of his depth, and for once, not even clearing his throat seemed to help; at the end of his tether, he looked pleadingly in the direction of the gentleman seated behind me. Yes, and it was then that the latter asked, 'Do you really like the name Edith?' I was not prepared for such a question. Of course I didn't like the name, who likes his name? My friend Gabrielle Konradi always called herself Gabriela when she leaped about in front of the mirror, and this impressed me. That I would have preferred to be called Marlene was my own deep secret. I was so surprised I could do no more than shake my head. But I was even more surprised when I heard him say, 'I believe it was your grandmother's name. Her mother's, too.' And when I looked at him hard, because all this seemed rather mysterious to me, he made a gesture and said, 'Nothing to be done about it. For the stage, of course, we can think up another name.' Imagine how surprised I was! Because he was taking me seriously when, all along, this had been nothing but childish nonsense. When I got home, my mother cross-examined me and I had to recount everything in detail, every last word. But about this business involving my name I told her nothing; that I preferred keeping to myself. Then this gentleman stood up and said, 'Very well, we shan't commit ourselves to anything, that isn't our affair. I just wanted finally to make your acquaintance.' And naturally I stood too, since he was the elder and was speaking to me, so we stood facing each other. It still had not occurred to me that this might be Papa. How could anything of the kind have occurred to me, I'd like to know? Do you know what I thought? Suddenly I was afraid one of the girls had ratted and this gentleman had been sent by the theater to look me over and judge whether I was suited for the dance. That came as a terrific shock, because I had no idea how I ought to behave. And besides, I had never really been serious about it.

But Papa came to my assistance as always. Just as the old solicitor there behind his desk was getting ready to clear his throat
really thoroughly, this gentleman looked at him with raised
eyebrows, and when I noticed this, I raised my eyebrows, and
turned and stared at him in exactly the same fashion. That's
what always happens to people when they're with Papa, they
imitate him without even thinking, it just happens automatically. And then he said . . . And yes, this too is characteristic:
he says exactly what you're thinking but don't dare say or even
admit to yourself, because you're afraid that if you did you
would be ridiculous, but then when Papa's said it, the idea
strikes you as axiomatic and you feel something like release. So
he said to Grieshuber, 'I'm awfully sorry, Dr. Grieshuber, but
neither Edith nor I have ever rehearsed this scene. And a scene
like this demands hours of preparation in front of a mirror—
like Gabrielle in her ballet slippers—before the proper expressions or the proper movements come. For if we were to make
one false move, the result would be disappointment; certainly
that old lady out there is quite disappointed—don't you think
so, Edith? But you see, Edith and I simply are not in a position
to accept these roles and play them as they were generally
played a hundred years ago—which is the way some people
still like to see them played in films. The newly discovered
daughter falls tearfully into the arms of the newly discovered
father—no, that just strikes us as childish. No one behaves like
that nowadays. But the question is how one does behave nowadays, isn't it? What do you think?'—He had turned to me. 'I
believe the best thing to do would be to go buy you some
stockings—that is, if you have the time.' Of course I had time.
I said thank you very much to the old lawyer and I also thanked
the old bat out in the waiting room, although there wasn't
any reason to. Afterward, Papa sent her a little bag of liqueur
chocolates. He asked me if I thought she liked cherries. And
then we bought the stockings. I walked beside him as though

we had gone for walks every day, and we didn't talk about anything in particular, just the ordinary things people say. But of course I was very proud and hoped that the greatest possible number of people had seen us together. As soon as word spread that the gentleman had been d'Arthez, the other girls envied me; they thought it must have been heavenly; I had to provide them with autographs. But there was nothing much I could tell them about him, so I found it necessary to pretend indifference. Yet somehow my life had changed. You see, I didn't see Papa again until shortly before I came here to Frankfurt. After I received my diploma, but before the university semester began, I spent two weeks with him in Berlin. Papa wrote me to ask my mother if she considered it proper and if she would agree. I was terribly afraid she would say no, but probably she was in no position to do so, and perhaps too this had all been settled in advance through the solicitor. Between his visit in Aalen and my trip to Berlin, that is to say, during those two years in which I finished secondary school, I wrote Papa from time to time—in fact, quite regularly. I always showed the letters to my mother, so she wouldn't think we had secrets. I'd write him only the day-to-day things, school outings and the books I was reading and so on. And Papa's answers were always short, thanking me for the letter but unfortunately he couldn't come to Aalen because he had to go abroad—things like that, as though we had agreed to the subject matter in advance. Yes, and imagine, he never signed, 'Your Father,' or 'Papa,' but always, 'Best wishes, d'Arthez.' This seemed perfectly proper to me, anything else would have been embarrassing, but I believe it annoyed my mother. Papa was doing all in his power to prevent my having any difficulties for his sake with my mother and the rest of the family. Everything was to remain as it was, that much was clear. To this very day I have no idea how all this was handled from the legal point of view—the divorce and so on, I mean. For certainly the arrangements made under the Nazis could have had no legal validity since the end of the war. The old solicitor explained nothing to me, and presumably Papa forbade it. I was given an allowance, although not a large one, and it was always given me by my mother; so it could as easily have come out of my stepfather's pocket. That is totally irrelevant. Uncle Lambert simply hasn't any right to complain and scold just because my stepfather was a Nazi. He couldn't have done anything evil, he is much too timid; no, I mean too weak—you understand. And besides, they all had to be Nazis if they wanted a position in the civil service, at least that's what I've read. My stepfather as a young man wanted to go into what they used to call the Ostmark, where teachers were in short supply and he would have better chances. That's the reason my mother married him, she wanted to get out of Berlin. And certainly they had to make up their minds quickly, so she remarried as soon as Papa had been arrested. And to think that she was already pregnant! How was she supposed to support herself? Uncle Lambert simply hasn't the right to pass judgment on her. And that's how we landed in Posen. After I was born, my mother had two more children there; the third was born later in Aalen. I can't remember anything about Posen, we were only there three years and I was much too small. Only our flight has left traces in my mind, because it was interesting. So don't let Uncle Lambert tell you any tales. From the very beginning, my mother couldn't stand him, or his wife either. At home I don't even mention him, to avoid unpleasantness. At first, when I'd just met him here in Frankfurt through Papa, I happened to mention him. My mother said, 'Him? He'd just better watch out. What a Judas! Brags he never collaborated, but with those trashy novels of his he was raking it in.' Simply better not bring him up, or discuss this with Uncle Lambert either. Naturally I was prejudiced against him, and it was all so new to me, but now . . . You see, I believe that Uncle Lambert is ashamed of himself for having ever written such novels, and that's why he's taken to calling himself Lembke again. I'm telling you all this just so you'll be careful. Do you know something? But perhaps this has already occurred to you. Older people never want to talk about the things they've been through, although it must have been very interesting and you would like to learn about it. They just brush the question aside with a gesture, or laugh, or somehow imply that nothing ever happened. This has often enough annoyed me—why, it's as though they didn't take us seriously. But no, that's not it either. I believe it's because they are sensitive, much more sensitive than we are, and that's why, again, we must be so careful. Now of course I don't include Papa. Papa is strong, and besides he has always been exactly the way he is now. But with Uncle Lambert this has only been so since the death of his wife. Yes, she did herself in, and just at the point when there wasn't any more pressure. Papa told me the whole story. In Wiesbaden, and not even this turned out to be something she could do right, just halfway; as Papa says, 'She was a woman who couldn't do anything right.' She took an overdose of sleeping pills but they caught her and pumped out her stomach. She had a weak heart; that was what finished her. Uncle Lambert sat by her bedside the whole time. He finally fell asleep for a minute and she died.

"She must have been a funny sort of woman. Not funny ha-ha, funny queer. Naturally I pumped Papa: what she was like, how she looked. But not even Papa could describe her exactly. 'Perhaps she was pretty,' he said. 'Yes, of course she was pretty, if she had been ugly I'd have noticed. Tall and thin and dark-haired. She parted it in the middle, I recall now, and her scalp showed through very white. I must have danced with her, that's when a man notices things like that. Not her coloring, or that she was pale, but there was something about her that made dancing with her unpleasant, as though one didn't know precisely what he had his hands on. You couldn't even feel

135

sorry for her, she left you so cold! And then those eyes of hers! Big brown eyes, but somehow pale too and always questioning —which was a nuisance. You felt guilty but didn't know of what, and that kept you at a distance.' Papa met her parents too. Her father was the representative of a tremendous English machine-tool concern, and her mother was English. Very correct, as Papa put it, much more so than the Nasemanns in Dresden. And the furniture too, old English furniture. Some of it later reappeared in Uncle Lambert's house in Zehlendorf but didn't seem to belong, neither the furniture nor the wife, and God knows it didn't seem the sort of thing for Uncle Lambert! And everyone acted as though nothing was the matter, which was spooky, as Papa said. Uncle Lambert's wife seemed to be the only person who didn't realize this. She read poetry. Papa wasn't particularly interested in poetry and didn't know exactly what poets she was reading. He did say that, whoever it was, it didn't seem to fit either but, all the same, it seemed to fit a little better than anything else she did; she was the sort of woman you read about in old-fashioned poems no one reads any more. But what could Papa do? He could hardly advise Uncle Lambert to drop her. Uncle Lambert just told him that he was engaged and dragged him off to meet his fiancée and her parents. As I said, everything was very fine, but somehow one couldn't believe it, Papa said. And one fine day the two of them went to England and were married there with orange blossoms and rice thrown after them and the rest of it. Papa was asked to be best man and go with them, but he begged off with some plausible excuse. Lambert's fiancée had almost gotten down on her knees begging him. 'It was most embarrassing,' Papa said. 'She claimed that if *I* were best man she would feel more sure of herself and then everything would surely turn out much better. I was positively horrified, because she wasn't just talking, she meant it.' You see, even before that, she had talked to Papa this way. Already at the party celebrating their engagement before

136

she had even properly met Papa, she forced him into a corner and appealed to him. 'I was scared out of my wits,' Papa said, 'and I tried to catch Lambert's eye. How could he let something like this happen? She actually grabbed me by my lapels! "You are his friend," she said, "you have known him since his youth, and much better than I . . . You need only say the word and I will vanish, the engagement will be broken off. I don't want to see him unhappy." ' What can a person do in a case like that? 'You can run away,' Papa said. He was still young and had never heard of women behaving like that. You see, she wanted to sacrifice herself, that was it. Now, if she really had been able to sacrifice herself, she might have been happy—but no one wanted her to sacrifice herself, or renounce a thing; so she did everything only halfway. 'Never sacrifice yourself,' Papa told me. 'It's a thoroughly rotten method. All you do is put the other party in the wrong and everything goes to hell.' But he only said this much later, and the circumstances were totally different. And of course at bottom Papa too had married the wrong woman, as I now realize, but naturally this is something I can't discuss with him. Yes, and later, after Uncle Lambert had married and moved to Zehlendorf, where he had that house—his wife's parents had long since emigrated to England because of the Nazis and had died in the meantime —later it was every bit as bad. In fact, it was worse. Papa didn't see Uncle Lambert often; usually they just met in town in a café when they had something they wanted to talk over. My mother couldn't stand Uncle Lambert or his wife, and to this day she says they were a lot of hot air. Papa didn't go out to their place for his own reasons; he thought it was too bad about Lambert. Papa didn't want him to notice that the situation struck him as spooky and he didn't see how anyone could stand it; that was too much for Papa. But Uncle Lambert managed to stand it all well enough, he seemed to take the situation for granted. He lived out there with his wife and wrote one novel after the other and earned piles of money. Once Papa dropped by before Uncle Lambert had gotten home. The maid let him in—yes, they even had a maid—and he walked through the salon, or some other room that led onto a terrace, and there he caught sight of Lambert's wife out in the garden. He was horrified. Oh, her name was Agnes, it just occurred to me. She was standing down in the garden beside a flower bed stroking the flowers! They happened to be hollyhocks, black ones—of course they had to have black ones . . . For God's sake, why do flowers have to be black? Papa was horrified because he suddenly recalled that he had seen this somewhere before. In an old gold-edged art book with tissue paper between the plates, back home in Dresden. It was still lying on a table long after everyone had stopped leafing through it. There was just such a picture in that book. The only difference was that the flowers were irises instead of hollyhocks. For the sake of symbolism, they just had to be irises, Papa explained. But precisely the same woman. She is standing there in the sun; she is wearing a white dress and her hair is dark. She picks at the flowers and, as she does so, a sleeve falls back to reveal the whiteness of her arm. And of course her smile is enigmatic . . . *Agnes* might even have been printed under the picture, for in those days that would have passed for wit. Or perhaps some other symbolic nonsense: 'The Women without a Shadow,' or the like. 'How anyone can live with a symbol, I do not know,' Papa said. Otherwise, Lambert was clever enough, as the success of his books demonstrates. If only he had been sickly, his wife could have picked at him and then she probably wouldn't have done herself in.

"But that was much later, in Wiesbaden. Why Uncle Lambert moved to Wiesbaden after he had to leave Berlin because of the bombs and then the Occupation, Papa didn't know. I like the town well enough, but Papa doesn't. Of course he appears there, in the Kleines Haus as well as in the Kurhaussaal.

Papa says that the Wilhelmstrasse is so full of old women, and all of them the widows of generals, one quakes in one's boots for fear!—he had never realized there were so many. And that explains the town's being heated from below by thermal springs to 140° Fahrenheit. Uncle Lambert lived in a sublet apartment with his wife. What he did in the year or more before his wife died, whether he tried to write another novel, Papa doesn't know. He knows nothing at all about that period, since it was then he had to find his own feet again. I asked him once if Uncle Lambert might have attempted there in Wiesbaden to write a book on the pattern of the earlier ones, but it hadn't worked out. And if his wife was as Papa had described her, when she realized that Uncle Lambert couldn't bring it off, she might have taken the sleeping pills because she didn't want to be responsible for his failure. Papa listened to what I had to say and remarked curtly, 'One can tell you have studied.' I was quite insulted, for really there had been no reason why I shouldn't have asked. But Papa commented that this was a novel which ought never to be written. If he says something like that, you can stand on your head, he still won't betray his real thoughts—at most, he just makes fun of you. Or he diverts your attention—Papa's good at that. For instance, he asked me, 'What became of the real Louis Lambert's wife? Her tombstone cannot even be located.' That is true, I read it afterward in Balzac. All we know is that she looked after her sick husband, but what happened to her after his death we are not told. That is the way things are: suddenly a woman is no longer interesting. Don't you find that positively unjust? She has her memories, and these are precisely what we would like to share. But no, she vanishes as totally as if she had never existed. Papa first had news of Lambert again long after his wife was dead and he was living here in Frankfurt as a librarian. The return address on the back of the envelope read 'Ludwig Lembke,' and the address the Goethestrasse. The address had been applied with a rubber stamp. Naturally, this struck Papa immediately. Previously, Uncle Lambert had his own stationery, engraved 'Louis Lambert.' So Papa realized that something had changed. As soon as the opportunity presented itself, he flew here and looked up Uncle Lambert. Since that day, I believe, they have been as close as they are today. Of course I can hardly judge, since this happened when I was a child and still lived in Aalen. Yet I wouldn't be at all surprised if they never discussed the past or old times when they are alone. They act as though all that is settled, as far as they are concerned. Yes, one time Papa said to me, 'That is a novel about a wrong name, the most terrible kind there is. You stick to Edith, even if you think other names are prettier.' Yes, and that reminds me of something else—but you won't believe it. You see, I don't believe it myself. I just took it for a figure of speech chosen because Papa wanted to say something nice about Uncle Lambert. With Papa, you can never tell for sure. One day he said, 'Lambert invented me.' Imagine. The ideas for many of the pantomimes that Papa performs were really the work of Uncle Lambert. Even before the war, but even more so now. Uncle Lambert thinks them out at night alone with his dummy, and then later they discuss his suggestion. It's true, I was there once when they had one of these discussions, and I was quite astonished. Of course, I had always supposed that Papa thought them all out for himself—even though my mother always claimed that it was Uncle Lambert who had corrupted Papa, as she put it. Papa himself says that he never had enough imagination, all he could do was execute the ideas Uncle Lambert supplied. Yes, this is hard to believe. And why is it no one knows anything about this? Actually, it should read on the programs 'Based on an idea by Louis Lambert' or the like. And then in all those interviews with Papa not a word, and you'd think Papa would have mentioned it, he isn't the sort of man to deck himself with borrowed plumes. Besides, he has no need

140

to, do you think? Papa says Uncle Lambert absolutely forbade him to mention his name and made him promise he would never divulge it. Previously, during the Nazi regime, Uncle Lambert might have felt this way to protect his books and his wife—that's understandable. But in those days Papa was not yet the celebrated d'Arthez. Yet today, with Lambert's wife dead and the political situation completely different, couldn't we simply use names? But still Uncle Lambert withholds permission. 'I'm his masterpiece,' Papa says. 'That's why.' As if that explained anything! His masterpiece, indeed, and that must never become known, otherwise it will miscarry."

seven

Doubtless Edith was mistaken about Lambert when she warned the narrator never to touch on suicide in his presence. He was beyond what people understand as despair. "This variety of negativism will scarcely do nowadays," he remarked once when the paper printed the news of some celebrity's suicide. "Not at all for TV," he added.

The narrator confesses that he sometimes feels a breach of confidence has been committed in putting down words confided to him in passing, simply because he happened to be present when the situation or the atmosphere prompted another person to say such things. For instance, Edith's whole account of her life at home in Aalen and about her father and Lambert. Were these facts really facts, facts that could pass as valid proof for a historian or for a man like Dr. Glatschke? Was it not the case that they had become facts only at the moment they tumbled out of Edith's mouth, and only because they were things with which she could not yet cope? Do we dare take advantage of such moments of helplessness? Would it not be more decent, rather, to cover up for her? And indeed for one-self, instead of mulling them over in these notes, trying to suck the last drop of life out of them? For the only thing astonishing in this whole account was Edith's having told it all that first evening in this fashion to the narrator, a person whom she had known only a few hours and who lacked any demeanor other than that prescribed by his calling.

Moreover, as they parted in the Elkenbachstrasse, yes, as she was on the point of unlocking the front door, Edith turned suddenly and asked, "Yes, now what about you? What's it like where you grew up?" To that, the narrator could only reply that he was unable to recall his parents, they had died in an air raid on Hannover. He had been evacuated as a small boy to a summer camp near Rosenheim. And so on. To all this, Edith only said "Ah!" and closed the door.

Perhaps it will serve to excuse the narrator that these notes (made, by the way, during the intervening year and most often at night, immediately after the events they describe had occurred) are being read through one last time on a boat bound for Africa, and that he is still making additions that occur to him only now, to round off this report. The ship vibrates. There is much one would like to cut. Due to the vibration, one must steady the hand that holds the pen with one's free hand—otherwise the pen would do the cutting on its own.

En route to three unknown years for which the narrator had to commit himself before the school near Frankfurt would accept him. Here it should not be forgotten that Lambert did not conceal his scorn for the narrator's decision to train for work in the underdeveloped nations. Lambert considered this mere romanticism and claimed that industry showed its shrewdness by exploiting what he termed the remaining shreds of emotionalism. "Underdeveloped nations! Don't make me laugh! Look at the Kaiserstrasse and the Goethestrasse and the Zeil, there's your underdeveloped nation. And you can seriously maintain that you studied natural law!" There was little to be said in answer, but nothing was necessary since Edith, who happened to be present, jumped all over Lambert. "And what are you doing about it over there in your library, I'd like to know! Or with your stupid dummy either, for that matter." And to shut him up once and for all, she added in indignation, "Papa would heartily second his decision, if he knew about it." All Lambert replied was "You poor innocents!" After that, he never brought the subject up.

As stated, the ship vibrates. One would like to know what will last. It is like a sieve: the things that gave one trouble and one thought important for that reason alone, they sift through. One does not notice this at once; everything is so new and unfamiliar, one hasn't time to think about what *is* familiar. One believes there will be time for that later, once the unfamiliar has become familiar.

The arrival at the station in Frankfurt was on time; actually, far too early. As always now, in the broad hall before the platforms American soldiers sit on their duffel bags, waiting. They are already tired. They were trained somewhere nearby and then transported in a gray bus to the Central Station. Now they are waiting to be shipped off to a war in Vietnam. That will last. Oh, not the war or what one reads in the papers or sees in the newsreels. Even the largest headlines pale. But the way they are sitting and smoking and waiting, that fatigue will last.

Then the others arrive, the people traveling on the same train, in the same boat. They all go through the gate together to the platform. Each carries no more than his hand luggage; the larger pieces have been checked through, perhaps even sent on ahead. There are a few relatives on hand, fathers, mothers, younger brothers and sisters. One is introduced and quickly shakes a few hands. But none of that will last. Suddenly Edith is standing there too, although it was agreed that she should not be present at this departure. No one could know in advance how it would be and what she would think after the train has pulled out, leaving her to go home alone. Isn't Lambert dead, and who else does she have? Does she have one real friend among the girls she knows? Obviously she cannot discuss any of this with her landlady. The woman is affable enough, certainly, but merely out of curiosity. Yet at the last moment Edith came, after all; and it was well she did so; it helped because of all those relatives who were there too. But not even that will last. What will last is what she thinks on her way home alone, even if one does not know what she's thinking.

Then the train starts rolling, the arrival at Bremerhaven, the embarkation, then one is allowed half a day off to visit Antwerp. One can write a postcard too; none of that is any different from before. One might even begin all over again as one began the morning in school. On the postcard there's a church or a city hall or a market, Gothic or perhaps Renaissance, but fairly gaudy. None of it will last. Nor will what one writes on the other side. The landlady will read it and look at the church and the market and the foreign stamps of course. Isn't her husband with the railroad, an engineer or something like that? Perhaps he was in Antwerp once and knows these sights. It will give them something to talk about.

But then the ship begins vibrating again and everything is blurred. The postcard falls through the sieve, the Gothic church, city hall and the whole marketplace. Wasn't there an accidental dog in the picture? Where is he now? And where is Aalen? Didn't one hear a great deal about Aalen recently?

Aalen must have been important if it was talked about that often. Weren't there ballet slippers in Aalen? What do ballet slippers have to do with Aalen? Is there a picture postcard of Aalen? Was Aalen home or was it a nightmare? On the ship there is an atlas. As a matter of fact, Aalen does exist, it's in Württemberg. Aalen must have fallen through the sieve into the atlas. Or into a history book. One could write a doctoral dissertation about this. Aalen hasn't lasted, but the ballet slippers have. They are too light, they do not fall through the sieve. They vibrate on the mesh.

And NANY Inc.? What's happened to NANY? Let's look through the porthole. Isn't that pink cloud of artificial fibers still flapping above the sea, the one that NANY spins over the Taunus foothills to evoke a song of woe from the local housewives? No, this cloud is black. It assumes the shape of a dressmaker's dummy. Her bosom swells. Does that mean we shall have a storm, Herr Kapitän?

Where has the family album gotten to, the one with pages edged in gold? Did it remain in Dresden to be thrown on the rubbish heap by the Marxists, or was it destroyed by bombs in Hannover? Where was Rosenheim? Where is Posen? In the archives it is written that a Rosenheim and a Posen exist. Where are the archives?

The ship vibrates. Why won't that redhead fall through the sieve, the one who plies her trade on the Augsburgerstrasse awaiting the death of someone's cancerous wife? And one hasn't even seen her! Someone merely mentioned her. Will she fall through the sieve only when the cancer patient finally dies? Wasn't a grocery store in Tegel mentioned? Who has ever been to Tegel?

What will last are the pictures that were never taken. The vibration develops them. What will last are words that were never spoken. The vibration makes them audible. Who said this? "Movement, because it inevitably creates resistance, brings a relationship into being which we call life. If resistance or movement gain the upper hand, life ceases." Who said this? "The angel who is borne along on the wind does not say, 'Arise, ye dead!' but rather, 'Let the living arise!'" Oh, a young man said this more than one hundred years ago and he only said it in a book, and only in this book does he die, and no one even knows where his wife is buried.

Books? Book? What ails the dressmaker's dummy that she grows two arms by magic, and not two black calico arms either, but the living arms in a sleeveless dress? Is it summer? Is it ever this warm in Frankfurt? And why books? Is one expected to read them? Why else are they being proffered? The ship vibrates so badly one cannot make out the titles any longer. But they are held quite close to the glass of the porthole. Close-up! Careful! The cellophane covering that white book jacket reflects the spotlight. Red and green spots race across it. There must be a traffic light close by. The titles vibrate. One of them reads *The Question of God* and the other *The European Point of View*. Why haven't these titles fallen through the sieve into some handbook or other? In every bookstore they have a big fat reference work and that's where such titles belong. What can one do with them in Africa?

Is it possible to make a living with books like these? Why would anyone want to display them in a bookstore window? Who could believe anyone would come in to buy *The Question of God* or *The European Point of View*? And with what patience that hand arranges these two books until they lie just so, where they will catch the eye of passersby.

But there is only one person who stops in front of that window past which so many people hurry. It is closing time and they hurry home. Neither *The Question of God* nor *The European Point of View* can divert them. And the person who stands there isn't interested either and will never read these books. And their titles will last only because that hand arranges

147

these books in the display. The hand and the arm prevent those books from falling through the sieve. Two books no one will ever read serve to make that arm and that hand visible. The arm is Edith's arm. It must be summer in Frankfurt if Edith wears a sleeveless dress.

She leans through the small door in the partition of yellow oak that separates the display from the shop itself. She supports herself with one hand while the other patiently arranges *The Question of God* and *The European Point of View*. She is completely absorbed in her task. As though she were setting the table and expecting guests. Or after looking in to see if a sick person were tucked in properly, she carefully tugged the blankets a bit.

And the ship doesn't stop vibrating.

Later—but when would this be? And where? Aren't both *when* and *where* totally irrelevant? Something is vibrating once more the way the plate-glass window of a bookstore in Frankfurt vibrates during heavy traffic, the ship around the machinery that propels it forward. And thoughts because they lack for words to which they can entrust themselves. Like the thoughts of a girl on her way home alone from the station. There is no *where* and there is no *when*.

This time it is the planks of a landing that are vibrating. Frail pilings carry the landing far out into a calm bay. Far in the distance lie two tongues of land that seem intent on touching, and if one almost closes his eyes against the glaring sunlight, one can make out palms and between them a channel and the sandbar in front on which the waves break. Now, that would make a lovely postcard. But the one who has walked out to the end of the landing doesn't have a camera and doesn't want a postcard anyway. Why has he stepped out into the midday sun that sears this bay? Wasn't he taught in that school near Frankfurt that it is better to keep to the barracks around noon? They may even have air-conditioning. Does this person, who no longer refers to himself as a narrator because it strikes him as too pretentious, want to try out the possibility of calling himself "I" out there alone on a landing in the midst of this tropical incandescence? Someone once advised him to.

At that moment the landing began to vibrate from the footfall of two little bare feet that slapped against the loose boards in running, loose boards that conducted this vibration out to the very end where this man stands who would like to think of himself as "I" and for this reason finds this hurried running a disturbance. For how can one say "I" to himself when he must turn around to look?

There stands a little black girl and on one hip she carries her tiny brother. His head is large and his thin legs twine round his sister's body. And four wide eyes take this great "I" in. And the free hand of the little black girl stretches out to this great "I" and her eyes say, Come on, don't you listen to the stupid people who told you it isn't right to give us anything. I know for sure you want to give us something.

But before we return to Dr. Glatschke and to the reports that the narrator was compelled to file in earlier days, a short note on Lambert's literary remains, which were handed over to Edith shortly after Lambert's death. The heart attack—or whatever is listed as official cause of death—occurred, it should be mentioned in passing, during a hot spell when the thermometer in Frankfurt registered more than 95°F. in the shade.

To designate these papers "literary remains" is surely too grandiloquent. Actually, it was merely three old faded blue folders into which Lambert had carelessly stuffed any paper he found in his pockets. There were even used streetcar tickets among them. Lambert was in the habit of emptying his pockets when he got home if he did not plan on going out later. He threw everything on the table and any piece of paper he saw he crammed into one of these folders that always lay on the table. Slowly they opened and finally gaped due to the amount and varied size of the material stuffed into them. Something was always sliding out and flying over the floor. The narrator happened to see this occur quite often. He would stoop to pick up the piece of paper, then hand it to Lambert, but Lambert never once put on his glasses before glancing at it. He always wadded it up and tossed it in the wastebasket. This seems to have been Lambert's only method of limiting the accumulation of these papers.

There were no letters of a personal nature. If Lambert received any over the last few years—which is highly doubtful—he would have torn them up immediately. The whole confused mass consisted chiefly of bills, receipts, income-tax forms, bank balances, postal money-order stubs and the like, wildly scrambled and devoid of any chronological order. Fortunately, a contract with a cemetery in Wiesbaden entitling Lambert to a plot for twenty-five years turned up, so it must have been his wish to be buried beside his wife.

The sorting of these more than merely accidentally gathered papers didn't take long. Edith and the narrator, who assisted her in the process, were through in little more than half an hour. Then they noticed certain notes, in Lambert's hand, scribbled on the back of insignificant restaurant bills that also contained the waiter's illegible additions beneath advertisements for beer or Cinzano; Lambert's notes appeared to have been written down in great haste with a ball-point. Obviously, Lambert had intended retaining some thought that had gone through his head as he ate, so that he could work it out later when he returned to his room. But by the time he had gotten home it was forgotten, and once it was stuffed into the folders, the narrator feels he can assert with some confidence, it was never looked at again.

Thus Edith and the narrator were compelled to sort through these papers a second time looking for such notes, but precious little remained even after this final sifting. Edith, who worked in a bookstore and understood more about this, was qualified to say that it possessed no literary value. Since, despite all his novels, Lambert simply did not count as a writer, the narrator had not reckoned with anything else. He was more interested in possible references to d'Arthez, but in this respect the notes were far from informative. With one exception, perhaps. This will be discussed later, but even here everything depends on the construction one puts on the words. The name d'Arthez occurs only once, in a very short note that Lambert jotted on the back of the bill from a dry cleaner where he had taken a suit and two ties. It read as follows: "D'A. Paris. Brick. Absurd pantomime?" Thus, it must have dated from the period after d'Arthez had been interrogated by Dr. Glatschke. Can one infer from it that, for Lambert, d'Arthez was no more than the character he portrayed in his pantomimes?

In any event, this was the only note that had a more or less precise dating. Although among the other receipts and vouchers a date appeared here and there, nothing proved that Lambert had used them to jot down an idea the same day. Any one of these scraps of paper could easily have turned up and been put to use at any time after that date. With some certainty this alone can be stated: all these notes dated from Lambert's residence in Frankfurt; that is to say, from 1949 or 1950 on. That can be unequivocably inferred from the papers he used. For example, there were library cards ripped in half—quite possibly due to their having been made out incorrectly. This shows that during the day, while working as a part-time librarian, he also took notes, was sometimes even stimulated to do so by the request for some book or by a cursory glance at its contents page. From Wiesbaden, from the period of his wife's death, there was not a single scrap of paper. Even the pieces that relate to this place and event are demonstrably written later, during one of his Frankfurt nights. And is chronology relevant? Edith and the narrator quickly gave up, and not without a certain shame at having attempted such a pedantic act. It could only have resulted in blurring the one valid picture of Lambert. The picture that will last for the narrator and will not fade through the action of cataloguing day, month and year is that of a man who stands at night at the window of his room in the Goethestrasse beside the silhouette of a headless dressmaker's dummy which does not reflect the green and red neon signs on the buildings and rooftops of a sleeping Frankfurt. The man is speaking; his lips move, that is no optical illusion caused by the red and green spots seeking a resting place on his face; no, he is really speaking. Whether what he says is relevant is unimportant; all that matters is that he speaks. No one can hear him, everyone is sleeping. There is no receiver tuned to this wavelength. Would this man go on talking if he had learned for certain that the receiver would never again be found, was lost among the junk in an attic, or covered with dust in a cellar? Perhaps a child will discover it playing. Or when they move again, the folks will ask: Shouldn't we finally throw that old thing out? Then one of them will fiddle with it and someone whose name we don't yet know will hear, and though the others will laugh, he will leave a changed man.

The man in this picture bears the name Louis Lambert. He bears this name rightfully.

The validity of this picture is proven by a note that shared a sheet of paper with separate figures and columns of figures. Obviously, Lambert had been figuring out what he could claim as deductible expenses on his income-tax return. The note follows:

> "Next door [written over a crossed-out "Above me"] Next door an aging writer paces back and forth, seeking in vain the first sentence of his last book."

Lambert had already said something like that to the narrator. This note demonstrated too the likelihood of an already mentioned suspicion of Edith's that, in spite of everything, Lambert still entertained the idea of writing a book, and a book totally different from his historical novels. At first, difficulties were created by two sets of initials or abbreviations under which the most varied notes seemed to be collected for some definite purpose. No matter how one arranged the scraps, the arrangement made no sense. There two abbreviations were *TdI* and *iml*. For instance, under *TdI*, these notes appeared:

"Twelve hours are easily enough filled."

"Three minutes after midnight? That sounds so poetic, but perhaps it's more accurate."

"The house detective, a very proper young man. The young lady at the switchboard wears earphones. She makes one connection after the other."

"Taking part at one's own funeral, of course. The tea wagon on which they roll the casket to the grave. A sociological phenomenon. Fine! Fine! Sociology on the other side as well."

"Merchandising loneliness. For instance, through setting up a station for the lonely, so called. Manifesto: Commitment to loneliness! Too clever by far."

" 'You cannot sit here,' the fat doorman says. On the steps leading up to the ritzy entrance. Columns and caryatids. Yes, where then?"

While under the rubric *iml* these bits appear that might equally well have borne the initials *TdI*, as for instance:

153

"In the park of the spa the station cannot be received. No-man's-land. Wilhelmine or Victorian."

"Politics? A way of filling leisure time and calculated in advance by the system. And how much leisure time there is! What can the second-rate do? Not to mention the third-rate! All of it abstract, because it's all *real*."

"Three likable young suicides. We were told we had more tact and that's why they could use us. Tact? What is that? Mightn't it be nothing more than apathy? This has to be thought through."

"Does this station always come through free of static? Not at all! Perhaps the static is what really matters. Individuals who hear only the static. That would be horrible. They don't even dare scream, since that scream would be marketed immediately. Therefore, one doesn't scream simply to avoid being marketed. Poor beast!"

"Your profession? —Intellectual. —Intellectuals have always given us trouble. —Now wait a minute . . ."

"The majority come on foot, that is true, but cars drive up as well. The doorman opens the doors. He even has a great hotel umbrella in the event of rain. That's reality for you."

"On the absence of Evil. Since when is Evil dead, Herr B.? What can you do with a religion lacking the notion of Evil? Without Evil, the world makes no sense. Where is Evil buried? There I would be buried as well. But I would have no murders out of simple indifference. That would justify no one's existence. Or at best only the professionals."

"To left and right the identical principles of organization, only carried to differing degrees of perfection. If one might say so, the Eternal Feminine—but in no misogynistic sense. This everlasting business of being consumed and disposed of. Not even melancholy, just plain exhaustion. That is worse than melancholy. Sympathy for the exhausted, yes indeed!"

"Careful about the use of the word *liber*! The original meaning perhaps: totally abandoned—by whom?—flotsam robbed even of the possibility of dying. Ahistoricity."

This selection of notes appearing under the above-mentioned initials was made by the narrator. His criterion of selection was determined by the question he was trying to answer: What had Lambert been mulling over all those years at the window? And behind this question, one other: whether these shreds of thought threw any light on the phenomenon who called himself d'Arthez—which is actually the only concern of the narrator's report. Naturally, such a criterion can be criticized. Edith, for instance, would probably have come up with a different selection.

The last of the jottings entered above, the one that begins with the word "careful," led to the deciphering of the initials. The abbreviation *TdI* stands for *Tod der Intellektuellen,* "Death of the Intellectuals" while *iml* stands for *inter mortuos liber,* "Free among the Dead."

"Death of the Intellectuals" was doubtless intended for a long time by Lambert as the title to a story or essay he planned to write; "inter mortuos liber" was to be its epigraph. Title as well as epigraph, however, were dropped. On a copy of the piece given it as a title Lambert had violently crossed it out, and not stopping at this, had added in large letters, NEIN!!! The epigraph too was crossed out, but much later, to judge from the color of the ink and the type of ball-point used. And again, scratching the words out did not seem to have satisfied Lambert, for he had added, "What ostentation!" On the basis of all this, we may assume that Lambert often read this manuscript through. A few corrections point to the same conclusion.

Edith was able to pinpoint this bit of Latin with the help of her boss, the owner of the bookstore, as a line from the Vulgate, Psalm 87. Lambert must have run across this quotation in the library, since there wasn't a single book in his room. This too is striking, particularly if one recalls that d'Arthez's apartment as well had been without books except for that lurid detective story. The narrator never dared ask why.

Edith also tried to ascertain if the Herr B. mentioned in these jottings was some person known to Lambert rather than a purely fictional character, but in vain; and besides, that was scarcely the point.

Well, what was the point, then? Edith and the narrator sat helplessly opposite each other after they had finished going through Lambert's papers and bills together. There the thoughts of the departed lay arranged in little heaps on the tabletop. A merely accidental arrangement of merely accidentally recorded thoughts. "What are we to do with them?" Edith asked, but when the narrator suggested they put them aside for her father, who might be interested in going through them himself, she said, "Papa certainly won't want them. No, he won't want to see them at all." Nonetheless, she fetched a paper bag from a drawer and fished out a few rubber bands. So that the slips of paper would not become scrambled again, the separate piles into which they had been arranged were secured with rubber bands. Then everything would be wrapped up in brown paper and secured with string. The narrator assisted Edith. He put out his index finger to help Edith tie the knot. The package was light: Edith held it over her head and let it drop to the table. "What do we do with it now? We can't simply throw it away."

"I could keep it for the time being, . . ." the narrator suggested. But that would have been for a scant four weeks. The date of his departure was already fixed, and the package certainly couldn't be carried off to Africa.

Now it lies in a crate, together with two trunks, in the storage vaults of a Frankfurt mover. The storage costs have been paid a year in advance, the receipt is in Edith's hands. Where else could one have preserved this package? The narrator hasn't a relative in the world to whose attic he could entrust his belongings. In her furnished room Edith has everything but space. And God knows it wouldn't do to send this particular item to her folks in Aalen. The package, along with the crate and trunks, was even insured against fire; that was required.

This package is a piece of the past, if you will, and that explains why it couldn't simply be tossed on the rubbish heap. But this must not be misunderstood: what matters in this case is not Lambert, or his jottings, or what one would call piety. Or, as people say, "In accordance with the wishes of the deceased." How can anyone know what the wishes of the deceased are? And add to that, the deceased in this case being Lambert! Free among the dead? That is a role that he rehearsed for many years, only to have it miscarry. But the attempt will last and the thoughts as well, even those that miscarried, thoughts uttered at a window. It did not matter whether they were heard. As thoughts, that was irrelevant, but nonetheless it is possible to come across these thoughts. Poor orphans! Innocents who only learned to think what was taught in the orphanage, perhaps they will come across these thoughts because they just happen to be bored, and imperceptibly the world will change.

When he speaks of Lambert, however, it is not the narrator's intention merely to cast a sentimental backward glance in his direction, nor somehow to save the honor of a shattered existence; no, it is only the image of d'Arthez that matters, this image that achieves living reality not in pantomimes or reviews or the monograph devoted to his career, but uniquely through the behavior of those for whom he is or was living reality. In this respect the childish reaction of a man like Dr. Glatschke too has value, despite this reaction being such that the narrator almost blushes to tell of it.

For this reason the narrator considers it proper that the only piece of any length by Lambert found close to completion, and as a matter of fact the one for which *TdI* was to have served as title and the above-mentioned Biblical quotation as epigraph, should appear only at the end of this report, since it quite unambiguously relates to d'Arthez. According to Edith, this tale does have literary merit. She even typed it out herself. She did not doubt that one of the better periodicals or newspapers would publish it. But under what name could this be done? Certainly not under the name Lembke. And the name Lambert had been misused for the purpose of publishing trashy novels. Neither Edith nor the narrator ventured to decide this one way or the other. In the end, this tale too was deposited in the brown package.

In its stead, here is a sketch or short story that treats of the death of Lambert's wife. Lambert had provided this piece with a title—and later placed a question mark after it. The title: "A Modern Orpheus." Here is the text.

> Permit me to direct your attention to that unassuming young man sitting so honest and patient beside the bed in which his wife is dying. Isn't that touching? He might have just as easily left this task in the hands of the hospital personnel. The nurse on night duty even advised him to take a nap. Or do you find it stands to reason that after twelve—or is it fourteen, I must check—years of marriage a man will keep his wife company while she dies?

It is neither touching nor does it stand to reason, ladies and gentlemen. You only think so because you have more imagination than that little man there, and because you cannot conceive of a man in this situation thinking of anything other than those years he has spent in the company of the dying woman and those years which he will now have to pass without her. And those of you who possess even more imagination, even if such imagination is totally senseless, will be able to put yourself in the place of the dying woman, and by means of illicit sympathy prolong her semblance of an existence.

A hopeless case, ladies and gentlemen. Just read the patient's chart. One should not waste sympathy on a hopeless case; mawkish sentiment is the only possible result. You've been warned. This little man attempted for twelve or fourteen years to turn a hopeless case into a hopeful one, until Eurydice liberated him from the arduous task of playing Orpheus by finally deciding to call herself by her own name again, Agnes in other words, and to have an overdose of sleeping pills.

Naturally the light is dimmed, as it should be in a room where someone is dying; still, you will allow me to call your attention to the little man's hat and overcoat. How orderly they hang on a hook beside the door. How's that? You would have thrown your coat over a chair? To have hung it up on a hanger strikes you as offensively particular? Stop and think: a coat is not subject to hopelessness, it can be used again tomorrow when the hopeless case has found its conclusion. When he leaves the hospital to make arrangements with the funeral director, who or what will protect the little man against the east wind that sweeps the streets? That coat, ladies and gentlemen, that coat!

Yes indeed, and something you have overlooked so far

because of the weary attitude the little man has taken on his uncomfortable chair—he hasn't even loosened his tie, and no one would have been offended if he had—why, how properly his hands rest on the thighs of those short legs of his! And the folds of skin that project ever so slightly over his collar! Doesn't that increase the confidence he inspires in you? Yes indeed, the very picture of a man who deserves his pension! But how could the wife of a man like that have taken sleeping pills? That is incomprehensible.

But what we have thus far overlooked is the little man's having closed his eyes. Not against the blinding light, since the light is dimmed. No, he is sleeping, and the reason he sleeps is because it is quiet. It was this quiet that he wanted to call his wife's attention to. It sounds a bit sentimental, but with his wife dying, we can allow ourselves some sentimentality. Just now he wanted to say, "Do you realize, everywhere we ever lived, it was so noisy we couldn't sleep without ear plugs. Either trucks rumbled down the street or women in the apartment over ours ran around in the kitchen in high heels. Or radios blared out of windows and children squealed in the gardens on either side. And every evening the lawn mowers went screaming across the little plots of grass! And jackhammers and drills followed us wherever we went. And later in the night came the jet fighters rehearsing for the next war. Who would have ever thought that quiet was so near, here in the hospital? Well, we finally made it." And perhaps the little man wanted to stretch out his hand once more to thank his wife but because of the quiet these good sentimental words remained unsaid and he fell asleep.

He slept without snoring. In a sitting position that could pass for a parlor trick. He did not dream—what was left for a little man like that to dream? All those useless dreams that sometimes even make one fall out of bed. Really, one should have begun life using sleeping pills.

And if one hears the faint squeak of rubber soles on the linoleum of the corridor, and the sister on night duty is coming, then all one has to do is open one's eyes, and no one will notice that one has been asleep. And the nurse will bend over the woman with professional self-assurance, the woman who no longer needs to play Eurydice, and taking the telephone from its hook, will call the assisting doctor to come and register the fact.

And Herr Lembke? Where is it written that Herr Lembke must bury his wife, slightly taller than himself, in Wiesbaden? Nowhere. Only afterward was it written.

D eight

r. Glatschke suspected there was a clandestine transmitter in Lambert's room. The narrator was responsible for this, but how could he have guessed that anyone would reach such a stupid conclusion?

This was due to the reports that he was required to file daily. After three or four days of acquaintance with Lambert, the drawing up of such reports had already become difficult. What was there to report, after all? His style of life was so regular, so dull, and this obviously the case for so many years, that it was impossible to add anything new, once this had been reported.

Furthermore, it should have astonished the narrator to discover that it was precisely this regular, dull way of life that aroused and strengthened Dr. Glatschke's suspicions. As he read these early reports, he could not suppress a repeated "Aha!" Why, he even praised the narrator's powers of observation. "Excellent, old fellow, excellent!" He rubbed his hands together when he said that; a disconcerting habit of his. "These people have an absolutely spooky gift for camouflage. But we'll get them yet!"

In his reports the narrator quoted all conversations without comment, but the implications were always misunderstood. For example, that in their first encounter natural law was discussed received an unexpected interpretation from Dr. Glatschke. "Natural law? Aha, we must be on the lookout for that in the future. Another euphemism for a subversive point of view. Excellent, old fellow!"

A few days later the reports were already growing thinner; for conversations of a purely personal or purely human sort the narrator did not consider himself duty-bound to relate; they were of no concern to Security. So he made the mistake of enriching his report with facts about Lambert that he heard from Edith, naturally without naming names or so much as hinting at her existence.

Before he came into a head-on collision with Dr. Glatschke, the narrator had never once set foot in Lambert's room in the Goethestrasse, but Edith, who had doubtless heard this from her father, had told him that Lambert was in the habit of standing half the night at his window. "Uncle Lambert is terribly lonely," she had remarked, and the narrator had foolishly allowed himself to mention the fact of his standing there, with the addition: "Obviously a very lonely man."

"A lonely man?" Dr. Glatschke cried. "Don't make me laugh! He lonely? He is far less lonely than you or I. Jesus Christ, you're naïve! What you take for loneliness is old guerrilla tac-

163

tics. We learned all that in the war. And the guy stands there at his window all night, well, it's clear as the nose on your face what *that* means. Excellent, old fellow."

Dr. Glatschke appealed to an expert from the investigation service. Although the narrator was not present, there could be little doubt as to what this step signified. Then when he was called in himself to describe Lambert's room for this expert and had to confess that he had not yet seen it, he was naturally asked how, if that were so, he could know that Lambert stood half the night at his window.

Since the narrator wished to avoid at all costs Edith's being dragged into the case, he made up the story that he had discovered this while inconspicuously making inquiries among patrons of the library and among the women selling milk or cold cuts in Lambert's neighborhood.

"Excellent, old fellow," said Dr. Glatschke as he exchanged a look with the expert from investigation. "You're on the right track. Just keep at it."

The story that the narrator hit on was impossibly stupid. How would the women who sell dairy products or groceries know that Lambert stood at his window half the night instead of sleeping? Dr. Glatschke was merely affecting belief and it was all too clear that, as of this moment, he no longer completely trusted the narrator, who, as it turned out later, was now being watched himself.

Much worse, however, was the shame this deception caused the narrator in the presence of Lambert or Edith. Should he warn Lambert that in all probability a microphone had been installed in his room? That would be betrayal of the authorities. But to refrain from doing so—would that not be betraying Lambert? And as for Edith, what right did the narrator have to listen to her innocent tales of her father? What a totally false situation the narrator had fallen into through no fault of his own! And whom could he ask for counsel? He had a large

164

group of colleagues and acquaintances—fine people, all of them, perfect for a Sunday outing or for having a drink with any evening. With them one talked about whatever it was the whole world talked about that evening, politics and sports, superiors and salaries, the latest film and girls, and when one of these people became engaged or married, one had a celebration and bought a present, or just flowers. But then there was no one he could take into his confidence; no, that simply would not have worked, for those dear friends would have stared blankly into his face and said—if anything—say, isn't it about time you found yourself a girl and settled down? And why ask for advice when everything was just fine? Exams had been passed, the doctorate obtained, one's position with the State was secure, the prospects good. One was twenty-seven. All that remained was marriage. What else? Here there was simply no place for a decision. Since this life was the one that all of them led and considered right and fitting, the very fact of one's finding it open to question and of asking for the substitution of something different, special, put one in the wrong in advance. And the narrator, as a matter of fact, up to that point had never had any doubts that he would go on and do what everyone else did.

At that time he did not yet know that Edith, five years his junior, had once been confronted by a similar dilemma, and that she had reached a decision on her own. She had not even discussed it with Lambert, and scarcely mentioned it to her father. She certainly did not so much as hint at it to her mother in Aalen. She had worked it all out alone. It would have helped if the narrator had only known this; his assignment had an inhibiting influence when he was in her presence. And it was the same with Lambert, although Lambert—and this was something novel—was the first older person in whom the narrator could have confided, but that was obviously impossible, since he had been assigned to keep an eye on him. Afterward, after the decision was reached so unexpectedly and the narrator, although he knew it was the right decision, did not have the energy to carry it out and therefore felt quite chagrined, it turned out that he need not have worried about deceiving Lambert. For Lambert had seen through him at once. How? Lambert never explained. All he said was, "At first it provided some amusement, leading you and your agency around by the nose, but after one day of that, I was sorry for you. In fact, I was furious that they were doing you dirt." But he did not let on. That was characteristic of him. On one of the scraps of paper he left behind he had scrawled, "The attempt at living with two truths extinguishes life prematurely." The narrator is quoting from memory. When Edith read this, her brow wrinkled. She asked what Uncle Lambert meant by that. She took it for a slap at marriage and getting married. But the narrator could point to the date on the other side, suggesting that this was one of the earlier notes and that it more likely meant that one could not be Lembke and Lambert at the same time. This slip they also placed with the papers in the brown package. Edith and the narrator studiously avoided the discussion of such questions, not because of Lambert's death, but because the narrator's departure was certain although the date was not, and both of them were rather saddened by the uncertainty.

Even the microphone concealed in his room was known to Lambert before the narrator himself heard that Dr. Glatschke had ordered that it be placed there. Men like Lambert and d'Arthez reckon with such acts and are not even disturbed. On the contrary, such things amuse them. "We want to keep them guessing. Otherwise, they would lose all justification for their existence," Lambert remarked somewhat later. As a matter of fact, he worked out in advance just what he wanted to say to disturb Security. Certainly some of the notes among the scraps in the brown package belonged in this category. He even pressed the narrator to shout senseless or ambiguous phrases into the microphone. The narrator refused. Edith, too, disapproved of Lambert's horseplay.

One morning the narrator was urgently requested to appear immediately in Dr. Glatschke's office. The narrator found him in a state of incredible excitement. "Just listen to this!" Dr. Glatschke shouted and immediately turned on the machine. The tape had obviously been rewound to just the right spot.

After an empty rustling that lasted perhaps a minute, Lambert's voice was heard clearly articulating the words "SOON! SOON! SOON!" Just those three words, and between each one a pause of three seconds. Then nothing but the empty rustling. It was spooky.

"Well, what do you say to that?" Dr. Glatschke demanded in triumph, rubbing his hands. "Now we have him. Is that Lambert's voice or isn't it?"

"Yes, that is his voice."

"And what do you have to say, old fellow?"

"Is there anything else on the tape?"

"Nothing. Not a sound. In fact, that's the point. Not even the sound of movement or interference. Well, how do you explain that?"

The narrator misunderstood this question and found himself in an embarrassing position. He believed that Dr. Glatschke suspected him of having been indiscreet and of betraying the microphone to Lambert.

"I didn't know you were bugging his room."

"You leave that to me. I asked you what you had to say about this program."

"Program? Is there something else on the tape?"

"But I just told you, total silence."

"Perhaps he was only talking to himself. You know, that's his right."

"Right?" Dr. Glatschke shouted.

"I mean, it does happen, if you're all alone in a room."

"Stop talking nonsense! Did you ever shout SOON! three times when you were alone in your room?"

"No, I have to admit."

"There, you see. And besides, Lambert was not alone. A female shape was to be seen standing beside him at the window."

"Female shape?"

"Yes, and almost precisely at the time he shouted. Lembke and this female stood at the window and roared with laughter. Read this report our agent handed in."

"They laughed?"

"Don't worry, they will laugh out of the other side of their mouths before long."

"How could the agent know that they were laughing?"

"You can see that. The woman almost fell over, she laughed so hard, and she would have if Lambert hadn't caught her."

"But we should be able to hear that on the tape!"

"A malfunction, obviously. That happens from time to time. It will be rectified, rest assured. But their laughter doesn't interest us, what interests us is the identity of that woman. A relatively fat one."

"Fat?"

"Yes. Buxom, it says. Rather peasanty, as the agent puts it. You know how these agents always put things . . . Hardly a lady, he writes. How he should know, don't ask. But all the same, whether or not she was fat, one should be able to establish with certainty. He does have night glasses."

The narrator's sigh of relief must have been audible. So it had not been Edith after all who was doing all that laughing. At the time the narrator knew nothing of the dressmaker's dummy. Whether or not other women visited Lambert at night was of no concern to him.

"I assume," Dr. Glatschke continued after noting the narrator's sigh, "that you would have informed us of this party, if in your inquiries you had met her or heard Lembke speak of her."

"A cleaning woman perhaps?"

"At one o'clock in the morning? Don't make a laughingstock of yourself!"

"I only meant to say that it may be a case of innocent accident."

"Accident!" shouted Dr. Glatschke indignantly. "Dear boy, when are you going to wake up? Can it be an accident that in Paris an underworld character named d'Arthez was murdered? That right here a Saxon goes around under the same pseudonym? A Saxon with a political past! And that this Saxon is in constant contact with another Saxon who plays the part here of a harmless librarian? Note that: librarian. Is it so as to be close to students? With people like this, there are no accidents. Remember that. And that SOON! he came out with three times, a code word. And repeating it three times will mean something too. One of the original tricks of secret organizations. Common words, everyday phrases, a sentence about the weather, a question about one's health, stock quotations and where one goes for a vacation . . . Previously these were difficult to decipher but it's child's play for our computers. Will you finally wake up, old fellow? I am not speaking as your superior but as your elder. If you expect to get ahead here, you cannot afford to be a dreamer or harbor illusions. Accident! Don't make me laugh! In our work, accidents don't exist—remember that. And the fat woman whom Lembke received, she's not an accident either. At the moment we do not know how she got into or out of the apartment house. In any event, not through the front door in the Goethestrasse or out the back door in the Rothofstrasse, where the garbage cans stand; they're both watched. Since three doctors have offices in the building, there is a veritable river of patients coming and going at certain hours through the stairwell—the elevator never stops running, as the agent puts it. There must be a great many sick people around. So it's only natural that from time to time a fat woman enters the building, that's obvious. But not one of those we've tracked down has any connection with Lembke. One is the wife of a butcher in Rödelheim. She has high blood pressure, our inquiries assure us. The other lives in Sachsenhausen, a widow and completely harmless, although she did move here from the East. None of that proves anything one way or the other. Here again we are up against one of the oldest tricks of such organizations, the use of women like this for the transmission of secret information. Yes, they can even turn fat women into fanatics, though it's hard to believe. Now your assignment is to find out all you can about this party. Question Lembke himself, but discreetly. That won't be difficult for you. You see, this fat woman is clearly a key figure. Once we have her, we will know a great deal more about the organization, and if circumstances permit, we will be able to take action. Oh yes, and one more thing. Your Lembke sometimes has a beer in a bar in the Taunus-strasse. Often he's seen in conversation there with a prostitute named Nora and with whoever is her pimp at the moment. Now, that is mighty suitable company for our university librarian, I must say! But we aren't concerned with morals, we're concerned with politics. And besides, we can't prove that Lembke is intimate with this prostitute. Be that as it may, you needn't bother. Our agents, who know everything that goes on in such circles, have proven beyond the shadow of a doubt that the fat party in question for whom we are searching is not identical with this Nora. In the Taunusstrasse, politics means nothing. So, old fellow, to work."

This stupid lecture by Dr. Glatschke has been included here only to illustrate the dilemma the narrator found himself in. Since he had never seen people living in any other manner and, in the homes and institutions he had been raised in, had never heard of other possibilities, he simply accepted as a matter of course that professional life and private life were unrelated spheres. Or that one could, to quote Lambert, live with two distinct truths. But now, for the first time, and indeed as a result of having made Lambert's acquaintance, this point of view had become questionable. Wasn't it really his *duty* to warn Lambert?

Fortunately, the necessity of reaching a decision was removed in this case by Lambert himself. Afterward, one couldn't help wondering how everything seemed to have happened of its own accord, as if by some well-thought-out plan, so to speak, to which only the narrator was blind. That afternoon, as the narrator entered the reading room as usual to pick up the books he had reserved for the preparation of his mythical research paper, Lambert motioned to him discreetly and with his lips mouthed all too clearly three times what could only have been the word SOON! Thus the narrator was freed from the shame of confessing the dishonesty of his behavior.

Lambert accepted it all with a shrug of his shoulders, both the microphone and the agents, no less than the fact that d'Arthez alone really interested the authorities. He even went so far as to offer his assistance in the composition of the narrator's daily reports for Glatschke. "We will harmonize them with what I say into the microphone," he said. "We can begin today, even converse a bit in front of the microphone. You'll see that this will raise you a great deal in Dr. Glatschke's estimation. We could also both show ourselves at the window, so the agent in the attic across the way has something to report. The main thing is to keep these people occupied. They only become a nuisance when left to their own devices. They must be fed a steady diet of harmless lies." As he said this, he drew the cover of a shoe-polish can from his pocket. A frog or a turtle with a crown on its head designated the brand. This cover fitted precisely over the microphone; and if one stuffed it with Kleenex or cotton, one could be certain that nothing would be recorded.

171

The microphone had been installed behind a picture, an etching. It hangs in Edith's room now, though she does not particularly like it. But since it was Lambert's, this does not disturb her. It is an etching of three centaurs as they might appear today if one ran into them on the street, except that the human part of their bodies as well as the equine portion is naked. One is a proud young female in sunglasses walking triumphantly down the street on high heels, which have replaced her front hoofs. She acts unaware of the sensation she creates. A young male stands there as if dumfounded and scratches himself with a hind hoof as though unable to make up his mind to follow her or decide what to say. And behind him stands another centaur, an older male, a bald-headed roué with a cigar, cynically sizing the girl up as she parades her bosom along the street. He will probably walk up and invite her to dine in a fancy restaurant and the young centaur will be left out in the cold. Lambert asked if the old roué didn't resemble Dr. Glatschke and, as a matter of fact, there was a vague resemblance. Later a second microphone was installed due to the suspected malfunction of the first, this time behind the molding, but this too Lambert sniffed out at once. Another shoe-polish cover put it out of commission.

That evening Lambert took the narrator to his room for the first time. A few words were exchanged in front of the uncovered microphone, although the narrator had pleaded with Lambert not to make him do this. But Lambert was kind enough to make this easy for him. All he asked was, "What did you say the name of that street was where the fellow was slain with the brick?" "Rue Lauriston." "Thank you. Our friends will find it easily enough." And with that he placed the frog king over the microphone. Next day, as was to be expected, it was only the words "our friends" that put Dr. Glatschke into a sweat.

Naturally the dressmaker's dummy, which the narrator saw

as soon as he entered Lambert's room, could not be shown at the window as long as he was there. Otherwise he would have had to answer questions about the mysterious fat woman the next day.

But even without the epiphany of the fat woman, the narrator's position vis-à-vis the authorities and Dr. Glatschke had already become untenable. In the long run, it wasn't working out to hush up the personal and human side by merely reporting completely immaterial actions and remarks, since the authorities only gave them a mistaken gravity. Men like d'Arthez and Lambert knew how to use a hidden microphone to make fun of Security with its comic pretensions; the narrator, however, was not up to such a role. In fact, it was incomprehensible to him how these men could manage to take as a subject for clever conversation these suspicions harbored against them. Why did they not protest and rise in revolt?

But Lambert was dead set against the narrator giving up his position. "Lying? Stuff and nonsense. What you refer to as lies are unfortunately the all-too-bitter truth for those gentlemen for whom you work. And precisely where in the anthill do you propose setting up residence, if I may ask? Where will you not have to lie? Are you in possession of a truth of your own with which you plan to live? If it should ever be your misfortune to find one, then you will have to adapt yourself to the law of depreciation—let us call it that—and live in accordance with this ahistorical law, Mr. Lawyer, until the law in question chucks you out as no longer serviceable. That happens from time to time. It is anything but pleasant."

So the decision the narrator felt himself obliged to make was postponed a bit longer. The decision was made inevitable by a letter d'Arthez wrote Dr. Glatschke concerning that murder in Paris. What could have moved d'Arthez to write a letter that no one had asked him for? Did he, like Lambert, merely wish to lead the authorities around by the nose a little, to get even with them for the annoyance of having been interrogated during his visit to Frankfurt? Or was his sole object, as Edith believed, an attempt to clear the name d'Arthez? Lambert had already received a carbon of the letter on the previous afternoon, so the narrator had seen it before Dr. Glatschke. The letter read as follows.

Sehr geehrter Herr Oberregierungsrat!
Will you forgive me for letting so much time elapse before communicating to you the results of the investigation that I promised to institute re that party slain with a brick in the rue Lauriston. The apparatus we have at our disposal does not function quite as perfectly as the police. If we wish to get at the truth, it must be by means of gossip circulated in bars and beds. This method entails the waste of a good deal of time, more than police methods.

The murdered man's legal name was René Schwab. This name, however, he used only exceptionally and rather as a pseudonym. Sulkowski, the name under which he was well known in literary and homosexual circles in the thirties—as inquiries in and around Saint-Germain-des-Prés will confirm—was the maiden name of his grandmother, an immigrant from Poland who married the Parisian jeweler Schwab, who died before the turn of the century. The murdered man was reportedly the illegitimate son of their daughter, which would explain his legal name being Schwab. Born when his mother was seventeen, he was left with his grandmother when his mother departed for England, where she evidently married several times. Perhaps she still lives there. The murdered man grew up in his grandmother's house. She was an extravagant, wealthy old lady who spoiled him in every possible way and he loved her dearly. There he must have come in

174

contact with artists and intellectuals at an early age. All in all, a background typical of the twenties and thirties in which the murdered man was to play his part with extraordinary and indeed widely feared talents. Widely feared, my informants say, due to his clever untrustworthiness, where, all expectations to the contrary, the emphasis falls on "clever." For a time the murdered man must have intended to become a priest or monk. He entered a seminary, where for a year he lived an exaggeratedly ascetic existence, but took to his heels a few days before his ordination. Of course this was very much customary among the demimondaine in those days.

In 1943, that is to say, during the German Occupation, the murdered man was blackmailed by the Gestapo, which had the goods on him—whether connected with his homosexuality or with black-marketeering is not known—and he found himself compelled to spy on Frenchmen deported to Germany for slave labor. My informants are uncertain whether this man actually caused any harm by means of denunciations. As far as could be ascertained, he spent a year and a half in Hamburg, allegedly collecting a lending library of some sort for the French workers. He is said to have run around with the French edition of Nietzsche's *Will to Power* in his pocket. In early 1945—in other words, just before the final collapse —he was evacuated along with his compatriots to the province of Schleswig-Holstein. He is supposed to have been killed in Neumünster, whether in an air raid or in a mass execution—they were not infrequent at this time— remains unclear. French men of letters who started investigations after the war were unable to locate his grave. Rumors, however, were long-lived: he had somehow managed to drop out of sight at the last minute, he was reportedly seen here and there—in Persia, for instance.

175

The suspicions of the Security Police that he was enlisted into the secret service of some other nation because of his Gestapo experience may thus be quite well founded. Ferreting out the complete truth about the murdered man's activities over the past twenty years, from the end of the war until his death, proved to be beyond our capacities, and also our interests. The murder in the rue Lauriston testifies to the likelihood of the rumor, and that is enough. And last of all, that the murdered man went by the name of d'Arthez is easily explained when one considers his literary background. In the seminary he is said to have been passionately devoted to the study of Pascal. This could not fail to lead him to the character in Balzac. As for me, my Parisian attorney tells me that I have no recourse to legal action in the case of misuse of this name.

My informants are unanimously agreed that the murder in the rue Lauriston can be nothing more than a somewhat tardy revenge on a collaborator. Despite the years that separate us from the circumstances of such acts, we must reckon with their frequent recurrence. The germ of revenge is one of the hardiest; even the most trivial occasion that reminds a man of the pain of a wound long since healed can rouse it to virulence. Some even claim that it can bring about genetic changes.

In the hope that these particulars which I have been able to gather may be of assistance to you and the authorities, I remain

Ihr sehr ergebener

Ernst Nasemann

As might have been expected, the narrator was called in the next afternoon to consult with Dr. Glatschke about this letter. Lambert had advised him that it would be preferable to come right out with the admission that he already knew it and thus spare himself the useless pains of feigning surprise. But even so, the situation was past saving.

Naturally Dr. Glatschke, already angered considerably by the contents of the letter, was further thrown off his stride by the narrator's admission.

"Well, I never! You've already read the letter?"

"Yes, sir, yesterday evening Herr Lembke showed me a carbon."

"Oh, a carbon. Very interesting. So the Saxon in Berlin considered it necessary to send his contact here a carbon. Quite revealing! And what did your Herr Lembke have to say about it?"

"Not much."

"Oh, *not much*, is it?"

"Of course we talked about the murder in Paris. You can imagine, I was surprised at the letter."

"Well, I never; the letter *surprised* you. And *what*, may I ask, surprised you precisely?"

"That the act was one of revenge. That was the first thing one should have thought of—and I hadn't . . ."

"Yes indeed, the first thing. And that's the trouble. How stupid we are, all of us, not to begin with first things first. And what did Lembke say to this?"

"I asked him if he thought that was so. He replied that d'Arthez—he never calls his friend anything but d'Arthez—certainly accepted it as the truth, insofar as one can talk about truth at all, or he wouldn't have written that letter. The case doesn't interest Herr Lembke at all."

"Oh, it doesn't interest the gentleman at all. He's only interested in that fat woman who's always up at his place. And what can you tell us about her?"

"As yet, nothing. It wouldn't do to ask him about her point-blank."

"And in his apartment, or his room rather, you have seen no clues as to her identity?"

"No, sir."

"Very well. These people are clever. Let's put this aside for the moment. Let's stick to this letter. You say that you discussed it with this Lembke. Did he bring to your attention the manifest threat that it contains?"

"Manifest threat?"

"Yes, in the last paragraph, where this amiable contemporary of ours threatens us with acts of vengeance."

"That . . . That hadn't occurred to me. I took that for nothing more than a simple logical conclusion."

"Thank you for your lesson in logic, old fellow. But can your logic explain why your friend Lembke showed you the carbon?"

"We had already spoken about the Paris murder at some length; I couldn't avoid it. Isn't it part of my assignment, if I am to gather information about d'Arthez? I have to win Herr Lembke's confidence, don't I?"

"You seem to have been a bit too successful in that department. Truly admirable. An entirely new method. In other words, your Lembke is aware of the fact that you have been assigned to him."

"Why, not at all. He knows that his friend was interrogated here because of that murder in Paris and he knows that I am acquainted with the case and that we are working on it. I had to give that away if I wanted anything from him. Otherwise, he has no interest in the case."

"This Lembke of yours, with whom you seem so astonishingly well acquainted, what, if I may ask, is *he* interested in?"

"I couldn't say. Perhaps in his job. No, not in that either. I haven't known him long enough, I suppose."

"And how is it that the conversation you had with him about this letter is not registered on tape?"

178

"The conversation? Oh, that's easy. He showed me the letter in the bar in the Rothofstrasse. That's it."

"Ah, how thoughtful of him. And afterward, up in his room, you didn't mention it again?"

"No, as I said, the case doesn't interest Herr Lembke at all. We talked about other things."

"Ah, other things. Am I permitted to ask what?"

"Nothing in particular. Things of no real interest."

"It would be better if you were to leave the question of deciding whether something is *interesting* or not in the hands of men who have more experience. You will forgive this observation. And how do you explain that these uninteresting things you said were not heard by our microphone?"

"Perhaps it was poorly installed. Perhaps we were sitting in the wrong corner of the room. I wasn't up there very long."

"Thirty-one minutes, old fellow. In thirty-one minutes a great deal can be said about a great many things. But, nevertheless, let us assume that a technical disturbance was the cause. That will be looked into. Let us return to this letter. That murder in Paris doesn't interest us much either. As a favor to our Parisian colleagues, I put in a call to the Hamburg office to have the information this letter offered checked out, but whether or not the information is true, the case can be shelved. But, in so doing, we do not shelve *the d'Arthez case,* which we stumbled on in the process. Let us suppose that everything contained in that letter is so. Nonetheless, the question remains: How did Ernst Nasemann and his "informants," as he calls them, in the space of two weeks, turn up more material about an obscure character, who had been given up for dead twenty years ago, than the Paris police, whom, God knows, I would be the last to accuse of incompetence? Doesn't this support the suspicion I have harbored from the beginning, that we are dealing with an organization of international proportions, in appearance a quite hardy group with long-term plans, in control of an astonishingly well-functioning underground system for the gathering of information? How are we to explain that this organization, which has obviously been in existence for decades, has thus far eluded the watchfulness of every state? This is a question that I have been mulling over as I read your reports of this subordinate character, Ludwig Lembke. For he is merely a subordinate character—of that there can be no doubt. I take him to be a rather lowly purveyor of information within the organization and nothing more, and I presume only unimportant information would be entrusted to him. All the same, that this organization is able to make use of such wretches as him indicates the existence of a terrifyingly widespread and carefully constructed network of agents, and for bringing this network to light—or at least one small corner of it—you deserve a tip of the hat. The job you've done worming your way into Lembke's confidence is remarkable. Thanks to you, we have come a giant step forward. You can depend on it, I shall give credit where credit is due. But this still does not answer the question why no one has investigated this organization so far. One excuse might be the number of pressing day-to-day problems after the war that engaged the attention of those organs of the State charged with the maintenance of order, problems which required immediate action; and for this reason the real enemy was lost sight of. There is probably something to this, but nevertheless the answer strikes me as far too simplistic. I believe that I have found a more plausible solution, and again thanks to your reports, old fellow. Yes, it's a fact, you needn't look so astonished. It was thanks to your rather uninteresting reports about this Lembke that I stumbled on the principle of organization. Yes, one might go so far as to say that it was your reports' general prosaicness which suggested this solution to me. These people whom God knows we must not underrate, even when, as this impudent letter demonstrates, they overrate themselves, appear to have learned something from the long history of secret societies and to have drawn the logical conclusions. All the historical revolutionary parties, call them nihilists, anarchists, Marxists or what you will—yes, even the Nazis worked according to principles which were historically outmoded and that is undoubtedly why they lost power after twelve years despite their totalitarian system—all these parties and organizations made the mistake of raising topical questions to become well known and win adherents. This only brought them to the attention of the authorities and one could take a stand against them or take countermeasures. This mistake of being topical, for we must call it a mistake—even the military and political guerrilla tactics presently in fashion are a mistake, inasmuch as they make the enemy visible and what is visible can be combated—this mistake d'Arthez and his comrades have avoided. The basic principle of this secret organization with which we are now dealing seems to be the exact opposite of all its predecessors, that is, they absolutely avoid taking a stand on the issues of the day. I wouldn't be surprised if there weren't an express prohibition of topicality, and that new members, on initiation, had to swear to observe it. Just ask yourself what this Lembke in the two weeks you've known him has said to you of topical interest! Nothing, nothing at all. Beautiful and not-so-beautiful sentences that could just as easily have been spoken a hundred years ago. Hasn't that occurred to you? And this letter isn't really any different. The nontopical as camouflage—don't you see what a dangerous principle that is? Yes, and in order not to become too conspicuous by this reticence, they even choose a superficial pseudotopicality. Parttime librarian, cabaret artist. Professions that superficially relate to the public. Superficially! Perhaps even teachers and priests. You believe they're talking about Cicero or religion, they practice their innocent callings, they baptize and bury and fly off the handle when it's a question of sex education, all of it a-political and not the least bit dangerous, and behind it the old conviction lurks, the conviction that the order for which you and I labor must be put down. The old nihilistic goal. And what discipline! What training their members must have had! What a principle of selection! And all of it directed toward keeping out of sight of the powers-that-be. In order to patiently build up an opposition. What long-range planning! Until the day that disintegration begins to show. The most terrifying secret organization in human history. The old methods for putting down insurrection are powerless against this, we must admit it at once. We are no longer dealing with just another ideology or sect, but with an absolute negativism. How do you propose to come to grips with absolute negativism? How do you bring it into court? It will simply slip through your fingers, you will find yourself trying to grasp the void, and you yourself will be contaminated without even realizing it. The police are powerless against this, old fellow. We are going to have to raise a whole generation of doubting Thomases whose job it will be to subvert this absolute negativism from within. Young people like yourself, you know. We are going to have to fight fire with fire. Once you know the principles, you can develop the antidote. It is a little late in the game, but still we have no cause for despair. For these people, otherwise so exceedingly clever, have betrayed themselves in spite of everything by their very solidarity, by this eternal use of "we." Read this letter from d'Arthez through again carefully. *We, we, we!* That first-person plural has become so natural for him that he no longer notices it himself. These people have gotten cocky because they've been able to give us the slip for so long. They are already issuing threats. But right here they have made a miscalculation. Now we have the goods. We can destroy this solidarity, we can gnaw away at it from within until nothing remains but a laughable shell. There is your task, *your* task, dear boy. Above all, I am thinking of you and young people of the same stamp. You were born for it. Without feeling confined by our old-fashioned methods—yes, our methods, I admit, are old-fashioned, and thus ineffectual—without being weighed down with a past, you can penetrate into this enemy's no-man's-land immune to the bacillus of nihilism, because since you were born you have been inoculated with it, so that the bacillus dies, and the enemy by his very lack of opponents begins to look ridiculous, and order triumphs! Yes, old fellow, possibly without knowing it yourself, you have already accomplished something in this direction. I am fortunate not to have erred in choosing you. Because from my point of view it was an experiment, assigning you to so dangerous an adversary as d'Arthez. That could easily have misfired. But my instincts did not lead me astray when I sensed that you were suited to this assignment. You can depend on it, this will figure in your record. That will be a big help to you in your professional climb upward."

Dr. Glatschke was positively dripping with benevolence. The role of the paternalistic superior who looks after the interests of his subordinates seemed to please him, but he also considered that this made him worthy of their confidence. In this particular subordinate Dr. Glatschke produced a most unpleasant sensation, since he had not the slightest notion of what could have occasioned his superior's enthusiasm. He listened to Dr. Glatschke without interrupting and without once wincing when his superior, in excitement, poked him in the chest with his index finger.

But the blow came like lightning. Despite his continuing attentiveness, it found the narrator in a condition of total unpreparedness. Had Dr. Glatschke been working up to this all the time? Could it be that his methods were not as old-fashioned as he pretended? Or could he really believe everything he said? In any event, suddenly the carpet was pulled out from under the narrator.

"Magnificent, old fellow, the way you've managed," continued Dr. Glatschke, after he had caught his breath. "In the beginning I was surprised when nothing about it appeared in your reports. I was flabbergasted, if you'll pardon my saying so. But now I understand. I can even say I endorse your technique. Here we have the new methods of which I was speaking. Your reports, you know, are read by others in the department, and you are right: it is better that your advanced tactics should not become generally known before their time. Absolutely magnificent, the way you discovered the weak link in the enemy's defenses. Take your time, take your time, for God's sake! We must allow ourselves as much time as the enemy if we are to mine his defenses. But that you realized all this on your own and discovered the one possible route into enemy territory, that simply cannot receive sufficient recognition. I can only express my gratitude on the part of the authorities. You see, I readily confess that no one here had so much as given this daughter of d'Arthez's a moment's thought. Now don't be frightened! You must get over that. This Fräulein Nasemann will remain your secret, I can give you my word, for what it's worth."

"You put a tail on me too?" asked the narrator.

"But that goes without saying, old fellow! Can that surprise you? Isn't that my duty? I am responsible for you, after all. You won't always be working under me, that's certain; but whatever post you next receive will be given you on the basis of my reference, and if I am to emphasize your abilities and suitability for our profession, I want to be able to do so with a good conscience. And what's the difference? You can be certain that from time to time I too am subjected to scrutiny. If the system we stand for is to remain intact, we must be able to depend on each other absolutely, and the only way we can attain certainty in this is by letting neutral agents judge our behavior. Oh yes, those agents! Most of them are quite primitive, but how informative their reports can be! Very often their grammar is faulty, but they always write without conscious reflection, without premature conclusions, without all the thoughts that you or I would have had in their place. Due to our professional zeal, we always make up our minds in advance, and for this reason we are likely to overlook the most important point of all. These primitive agents, on the other hand, see nothing but those trivial details that escape us. And it is invariably a trivial detail that gives someone away. Look here, it reads, 'He took her arm in his.' Well, why shouldn't one take a young lady's arm? We wouldn't have bothered to mention it. Or here: 'She drank tea with lemon; he drank a cup of coffee. He smoked six cigarettes, some of them just half.' You smoke too much, old fellow, you're nervous, if you will forgive my saying so. Or here: 'He mostly just listens, she talks a blue streak.' Good, good! You made her sing. That is a great art. Now, what else have the primitive types noticed? We must not let their style put us off. 'He wanted to foot her bill for the tea, but she turned him down. He helped her into her coat.' Naturally one helps a lady into her coat, but an agent thinks it necessary to mention the fact—that's the difference. And then he actually apologizes. 'They were standing a long time in front of her door in the Elkenbachstrasse. As it was late already and there was no traffic, the couple could only be watched from a distance. They talked incessantly. Their voices must have been very loud, because a window went up on the fourth floor and then shut again with a bang. At that they parted.' Yes, and now we have reached a point that will amuse you. Our agent believes he must emphasize the fact that there was neither an embrace nor a kiss. Typical! Why should one even bother to mention it, particularly in a classified report? But to these people such things are important, they never think of anything else. This is really a classic example. In your case, I call it admirable tactics the way you nurtured this young lady's confidence. Certainly she would have had nothing against your putting your arms around her and kissing her; perhaps she had even counted on it and even

185

now wonders why nothing of the kind occurred. And therein I see your adroitness. Thanks to your reticence, you have made this young lady worry about you, so next time she will tell you even more about herself. I congratulate you, old fellow. Such adroitness is truly astonishing in such a young man. After all, we are all only human. As I said, I understand why you mentioned none of this in your reports. Out of modesty and because you wanted to be able to present me with the goods. You were afraid, were you not, that I would take all of it for a mere infatuation and make fun of you, if any mention of it appeared in the reports to the authorities? But now you know me better and realize that I admire greatly the manner in which you have approached this case. I am fortunate in having you as a co-worker. Keep up the good work!"

The narrator saw himself the victim of a system that he had formerly considered so stupid. Certainly his reaction was ill-considered. He was pale with fury and, what made him even more furious, Dr. Glatschke had noticed it too and rubbed his hands in amused anticipation. What satisfaction it must have given the man when his victim pushed back his chair and stood up to stutter about his "private life." That was only delivering Dr. Glatschke a whip with which to beat him.

"Private life?" he asked, feigning surprise. "Did you say *private life*? Don't be a child! Private life! What an antiquated notion to be trotted out in these official chambers . . . Yes, haven't you learned by now that we who have the honor of watching over the security and good order of the community *have* no private lives and indeed should have none? Very well, you are still young, younger than I had supposed. I will keep this to myself, for if such a remark were to appear in your file it could only serve to injure your career. Private life! Don't make me laugh! A few days' acquaintance with a young lady and you call it *private life*?"

"I do not wish the name of this young lady . . ."

"What a tone you are taking, Herr Doktor! And as for your wishes, unfortunately they do not carry much weight with Security. The young lady whose name you do not wish brought up again is not a part of your so-called private life but the daughter of a suspect, and as such occupies a place on the list of those whom it is our duty to keep under surveillance. Although I am prepared to admit that the young lady is up to no mischief—I even assume that she is innocent—still, her contact with suspects has contaminated her; presumably her very innocence and lack of suspicion are exploited to lure others into their net. These people are absolutely without scruple. Let me warn you as an older man that the daughter of this d'Arthez is no fit object for your affections. Think about it. I do not want to hear anything like this from you again. And moreover, are you aware of the fact that just six weeks ago this young lady broke off her official engagement to a promising young man and gave no reasonable grounds whatsoever? No? She didn't tell you about it? Strange! A strange private life, wouldn't you agree? And at the same time a fact well known to us. The young man in question has just passed his engineering examinations in Darmstadt, and *cum laude*. Immediately he was offered a position with one of our industrial magnates, a position with unlimited possibilities for advancement. That is no secret, old fellow; engineers always interest us in Security . . . And your young lady for almost a year 'went' with this young man, as people say, or rather she 'drove' with him, I should say, for this young man had a small car at his disposal. Even the license number is on record, if you want to check. Not only did your young lady visit the young man's parents—good solid people, his father has a position in the postal service—she even took her fiancé to Aalen to meet her mother and stepfather. Not to mention regular weekend trips into the Taunus, the Odenwald or along the Rhine. Yes, she even went to the ball of the Darmstadt Student Association, if that means anything to you. There you have your private life, Herr Doktor, and the authorities seem to know more about it than you do."

At that, the narrator left Dr. Glatschke's office, sat down at his desk and wrote his letter of resignation. It was this which Lambert termed an ill-considered reaction. In the letter he gave no grounds, and above all avoided any reference to Edith Nasemann, since he did not wish to add instances of her name to those already in the files of the Security Police. But the narrator felt totally helpless, which was the worst of it. And he was to continue feeling helpless for a long time. It was no easy matter, growing accustomed to this feeling. He would have thought himself a coward had he sent this letter of resignation by post. For this reason, he waited until after lunch and returned to Dr. Glatschke's office with the firm resolve not to allow himself to be goaded into any sort of argument but simply to hand in his resignation.

"Well, I never!" said Dr. Glatschke. "And how do you arrive at this, Herr Doktor?"

"I do not consider myself suited for the post."

"Really? You don't consider yourself suited for the post?"

"If you prefer to have the dismissal proceed from your side, I have nothing against that either."

"Really, you have nothing against that either? Why, thank you."

"I only mean to say that I forgo any appeal. I am prepared to say that in writing."

"Princely of you. Thank you."

"Whether resignation or dismissal, it is irrelevant to me. Excuse me, but I do not wish to discuss the matter."

"Aha, once again there is something you do not *wish*. You really do have a great many wishes! Is it true that your father was president of the Superior Provincial Court in Hannover? What would he have said to these noble wishes of yours?

188

Please go now. The authorities have no use for people who desert them for nothing more than a pretty face. Good day."

That was that. Then suddenly after he had shaken hands with his astonished colleagues and taken the elevator to the ground floor the narrator realized that he had expected too much of himself, he was not man enough for the decision he had made—the decision? What decision? And if a decision, who made it? His knees were trembling when he reached the street. His own voice sounded strange to his ears when he sat down in a coffeehouse and asked the waitress for a cup of coffee. Couldn't everybody see the change? The waitress looked after him distrustingly—he had left far too large a tip on the table.

It was better to go home and hide. Home? In other words, to his one-room apartment. The concièrge was sweeping and tidying up the foyer. "Closing time early today?" he asked. Did he already *know*? How had it happened? Two weeks earlier, everything had made sense—and now? Simply because a total stranger named d'Arthez had winked at him? Perhaps he *hadn't* winked at him. What nonsense to claim such a thing. And even if he had, the whole thing could not be blamed on that one wink. Ridiculous!

And Lambert? The narrator was not equal to sitting alone in his room. He had no assignment now. On the contrary, he had been dismissed from his assignment. But had he not already confessed to Lambert that it was only in his capacity as an employee of Security that he had forced his acquaintance on him? Lambert wouldn't miss the narrator any more than he missed anyone. Lambert missed no one. Without letting him down, he could simply disappear. Perhaps he would say something about it to his comical dressmaker's dummy and shrug his shoulders. And what would he say to Edith Nasemann when she asked after the narrator? Naturally she would ask. Yes, she

189

must be saved from all this. Wouldn't Dr. Glatschke lose all interest in Edith Nasemann if his spies were to tell him that the narrator was no longer seeing her? Then of course he could write her later on and explain it all, and beg her pardon. Yes, later on.

The narrator did not go to the reading room. He waited on the steps at the entrance to the library until Lambert finally came out. The narrator wanted to keep the scene as short as possible, he wanted to shake hands and say goodbye. Naturally, he would have to explain why he would not be visiting the library any longer. Perhaps it would be best to say he had another assignment, or something like that. But as has already been remarked, as brief as possible.

But that is not how it happened. Lambert already seemed to know. He didn't even begin by asking, "Why weren't you in the reading room today?" although that would have been perfectly natural. He simply nodded to the narrator and said, "Come on. Let's sit a moment in the park before we take a streetcar to the restaurant." He looked exhausted. The climate in Frankfurt did not seem to agree with him. He really did look terribly tired. Perhaps he always looked like this and this was just the first time the narrator noticed. It would not do simply to blurt everything out.

So they both sat there on a bench in the park for a while without speaking. The sun had just sunk behind the foothills of the Taunus. The west windows of the library reflected the deep red and it seemed as if a costume ball were in progress inside, for which all the lights had been hung with red lanterns. The people on the street noticed nothing, the evening traffic hurried on as usual, but sitting on this bench, one noticed.

Suddenly Lambert sighed and said, "Too bad d'Arthez isn't here." The narrator supposed that the windows had prompted this, their glow was so unreal, but he was mistaken.

"I only came to say farewell, Herr Lembke," the narrator hastened to add. "Not because I am in need of help."

"Stuff and nonsense! Be glad that you need help. Oh well, let's go eat something first. I think the Central Station would be best."

They did not speak on the street. As so often, though, Lambert made fun of the sign on the streetcar that indicated that it had no conductor—*schaffnerlos*. "Oh, the gravity of that *conductorless*!" he sighed.

In the main hall of the Central Station, American soldiers were patiently sitting on their duffel bags waiting to be transported to a war. Lambert stopped for a moment, his forehead wrinkled, but then he pulled the narrator into the waiting-room restaurant. "We'll eat first. You must be hungry. Don't talk nonsense, naturally your stomach is empty. You have tried the truth, that makes a man hungry. Oh, you poor innocent! Here's another who would tell the truth before he has learned how to lie."

Afterward the narrator told the whole story of his resignation and what led to it. It was not possible to leave out all mention of Edith. Lambert would notice anyway that his involvement with her had contributed to his decision.

"Was your father really the president of a Superior Provincial Court?" Lambert's asking this came as a surprise. "Incredible! I've written some pretty trashy novels, but I never would have dared to use that fact as a weapon the way Dr. Glatschke did. Life is even in worse taste than one had supposed. How are your finances?"

The narrator explained that he had a little money from his father, and he had also received war indemnities. Until he reached his majority he had been a ward of the court. And an old aunt had left him her belongings. Their sale had brought a small sum. His guardian had invested his small capital in government bonds and the accumulated interest would just about enable the narrator to live for half a year without another source of income.

"You lucky dog," Lambert remarked.

Together they strolled back toward the center of town along the Taunusstrasse. Near the arcade, one of the girls stood bargaining with an American. Lambert nodded to her and she nodded back over the American's shoulder. He turned around suspiciously. Lambert said, "That's Nora. Can you believe it? Nora! And it's her real name . . . She showed me her papers to prove it. Come on, we ought to drink a beer." At that he turned sharply to the right into a small bar. The narrator had passed it often. This bar seemed to be headquarters for the girls and their friends and for this reason he had never set foot inside. Lambert, on the other hand, seemed to be well known to everyone. The man behind the bar greeted him, and they had scarcely sat down when a man with a black mustache had elbowed his way to their table to say, "Nora is outside."

"Yes, I saw her. Well, how's life? A beer?"

But the man preferred a Coca-Cola. It's just like the police, Lambert explained later; on duty they won't drink. During their conversation the man glanced occasionally at the narrator with his restless eyes.

Lambert calmed him down. "The young man is new here. We were on our way from the station. Well, Nora has her hands full. Some other time."

"Did you really want to introduce me to this Nora?" the narrator asked once they were outside.

"I just said that to calm him down. He isn't worth much but you don't have to lie to him and that's something. Nora's the same. Nora is as hard as rock in spite of all that meat. She wants money and that's that. A cold career woman. Once I gave them some advice on making out their income tax and since then they trust me. And maybe too because I take their profession seriously. I have even had the rare honor of being received on a Sunday in their apartment, and all because of that income-tax statement. They have a two-room apartment in a block of new apartments—I forget the street, somewhere to the west of the Mainzer Landstrasse. A very tidy apartment. A crocheted doily on the table and figurines everywhere. No naked women, just porcelain animals, perhaps even Royal Copenhagen. Why, there was even the lady about to throw her golden ball, standing there on the credenza, exactly like one my parents had in Dresden. A real showpiece. Of course there were flower boxes on the balcony. Fortunately I had brought a bouquet, five roses bought in the Central Station. That made her so happy I was asked to stay to dinner. But as I said, in business matters she's hard as rock. Certainly, if you wanted her to, she could mother you too. And she would mother you a damn sight better than any woman who considered herself the motherly type, but it would cost you something extra of course, it's more tiring. All the same, no matter how often I've talked with her in this bar, I've never dared ask what those flower boxes and the lady with the golden ball *mean.* She can't even deduct her porcelain from her income tax since she never uses the apartment for professional purposes. Perhaps being named Nora explains it."

In the Goethestrasse they stood for a long time in front of a toy shop. "At closing time they always turn off the current," Lambert complained, pointing to an electric train in the window with its tracks, tunnel, switches and signals. It all lay motionless in the half-light. Lambert almost had his nose pressed against the glass. He was looking for something. On other evenings, too, he had stopped in front of this window. It wasn't the electric train or the installation that interested him, it was the stillness. "Well, that's the past for you," he spat out angrily. "During the day you notice nothing because the little train rockets along the tracks and the signals blink on and off, but when the current has been cut off, one wonders where one was. In a train? In the waiting room? Or was one the station-master in a red cap? And in the morning, when they throw the switch, one will be able to flag trains down again."

The narrator too felt his interest in the subject growing. It occurred to him as he stood in front of the display window how often he had sat in trains looking out at little towns flying past with their little houses where a woman is cleaning the window or pushing a baby carriage in a small garden with tiny fruit trees—yes, how could one even get to that house? It lay way at the edge of town. Did one need a car, or was there a bus into town? For the husband in the morning and again in the evening and for the wife when she needed anything special. And in that case, who looked after the baby? A neighbor's wife? Did the neighbors get on well? Yes, which road leads there? Is it a dirt road or paved? And if the couple want to go to the movies, what do they do? The landscape is attractive and the house commands a view from a hill. The air, too, must be pure there. And mail? Perhaps these people don't get much mail. And what about the trains that whiz past daily in the valley on that great stretch of track? Do they ever wonder who is sitting in those trains and why and where he is going? And when the current is turned off suddenly? Then the woman's hand with its dustcloth remains stuck to the window and down below in the stationary train a figure sits with a cigarette in his hand but the cigarette no longer glows. And everything that everyone thought no longer counts . . . Yes, before this the narrator had often asked himself: What sort of life do people live here? Certainly it must be a good life. But Lambert answered this for him: "The life they lead is horrible. But luckily they don't know it. The ones who do are finished."

This time, however, he asked suddenly, "What about Berlin?"

"What would I do in Berlin?" asked the narrator by way of a reply.

"Oh, just a suggestion. I mean, because it all began with d'Arthez . . ."

"No, absolutely not."

"As you like. Good night."

nine

There is all the time in the world to talk about d'Arthez. For the moment it was Edith who quite rightly occupied the narrator's thoughts.

That very night, moreover, Lambert removed the shoe-polish lid from the microphone and recited:

> DO NOT BE SAD, FRIEND, DUE TO THE MANY WARS THE ANGEL WITH THE ABSOLUTE NEGA-TIVE HAS BEEN DELAYED. BUT HE HAS AL-READY REACHED THE BORDER.

And immediately thereafter he showed himself at the window beside the dressmaker's dummy.

Lambert related this to the narrator next day or the day after that. "Your Dr. Glatschke himself suggested that nonsense about the absolute negative. And as for the word 'angel,' he will surely discover in the dictionary that it comes from the Greek for messenger. That will give the authorities some work! Yes, and what do you say to 'reached the border'?"

It appeared that Lambert planned a whole series of such communiqués in which the words "angel" and "border" would figure, and this for the sole purpose of leading Dr. Glatschke and his agency around by the nose. But those days the narrator was in no mood for such pranks. Before that there was a Sunday afternoon that he cannot yet recall without real dread. If there is anything that fits the childish concept of "absolute negativism," then it was this Sunday afternoon. It was like a sudden collapse. He even knew about it in advance and could do nothing to forestall it, and this very certainty too was one of the things that brought on the collapse. Even the very church bells which professed to bring this Sunday afternoon to a close were one more instrument of torture. The wind carried their droning sound from the cathedral and other spires. Why did no one throw himself off the roof of one of the taller buildings this Sunday afternoon? Or in front of a train? Neither a scream nor the squeal of the brakes could have been heard. Only church bells. Perhaps this is the kind of past Lambert spoke of, this certainty of the possibility of collapsing *at any given moment.* Perhaps, too, this explains d'Arthez.

That remains to be seen. Or not. What seemed most important then was to protect Edith Nasemann. The narrator had made up his mind not to see her again. For after all he alone was to blame for the authorities having taken notice of her, and thus it was his duty to see that she was cleared of any suspicion.

But this could not be done. Naturally, she learned from Lambert what had happened to the narrator. Indeed, Lambert, to inform her at once, made an exception to his rule never to visit the bookstore. She was quite agitated, and particularly furious with Lambert. She imagined that his jokes and ranting before the microphone were the chief cause of the narrator's resigning his post. It was almost impossible to persuade her of the incorrectness of this view, as one could not come right out and tell her that it had been for her sake that he had resigned.

And besides, it made absolutely no difference to her that she was under surveillance. Why, it seemed positively to amuse her! During the day she occasionally walked to the door of the bookshop to look for someone lurking about in the street. Given the chance, she would have asked the fellow if his feet were cold. Once in a restaurant she suddenly turned around and nodded toward another guest: "Do you think that's him? Shouldn't we invite him over?" And one night at her door she asked the narrator to come upstairs with her. "My landlady worries herself sick about me as it is, the poor old soul. We can pull the curtains and turn down the light. That will give your Dr. Glatschke his money's worth."

It was at this time that her broken engagement came up, though quite by accident. "Uncle Lambert is a disappointed man," she said. "You don't mean to model yourself on him and live like that, do you? Anyway, what are your plans?"

The narrator assured her that he was certainly not modeling himself on Lambert. Someone with his legal training had a great many possibilities of employment in industry or with one of the big insurance companies.

"You aren't going into industry!"

"Why not? It's one way to earn a living. Private business pays quite a lot better than the state."

"Oh no, you mustn't!" said Edith. "That would be the end."

Her aversion to industry was not due to NANY Inc. or to

198

those relatives whom she couldn't stand; it had to do with her ex-fiancé.

"Do you know what 'old boys' are? In a Student Association that's what they call the alumni. Often they aren't even old, but that's what they're called. They are men with money or with influential positions, owners of factories, directors, chief engineers and the like. They also put up the money for the association, since the students could hardly afford it alone. I've seen it all with my own eyes. At first I thought nothing of it, I thought this was the way things had to be, and besides, why not? But later . . . At the time I had already left the university. Volker didn't mind. Yes, his name was Volker, but that wasn't his fault. It's just another name popular with the Nazis. He said, 'Why do you need to study, there's really no earthly reason.' Just *that* annoyed me. Oh, I would have married him all the same, but phrases like that . . . He didn't have to sound so sure of himself. But these 'old boys' too are always so sure of themselves, you know what I mean? There they sit as though nothing could possibly go wrong and drink their beer, even pay for the students' beer and sing stupid songs. And then again there was Darmstadt and all those kids studying physics and the most modern subjects. I couldn't discuss any of this with Volker. Yes, that was how it began. I didn't want to have to drive to Darmstadt and be with his gang for some big celebration. It made Volker quite angry. He said that the 'old boys' were perfectly nice and always found you an opening in their factories, it was important to have connections. Romanticism didn't pay for the groceries. Yes, he called me a romantic. Every time you find something ugly which they consider beautiful, that's what you're called. They simply won't take you seriously. At the same time Volker was talented, certainly much more talented than I, and for this reason I thought this was the way things had to be. And at home in Aalen they were so enthusiastic about him. We drove there once, we were as good as engaged. I had to show him to my mother at least once, it's expected. But I never showed him to Papa; it struck me as embarrassing somehow, I just couldn't see them together. For this reason I kept on hesitating and looking for excuses every time Papa came to Frankfurt. And I could tell it made no difference to Volker, and that particularly hurt my feelings. I believe he felt that since my father had been divorced from my mother for more than twenty years he did not require any special attention. That's the way I see it now; then I thought I was simply in the wrong. Volker was always so proper. I even introduced him to Uncle Lambert. And there, too, Volker behaved so properly, and yet . . . so . . . so superior—you know what I mean? I couldn't even bring myself to look at Uncle Lambert. He never said a word about Volker, I'll have to hand it to him; of course if he had, I'd have gotten furious and defended my fiancé. And when I finally broke with Volker I merely mentioned the fact to Uncle Lambert in passing, and he acted as though the matter didn't interest him. Volker invited Uncle Lambert along on a drive up into the Taunus that afternoon. Can you imagine how embarrassing that was! Uncle Lambert politely declined, pleading that unfortunately he had a great deal to do. I believe it was a Sunday. And afterward, when we were alone once more, Volker remarked, 'What a clever man! I didn't know there were any left.' Imagine, a clever man! But at home they carried on something awful when they learned I was no longer engaged to Volker. My mother gave me no peace! Once again I had missed a great chance because of my pigheadedness, and did I think I was anything special, and who had convinced me I was? She meant Papa, of course. I didn't bother to answer. And they had been furious in Aalen when I left the university. I didn't have to tell them anything then and now I wouldn't and don't, but in those days I still thought it was my duty. They always believe I must be under someone's evil influence. And by that *someone* they mean Papa or Uncle Lambert. I wrote my mother to explain that I wished to become independent as soon as possible and earn my own living; if I went on with my studies, it would be three or four years. This certainly must have astonished them; they took it for granted that Papa gave me an allowance. And he did, indeed, and I could have had a great deal more if I wanted. But I didn't. I will not live at his expense, I don't care how much money he has. And it's for his sake, too, I don't want to. During the summer vacation I was already helping in the bookstore to earn a little extra money. Yes, and for another reason: so I would have an excuse not to go home to Aalen, that's true. At home they scolded me, saying it was certainly silly and so on. Volker too considered it unnecessary. In Aalen they fell for him as soon as they saw him; my mother in particular was wild about him. Yes, he was very good-looking and behaved so correctly and anyone could see how capable he was, and how far he would go. In Aalen they saw this at once. And Volker too seemed to feel at home there. I was dumfounded. It even annoyed me. He fitted right in, that was the trouble. He sat on their sofa and talked to my stepfather. My mother poured him a cup of coffee or a glass of liqueur and served him a slice of cake. And then she came in with some fruit and asked me if I wouldn't peel an apple for my fiancé. I was so taken aback I said, 'He can peel it for himself if he wants one.' And my mother sighed and said, 'Little monk, little monk, you've chosen a difficult road!' I almost exploded, I was so furious. That is so like her, coming out with an old proverb whether it's appropriate or not. And what do you think? She peeled an apple for Volker and he . . . he let her, as if what she did was perfectly natural. Do you know how he was sitting? Like one of those 'old boys' at the Student Association. Exactly. He wasn't fat yet and he did not smoke a cigar. And I wouldn't have cared if he had been fat—as they grow older, many men get fat; that's not what I mean. But that he sat there as though that's the way everything was meant to be and so satisfied with it all, talking to my stepfather and allowing my mother to wait on him hand and foot—that was it, that's what made him seem fat and an 'old boy.' On the drive home we almost broke off with each other. He had felt so perfectly at home in Aalen he couldn't stop talking about what a happy family I came from. I didn't want to blacken my own name. What could I say? I said nothing, I pretended to be exhausted. I must have spent the whole drive thinking about Papa. Otherwise I would have broken with Volker then and there. I didn't dare yet. I was thinking that once you give your word you have to stick by it. Who can you go to for advice when everyone is against you and claims that you want something special for yourself? I want nothing special. I just cannot imagine being married all your life to a man who sits on a sofa like that, smoking a cigar and letting people peel apples for him. Please don't laugh. Of course he can smoke cigars if he wants, and I will peel his apples for him too if that is absolutely essential. I mean . . . You know perfectly well what I mean. And as I said, they were so enthusiastic about him in Aalen and when I hinted that I might give up my studies they winked as if to say: Oh yes, dear, now that won't be necessary any longer . . . The straw that broke the camel's back. I almost went on with my studies, just to make them mad. As though that's why I stopped! I stopped because I saw that I was too dumb to study, it merely bored me. Selling books isn't very interesting either. People are always buying books you wouldn't read yourself and you aren't allowed to say so. But at least they are people, not like professors and students, who use the most complicated expressions to discuss the simplest things—so that you feel stupid. No, I'm not made for that. But that isn't what I wanted to talk about, but how I broke up with Volker, so that you don't get the wrong idea. And 'broke up with' isn't right either, it sounds so mean. What do you think? I even cried my eyes out afterward. And in spite of telling myself at least ten times: You don't have to cry about Volker. He'll easily find another more his type. Probably I was only crying about myself because nothing ever turns out right for me, and the others are right when they reproach me with never knowing what I really want. Of course Uncle Lambert realized at once that I had been crying. I ran straight to his place that evening, I couldn't stand being alone. I said nothing about it to him, at least not that evening. Later I merely remarked when the subject came up, 'Oh, that all ended ages ago.' Of course Uncle Lambert noticed at once that something had happened, but he doesn't ask questions. You know how he operates, he asked me to dinner and simply to oblige I accepted, although I had had it up to here. But what are you supposed to do when you have no one to go out with? If you go to a film by yourself, it just makes you sadder. I'm only telling you all this so you won't take a job in industry. Really, then you're lost. Please don't laugh. I am *not* a romantic, no matter what people say. You see, it was another Sunday when I definitely broke off with Volker. Yes, the relationship dragged on for a few weeks longer. Volker never noticed that anything had changed and I thought no more about it myself. I thought that's the way things have to be. But then he picked me up in his car like any other Sunday. We were always taking little outings and eating somewhere on the road. We drove on the side roads because there was never much traffic and because of the landscape and the picturesque villages. Volker worked out our route in advance on the map. And outings are healthy, I have nothing against them, the air is so bad in Frankfurt. This time we drove down the Main, on the left bank at first—yes, I'm sure it was the left bank—as far as the Rhine, and then a little ways farther where the country is so flat. And somewhere we stopped and ate. I'm always forgetting the names. Volker points out everything: Over there is Oppenheim—or whatever widening in the road it happens to be. He knows all this like a book. Yes, and then we drove back up the

Main, but this time on the other side. Volker wanted to show me the factory where he had been promised a position as soon as he had passed the examinations. He had connections, you see; the chief engineer was one of those 'old boys' that aren't so old at all. A gigantic concern! Oh, not NANY Inc., don't believe that for a minute! Perhaps it was even larger. Volker was terribly proud. But I have nothing against that, it's understandable. Naturally you cannot visit the plant on a Sunday, that wasn't even what Volker had in mind. He drove me around the development where their employees live. A brand-new development, and so clean. Volker drove quite slowly down the streets so that I could see everything; he was so enthusiastic. Why, they had planted trees along the streets, although they were quite small and needed the protective mesh around their trunks. And there was row after row of houses, one like the other. Or perhaps not, I won't swear to it. Perhaps the architect thought up something different for each street, but if so, the difference was not striking. All of them little one-family houses, one next to the other. One front door stepping in to replace the last, with a big window beside it. Nothing was different but the curtains. And over these the bedroom window, and there may have been a little attic window over that, I didn't notice. And in back a narrow garden for the children or vegetables. Each garden met the garden of the house on the next street. It all formed a perfect square. Oh, and I almost forgot that the balconies on the back of each house were all painted different colors—the railings, I mean. Pink, blue, orange, white too. Certainly, you could choose your color. And on every corner there were shops, dairy products, a butcher, a bakery. Very practical for the housewife. "It saves a lot of time," said Volker. You see, we were going to live in one of these houses. Volker asked if I didn't want to see one on the inside. He knew someone who was living there already. I just shook my head, and that was all right with him too, because it was Sunday and he didn't want to disturb those people. And there was a central square too with a modernistic church—what a comical spire! And the heat for each house in the entire section came from a single plant! No work and no dirt! We drove around the square. They had planted begonias and roses, all of it looked quite new. 'Do you like it?' asked Volker. And then we drove slowly into another development. Here too there were one-family houses, but they were somewhat larger and the gardens went all the way around, but otherwise they were similar. 'We'll move in here later,' Volker explained. 'In a year or two, I hope. You see, this is where the higher-ups live.' And Volker really was talented, so it probably would have taken no more than a year or two. It all seemed to make perfect sense. 'Aren't you at all happy?' Volker asked. How could I tell him? No one ever thinks of telling us how we should go about telling a person something like this. And he wouldn't have understood anyway. He thought I was tired out from the drive, for I had closed my eyes before we headed back to Frankfurt. The whole time I was planning how I would tell him. It was awful. We were getting closer and closer to Frankfurt and the traffic demanded his attention and I still hadn't told him. Only in the Elkenbachstrasse, after he had already pulled up in front of my door, did I say it. It would be better if we saw no more of each other, or something like that. At first he didn't understand, but after a moment he understood. That was worse. He asked, 'What did I do wrong?' and 'Won't you think it over? You're just exhausted.' Finally I just turned and said, 'Good luck! And thanks for everything.' I left him sitting there in his car and ran into the building. Upstairs my landlady asked, 'Well, Fräulein Nasemann, back so soon?' My room doesn't face the street, so I couldn't look out to see if Volker was still sitting down there in his car or not. I came close to phoning him in Darmstadt to make sure nothing had happened and to apologize and tell him I hadn't meant it the way it sounded. And that's why it was better to leave the house and pay Uncle Lambert a visit. Naturally, my landlady had her own ideas."

So she had run to the same Uncle Lambert whom she called a disappointed man and warned the narrator to beware of.

"Don't you have any relatives at all?" she asked him.

"No. That is to say, perhaps there is still one cousin living in America, in Bloomington, I believe—the name has stuck in my head, I've no idea where it is. A cousin once removed. My aunt used to write him at Christmas, or was it New Year? He may have died ages ago."

"And friends?"

"Lots of them, of course. From the university and elsewhere. Some of them have married in the meantime, but all the same they're nice."

"Why don't you talk with them about this Dr. Glatschke and your position?"

"They all have positions of their own, even if they aren't all of them with Security. No, that won't do."

"And Sundays?"

"What about Sunday?"

"What do you do on Sunday?" Edith asked angrily. It should be pointed out that this conversation took place on a Sunday morning and indeed in the Taunus Park. Edith and the narrator were sitting not too far from the gigantic scantily clad figures that have something to do with Beethoven, as anyone knows who has read the inscription. But that isn't the point. Not far from them sat another couple. More precisely, they were not sitting. The young man was lying on the bench, sleeping with his head in his girl's lap.

"Yes—now what do I do on Sundays? If I'm asked out, I always accept. An outing, we go swimming or out to Sachsenhausen for the hard cider. It's always nice. Yes, and if not that, I stay home and work or read. There is always something to do. A report or something."

"Yes, and *now?*"

Edith meant, by this *now,* now that you have no more reports to write. The narrator had not yet thought of this. He had no way of knowing what a wicked Sunday afternoon was in store for him. There on that bench in the park everything still seemed to make perfect sense. He had even managed to forget that quite possibly back there in the bushes lurked someone whom Dr. Glatschke had told to keep an eye on him.

"Too bad Papa isn't here," said Edith suddenly. "He will be in Berlin for the next three weeks, I believe. And whether or not he then comes to Frankfurt I can't say. Why don't you fly to Berlin? You do have the time now, and you might even be able to stay at Papa's if I write him in time. It wouldn't cost much. Why do you laugh?"

"I'm not laughing."

"Yes, you are. I'm only suggesting it because you don't have any relatives, or anyone else, for that matter. And Uncle Lambert is just not the right person. Not that Papa could get you a job—although he might, actually. He has so many connections —thanks to TV, everyone knows him—but certainly he could give you some good advice. You're laughing again."

"But I'm not laughing."

"Oh, yes, you are. You're making fun of me. Just like Uncle Lambert sometimes. I'm certain he has persuaded you that you're a writer!"

"Me?"

"Yes, because he was a bad writer himself."

"All I need to do is begin a letter of condolence and I start to stutter!"

"A letter of condolence?"

"Yes, or birthday greetings. My literary abilities will do for a report for Dr. Glatschke and nothing more."

"Don't start talking nonsense. I'm dead serious. Papa won't give you advice directly, that's not his way. He behaves as though nothing interests him. Yes, you'd even think he wasn't listening, and perhaps it really does bore him too, but then afterward, after you've been with him, everything is so clear you wonder why you hadn't thought of it yourself immediately. It's different with Uncle Lambert. I don't mean to sound as though I have something against him; on the contrary, I like him a great deal. I only want to do what I can to prevent him from influencing you. All that business with the dressmaker's dummy. Oh, it's all clever enough, but who can live like that? And that he was never happy with that wife of his, nobody else can be held responsible!"

"He doesn't seem all that unhappy to me."

"You see, you see! And all the same he's enormously unhappy. Even Papa wonders how he stands it, and Papa *knows*. He once remarked of Uncle Lambert and his wife that unhappiness had welded them together in such a fashion that any attempt to be truly happy or make them happy called their very existence in question. Unhappiness had almost become a sort of happiness. But that isn't what we were discussing. As if I hadn't known that Uncle Lambert was at the bottom of this! Him with his stupid chatter about our having no past. What nonsense! As if we had no past! You with your boarding school and wherever else it was you grew up. And I was born in Berlin and then spent several years in Posen while I was still a baby, and then Aalen. Why should Uncle Lambert give himself airs about that stupid past of his? And to think that you let yourself be taken in by stuff like that!" Edith was so furious she seemed on the point of standing up.

"But didn't you break off that engagement all by yourself?"

"Well? Don't I have the right to break off an engagement? And what does that have to do with it?"

"Nothing, but you didn't ask your father for his advice."

"Why should I ask him for advice? I simply did not want to live in one of those houses and I didn't need Papa to tell me that, and besides . . . But we aren't talking about me. You're trying to change the subject."

"No, I only meant to explain why your suggestion that I fly to Berlin . . ."

"But that is totally different. Papa will certainly be over-joyed."

"I have too much respect for your father . . . Please, will you try not to interrupt, the business is already difficult enough to explain. I don't even know your father personally, there was only that moment there in the office when he winked at me . . ."

"You see, you see!"

"And that could have been my imagination, stimulated by what he said to Dr. Glatschke. But, all the same, I do have the greatest respect for him. Not because I've seen him on TV, and not because I've read all the things written about him—none of that could have made me *respect* him. But what you have told me about him, and what Herr Lembke—or Lambert, if you prefer—has related, that . . . that . . . And Lambert scarcely *said* anything, you needn't worry, just the barest irrelevancies. Everything I know about your father *you've* told me. Nonethe-less, it is crystal-clear what Lambert thinks of him. It is as though your father were present when Lambert speaks. Do you understand what I mean? You see, this is all very hard for me to put into words. Yes, and then your father refused that inheri-tance, that share of NANY Inc."

"But what has that to do with you?"

"With me? Why, nothing. But naturally I pondered it a great deal."

"There's no reason to. If you knew the people involved, those so-called 'relations' with all their money, and how they treated Papa . . ."

"Nonetheless, this caused your father quite some uneasiness on your behalf, that much I know."

"That was totally unnecessary and I told him as much. It should have been clear to him whose side I was on. And if Uncle Lambert doubts it, then he insults me."

"On the contrary. Lambert never doubted for a minute that this inheritance must be refused. But you forget I am a lawyer —which explains my pondering, pondering the motives of a man whom I deeply respect. No, please don't interrupt. I too have inherited a little something from my parents and from an aunt and also I got an indemnity, for being a war victim or a war orphan, what's the difference? None of this did I refuse; I wasn't even in a position to do so, since I was not of legal age. But I never even gave it a moment's thought. Now, for the first time . . ."

"But the case is totally different—you needed the money for your education."

"This has nothing to do with money. Certainly it was not money which decided your father to refuse the inheritance. And it certainly wasn't the money that made him hesitate or take you into consideration. That is perfectly obvious to me. No, he had to ask himself if he had the right to demand something of you which was a matter of course for him."

"How's that? What did he demand of me?"

"To live as a free person. Or, in other words, without a connection to any group whatsoever. What hackneyed words these are! Forgive me. It is for this reason that I so deeply respect your father. Precisely for this reason."

"Well, what then? What are you driving at?"

"I was only trying to explain to you why it is absolutely out of the question for me to fly to Berlin. No, please, why are you making this so difficult for me? It has never been my habit to talk about such matters, and now that I'm trying, it only sounds like a report on some subject of no personal concern to me. You might almost say that I cannot believe what I'm saying myself, since God knows I could refute every word of it. I could refute myself better than anyone else could, logically and to the point—that wouldn't be any trouble—but what would be left then, I ask you? What would be left of *me*, I mean. This question never used to give me any trouble, and you mustn't think I spend all my time trying to psychoanalyze myself. Things used to function so perfectly all around me, all one had to do was set his course accordingly and everything followed like clockwork: waking up, going to school, lunch, play; and later in life it was no different: courses, examinations, outings and dances. Yes, I can even dance, if not particularly well. Those rows and rows of little houses would never have caught my eye. Forgive me for bringing it up. But since I've known your father . . . All right, I don't really know him—there's an example of how easily I can be refuted. But nonetheless, there your father is, and he exists for me too. Just the fact that in spite of his having done nothing wrong he can arouse such hate in Dr. Glatschke proves that *he is there*. And for me too. I never stop turning around to see if he isn't there."

"This is nonsense."

"Of course it's nonsense. I told you so myself."

"And it's nonsense your always calling him my father. Are you trying to make fun of me?"

"Pardon me, that is the way I was brought up, I never learned any other way . . . I certainly can't call him Herr Nasemann. And d'Arthez? No, that would be too . . . too . . . yes, too *intimate*. Please let me have my say, I'll be through in a moment. God knows it's no fun for me trying to talk about things that I don't know how to talk about. I don't doubt that your father would receive me graciously if I arrived with a letter of recommendation from his daughter. Pardon me, 'letter of recommendation' was another incorrect choice of words. Perhaps he would even help me find another position if I were to ask his assistance; I have no doubts about that either. On the contrary! On the contrary! Forgive me, I didn't mean to frighten you. Even that kid over there with his girl has woken up. There, you can see for yourself, all my arguments work against me; I have no evidence at all, so I protest loudly in spite of my good upbringing. But this business of dropping in on your father really won't do. That would be too dangerous. And I don't mean for me . . . And I keep using words that I don't want to use . . . No, I mean something like this: supposing I let your father help me, well, what then? Suppose I were to see him later on TV, I'd laugh like everyone else and then turn off the set. Well, where's your father then? Where is d'Arthez? Snuffed out! And I did it. No, that would be unconscionable. Come, perhaps it would be better if we moved on. We're only disturbing that couple. Both of them must think I'm nuts."

Everything had been said, however inadequately. Had Edith understood, and if so, was she annoyed or was she sad? In any event, they walked silently between the flower beds to the Opernplatz. And on the pediment of the ruins of the opera house there stood for all to read those extraordinary words: TRUTH, BEAUTY, GOODNESS. Edith, who must have learned this at the university, had once explained to the narrator that this quotation from Schiller wasn't Schiller's at all; it came from some Scholastic philosopher, and the ancient Greeks had already set the true, the beautiful and the good on the same pedestal. But this wasn't the point.

They crossed over to Zurich House and then into the Rothschild Park, passing the dog run. A tan dog, an Irish terrier, was racing like mad in a sort of squirrel cage, a Rhön wheel, which had been placed there to provide dogs with exercise. From time to time he jumped out and tried with his teeth and much growling to stop the wheel, then jumped in again and raced like mad till he dropped. Edith warned the child who stood beside the wheel that the poor animal could have a heart attack. And to the narrator she said as they passed on, "You needn't see me home."

"Don't we want to have a bite to eat somewhere together?"

"No, there's food in the icebox. And this afternoon I have to wash out a few things."

Nonetheless, the narrator walked along beside her. They were headed in the same direction anyway, for a few more blocks, before Edith had to turn right and the narrator to the left.

Suddenly she asked, "Are the documents relating to Papa's arrest still in the files?"

The narrator explained that, if they were, it was pure accident, the Nazis had burned everything they could. "Too bad," said Edith. "I'd like to have known who denounced Papa."

The narrator asked why she wanted to know.

"Not for revenge, no. You just finally want to know for sure. I thought that perhaps you could find out through your office. But now that you no longer have an office, well . . . And perhaps it doesn't really make any difference."

The narrator said that nonetheless he could ask a friend to track it down.

"Oh, forget it. Don't cause yourself any trouble."

With that she said good-bye and turned right on the Grüne-bergweg. She walked quite fast and did not once turn around. Should the narrator have gone running after her? The Elkenbachstrasse was a long way off and all that about dirty clothes might not have been so important after all.

And why had she suddenly asked that question? She had never before brought up her father's arrest. Since d'Arthez never spoke of it himself and obviously viewed with indifference the events leading up to it, why should his daughter have taken an interest in them?

Of what possible use could it be to the narrator, for example, to discover how his parents spent their last hours? Did the bomb which fell on their house in Hannover kill them at once or did they slowly suffocate in the cellar? And what did that father whom he knew only from a few old-fashioned photographs think as he died? Certainly he would have considered the whole business a rather unseemly mess, what with the very strict view of right and wrong his position as judge of a Superior Provincial Court imposed upon him. The narrator's aunt or great-aunt used to make fun of this. Once she told the judge how she had smuggled in some trifling object, absolutely scandalizing him. They almost stopped speaking. But such anecdotes seemed to come from another world. And why stir up such a past?

As the reader will have noticed, the narrator did not chase after Edith, whether or not he should have. And at that moment began his Sunday afternoon, although he may not have been aware of it immediately.

How did it happen to Edith's father, back then? Perhaps he was on his way home just as the narrator was; it might even have been Sunday. When he reached his front door, two men walked up and said, "You'd better come with us." It could as easily have occurred in the cinema after the main feature. The rest was inevitable.

But two men were not waiting for the narrator at his front door.

He had to get through this Sunday afternoon alone.

Sunday afternoons had always been a bore even back in the dormitory at the country school. One looked forward to Sunday and instead one was faced with Sunday afternoon. The students who had relatives in the vicinity went home for the weekend, and when they returned Sunday night, many of them bragged about their experiences and sometimes even had something new to show for them. But those who had stayed in the dormitory because their parents lived abroad didn't know quite what to do with themselves. There were always the possibilities of swimming, going for walks in the woods or playing football. One could even take a book out of the library, but then all one heard was "You grind!" so it was better just going along with the rest and doing what they did; there would be no cracks. The headmaster and his wife were friendly. In the afternoon they served cake with whipped cream, true enough, but it was a strain and tiring and one no longer looked forward to what one had planned to do. Next Sunday, perhaps.

The narrator had no cakes and no whipped cream at his place, but there was a loaf of bread and some butter and the end of a liverwurst in the icebox and that would do. And there was enough coffee in the can. In the kitchen alcove there was a Formica table that folded down from the wall and one could eat there. Why take plate and cup into the main room? Moreover, the place had just been cleaned. This one-room apartment was cleaned on Fridays. The management arranged it all. One did not even know the cleaning woman, one just added something extra every month when the time came to pay the rent. And the bed folded down too. One folded it back against the wall before leaving each morning.

It all cost quite a bit, but the narrator felt he could be proud of his small apartment. He had moved in a year and a half ago, saying to himself, "This is a beginning. This is the way one lives if one has had a decent home." The cupboards were all built in, the kitchen alcove even complete with pots and pans and the rest. All one needed were a table and a couple of chairs, perhaps an easy chair. And a carpet, of course. But it was a beginning. The only piece of furniture that the narrator had kept when he disposed of his great-aunt's estate was an old desk. It did not suit the room. It took up too much space and was otherwise impractical. Perhaps it would have to be shed along the way. In the drawers, instead of papers, lay underwear and shirts. It was a nuisance. Every time he wanted a shirt, the writing surface had to be cleared and then folded shut.

Very well, if Edith was going to spend Sunday afternoon washing clothes, then the narrator felt he too could do two nylon shirts and a pair of socks. But in ten minutes they would be done and hanging up to dry in the shower. Surely Edith needed more time for her clothes.

But what would she do next? Shouldn't they have made a date to go to the movies later? Perhaps there was one with a scene in which two men speak to a third standing at a bar. "You'd better come with us. Make it as inconspicuous as possible." One accepts it so easily, although it lies completely outside one's own experience. One really believes that this is the way it happens. In the short intermission between the newsreel and the main feature, one can eat ice cream.

During his interrogation by Dr. Glatschke, hadn't Edith's father when asked if he made notes answered, "But that would be highly imprudent of one of us?" What did Edith's father mean by this? What had he meant by "imprudent," and what had he meant by "one of us"?

Many weeks later, perhaps only a few days before his death, Lambert said, "The important decisions are all made on Sunday afternoon." That was in his room in the Goethestrasse and it must have been six o'clock in the evening—one could hear the tolling of the bells of the cathedral and the other churches. Lambert was always complaining about this silly anachronism; when the wind blew from a certain direction, one couldn't hear oneself think. At that time the microphones had long since vanished from Lambert's room. Lambert regretted this, as he would have liked to tape the noise of the bells as a little joke on Dr. Glatschke.

At that time the narrator did not understand Lambert's drift, but it would have been useless to ask him what he meant, since nothing further could be pried from him. Lambert would only have made fun of him. But now, so many months later, the narrator believes he understands what Lambert meant. He meant precisely the opposite of what he said. In other words, what he called the important decisions are *not* made. They are not made because everyone is so exhausted by a Sunday after-noon, and by the ringing of the church bells, that no one is in a position to decide anything. And that, according to Lambert, was the great decision. And of course one can also go some-where and dance until he drops.

In another epoch, as we know from our reading, sometimes a man would step to a window and gaze down into the street. Behind him a voice would ask immediately, "Wouldn't you like another slice of cake?" But it could also be that this person who walked to the window was alone in his room and no one asked if he wanted another slice of cake. But that is immaterial; what there used to be on a street to look at has not changed. Perhaps there were more baby carriages in those days—that could be. But, on the other hand, the baskets in which they are now car-ried can be picked up with one hand and fit neatly into an automobile. "Drive carefully, Christian!" It is difficult as hell to avoid a squabble on Sunday afternoons; one must put all one's mind on avoiding them. "But the gloves that match your suit have been mislaid again . . ." And "You know how your sister-in-law Mitzi is always insulted if we're late. And Uncle Adolf is such a sweetie, but that venomous housekeeper of his . . ." Happily, the car isn't slow starting—small mercies! And on a visit to your sister-in-law and to Uncle Adolf you have to watch your p's and q's. "What? You're going to Italy? In Spain, every-thing is much finer." "Wouldn't you like another slice of cake?" Yes, for God's sake, yes, so that old housekeeper doesn't have her feelings hurt and take it out on Uncle Adolf, the old sweetie, once they're alone again. "Drive carefully, Christian." All flows back, all repeats itself. A pleasant afternoon without arguments. An important decision.

Will you stop trying to stuff that shitty cake of yours down my throat!

That would be the less important decision. But back then one did not use such language. Today, after two wars, such language has become so common, even when the day is Sunday and the time afternoon, that it won't even do any longer for so much as a small decision. Long ago, if we are to believe what we read, nobody walked to the window on a Sunday afternoon to scream before making his small decision. For, if he had, it would have been printed. All the papers would have carried it and everything would have been perfectly unambiguous. But they reached their small decisions in silence. "Sudden and unexpected," as they used to say in death announcements. That was bad. That was unseemly; it only produced a commotion in the household and on the street outside and in the Sunday afternoon as well. The police arrived with their blue lights flashing and made inquiries on other floors. At an hour when the children had to be gotten to bed and one wanted to check the results of the day's soccer matches. And one said to the police, who took it down: As if I hadn't seen this coming. Didn't I tell you, Christian? That young man will come to a bad end! He never said hello on the stairs. He was always so silent that he gave you a start. I'd come home from shopping and feel around in my handbag for the key and suddenly he'd go by, as if he'd materialized right then and there. That behavior only leads to the worst. No, not one girl ever visited him. What do you say, Christian? Wouldn't we have known? In this building you hear *everything*. He lacked contacts; otherwise, this never would have happened. Oh, there he goes . . . And such a *fine* young man, a real shame. I don't want the children to see it when they carry him out. What do you say, Christian?

No, Herr Lambert, suicide is not a part of natural law, it's a matter for the police. A transgression, if you will. A transgression of Sunday afternoons—that could be its definition. "Public nuisance" would be an exaggeration. Even suicide is not that public. A slight disturbance, that's all. A tiny decision.

No, no visits from girls . . . And you, Herr Lambert, are

you standing at the window with that dressmaker's dummy? Or . . . ?

And if a person does not have what you call a past, Herr Lambert, how can he expect girls to visit him? If they did, he would be lost—what would he have to hold on to? The girl? A dressmaker's dummy?

Outside, it grows darker. The narrator puts on his coat. He does not turn on the light, he does not look in the mirror to check the state of his tie. If Dr. Glatschke has an agent posted on the street, he will be wondering why the light hasn't gone on. He will mention it in his report, for certainly it means that the party up there intends to slip out. If one had only had a glimpse of these reports, one would have something solid to go on, the facts. What do you say, Christian?

Where is a young man to go late on a Sunday afternoon as the cars return in packs from their outings? A young man without a past and without a girlfriend and for the last few days without a job?

Where is he off to? For an agent, if he's on the job, this will be no riddle. The young man will be hungry. He had no midday meal, that's certain. There, he's already studying the menu that hangs in the window of a little tavern. Why doesn't he go in? Doesn't he like what they're serving?

No, Herr Lambert, let's stick to logic. There are two parts to suicide: *sui* and *occido*. The word betrays the fact that it takes two. A self is necessary. It is not as easy to extinguish a nothing as a self.

And the young man walks on. His feet are carrying him without his knowledge to the Central Station. Does he hope to run into Lambert there accidentally?

But the agent will think, Now we're getting warm. He must pick someone up. A woman? An accomplice? Keep your eyes peeled!

The narrator goes straight to the main hall that leads to the platforms. He stops neither at the florist nor at the book counter. Nor does he stop before the boards announcing arrivals and departures. He appears to know what he wants. He walks right up to a stand and orders a pair of sausages and a roll, with mustard of course. And he takes the paper plate to one of the high tables where one eats standing up, and takes a bite of sausage after dipping the end in mustard.

Is the agent expected—if an agent really has been tailing him—to order a pair of sausages too and stand at a nearby table? It would be a good way to keep an eye on the suspect.

Why did he look concerned about the woman squatting on the floor near a wall surrounded by bundles and bags, with a child leaning against her asleep? An Italian woman, or Spanish, from some place Down There. Is she waiting for the arrival or the departure of a train? She stares indifferently into space and waits and waits. But that can be a trick arranged with the suspect in advance. Is he going to try to smuggle information abroad through her?

Is he waiting for a sign from one of those men who stand around in little groups, gesticulating wildly with foreign newspapers and arguing in foreign languages about the results of Sunday sports matches in their homelands? Why else should he be looking at those men?

"They have no imagination at all," says a voice close behind the narrator, and though said only in passing, these words bore deeper into the narrator's silence than the loudspeakers shouting across the station over his head.

The narrator starts and turns around. Someone is standing beside him at the high table who also eats sausages with mustard, with much more mustard. A little man, a gentle man. At first, all one notices are glasses with narrow gold frames—because the station lights are reflected in them—but then one notices the pale skin and pale lips, the mouth turning up at the corners. And last of all one penetrates through to the eyes, which reject the very men they contemplate.

"Imagination on a Sunday afternoon?" asks the narrator. "That might be dangerous. They have no women."

The other looks up at the big clock. "Sunday afternoon is over."

Since in order to do this the man had to crane his head, the narrator could see that he wore a cassock under his dark gray raincoat.

No, not even Dr. Glatschke would dare send out one of his agents disguised in a cassock. At that, the narrator apologizes. "Excuse me, when I mentioned women I really meant nothing at all. I took you for someone from the Security police."

"Security police? Does it really exist, then?"

"Indeed it does. An institution totally devoid of imagination whose one concern is security—for which they constantly fear."

That agent, if he is around, will write in his memorandum: A man disguised as a cleric exchanged a few words with the suspect.

Dr. Glatschke will be dumfounded. He'll ask: Do they really have a network set up that includes men of God? Then the greatest tact must be employed.

"Pay no attention to my uniform," said the other, pointing to his cassock.

"Imagination?" asks the narrator. "A Sunday like this resembles a stroke that paralyzes speech, it's terribly difficult to start all over again. You see, I'm a lawyer. What do you mean by imagination? Do you mind my asking?"

"The perception of things which are not considered possible, but perhaps there are other, better definitions. What has always stood between most men, including us, and this perception is our past."

"Past?"

"Or call it the passive intelligence of nature, if you prefer.

But it's train time. I'm on my way to Passau. Trains are always leaving for the past. I am a professor of theology."

He raised the satchel that stood next to his feet. It looked quite heavy. "A whole sackful of concepts for my students. Instant concepts . . . What were you saying? A stroke paralyzing speech? A fine expression, I must make a note of that. If a man can no longer speak, he must make do with concepts. Cheerio!"

The other tossed the empty cardboard plate into the trash basket under the table. Will that agent, if he's really here, paw about in the trash until he's found the paper plate? It might contain scribbled information.

But the other has already pushed his way through the crowd at the gate. For a moment he is no longer to be seen, he is so small, but beyond the gate, out on the platform, he turns around to face the narrator, who still stands at the high table, and waves with a smile.

The agent, if he is there, will write in his report: The party disguised as a cleric took such and such a train for Passau. Before climbing aboard, he made a sign to the suspect. Poor Dr. Glatschke will be worried to death. He will have a question for his subordinates: How did it happen that our dossier mentioned no connections with the church? Must I always remind you how important thoroughness is? Get me the faculty roster of the Passau Seminary at once. But with all possible discretion. We cannot allow ourselves . . . The narrator leaves the table and the station. Only when he is well into the passage that leads under the Bahnhofplatz does it occur to him that he has forgotten to check if the woman is still squatting on the same spot with her child and baggage. Something makes him laugh. A girl walking toward him seems to think the laugh was meant for her. What makes him chuckle quietly to himself is realizing that it also constitutes a kind of past to have talked with a cleric over sausages in the Central Station, with a cleric who calls his cassock a uniform; yes, and to have discussed perception and the like, despite the mustard and despite Sunday afternoon and paralysis of speech, and despite the loudspeakers too. Naturally it isn't *much*, one can scarcely call it something to hold on to: someone waves from the platform and the gesture scares away a whole flock of concepts. Should Lambert be told about this? Will he be at home? One cannot tell from below in the Goethestrasse, since his room is set back. There's a little balcony in front with a railing. In order to catch a glimpse of Lambert, one would have to climb to the attic across the street in the Kleine Bockenheimerstrasse that Dr. Glatschke rents.

Or would Lambert be with his Nora—for a little conversation, as he called it. Because everything is clear and presents no problems while you're conversing with her, Lambert says. For even he must find it rather difficult to spend a whole Sunday afternoon alone with that dressmaker's dummy making notes he must realize lead nowhere and are nothing more than a way of passing time.

Nora isn't standing in her usual spot near the arcade; otherwise one might have nodded to her. Nor is she to be seen in the snack bar. On a Sunday afternoon of course she must often be consulted in a professional capacity. Or could she have left with Lambert? Not to go over the assessments for the income tax, Sunday afternoon is not the proper time for that, but, as already suggested, because a dressmaker's dummy is insufficient for conversation. A certain minimum of words and answers must be a biological necessity. One always says good morning to the women at the bakery, and when the wife of the cigarette dealer is on duty, one asks her how the baby's doing who lies behind her in the tiny premises. And one has a sympathetic look for the butcher when whoever it is upstairs practices the piano.

But how will Lambert behave? Will he say something on the street like: Do you have time for me, baby? And will she answer: Come on, kid? Would she really call Lambert "kid," as is the fashion these days? Her calling him Ludwig or Lembke is inconceivable. And what do they talk about on the short walk to the hotel? Do they walk arm in arm? For the idea of Lambert's throwing his arm around her is inconceivable again. They will walk along next to each other, the way man and wife walk home on a Sunday afternoon, with total certainty as to what they need each other for. Will Lambert ask: Well, how's business? to which Nora will naturally reply: Oh, so-so. Or will he say: That's a new dress; pretty, I noticed it at once. But isn't it rather cool? But not many words will be necessary, it isn't far to the corner of the Niddastrasse. Or is it that hotel in the Weserstrasse? One has to be quick-witted if one isn't to be knocked over by the young men who troop from bar to bar.

All this one has seen in the movies. Also how Nora strides into the hotel straight up to the fellow sitting in a glass booth, who scarcely looks up from his newspaper. He hands her a key. Nora takes it and the two of them head up the dark stairs. That it must already be dark, one also knows from the movies. Does Nora prefer to return to the same room over and over? About such arrangements one knows a great deal less.

The room will be on the third floor. Nora will unlock the door and shove it open. A quick look will assure her that the place has been cleaned and the curtains drawn. Naturally she will have already switched on a light. Aren't you coming? she will say to Lambert, who still stands at the door, and later when she has locked the door from inside, he will still be standing there looking helpless. Nora has seen it before. But she has an easier time acclimating, she brings her own smell with her, while the absence of personality that the odorless air of a hotel room betrays never fails to surprise a man. He will find his feet much faster if a slight smell of onions wafts through cracks in the window from a hash house next door.

Nora deposits her heavy handbag on a chair and minces in her high heels in front of the mirror. For a moment she has totally forgotten that a customer stands beside the door waiting for her to attend to him. She observes herself critically and does not appear too happy with her reflection; she turns a bit to one side, for the profile, and tugs at her dress here and there. Then she draws closer to the glass and examines her makeup. As she does this, she lifts her complicated hairdo loosely from her neck with both hands. This can last only a few seconds—until she notices a man in the mirror standing far behind her at the door. She recalls that she must offer herself. She turns around quickly, stepping out of her shoes in the process. They hurt her feet. She kicks them negligently aside and trips in her stocking feet toward Lambert. That she runs barefoot rather than on high heels means that all there is to hear is a gentle thump-thump-thump, which is considerably more pleasant. And this is not a refinement; any woman who has spent the whole day on her feet is happy to be out of her shoes for a moment. But it is a good beginning, nonetheless. And naturally, as she runs she smiles—that is expected.

Furthermore, this man presents no difficulties. You know him, and you know what he likes and how he expects you to behave. He is a regular customer, and it's advantageous to have a few of them, so you do what you can to keep them. There are others who pay better, it is true, particularly if they're drunk and want to show off, but on the other hand this often ends in a row, or they expect the most impossible things of you. But this guy here is a decent regular, already rather old; mid-fifties, he says. Probably a widower, or his wife left him. Certainly a public servant with a pension assured. Somebody will get that pension when he dies . . .

225

He wouldn't be much trouble for a woman who marries him. Every morning he goes to the office. You'd have to wave at him from the window or the balcony, certainly he'd like that, and then every evening the same bus would bring him home, and he'd look up to the window to make sure he's expected. If, for instance, you moved out of town into the new apartment houses going up northwest of Frankfurt, no one would know you. Or perhaps as far as Bad Homburg, which isn't really much farther. There are new high-rise apartments there as well. Lissi moved in there with a widower from the Gas Works. They ask three months' rent in advance, but the air is so much healthier than here in Frankfurt. Lissi even bought garden furniture for the balcony, where she can relax with a view of the Taunus hills. And certainly a café isn't far off if the balcony gets too dull. But there are no more run-ins with the police. No one sidles up whispering: Watch it! they just picked up Fritz (or Charlie). Your husband comes home on time every evening and you sit around. And Sundays too, but there's always a movie house if you aren't up to Sundays together.

Now why are you standing there looking like a lost soul? Nora asks and walks toward Lambert with a smile. This man, she thinks, wants to be given the feeling that you've been waiting all week long for him. That explains her throwing her arms around his neck as she stretches on tiptoe since she's in her stocking feet, although with her pompadour she does not look much shorter than Lambert. But he will appreciate your behaving a little like a child and cuddling up; it shows how you trust him, how being with him puts you in seventh heaven. There's nothing I'd rather do, kid. Yes, this is one of those men we have to do our best to make everything easy for. He believes as some men do that they must always apologize for needing a woman, and for a girl allowing herself to be exploited in this way. And naturally Nora presses her body against Lambert's, as one

226

would if one felt trusting and wanted to cuddle up. Then she kisses him, at first just so, but quite tender; then she throws herself into it, opening her mouth.

Couldn't Nora be mistaken about Lambert? Didn't he once remark: You couldn't change a thing about Nora without spoiling her? While she kisses him so passionately, won't he be thinking, That will *do,* baby. We aren't as close as all that. Yet what good are such ephemeral reservations? Nora knows what she's doing, and who would want to hurt her feelings? The original plan, a rather tired old Sunday-afternoon plan, is about to be realized. The process can no longer be arrested. Let us leave the whole thing to Nora, who knows a great deal more about it.

No, Nora is not mistaken about Lambert. She draws back a little to disengage her face and asks: Well? Then she pulls loose from his embrace and with a few experienced movements begins undressing. All this the movies have shown us often enough. And Lambert? All the same, there are nuances that a camera would miss. Lambert, for instance, instead of watching Nora undress, walks to the vanity where she left her bag under the mirror and, while her back is turned, drops in a bank note. We may assume that he has had that bill in a pocket of his jacket, so that he would not have to fumble for it in his wallet.

Now that was one of those nuances. Naturally, Nora would not have stopped listening attentively just because she has her dress over her head or has bent over to remove her stockings; on the contrary, with her ears she followed what Lambert was doing, and waited for the click of the handbag. You have to watch out no matter who . . . She certainly would not have let just anyone get near her handbag; that's the stupidest thing you can do, and if money is missing afterward, you've no one to blame but yourself. And there is no one else whom you'd allow to choose what he's going to pay; if you did, you might as well go down for free. But this is a fellow you can count on. When you look into your handbag afterward, you can be sure you'll find the money. And it will be enough.

How does one know for sure how much is enough these days?

But Nora feels sure that this is a fellow who is happy if you don't pay too much attention to the money angle, but instead allow him to play the daddy who secretly slips a girl some money. Men like that are usually sentimental, and you have to reckon with this. Should a girl chirp "Thanks!" when she hears the purse snap shut? Wouldn't it be wiser to run over at once and hug him out of gratitude? Even if you aren't completely undressed . . . That might even be better, you know, so that this sort of man can accustom himself gradually to your body and not suffer shock at nudity too suddenly revealed . . . That too is something you know already. Yes, and what a touching scene for the camera. A girl no longer fully clad embracing an aging gentleman. That's how deeply she trusts him.

And Lambert? This is not a situation in which one can get by without speaking a word, even if the woman takes off her clothes without being asked. Even if Nora should be wrong, and Lambert not the least bit sentimental, the very nature of the situation requires that he take his cues from her. At the very least, one or two words must be exchanged, the ones which have been exchanged since time began. They don't have to be genuine, but to maintain the proper temperature they are absolutely necessary, for even the warmest body can turn unexpectedly cold and hostile.

Thus, as Nora finishes undressing, which won't take long, and after she picks up her clothing and arranges everything piece by piece over the back of a chair, or while she stretches awkwardly as a woman must to unfasten her brassiere, or while she's bent over slipping out of her stockings, Lambert might say: You get prettier every time, baby. For that is something she likes to hear. The words are not convincing, but the tone of voice with which they are said is. Or is Nora already sitting on his lap letting herself be caressed? That would indicate much more warmth, indeed a temperature at which the sound of the word love is no longer ridiculous, although to this sound Nora would surely react with an Oh, come on!

All this we can confidently leave to the cameraman. A camera can reproduce this with more dignity than the original has. But a bit later the camera too will be embarrassed, for this "bit later" is not photogenic. It won't do, spoiling an amusing Before with a boring After.

Saying thank you to Lambert and just letting him out would be impossible. And as for Nora, she does not object to a man watching her undress, how could it be avoided, but no one wants a man standing around when she's dressing. It makes a girl nervous.

"You'd better go first, kid," Nora says. She is not going to stop calling him kid, it is a habit. And she is not quite half his age. With a man like that, it might even pay to kiss him a quick goodbye on the cheek, something you'd hardly do with anyone else. Even if he wasn't in the mood today to tell you that you get prettier every time. It's something for him to remember Monday in the office, how stunning it was, little Nora stretching on tiptoe to give that good-bye kiss, and how she hid behind the door as she opened it in case there was anyone in the hall, and called through the crack as she closed the door, "Come back soon!"

Then one hears her inside turning the key in the lock. For some unknown reason, Lambert tiptoes down the stairs, although in this hotel such solicitude is not required. The man downstairs in the glass booth doesn't even look up—the guests would not like that. Should you wait for Nora in the bar and ask if she'd like a drink? No, that would be a nuisance, for after all she's on the job and must make her time pay. What business is this of yours, Mr. Narrator? Why don't you pay this Nora a visit yourself if you're so curious to know the exact procedure? Nothing can stop you. It certainly cannot prejudice your position, you have already lost it, and if there is an agent on your tail and he has an eye on you as you enter that hotel with Nora to spend half an hour, it will draw no more than a smug I saw it coming from Dr. Glatschke.

That, instead of going yourself, you send Lambert in your place . . . Isn't there something about this which is . . . which is, shall we say, humiliating?

In order not to run into Lambert in the Goethestrasse—since it was just within the realm of the possible that he really might be returning from Nora, which would be embarrassing—the narrator on his way home turned into the Kleine Bockenheimerstrasse, one of those poorly paved narrow alleys that survived the destruction of Frankfurt. Such alleys are more durable than the grand boulevards resplendent with luxury shops. It was here that this long Sunday afternoon found its dubious conclusion. Dubious because it brought to mind a small piece of the past that in the future too may be an occasion for misunderstandings.

For as the narrator hesitated in front of one of the many small bars of various coloration, its door swung open and for a moment the whole alley rang with voices and with music from a jukebox. And out stumbled someone who had obviously had too much to drink.

Everyone knows what a high crime rate Frankfurt has. For this reason the narrator stepped aside quickly in order not to get himself knocked down by this drunk. But he was not quick enough. For this unknown man had recognized the narrator and began to curse him out, and in Frankfurt dialect, to boot.

"Oh boy, I was just waiting for you, Miss Priss. You can tell your lousy chief from me that if he wants me checked up on he had better send someone who knows his job and not a little snot-nose who shows his hand half a mile away. And if he doesn't like the way I do my job, he can do the dirty work himself and have himself a ball every night up there in that attic window. I'd like to see the cold he gets. You can just tell him from me, you . . . you . . ." he shouted after the retreating narrator, who found it impossible, unfortunately, to vanish quickly into one of the side passages that lead into the Grosse Bockenheimerstrasse, since they had all been padlocked for the night. "Imagine, a jerk like that has a degree and can call himself 'doctor.' You ought to be ashamed of yourself, you . . . you . . ." the narrator could hear in the distance.

The humiliating conclusion of a humiliating Sunday. It was followed by a sleepless night.

Who nowadays can survive a sleepless night? Security considers them so common that they recommend a sleeping pill.

The narrator had no sleeping pills. He tried to throw himself on the mercy of this first sleepless night.

ten

Nonetheless, the narrator did suffer a relapse, if only for Edith's sake.

The next morning the narrator phoned one of his former colleagues in another division to ask if they might meet that afternoon.

This gentleman, whose name is Maier, was less concerned with politics than with the smuggling of drugs. Since the drug traffic was organized on an international scale and frequently encroached upon the political sphere, Security had made it their business to keep their eyes open here too.

The narrator asked Herr Maier not to breathe a word of their meeting, which only strengthened the latter's suspicion that the narrator's dismissal had been a put-up job, designed to throw some suspect or other off the scent. Would Herr Maier be so good as to ascertain whether the documents relative to d'Arthez's arrest in 1941 were still extant? The name rang a bell. "Weren't there inquiries from Paris? I saw the tracer myself. But it is a name that never came up in connection with drugs."

The narrator explained that he was not interested in the man who had recently been murdered in Paris; it was the well-known German actor whose legal name was Ernst Nasemann, related to NANY Inc. Dr. Glatschke had political grounds for taking an interest in this case.

"What does your Dr. Glatschke want with old dossiers from the Nazi period?" asked Maier in dismay.

"From an arrest twenty-five years ago we may be able to deduce something about this character and his present conduct. We are absolutely in the dark and, besides that, have to be quite careful not to irritate NANY Inc."

"The guy's a Commie?"

"On the contrary, Dr. Glatschke suspects him of connections with the extreme right. The tracer at least justifies your looking into the matter to see if possession of drugs wasn't used as a pretext at the time of arrest. They say things like that happened already in those days. NANY was what used to be termed an essential industry, and certainly the Gestapo would not have wished to compromise its owners. Perhaps it might still be possible to put our finger on the party who denounced him."

"Denounced him!" snorted Herr Maier contemptuously. "What system ever gives away the names of its informers?"

But the mention of drugs had aroused Herr Maier's interest. He even went so far as to thank the narrator for the tip. For his part, the narrator implored him to keep the matter strictly confidential, not even to mention it in the office—all of which only stimulated Maier further.

Immediately thereafter, the narrator was reproaching himself again for getting in contact with Security in such a manner and above all for heaping new suspicions on Edith's father. Luckily, none of this led anywhere. None of the remaining documents from the year 1941–42 related to this case. Nor had any been found during the various so-called compensation and reparation hearings after the war. Ernst Nasemann's reappearance at the end of July 1945 was officially noted by several departments. With this the competent authorities had been quite busy at the time.

In Berlin toward the end of July 1945 an American MP patrol picked up a man in tattered clothing. He was in a state bordering on total physical collapse. He could not have gone another ten paces without dropping. This condition did not appear to be simulated. The man was obviously homeless, although he claimed to be looking for his address—so far without success. As noted in the dossier, he answered all questions in almost perfect Oxford English. This merely served to arouse suspicion. In the guardroom the man explained that he had been freed from a concentration camp but that it had taken him all this time to make his way through the Soviet Zone of Occupation. He gave his name as d'Arthez, alias Ernst Nasemann. In reverse, in other words. Not Ernst Nasemann, alias d'Arthez. His profession: actor. He had no papers.

Due to his critical condition, the man whom they had just seized was first placed by the American authorities in a prison infirmary.

Not a word concerning the three months between the dissolution of the concentration camps and d'Arthez's arrival in Berlin could be turned up in the archives. Obviously, it did not interest the Americans—which is understandable. In those days there were cases like this by the thousands. Someone would surface again after an absence of seemingly impossible length. The authorities were only interested in establishing identities.

What had to be determined in each case was whether this might not be a Nazi official attempting to escape justice under a false name. Moreover, even so soon after the end of the war, the authorities were most intent on preventing the Russians from infiltrating spies.

The identity of this d'Arthez, alias Ernst Nasemann, was established relatively quickly and without difficulty. The names of more than twenty witnesses whom there was no reason to suspect figured in the dossier. Among them were a former concierge from the Academy, former neighbors and the owners of shops in his old neighborhood, even one of his fellow-prisoners from the concentration camp. Sybille Wuster, who at one time had been in the theater with d'Arthez, was on the list as well.

Above all, however, the greatest weight was given to the identification of d'Arthez by his brother, the Herr Generaldirektor Otto Nasemann, chairman of the board of NANY Inc. He was living in Bad Königstein at the time and was already negotiating with the American authorities and various American banks for the permits and loans required for the reconstruction of the Dresden plant in the vicinity of Frankfurt. For this reason, the military government had facilitated his flying to Berlin, otherwise impossible in those days.

With open joy, he immediately recognized his brother, who was still in an emergency ward; only then was he finally moved to a private room. The press had been invited and in the archives lay photographs of Otto Nasemann at the foot of the bed with the emaciated d'Arthez in the background. These pictures and the interview appeared in foreign papers as well, for a scene so characteristic of the times was of universal interest— particularly when an international industrial concern was involved.

From the interview which Otto Nasemann was only too happy to give, one learned that the family had heard nothing of this lost son and brother for many years and that hope had long since vanished of ever seeing him again. "The events of the war and the air raids, gentlemen, how many victims they claimed! This is something we need not discuss. Nonetheless, it increases the joy I feel at finding my long-lost brother again here! I cannot begin to express my gratitude to the American authorities for taking care of him. When I received the telegram, I had to exercise the greatest caution in making its contents known to our old mother, since for a woman advanced in years and exhausted by the forced emigration to the West, this happy shock might have proved too much. My only regret is that our father did not live to see the day. Thus for his sons remains this most compelling of tasks, the rebirth of the firm he founded and its renewed development along the lines he set forth. This will cost us much labor and self-denial, and we wish to express our gratitude to all those who aid us in this great work with their faithful optimism."

This mixture of purely human destiny and the will to industrial survival doubtless served NANY Inc. as a powerful advertisement. That day Otto Nasemann brilliantly anticipated the sort of advertising now in general use. In the finance section of the newspapers in the summer of 1945 there were favorable prognoses for the owners of NANY shares and hints that foreign capital was being invested in the firm. No interview was granted by the other brother, however. He lay there in the background very effectively. One saw a doctor and a nurse on either side of the bed who seemed to be guarding the patient against reporters.

What naturally strikes one right off is the total omission in these circumstances of any reference to concentration camps. Clearly, Otto Nasemann would not find it in the interests of his firm to mention matters of so personal a nature. One's private life was no business of the public's, although experiences such as these were common to many families. Otto Nasemann could not have guessed that his brother, if for very different reasons, might have been in agreement with this particular silence. But in any event Otto Nasemann would scarcely have given this a thought. It is possible that at this very moment, as he lay in bed mutely listening to Otto's effective rhetoric, the idea of acting out pantomimes came to full fruition.

The family's claim of ignorance as to the whereabouts of their long-lost son became subsequently untenable. NANY Inc. was an essential industry and enjoyed excellent connections with the highest echelons. Among other things, the firm supplied the Wehrmacht with parachute silk and camouflage suits. And as the leftist press maliciously revealed, NANY Inc.'s bid to deliver a durable regulation fabric for the uniforms of concentration-camp prisoners was accepted by the Gestapo. This the firm has never denied. It would be ironic indeed if for more than two years d'Arthez had worn a uniform made of fabric manufactured by his father's company.

Thus, one can readily assume that this thoroughly distressing arrest of his son must have led the firm's president to conclude an arrangement with the authorities that was satisfactory to both sides. As already pointed out, at the reading of the will Otto Nasemann boasted that his brother had NANY Inc. to thank for his life. There might be something to this. On the other hand, it might not have been precisely a disadvantage to have a former concentration-camp inmate in the family immediately after the breakdown of Nazi Germany, as if their own integrity were proven by his existence.

That the estranged wife of Ernst Nasemann was not appealed to in establishing d'Arthez's identity scarcely requires comment. Perhaps her place of residence was not then known.

On the basis of this identification, d'Arthez, alias Ernst Nasemann, received new papers from both the American and the German authorities. As soon as he had recovered, he found that his American papers possessed the added advantage of enabling him to reappear at once on stage.

And none of this was altered by another incident that occurred three or four months later and which is noted only briefly in the dossier. The Soviet authorities transmitted the unreasonable request that the case be reopened and his identification be subjected to further scrutiny. In the northern foothills of the Thuringian Forest, the corpse of a man had come to light. Children had discovered it while gathering mushrooms. Of course the decomposition of the body was far advanced, but the clothing was indubitably that of a concentration-camp inmate, and the number printed on the material was that under which Ernst Nasemann was listed. The Russians had arrived in time to seize these records. Alongside this man, who had been shot in the head, lay an army pistol. Whether it was murder or suicide could not be determined. No one appeared to have been willing to go to much trouble . . .

At that time such cases were far from unusual. The American authorities took this for mere chicanery on the part of their Russian colleagues. They did call d'Arthez in once more, however, but since he was unable to give them any clues as to how the victim might have come by his uniform, they dropped the whole matter as inconsequential. Nor did the Soviets discover the identity of this corpse. In those days corpses by the thousands remained unidentified.

The only remarkable aspect of this incident was that it prompted one of d'Arthez's first pantomimes. It must have been performed quite often in the first few years after the war. It was made into a one-reeler as well. One sees it repeatedly in any series devoted to the genre.

When the narrator happened to question Lambert one day about the above-mentioned film, as to whether it might not represent the transposition into art of a real-life experience, Lambert answered gruffly, "But it's an everyday sort of theme!"

In any event, he was always poking fun at the phrase "real life." The narrator forgets whether he heard this remark, typical of Lambert—"Why not 'real death,' that would be more accurate?"—from his own lips, or ran across it only later among his papers.

To return to this pantomime or one-reeler, its title alone was ambiguous: "Camouflage Suit." Perhaps it was intended to lead one astray. Anyone interested in the matter should look up the innumerable reviews of the epoch; attempts at interpretation were legion. They were not all hymns of praise either; it was also panned. Certain critics were scandalized because in their opinion this pantomime took a terrible human experience and trivialized it for the sake of a good laugh.

The stage represents a wax museum. Among other figures there was a beautiful young lady in a hoop skirt and a rococo coiffure offering a glass of champagne to the audience. It is the Marquise de Brinvilliers, famous for concocting poisons. In the foreground, on a straight-backed chair, sits a well-known murderer of women from the first years of this century—as though he were seated in a doctor's waiting room. His beard is unusually black; otherwise, he looks quite ordinary. He stares at his hands, bemused. Obviously he has just strangled one of his victims. Other well-known mass-murderers are present.

Neither Hitler in his ridiculous uniform nor other prominent Nazis are anywhere to be seen. This absence was criticized at the time in some quarters. Lambert talked about this in greater detail than was usually his custom. The scene would have been deprived of its entire impact, he explained, if any topical reference had been made.

The door at the back of the stage is cautiously opened from outside and d'Arthez peers in. When he catches sight of the figures, he pulls the door almost closed in fright. He repeats this two or three more times before he is convinced that these are only wax dummies. Then he slips inside and peers out the back way before closing the door, to make sure he is not being followed.

The pantomime is unusual in that here d'Arthez does not appear in his world-famous costume, that of the traditional British diplomat—or more precisely, most people's notion of one—but as the inmate of a concentration camp. Naturally, his clipped English mustache is missing. The shapeless KZ uniform gives him a clownish air. And indeed the first half of this pantomime is unusual in that d'Arthez is exaggeratedly playing the clown. Certain critics of the day pointed to this part with amazement, and between the lines one hears them sigh: What a clown he would have become—had he continued in this vein!

As d'Arthez advances toward the Marquise de Brinvilliers, who offers him a glass of champagne, he declines the honor all too modestly, making a few stiff bows, apologetic gestures, and finally attempts to get behind her so as to hide under her hoop skirt. He even goes so far as to lift her dress to see if he can conceal himself beneath it, but because of the wooden stand there is no room for him. As just mentioned, all this is acted out with an exaggerated air of comedy. The public must have laughed a lot.

He greets all the other figures in the same way and then walks behind the old-fashioned lady-killer, who sits solidly as ever on his chair. D'Arthez puts his elbows on the figure's shoulders and relaxes there while quietly contemplating the situation. A photograph of this grotesque pose somehow finds its way into practically everything written about d'Arthez.

This is the turning point in the film. Suddenly the concentration-camp inmate resting there in comparative calm catches sight of himself, that is to say, of a wax figure of d'Arthez as we know him at present, of a spruce gentleman in a dark jacket and striped trousers, with a black homburg allowing only a touch of gray to show at the temples—not to mention the small mustache. But this elegant gentleman holds a pistol. It points at the KZ inmate.

The inmate recoils, raises his hands quickly and reels forward. As if by command, he lurches backward and almost trips over the lady-killer, who has been sitting there the whole time. To keep himself from falling, he hangs onto the latter's hands, then helps himself up, not without dusting off the murderer apologetically. Then he slowly walks with raised arms toward the elegant gentleman. All played very much in the style of a clown.

This is followed by the famous scene in which they exchange costumes. It requires some time and much comical mimicry before the prisoner comprehends that the gentleman with the pistol intends to force him to change clothes with him. How can that be? Can anyone wish to change his well-cut suit for the grimy, shapeless overalls of a prisoner? Why, it isn't possible! But sometimes an elegant gentleman has very perverse ideas—the boredom of wealth makes them that way—and moreover, with a pistol pressed almost against your nose, it is wiser to comply. A pistol is usually loaded.

To simplify the otherwise complicated procedure of exchanging costumes, the inmate already wears the other's costume, except for the jacket, under his KZ overalls: white shirt, gray vest and striped trousers. Therefore, he need peel off only the overalls and dress his likeness in them. Of course, in order to do this, he must first remove the homburg. This he does with a maximum of apologetic mimicry. The former inmate, still in his shirt sleeves, admires the fabulous hat and puts it on.

Then he unbuttons the wax dummy's jacket, taking great pains not to tickle him. One imagines hearing his constant apologies. First he disengages the left arm, then he goes behind the figure to do the same with the right arm. But if a gentleman is holding a pistol, it is hard to help him out of his jacket. In his zeal to exchange costumes, the erstwhile prisoner has completely forgotten the revolver.

It falls out of the dummy's hand and crashes to the floor. D'Arthez stiffens; he looks exactly like a waxen dummy. Only gradually does he appear to conclude that he has nothing to fear, so he finishes removing the jacket. Now he works without apologies and in comparative haste. As he does so, apparently unintentionally he kicks the pistol to one side.

He drapes the jacket over a chair and begins immediately to dress the dummy in the KZ overalls. He does this rather hastily and without any consideration whatsoever. He fiddles with the overalls at neck, arms and legs until they sit properly and then steps back a few paces to examine his handiwork. He appears to be dissatisfied, and returns to tug at the overalls a few more times, even casting an eye at the Marquise for advice as to what might still be lacking. Finally, however, he gives up with a shrug. In other words, he simply takes the jacket from the chair and puts it on. As he does so, he walks to a mirror.

He is no more satisfied with his own appearance than he had been with the dummy's. He straightens his tie and pulls down the vest, turning one way and then the other in front of the mirror to examine the fit of his jacket. But it fits him perfectly. What can be the matter?

Perplexed, he slowly fingers the collar of the jacket. When his fingers reach the left lapel, he winces. Obviously, he has hurt himself, and a finger of his left hand even seems to be bleeding—at any rate, he sucks at it. What could have happened?

Pinned behind the lapel there is a party emblem, and d'Arthez pricked his finger on the pin. Ahah, that explains it.

D'Arthez has already become in his behavior quite the d'Arthez everyone recognizes. He holds up the party emblem before the still peacefully seated lady-killer and the Marquise, then walks over to the dummy in the overalls and pins it over his heart.

Then he bends over for the pistol, wipes off the fingerprints with his handkerchief and places it in the dummy's right hand. He bends the dummy's arm to aim the pistol at its head so murder can pass for suicide, and at the same time he tears the mustache from its waxen face with a calculated gesture. At that we hear a shot, but ridiculously feeble—as if from a cap pistol. With his foot d'Arthez gives the figure a careless shove and invisible wheels whisk it offstage.

As for d'Arthez, he negligently slaps on his mustache, examines his reflection once more in the mirror while pulling on his gloves, then tips his hat politely to the stolid lady-killer and, with greater respect, in front of the Marquise. As she still proffers champagne, he declines with a short but avuncular nod before leaving the scene.

In an interview that he gave much later in New York, reproduced in part in the often-cited picture biography, there is a remark that may throw some light on his pantomimes, on the one just described and on others as well. The American reporters ask him in disappointed tones why he has always refused to talk about his experiences in the concentration camp. Isn't it more or less his duty to make this known to the public so that similar incidents can never occur again? (Never mind the large sums that any of the big newspapers would pay for an exclusive story.) At this, d'Arthez is reported to have asked in surprise, "Have I ever refused, gentlemen?" But one of the journalists, more persistent than the rest, was not put off by this characteristic reply. "All the same, sir, we have the impression that you intentionally withhold the truth and that your admirable pantomimes are a means of hiding the truth from us."

In the interview we read that this statement affected d'Arthez deeply. Whether his pain was only an affectation, we can no longer decide. He is supposed to have answered this persistent reporter as follows: "That is the most caustic criticism my theatrical offerings have yet received. Oh, yes indeed, it is, gentlemen! But since you have brought up truth and claim that the public has a right to hear it, let me confess that I have always been afraid that I might be betraying far too much of the truth.

243

Every time I appear on stage, I am terrified lest a voice from the audience ring out: Won't you please stop pestering us with your personal experiences! No one is interested, and besides all this is now passé. Such a shout would finish me forever as an actor, and you might say as a human being as well. For we might as well admit it, gentlemen; everything my generation may have experienced or failed to experience may still make for a small literary sensation—that is something that you members of the press can judge better than I—but as for the experience itself, or what you choose to call the truth, it certainly no longer counts for the present generation, and least of all for this fortunate land of yours, which has been spared being a battlefield twice in forty years. Thus it would be ridiculously presumptuous to call this the truth, and anyone who did so would rightly be called a bore, as—if I am not mistaken—you term such people."

D'Arthez recovered rapidly. As early as the fall of 1945, he was appearing in a small, run-down nightclub in Berlin. He already appeared in the role he has played ever since. In the winter of the same year, he made his first tour in West Germany. For this he must have had the backing of the American authorities. The pantomime described above was filmed in 1946.

From those documents which Herr Maier communicated to the narrator, nothing more was to be learned. Herr Maier, by the way, had already lost interest. There had been no allusion to drugs whatsoever.

So there was no word about his arrest, or about his internment, or what he suffered in the camp, but above all nothing about those three months that passed between his being turned loose or escaping and his surfacing again in Berlin. Obviously, these three months struck the authorities as nothing out of the ordinary and they never thought to ask about them. But for the narrator, thinking about them twenty years later, these three months seem more important than anything else, more important indeed than the grounds for arrest about which Edith wished to know the truth.

Certainly Lambert knew more about this; presumably he was the one person to whom d'Arthez would have told the whole story. The narrator did his best to get Lambert to talk by pointing out that many questions touching on d'Arthez were also of purely legal interest, but Lambert recognized this maneuver for the pretext it was, and made fun of the narrator. "These are private matters," he said, "the only moment when one really must insist on privacy. Some people will turn to God in horror and, in doing so, fall on their faces."

Of course it was a pretext, but all the same the question is still of legal interest. If, say, one succeeded in observing the steps that lead from the breakdown of a totalitarian order to the provisional attempts to establish a new legal system, one could explain more than d'Arthez's personal fate; a whole important area of contemporary history, of which this personal history forms a small part, would be illuminated. Doesn't the mere fact that our lives at one time had a certain gap having no history of laws, during which nothing but keeping alive counted, throw some light on the way we live now? Weren't many of our laws a kind of barbed wire, a kind of protection against the possibility of the recurrence of such a gap? Had men and women become aware of still other laws during that lawless period, laws whose possible reappearance in their lives so terrified them that they took exaggerated and anachronistic provisions against just this possibility? And how is an individual to retain his identity if the whole era has lost its identity? What kind of identity can it be that one military authority or another has to confirm with its seals and stamps?

Lambert refused to consider such questions. He felt that only a philosopher could concern himself with them, a philosopher, moreover, who had not gone through any of this, because for anyone who had, these things were so much part of his life that he didn't even know the right words for them any longer.

What was it that made the nearly starved d'Arthez push his way through the Thuringian Forest, that gave him the strength to reach Berlin? He might easily have fallen by the wayside like the body found at a later date. Why, during those three long months, did he refuse to give up? The old-fashioned claim that a man yearns to return to the origin or focus of his life was meaningless in d'Arthez's case, since he had nothing left to call home and since Berlin for him was just one more destroyed city.

These three months were so fascinating to the narrator precisely because such notions as origin or focus of life offered no explanation at all. For if there can be gaps in one's life, no matter whether they last three months or only a single Sunday afternoon, these gaps still color or discolor all those things that we take for granted and consider the natural habits of existence.

How would it be if d'Arthez not only had known the man who was found in the underbrush on the edge of the Thuringian Forest but had actually killed him himself? That is no more than a hypothesis. That is, it might have happened that way, and even if it didn't, one can regard it as an insignificant possibility since it should have happened that way, and that alone counts.

Let us imagine that the two men meet after they escape from the concentration camp. The direction of their flight happens to be the same, although their escapes have quite different motives. Let us imagine further that these two men were anything but strangers and that this encounter was far from welcome. For what they had in common, the desire to flee as quickly as possible from a distasteful past and to abandon their different identities, was completely frustrated by this senseless encounter at the edge of the forest, almost as if neither of them would be allowed to cut loose from his past, not even in the forest of an almost uninhabited region.

One of the two men was the inmate of a concentration camp with a number instead of a name, and his reason for fleeing could not have been more obvious. The other need not have been the commandant of the camp—higher-ups usually have safer ways of escaping—and, besides, the commandant would scarcely recognize any of his prisoners, since for him they were nothing more than a faceless mass. No, the other would have had to be one of the underlings, one of those ordered to carry out the atrocities, who followed these orders to the letter. Was this particular KZ inmate for some reason or other—one need not explain it by the influence of NANY Inc., it could have been mere chance—given office work or commandeered by the lesser despots to wait on the underlings at meals? Here we are in the realm of speculation where one has to depend on the reports of other inmates. What makes us assume that our guess is right is the later reference to a kick in the pants with which a man condemned to death is dispatched into freedom. This remark we owe to Lambert, but it certainly might have originated with d'Arthez.

So what we are dealing with is nothing less than an encounter of executioner and victim, except that these titles are no longer appropriate since both men find themselves in the same situation, that is, in flight. Each represented for the other a past that was precisely what he was fleeing from. This unfortunate encounter then demands an immediate decision. Not in the spirit of revenge. Revenge is directed backward. It tries to set right an unjust past and this explains why revenge is never satisfying: the avenger is living in a past that is no longer valid. No, something more was at stake at this meeting on the edge of the forest than revenge for a kick in the pants or an attempt to protect oneself from someone's revenge. What is punishment, anyway? This concept presupposes at least a modicum of accepted order. Who thinks of punishment when there are no more laws to demand it?

Doubtless, this encounter found the former KZ inmate in the more favorable position, simply because, as a victim, he was accustomed to accept privation, torture and death as natural conditions of existence. Thus a creature becomes tough and unassailable in the face of adversity. Instead, the privileged executioner falls prey to every little draft once compelled to leave his central heating and the overstuffed chair at the heart of his regime. And even if he is better-clothed than the prisoner, we must remember that the encounter took place at the end of March or the beginning of April, and that even in April the nights are quite cold. And the following, somewhat marginal question occurs to one as one contemplates the situation: might the irony of fate not have seen to it that the clothing of this particular inmate was manufactured by NANY Inc.? That could have been ascertained easily enough since the synthetic fibers from which NANY wove the cloth would have lasted even though the corpse had decomposed. But no one at the time had troubled to investigate this question, particularly when the production of cheaper but more durable material for the uniforms of KZ inmates was never considered a war crime.

And yet at this encounter the concern of both parties could only have been clothing. In this respect, too, the inmate was much better off. As things had turned out, it was obvious that a person in KZ garb had the decided advantage, while a man dressed in civilian clothes, clearly not his own since they did not fit, who had no papers, could only elicit the gravest distrust.

How long these two were together—a day, a night, a few hours—we cannot know. Did the former executioner consider it necessary to apologize for his behavior of the day before and explain it away by claiming that he had been compelled to play the executioner? Were that the case, the victim would certainly have tried to make it easier for him—that is part of the psy-

248

chology of the victim. The inmate could have answered something like, Well, let's just not talk about it, that's over and done with.

Yet would the executioner have been persuaded of the indifference of the victim? That is hard to believe; he has been an executioner far too long. He will still be thinking in terms of executioner and victim and thus expect the victim to look for the opportunity to turn the tables and play executioner. For an executioner is only accustomed to kill, not to death.

This is the executioner's advantage over the victim. Let us try to imagine the two of them running into each other at the edge of the forest. It is quite possible that the former executioner was there first and then hesitated as to his next step. Before him lay some open country that he had to cross. In the distance, one could make out a village with a steeple. How was one to behave in this outside world to avoid the suspicion of ordinary people?

And at this instant, behind him, he hears a rustle in the bushes and turns to see a starving KZ inmate approach unsuspectingly through the trees. An inmate who yesterday was absolutely in his power. An inmate still wearing the camp uniform. Was not this an act of God to solve his dilemma?

There was no choice, particularly if we realize that the executioner had at his fingertips one other advantage from the day before: naturally he had taken his pistol with him.

The executioner probably aimed at the inmate at once, and the inmate, accustomed to thinking of himself as a victim and to looking into the muzzles of pistols and waiting for them to go off, would have raised his hands and even clasped them behind his head, if that was what was expected, and patiently waited. More complicated reactions were not required; everything had been rehearsed, as it were, and performed often enough.

Why wasn't the shot heard at once? Perhaps because the

stage was different from the one on which this play had so long been acted out. Missing was the dependable scenery of the orderly camp where a shot was nothing out of the ordinary. And how far would the report carry if one fired at the edge of the forest, in the very teeth of the freedom beginning beyond it?

Probably both of them, executioner as well as victim, failed to evaluate this change of scenery properly, as they began playing the roles so often rehearsed. Unintentionally, this new scenery gave their drama an unforeseen conclusion.

As remarked, the victim waited patiently for the shot to be fired; as a victim, he had waited often enough for this. And the executioner as he observed this defenseless expectancy would have felt himself reinforced in his accustomed role. Why hurry? You always have time to shoot somebody. The stupid jerk stands there so obediently.

Besides, isn't it harder to undress a corpse? Not to mention the fact that the uniform will be covered with blood, which would make a bad impression on people. Well, then.

This is how it came to the change of clothing. At the moment it seemed to the executioner that slipping into the concentration-camp overalls was the best idea; the way he saw it, this was likely to improve his chances of survival. What to do with the victim after he had his clothing didn't have to be planned ahead, it was an everyday act. And the victim simply did not think about it.

He pulled off the overalls as ordered. It didn't astonish him that his executioner removed his jacket and dropped his trousers. As it had been ages since he had been astonished by anything, he did as he was ordered. He did not even wonder at the magnificent gesture, magnificent for an executioner, with which he was ordered to pick up and put on carelessly cast-off trousers and jacket. Why should a victim be astonished at the moods of an executioner?

Here, however, the executioner made a miscalculation that

was to prove decisive. It had not occurred to him that a change of clothing could so totally alter the situation. He had never learned any other role than that of executioner; it was a role cut out for him.

For the pistol was a part of the costume that he had just laid aside—inmates of concentration camps, as any schoolboy knows, are never shown with a pistol. And thus he laid the pistol aside too, if only for a moment and if only to let out the belt that had been fastened around the meager waist of a starving prisoner and would not fit the normal girth of an executioner. For this, one needs both hands; the buckle is rusty. It may even be that another hole must be made. The easiest thing would be to order the victim to help. A victim always obeys. And so does this one. He even kneels to straighten the legs of the overalls. And when he has gotten up again, he steps back to see if the overalls fit properly. For it is only natural that in a camp the prisoners' overalls have to be worn according to regulations, and if one forgets, he is punished.

Meanwhile, he has picked up the pistol, only because regulations required it. To allow an executioner to stoop for anything would be insubordination.

The former victim may even have offered the former executioner his pistol with a friendly smile; for neither the victim nor the executioner will have realized that by exchanging clothes they had exchanged roles. Instead, they went right on playing the game that habit dictated. The trees surrounding them at the edge of the forest, their only audience, must have shaken their heads at this theater of the absurd.

Yes, and as the executioner disguised in KZ clothing reached for the pistol that he no longer had a right to, it went off. The play in which they performed seemed to have invented this new ending all by itself, and it suited the new scenery. The onlooking trees must have heaved a sigh of relief. Chance it was not! Chance is far too cunning to let anyone see into its

251

hand. No, this is a *logical* conclusion, easily understood both in legal and in psychological terms—in hindsight, as one returns home from the theater. It isn't necessary to include the part where one drags the dead man by the feet into the bushes and drops the pistol beside him. What can one do with a clumsy pistol? Putting it in one's pocket would only serve to chafe one's bones, because one's bones are covered with nothing but skin. Perhaps as a future item of exchange? How could a man standing on the edge of the forest know whether or not such an item would have any value out there beyond the farther edge of the forest?

Onward, then. Three unknown months lie before us.

eleven

According to criminologists, as a rule a criminal after committing a crime has only one urge and that is to work off the crime in the arms of a girlfriend or a prostitute, and as he does so, he is bound to boast of this deed. This "rule" provoked one of the narrator's professors to ask: "And who does the detective run to after he sends a murderer up?"

Disregarding for the moment that this change of clothing was not so much d'Arthez's deed as something done to him, to which he was exposed, as an individual is at birth when he is squeezed through the gate through which all children enter life, involuntarily surrendered to the arms of Fate—

—from which there can be no turning back— And this allows of neither affirmation nor remorse as a deed does—and one cannot awake from it as from a dream in which one has done something strange— And it cannot be worked off by throwing oneself into the arms of a prostitute—

disregarding for the moment that none of this need have happened this way, that it is nothing more than an attempt at interpretation on the part of the narrator, who may possibly be trying to interpret himself when, in explaining a character whom he respects, he stretches him this way and that until he finds him malleable—

disregarding, moreover, the three intervening months that remain completely unknown, totally outside our ken, beyond the boundaries of speech, three months of dreamless nothingness that swallow up every cry from beyond—and were anyone to try to reconstruct it on the basis of some old document which had fallen into his hands, in hopes of making a deal with the television people, he would not be able to find a single buyer who felt it would create a sensation—

disregarding all of this, it is hard to imagine that d'Arthez had nothing more pressing to do than to confide in a woman.

Not simply that d'Arthez's confiding in a woman does not happen to suit the narrator. For it is all too true that the narrator himself often longed to confide in Edith, and that even now, writing this report as the steamer vibrates, he is tormented by regrets that he never did so. Even as the train pulled out of the Central Station in Frankfurt, he had to get a firm grip on himself not to jump from the train at the last minute and fall into Edith's arms. "Why don't I simply stay with you?" But the train pulled out and they only waved.

For what in God's name had the narrator to confide? Nothing at all. He would have been deceiving Edith and one day she would have recognized the deceit and the discontent in the world would have increased.

No, d'Arthez would not have confided in a woman anyway. The matters involved are such that a man would not dare communicate them to a woman if he did not want to expose her to the danger of annihilation.

When asked whether she had ever read d'Arthez's palm, was this what the Woman in the Window in Berlin meant? "I'd have known better." Did she mean—assuming of course that there is anything to palmistry—that only because of those things we cannot confide, which for this reason one dare not touch on, can a man and a woman enjoy mutual respect?

For this Woman in the Window—it's odd, if one calls her by her legal name, she loses all reality—Edith evinced mingled skepticism and fascination. Naturally, she assumed that in the old days when they had both been acting students, her father had fallen in love with her. She even asked the narrator, although he had never met her father, if he too didn't believe her father would have been happier with this woman. She would probably have nothing against it, even applaud, if her father were to marry her now.

Of course Edith could not discuss any of this with her father, but the woman herself was much too intelligent, or, if you will, much too sly, not to have fathomed Edith's thought. She laughed good-naturedly.

"You know, dear, once we've realized how powerless we are against our own stupidity, we no longer rack our brains trying to be happy or trying to make someone else happy. But don't let me destroy your illusions, see for yourself. No matter how things turned out, your father would never have married me, I'd never have married him. We were never that stupid. We'd have done each other in for sure, and the only question would have been who was quickest on the draw. Yes, young man, things like this do happen, don't look so shocked. There's nothing about them in your law books, naturally."

She said all this when Edith and the narrator visited her in

Berlin, that is to say, shortly before the narrator's departure for Africa.

"One gets wind of your father only from time to time. And that turns out to be an advantage; otherwise, one would get ideas. So you say, Ah, that's how it is, and you're on your own again. Do you two remember a short bit he used to do? Beginning of the fifties, I believe. But of course, you two were just children then. This was the shortest bit he ever played. He comes on stage in his beautiful suit and he's hardly in the room before a bee or a horsefly is flitting around him. To begin with, he only waves an arm, or maybe it was his hat, to chase the creature away. And apparently it works, since the buzzing fades out, but just as he puts his hat back on, the creature stings him in the hand. Your papa gets stiff as a board, that's something he does marvelously, and then he lets fall with the other hand. The scene as such only begins at this point. He contemplates the dead fly with thoughtfully wrinkled brow, then taking him tenderly between thumb and index finger, bears him solicitously and ceremoniously to a little table on which a small box lies, a sort of little jewel box lined with cotton or satin, yes, and inside there's a necklace with a cross, silver or gold or whatever— He takes the necklace out and sets it on the table and in its place lays the dead fly. For a moment your father remains standing reverently before the box, then he closes it like a coffin. He looks around the room and then breaks two flowers from a plant standing somewhere and lays them on the tiny coffin. It is then that your papa notices the necklace and places the cross at the head of the coffin. If I'm not mistaken, he also lights a candle, but it may be I'm just imagining the candle. In any event, now everything is in order. Your papa stands erect before the bier, holding his hat over his heart the way elegant people do when they pray. At the same moment a harmonium strikes up a funeral march and your papa marches out with such dignity. The largo gradually in-

256

creases in volume. The scene was later censored because some church or other got upset. A cross for a dead fly and the largo besides. Could anything be more reverent? But no matter how careful you are, people will find something to get upset about. Stupidity is even greater than one had imagined. Yes, and when your papa paid me a visit after this, I told him right off. So, that fly was meant to be me! He laughed in my face. Well, young man, why do you get so excited about those three months? Do you actually imagine that her father ever told me anything about this? First of all, there is nothing to tell; and second, it isn't necessary to *tell*, you know all there is to know beforehand—if you don't, no amount of telling is going to make it comprehensible; and third, it's irrelevant whether it last three months or ten seconds. In poor Lambert's case it lasted almost ten years, or was it longer? That's bad, of course. And above all, because no one can be of any help. In her father's case it lasted three months and that was that. A day came and it was all over; he could laugh at himself. That's all there is to it."

Judging by her looks, no woman could have been a worse match for d'Arthez, at least with the public d'Arthez. When she addressed the narrator as "young man" and observed him in her unsettling way through eyes like slits, surrounded by innumerable wrinkles, she sometimes looked like an ancient and very cynical witch. But then again often it appeared that she had forgotten her visitor, although she was still looking at him; this was even more unsettling because one suddenly ceased to exist. It seemed as though she was hearkening with wide-open eyes to something going on outside, looking a bit melancholy and helpless, like a young animal, a female tiger or wolf listening to her mate's call which she must answer in spite of herself. At such moments one asked oneself full of terror who this woman really was and what she thought when she was alone once more in her cheerless room.

257

Afterward Edith defended her passionately, in a manner that was quite out of keeping with her and quite superfluously too, since the narrator had made no disparaging remarks. Edith claimed that her unkempt, lank, greasy gray hair, the stained collar of her dress, the shabby braid, the button that dangled, and the fingers yellowed by nicotine were only a costume, like her father's mustache and formal tailoring. This was only partly true. Admittedly, the woman said this much about herself: "When all these little dolls stinking of soap sit down across from me and I unfold their soft little hands, they almost wet their pants, they're so terrified. Then I can tell them anything I please, they'll believe anything. Really, dear, it's no trick predicting their futures. Money, bed and social pretensions. Of course you have to try harder for the people off the street since you can't fool them and they really want to know something. With them, you have to be honest."

All the same, it would have been interesting to see this woman with d'Arthez.

Naturally, she paid him a visit as soon as he turned up in Berlin. "I read it in the papers. The papers were funny in those days, not like today. I went right over to the hospital. I say 'went right over,' but in reality it was more a forced march—there were hardly any streetcars then. Well, I had nothing else to do but try to keep my head above water, and a little exercise is always healthy. And at the hospital two clean-cut American boys asked me if I could identify him. Of course, if it's him, why not? And it was him all right, even if he was only a skeleton with the eyes of some terrifically unstrung saint in an icon. 'Well, love,' I said, 'you *have* been through the mill.' And he grinned, or tried to grin, he even tried to raise an eyebrow. You could see every muscle, every tendon. Old Ernst, all right. 'Don't strain yourself for my sake, love. The girls have told me not to get you excited. And I haven't gotten any prettier in the meantime, I can tell without your smiling. Well, then, let the girls here nurse you back to health, then pay me a visit and we can laugh about it all. "Bye-bye now," as everyone's saying.' Yes, I called him 'love,' but don't think that means anything, dear, it's just left over from life in the theater. So, one day your father turned up at my place looking well fed again, and under his arm a bottle of Gordon Dry he'd swiped from the Americans. 'Those your new duds?' I asked, and we nearly died laughing. And naturally I confessed all my sins. You see, we had lost sight of each other for some time, more due to my marriage than his. Besides, your mother was never precisely my cup of tea, if you will forgive my saying so. No, my stupidity was even greater. Would you believe it, children, as sure as I'm sitting here saying all sorts of grand things, I fell for a pair of fine black trousers. I was swept right off the stage as a young thing and married that pair of black trousers. And naturally a pair of shining boots went with them, and the well-cut jacket of a uniform. It's unbelievable. So this handsome young SS officer —not a monster, lord, if he had been a monster as they're all described these days—nothing more than a handsome blockhead. God rest his soul, he got his somewhere in Russia, fortunately for him. By that time we had been divorced for years. It only lasted a year and a half. No children, and in those days that was sufficient grounds, maybe I did what I could to keep from having any, that is also possible. Yes, things like this do happen. But once you've committed such folly, there's no longer any possibility of taking yourself seriously again, and that is worth something too. Just as you can't take these little dolls seriously, rushing here straight from their bubble baths wanting to know something about their future. Future! As though they had a future! But don't let my turn of phrase disconcert you, dear, find out for yourself, that's all right too. I only mention all this nonsense because there was a time when I couldn't move in the same circles as your father. I would have scratched his eyes out if he had so much as raised an eyebrow at me. And then they pinched him. And then there was a war on and bombs were falling. You know, the usual routine . . . No one had any time to think about happiness or other abstractions. And you want to go to Africa, young man. Do you have to? For three years? Who talked you into that? It had to be Lambert! Okay, okay, don't get excited! I know it's none of my business . . . But don't think the girl is going to wait for you. If that were the case, everyone could go to Africa, a fine kettle of fish, and at home the silly goose sits waiting. And don't you get such ideas into *your* head, dear. Characters like Solveig are a male invention, so that there will always be someone to look after them when they come home with malaria. No, put that right out of your head. Instead, tell me about Lambert. Your Uncle Lambert, as you call him. How was he able to change his coat so fast? Is it true he was asleep when his wife finally died? Your papa told me something of the kind. That was the first intelligent thing I ever heard of him doing. Yes. Yes, indeed! Don't act so horrified. That wife of his should have croaked long before that, for years she hadn't any blood in her veins, nothing but poetry and the fashionable philosophy. You'll find them by the dozen at any cocktail party or opening. If only it were a put-on just to catch a man, but no, they actually believe it all. It makes you feel sick. The only thing to do is take to your heels. And what kind of man can listen to such stuff? Yammering about Literature morning, noon and night. Brrrr! It makes you lose your appetite . . . And you even feel uncultivated on the rare occasions when they keep their mouths shut. And your Lambert in the middle of that! What could have possessed him? I only saw that wife of his two or three times at some party or other. She was one of the living dead, and a blind man would have noticed it. Your blood ran cold at the sight of her. And poor little Lambert had to fall for the idea of keeping a creature like that among the living by marrying her. A woman like that would have turned Hercules to a shadow in nothing flat. But it's none of my business, my own folly is enough for me. And it was none of my business at the time. Lambert could marry whomever he chose and run after trouble with open arms. But the fact that he fell asleep before she died, that impresses me. Good old Lambert. Well now, why don't you two run along and leave me alone. As for your future, you'll just have to figure it out when it comes. And if your young man is going to fall in love with a black girl, there's nothing about it in his palm. But that has nothing to do with fate or related nonsense. Scram! Clear out! Do you want to drive me wild! Who is responsible for things working out this way? Oh, come here and give us a kiss. And that I'm in tears means nothing at all. All old women cry when they see one more lamb elbow its way to the slaughterhouse thinking everything is getting better all the time."

twelve

And Lambert too was furious when the narrator appeared on Monday following that Sunday afternoon.

He hissed to the narrator as the latter entered the university library, "Well, did you pay Nora a visit?"

"But . . . wasn't it Sunday?" the narrator stuttered.

"Yes, so we noticed. Edith dropped by to see me during the evening."

"But I thought . . . Edith?"

"Yes, Edith. Who else? We'll talk about it later."

An hour and a half later, as the library was closing, the first thing the narrator did was to tell him about the agent he had run into in the Kleine Bockenheimerstrasse. Lambert waved this away contemptuously.

"I've known about that for some time now. I invited the concierge to have a beer with me in that bar in the Rothofstrasse. Can your Dr. Glatschke actually believe he can put something over on a concierge? Not to mention the man's wife! What a bunch of children you have working there in Security! Can those idiots seriously suppose that the woman didn't notice at once what sort of person had been sent up to her attic? And besides, a guy that drinks and staggers around in the street? But the worst of it is, the poor bastard is in some sort of trouble. I asked Nora about it."

"Nora?"

"Of course, who else?"

"So you *were* with Nora!"

"As a matter of fact, yes, if you don't mind. After Edith left, I set out for the Taunusstrasse. See all the trouble you caused!"

"I?"

"Yes, who else? To ask Nora if you had spent any time with her."

"I?"

"For God's sake, will you cut out that moronic I, I, I! Do you suppose I would have put on my shoes again late at night for that damned agent? His face rings a bell, though; I must have seen him once before. That's why I asked Nora about him in passing; they all know each other in that milieu, even the stool pigeons. Naturally Nora was suspicious, but finally she called her friend over from the bar, and the matter struck him as important enough for him to hurry off to warn someone or other. Frankly, I didn't really comprehend what it was all about, and it hardly interested me. Obviously common jealousy is at the bottom of it. You see, these people still experience such things. But they don't like it at all when one of them gets knocked off, it only leads to a run-in with the police and brings business to a standstill. For that reason they stick together and do their best to prevent things from happening. What a clumsy oaf Dr. Glatschke is, just because he doesn't know a thing about life. Isn't it just like him to choose a rascal like that as his spy, one that's going to get killed? But that is none of our business. Sorry, I thought you were more intelligent. Now don't scream 'I' again! For a change, why don't you scream 'self'? You see, apparently they've started to draw a distinction between the ego and the self. But don't ask me what this means, I only saw a book with a title like that. Perhaps we should tape something about this for your Dr. Glatschke. If we don't understand it ourselves, it's certain to confuse him totally. For instance, in the form of a hit tune: 'Nora, throw your ego out/ And be your own sweet self!' Well, come on, we can discuss all of this over dinner."

Lambert whistled several melodies to see if they fit his text. In self-satisfaction he grunted something about becoming a song writer.

This time they ate in the beer hall on Rothofstrasse. Lambert was known to everyone at the bar and seemed on particularly good terms with the big blonde who worked the tap. The noise was overwhelming, the pinball machines never stopped rattling and clanking.

Lambert ordered cold cuts and was outraged that the narrator wouldn't eat the same.

"Are you already having to pinch pennies?" he asked.

Then as he carefully cut into the fresh liverwurst he told the narrator what he had confided to the microphone the night before.

"Wait a minute," he said and felt for a scrap of paper in his pocket.

"It won't do coming out with such stuff extemporaneously. I wrote the text on my way home from Nora. I even tried to give a worried ring to my voice before I removed the red frog king from the microphone. Here it is, listen.

ATTENTION! ATTENTION!
CALLING ALL THE FROZEN PEOPLE!
SOMEONE IS PLOTTING TO THAW US OUT!
THAT COULD MAKE A STINK!
BEWARE OF CONTACT POISON! ON THE ALERT!

With all the shortwave static. How do you suppose your Dr. Glatschke will react to that? Politically inflammatory! Unwieldy past! Stink! It was *you* who made me broadcast that. I was simply furious with you. No, no, quiet down, not you really, I broadcast it more for Edith's sake."

"Edith? What has Edith to do with it?"

"Her curiosity, old fellow. God damn! Curiosity in reverse; in other words, perverse. Only the smell of corpses can result. A stink. As already mentioned, moldy literary sensationalism. Small wonder the dead prefer staying dead. But naturally Nora was most suspicious."

"Nora?"

"Yes, who else? She doesn't like it at all, being asked about her visitors, which is only understandable. Not because she believes in discretion, but because she's afraid of the police and the competition. But in the end I got out of her that you had passed by and even hesitated for a moment in front of the arcade. Nora didn't see you, she was busy elsewhere. Someone else did. Someone always sees anything that has to do with the profession. And then they report you went on without having asked after Nora. Sorry, I gave you credit for more sense. Edith always gets furious when I call you innocents, poor little orphans; but it's *true*! Well, to quiet Nora down—she was so suspicious—I sat and discussed income tax with her and her friend. It's a dependable topic that says something to each and every one of us. And damned if the evening didn't cost me money! It was Sunday night and business was booming. I had to make up Nora's lost income somehow. So I slipped a bank note into her purse, and all just for you. That explains why I'm furious with you. Now. That will do.

"You see, it was there I had a tremendous idea—talking about income tax. And it's an idea that can be realized, it was always in the air and still absolutely modern. I attempted to generate some enthusiasm for it in Nora and her friend and their pals who happened to be sitting around. It goes without saying that an organizer is needed, and I'm too old for the part, so I suggested you. You have legal training, you know the ins and outs. And if you didn't have those wild ideas about under-developed countries and helping them evolve, I really would advise you to accept the post. You could make a fortune. Think it over, won't you, before you make up your mind about under-developed countries. What I am suggesting is much more modern and has a better future. And your Dr. Glatschke will be dumfounded. What is the poor bastard trying to do? All of it strictly within the law, you understand.

"Very well, then, all that is involved is the girls!—staging a protest march. The preliminary propaganda of course has to be thought out in the greatest detail. Without experienced advertising men and psychologists it won't work, but the brothers will be pushing their way to the ticket window as soon as they get a whiff of the money, no doubt about it. The question of income tax alone is a good enough slogan, but it won't do for a prolonged campaign. There will always be a few people who whine about their duties as citizens and even pretend they enjoy paying their taxes. This must be reckoned with. No, we must appeal to a deeper instinct.

"Frankfurt seemed to me the best imaginable place to begin. Berlin won't do, because of the Wall. Your Dr. Glatschke would begin raving about Communist infiltrators and rob us of our effect. And Hamburg won't do. The film industry has played out the red-light district there, and besides, we aren't interested in the movies. But a faceless international depot like

Frankfurt with its airport can be won over to such a European Idea . . . Listen to me, ideas breed ideas! The European Idea just came to me and it would be great for our campaign, and on banners. In the twinkling of an eye, dear old Europe could gain some ground. This must be thought through. Yes, a blow at Americanization. People over there will suddenly feel they're backward, especially after noting our negative effect on their balance of payments. Confronted with the European Idea, as long as it isn't laid on too thick, even your Dr. Glatschke will have to capitulate.

"So, a protest march staged by the ladies, beginning in the Kaiserplatz, then by way of Goethe and the Frankfurter Hof to the Hauptwache with a bit of the Zeil and ending on the other side of the Liebfrauenberg at the Römer. The classical tour, and not too long for the ladies in their high heels. In the vanguard, the first category in their Mercedes blowing their horns. These veritable paragons must by no means be absent. And they will play along, never fear. Not out of a sense of comradeship, for God's sake no, but because the problem affects them even more than it does the humble foot soldiers. For example, can a Mercedes be deducted from income as a business expense? It simply won't do for the hard-working, tax-paying bourgeois lady to be discriminated against in favor of the male industrialist, it's unheard of. As a lawyer you should take note of this, for such anachronistic injustice should at last be attacked from the academic side.

"But one thing above all will assure the success of our undertaking: this protest march has to unroll in a respectable fashion. Or let us say well bred. Everyone involved must realize that the problem attacked is of vital concern, that a constitutional question is at stake. They must feel this so strongly that even the Supreme Court in Karlsruhe cannot overlook it. And, it goes without saying, there must be neither nudity nor sex. Leave that to the film industry and illustrated magazines;

they're not really interesting. The dresses should be whatever length fashion dictates. Elegant but free from extravagance. Anyway, I believe this is something we can confidently leave to the ladies. And all the dress shops will be sold out a day in advance! And the hairdressers will have had to work overtime. In point of fact, the increase in turnover is not to be imagined. We'll surmount the financial crisis! The bankers will prick up their ears.

"I'm convinced that they will spend the whole day trying to reserve good parking spaces for watching the parade . . . Possibly there will be scalpers selling such spaces . . . But please note that any personal advertising will be dealt with quite severely. For instance, a lady waving to a potential customer, or vice versa. That could only create a situation in which the police would be forced to intervene. Very well, in the Römer, as the parade breaks up, there might be a fair, with stands selling sausages, and others where the ladies can shoot to win dolls that squeak 'Mama.' Also rides that make their skirts fly over their heads. No taboo will be broken. No one can take exception to a bit of folklore—as long as it is kept within certain bounds. Yes—and as for the music: it won't work without music! Naturally they can't play the 'Badenweiler March' because of its unfortunate associations, and due to the international character of the parade the national anthem won't do either, although it occurs to me that the 'Marseillaise' would not be out of place. No, perhaps a band composed of panpipes and harmonicas should precede the whole. And why not such good old songs as 'Must I go, I must go,' and 'Now let us sing praises to our dear homeland'? They are quite suitable and we cannot consider what we ourselves would like, we must keep in mind how conservative the ladies are. Yes, and as the parade dissolves on the Römer, the band could strike up 'I lend myself with heart and hand.' Solemn and in the tempo of a chorale. That would be most appropriate. It would demonstrate the readiness of these taxpayers to serve their fatherland, that the only equality they demand concerns taxation.

"And since we are speaking of equality, it is to be expected that the ladies will have the artists on their side, because they too work hard but are not in the mainstream of society and enjoy neither tax benefits nor old-age pensions. Banners should be designed by the most famous painters. However, no bare breasts or naked buttocks! Obviously such clichés shouldn't be part of such a serious occasion. Oh, perhaps here and there an attractive navel, that would be possible, but for the most part a certain re-mythologizing would have a greater drawing power. There is already a need for it. And I expect great things of the poets! Their hymns will be discussed in the Sunday supplements.

"But these are nothing more than suggestions. In the preliminary phases of organization I would advise you to concentrate on the notion of increasing turnover. In your brochures such words as 'index of industrials,' 'return,' 'investment,' 'consumer goods' and the like cannot appear too often. We must get the support of the stock market but without manipulation; and unofficially, from the grass roots. You see, this concerns more than one or two branches of industry like the world of fashion and the cosmetics empire. I have already alluded to the automobile industry. But think of hotels and restaurants, and behind them agriculture, imports and exports. And for all that, airplanes and ships are required. The airlines will have to add charter flights, and not simply for all the foreign tourists; no, a demand will also be created that only the import of foreign women can satisfy. Why shouldn't they too be allowed to participate in the realization of this great Idea? Out of gratitude, they will spread it over the whole world. Yes, with caution and without any antimilitaristic intent, we might appropriate such phrases as 'nonviolent action' and 'peaceful penetration.' I would advise against such Biblical slogans as 'On Earth Peace to Men of

Good Will,' at least for the time being. Everything which might suggest that we are *anti* anything must be avoided.

"Imagine, all this in Frankfurt! Just picture it! Goethe and Rothschild! The synthesis was already in the air. At least we have gotten far enough to make it a reality.

"Someone objected that we will tangle with the housewives of Frankfurt. There you have another example of how psychologists trap themselves in the web of their own abstractions. Naturally, whenever a housewife bumps into a neighbor on the stairs or out shopping, she'll feel obliged to remark, 'Have you heard? Isn't it a crime?' And of course they aren't exactly going to wave to the girls in the street as they march past, far from it. But they will turn off the vacuum cleaner and the utility companies will register a definite decline in consumption at a certain hour. Not a great loss, because the decline will be recouped a hundredfold later on. Yes, the housewives will be standing behind the curtains, watchful and critical, spying on this parade. One must keep up with the times . . . Who concedes the race willingly? And leaving axioms aside for the moment, our brochures should point out that actually the hardworking, self-sacrificing housewife suffers the worst tax discrimination of all. One should come forward with statistical findings—for instance, the number of miles a housewife walks each day, compared with a streetwalker. One might subtly imply that if we must speak of prostitution then it is the housewife whom men ruthlessly exploit, wear out, prostitute. Letters from readers must fill the newspapers with appeals to the Woman's Right to Happiness and Tenderness. And shouldn't we finally make full use of that happy American invention 'mental cruelty'?

"No, old fellow, it isn't the housewives, the problem lies elsewhere, and if we can't find a solution the whole business will collapse. For a whole hour I talked to Nora and her colleagues seated around the table. The ladies' friends sat beside them. All of them reasonable, sober individuals, without illusions and keen on their own advantages. In this unromantic atmosphere one feels able to breathe again and in spite of everything to believe in the future once more. But no! The conservatism you meet with in this milieu can drive you to despair! We live in the days of space travel, of hormones, of dialectical material- ism and second-generation computers that look after our yeses and nos—marvelous fruits of progress . . . But no! In this mi- lieu everyone is so damned conservative that the old-fashioned code of behavior of a thousand, five thousand years ago is still preferred to modern methodology. If this were to be explained by a sense of history, by a feeling for the effective costume . . . But no! In their environment they hold on to their religion. It is absolutely depressing. You end up feeling frustrated. Nora wouldn't even take me seriously.

"Yes, old fellow, if you insist on helping countries *evolve*, then why not right here?

"But let's talk about Edith."

thirteen

One should not forget that almost a year and a half separate the narrator from the events he reports, or that upon hearing this unexpected "But let's talk about Edith" he could not have guessed that Lambert was soon to die. Lambert's death and the emotions it aroused have colored this scene. Nor at the time did the narrator know about Lambert's own attempt at self-interpretation that was found among the papers he left. This attempt, which bears the title "Complications" and which the narrator has appended to the end of this report, appears to explain how Lambert and others of his generation saw themselves and why they tried to erase any clear picture of

272

themselves as soon as one began to emerge. "Complications" contains the curiously paradoxical sentence: "We need transmitters of information who can hold their tongues." Since he came across this sentence, the narrator has not been able to put it out of his head, and if he has understood it correctly, it must have been anything but easy for Lambert to drop his digression about Nora and suddenly turn to Edith.

However, only this much is certain and open to no objections: the sudden turn that the conversation took occurred in Lambert's room, where he had invited the narrator after they dined together. Lambert spoke facing the window, as was his custom once he had made sure that the concealed microphone had been disarmed.

The narrator was sitting at the table behind him, but on a diagonal, so that he saw the speaker's profile as the light of the neon sign colored it green, blue, red.

It is quite possible that the narrator's first reaction was to jump up and protest, perhaps with the childish statement, "I don't want to talk about this, it's a private matter."

In hindsight, one is ashamed of oneself, because now it is clear that it was not the narrator but rather Lambert whom this conversation left defenseless. Perhaps his shame explains this report—in the sense that the narrator wishes to make up for it. And also that the narrator so timorously avoided meeting d'Arthez, and instead sidestepped the issue by committing himself to three years in Africa, may have been caused by the desire to expose himself first to defenselessness before posing with affected confidence in front of another vulnerable person again.

Lambert even brought up the narrator's father during this conversation. "Even if you never knew him, consider what this president of a Superior Provincial Court in Hannover must have thought as his world came down around his ears while you were being cared for in Rosenheim or beside the Ammersee. You see, his thoughts matter, whatever he was thinking

273

down in the air-raid shelter before it caved in. And certainly for the sake of your mother and the other people crowded in the shelter he would have behaved as though nothing had gone wrong and the crazy world could be set to rights in short order. Those are the thoughts, old fellow, that matter and it's worthwhile trying to think them through."

Yes, he even went so far as to ask, "What's d'Arthez to you? You busy yourself with him as though he were a matinee idol instead of paying attention to your own affairs. What's the good of that? What do you end up with, after your pseudoscientific curiosity and Security Police methods have exposed a few facts? Less than a dressmaker's dummy, the mere picture of a dressmaker's dummy. Why else did we dream up that skit that was played a few years back? Yes, I contributed a little to its success, but the original idea was my friend's. One day he said to me—yes, it was right here in this room—'We have to destroy their desire to turn our past into literary sensations!' The first idea I had was of spoiled food nauseating a man so that he must finally stick his finger down his throat. But that wouldn't do for the mass media. The skit might have presented a buffet, with all the old-fashioned specialties, beautifully garnished but already putrescent. But d'Arthez would have been the last person in the world to be taken in by rotten food; and besides, the skit was not to overstep the limits of a pantomime. And to have had him clear the table by pulling the tablecloth out from under all that trash would have been too didactic. 'Never try to instruct' has always been our motto. So we agreed on the pantomime with the mirror. D'Arthez stands in front of it adjusting his tie and vest. Then he pulls a window shade down over the mirror and starts to leave. But then he turns around to lift the side of the shade slightly to peek in. He sees nothing, of course, thanks to the shade. Satisfying, but not completely. D'Arthez glances about him. There is a clothes stand nearby on which hangs a suit identical to the one he is

274

wearing. Pushing this in front of the mirror, he adjusts everything and even sticks a flower in the lapel. Quite satisfactory; in
fact, just right. Once again he walks to the mirror and stands to
one side of it. He jerks the shade and it winds itself up with a
bang. Everything is perfect. In the mirror we see the clothes
stand, and before it the clothes stand itself.

"That does perfectly. Your Dr. Glatschke can choose which-
ever he prefers to analyze, the clothes stand or its reflection.
Where is d'Arthez? He left hours ago, but not before he had
politely tipped his hat. Do you expect him to call out from the
wings, 'Here I am, here I am!' in order to explain his life story?
And what sort of explanation would that be? God forbid! There
is no backstage in this skit. Only a Here and Now into which
people would tumble as into a crevasse.

"You know, you drive me to distraction. Because you compel
me to speak of things which are so much a part of me I don't
have to talk about them. I far prefer just shouting something
into the microphone to keep your Dr. Glatschke busy. For instance, the motto on the gutted opera house. Attention! Attention! TRUTH, BEAUTY, GOODNESS! They would take them for code
words, of course, for an invitation to flock together in the
square in front of the ruins of the opera house and from there
to proceed to blow the system sky-high. But we were speaking
of Edith. Now don't go through the roof. For all I care, you can
take her out, go for walks, drink coffee together as much as you
like. You can fall in love with her if you choose, that's your
affair—and Edith's. But your Security Police methods I simply
will not have! You'll ruin her with them. You see, she already
has a tendency in that direction. She will take all your fine abstractions at their face value and try to translate them into everyday life. In a man, that would be either pedantic or comic,
but for a girl it's sheer suicide. I once knew a woman who tried
to live poetry—don't laugh, this really happened: it was like
pernicious anemia—and at the end of it, sleeping pills. If only

she had slipped a dose of arsenic into her husband's morning coffee, that would have been poetry, that would have been natural law, that would have been truth, beauty, goodness.

"Now, Edith came running to me yesterday evening in a terrible state. I tried to fill her with pizza at the Milano. That you should have run away from her at noon was perfectly normal. A woman must get used to things like that, and the sooner the better. One must somehow make his separate peace with these damned natural laws. Forgive me, I can't help poking fun at that favorite concept of yours. But it is intolerable that you should have let her convince you to snoop into her father's past using the Security Police. And not because there is anything there that should be hidden; no, the reason is that whatever you find in his dossier will be wrong. Anything that finds its way into a dossier has nothing to do with reality, it represents only a reality manipulated by the authorities.

"Very well, Edith suspects the woman who bore her of betraying her father to the Nazis. She would like to be certain about this, once and for all. That's just the way she is. Look at her forehead, how round it is, as if to show that she is bound to run head-on into various walls. Unfortunately, however, this wall is an elastic one and she will never butt her way through, and the truth that she senses behind it is also an elastic truth. The woman whom she supposes to have betrayed her husband was nothing but a female animal with the mother instinct. Here we have already one of those truths that it is wiser to hush up than to tell Edith, for the woman is her mother, after all. Whether this woman behaved decently or not is irrelevant. One merely becomes ridiculous, bringing up concepts like guilt and conscience to condemn a mother animal. *Non compos mentis* might be brought in as an extenuating circumstance, but that is a purely male argument, and how would you go about identifying what can be termed *compos mentis* in the world of women?

"Why is one forced to talk about things that are so obvious?

Proud mother animals are always in the right and that's why we have Security. The difficulty is only that all their neat laws are invalid in cases of exterritoriality; hence their infernal hatred.

"D'Arthez was not brought down by an inferior woman, but because he was already exterritorial. That is the unadorned truth. Anything else is a defect so trifling that it doesn't even count. If guilt is mentioned in this connection, then it is all d'Arthez's, since at that time he did not realize that his exterritoriality should be hidden or camouflaged. He had to go to a concentration camp to learn that lesson. And what gets under your Dr. Glatschke's skin is his somehow sensing this exterritoriality without being able to prove it, since not only does d'Arthez behave correctly, but he's related to NANY Inc. as well.

"Instead of writing about such unfamiliar things as natural law, you should rack your brains about the laws governing exterritoriality. Certainly they exist too. Unfortunately I cannot assist you, although I do think about the matter from time to time standing here at this window. But one of the first laws must surely be that a man dare not let his exterritoriality show, and it was this basic law that d'Arthez failed to observe. He even went so far as to boast of his condition. What is there to boast about?

"The final cause leading to his arrest was a very simple one, and you must explain this to Edith. To this day he has a tendency to make everything too obvious. He *is* an actor, after all. Every time we discuss a new pantomime, my sole task is to try to discourage this obviousness. We often fight about it. His theatrical temperament always runs away with him. And over and over again I try to make him realize that what really counts is only those things which are so much a part of one that they don't require expression. I had to learn that first myself. And naturally it puts people off, they feel offended. They come asking: Why won't he *talk* to us? Women in particular come in droves and each one thinks, *I* will be the one who makes him speak.

"But as I said, at the time d'Arthez did not know that he was exterritorial by birth. You see, that happens too. I cannot imagine why nature allows herself such experiments. Now, I was *not* born exterritorially, no indeed. I only fell in by mistake or out of a false ambition. Oh, I have some of the habits, it was unavoidable, but my constitution is not suited to exterritoriality. Yes, there are cases like that too. And perhaps for the very reason that I do not belong there, I can tell d'Arthez, who does, what he should or shouldn't do, better than he can tell himself. But at the time of his arrest we were not seeing much of each other. And besides, he was not d'Arthez then, he was a rank amateur who did not yet know his role. A director—what was his name, he must be dead by now—started him out on the wrong track. Actually he had already recognized 'd'Arthez,' but only halfway. He had advised him to play all the good, old-fashioned roles, only to play them a bit too earnestly—to make people laugh. It worked; of course they did laugh and they went home satisfied. But it was all wrong. The laughter did not go far enough.

"Nor did it go very far against the Nazis. It was already fashionable to make jokes about them, but the Nazis thought that if that was all people did they wouldn't get any silly ideas into their heads. But in d'Arthez's case they saw that the situation was more dangerous, and they saw this earlier than he did himself. Yesterday evening I tried to explain all this to Edith in an effort to put out of her mind all that nonsense about her mother being to blame. That would be tantamount to degrading the concept of guilt, but naturally we cannot tell Edith this. It would make just as much sense to take the blame myself because at the time I failed to dissuade her father from performing this pantomime. But, as I said, we saw little enough of each other in those days. I didn't even see the skit in question.

"From what I heard, the set represented an authentic reconstruction of what used to pass for a polling station, set in either a school or a café. There was a long table for the so-called poll officials and the ballot box, and stage-front, the poll booth. It consisted of a lectern surrounded on three sides by screens. Poll booth! What a word for it. A portrait of Hitler on the wall, it goes without saying. One of those in which he has a brown uniform but no cap. He holds the cap in front of his genitals like a lid. It's one of the funniest pictures in the world; a venomous caricature, actually, since it bears as legend DER FÜHRER. The awful truth is, no one could see that it was funny any more. Nowadays such a thing cannot even be imagined. Oh, and stage-front, next to the poll booth, stood a Party poster. Nothing but an enlarged ballot on which a single circle was printed to receive the voter's X. On the poster this X had been inked in vigorously and very black. Yes, there was only one circle. In those days such a thing was called an election; 99.5 percent of the vote one knew in advance, *everyone* knew. And there may have been an arrow pointing to the X so no one could possibly miss the point, and the words SHOW THE FÜHRER YOUR GRATITUDE! That's the way it went.

"I can only describe this to you as it was described to me, but that is the way it must have been. D'Arthez—or let us call him Ernst Nasemann—enters the polling station and bows politely to right and left. He looks like the average fine young man, with a wife and child at home, but not married for very long. And naturally somewhat embarrassed and uncertain, faced with the red tape that he must contend with. But in those days everyone was aware that if he did not throw himself wholeheartedly into the red tape he was in for trouble. There were Glatschkes enough back then and they would have found out

279

in no time. At the very least, he would have lost his job, and that he couldn't do because of his wife and child. So the young man walks up to the long table behind which we must imagine the poll officials and presents his papers, smiling politely, with a little bow to the emptiness. While his papers lie there and his name is checked off on a list, a voice murmurs behind him, a voice the spectators could identify as that of the portrait of Hitler. It murmured, 'Die Vorsehung!'—'Providence.' And it was precisely the tone of voice Hitler used for this word. The voice was imitated to perfection. The young man standing there at the table has no idea where this voice is coming from, he recoils, then a moment later smiles at the officials, whom we must imagine behind the table. This smile was far too un-ambiguous. In those days d'Arthez's acting was still very clown-ish. I mean by that, the old-fashioned asides he made to mime his helplessness and embarrassment. Then the young man moves down the table to the next official, the one who hands him the ballot. Once more the voice murmurs 'Providence!' and once more the young man recoils and then smiles. He takes the ballot and green envelope that are handed to him. He examines these papers, even turning the ballot over to look at the back side. Then he reaches the poll booth with a grotesque little leap. Far too grotesque. Obviously one of the officials snapped at him not to muck about, holding up the works. Once again he bows quickly, then directs more apologetic gestures toward the table. The young man enters the poll booth at last. He looks around inquiringly, as if to ask: Is this the proper procedure? He lays his ballot on the lectern. He pulls himself together and brings all his concentration to bear on his choice.

"I really would have enjoyed seeing this little scene, it must have been magnificently executed, already d'Arthez as we know him today, at least to judge from what I was told the next day. The young man takes a pencil that hangs there on a chain and tugs the chain once or twice to make sure it's long enough, then he places his left elbow on the lectern and his head in his hand, so that he can conscientiously deliberate in peace and quiet how he should vote. He looks almost as if he were going to write a poem. All this time he shifts from one foot to the other, his concentration taxes him so. Once or twice he even goes so far as to touch the card with the pencil, but no, something like that must be deliberated carefully, one dare not be in too much of a hurry. Unfortunately, the conscientious young man is disturbed in his deliberations. The voice is murmuring 'Providence!' continually. And indeed it gradually speeds up, becoming more and more impatient, louder and louder. Our overtaxed voter hears the racket, of course, but at first he thinks it must be his imagination and wriggles a finger around in one ear, but the racket doesn't stop. Then he lifts the top of the lectern: nothing inside. He also examines the cracks in the screen that stands on three sides of the lectern: no microphone, no loudspeaker. The young man can no longer endure this uninterrupted bellowing, he puts his hands over his ears. Just then the poster with its arrow pointing to the single circle catches his eye. That comes as an inspiration, indeed as deliverance of a sort; and, in fact, the bellowing lets up somewhat. But, just to be on the safe side, the young man turns the poster around to see if there isn't another circle on the back, but all he finds is empty cardboard—and the voice bellows 'Providence!' with such indignation that the young man lets the poster fall in terror, rushes to the lectern and draws an X in the circle as desired. As d'Arthez jams the ballot into the envelope, stumbles to the ballot box and drops it in, the word *Providence* too seems to stumble, first loud, then soft, deep in the bass, then high in the treble. A great deal of effort must have gone into the production, as someone told me who had seen the performance and just got out before the whole audience was arrested. In any event, d'Arthez stumbled like a sleepwalker toward the exit to the rhythm of these noises. The audience already guessed or at least feared where this irresolute zigzag would lead him, and they weren't disappointed. D'Arthez came within a hair of colliding with the over-life-size portrait of Hitler. One second before it was too late, he appeared to come to. He took a step backward, pulled himself together, stood erect, clicked his heels, jabbed his right arm straight into the air in what was known then as the German Greeting and bellowed, 'Heil, mein Führer!' What was so sidesplitting was his choice of a particularly low Saxon accent for bellowing these three words. Naturally, the audience collapsed in such prolonged laughter that the final joke was lost on them. For this scene had been so timed that at this point the voice shouting 'Providence!' receded to a squeak, as happens when a tape recorder is suddenly turned on 'Slow.' In this case, then, the first syllable of *Vorsehung* was still distinguishable, while the rest, the *se* and the *hung*, were spun out at such length that in the end there was only the empty swish of the machine. In the meantime, d'Arthez left the polling station—the stage, in other words. Not a bad idea, even if the effect was lost, due to all that laughter.

"D'Arthez was arrested as soon as he stepped offstage. He didn't even have time to return and acknowledge the audience's applause. And presumably the applause stopped abruptly too. Everyone tried to get out as quickly as possible. Now what does that woman have to do with any of this? She was with child, in the seventh month, I believe. Perhaps she was sitting at home listening to that stupid schoolteacher tell stories of Germany's future greatness. What does that have to do with d'Arthez? Even if she did behave pretty shabbily later on. That is, shabbily according to the prevailing moral code—which says a wife should stick by her husband when he brings about his and his family's ruin through political acts—although the reasons behind this moral code will scarcely bear scrutiny. Still, what is it but the end of a disagreeable marriage? In other words, just a private, petit-bourgeois affair.

"Yes, this is how it should be put to Edith. It was only for the sake of the child which she was carrying that her mother decided to divorce her father. That at least sounds *logical*. I am not a woman and you aren't either, but the point is to make Edith believe that this is how *we* understand the affair. And if there is still any doubt in her mind, then she will just have to struggle free of it on her own; she can try something else herself if her mother's act doesn't meet with her approval, but it is not up to us to make up theories about how a woman should behave in such a case.

"Can you believe I actually enjoy defending this worthless person? But it's got to be done; for Edith's sake it's got to be done. And so you won't cause any more trouble with your confidential files. And for d'Arthez too. Do you really imagine that his life would have been any different if that bitch had not betrayed him at that time? Damn, how simple everything would be! All one need do is marry the right woman and everything works out fine. Yes, just tell Edith that, even if it does hurt her feelings. It won't really hurt. And she can argue with you if she pleases. Who's stopping her?

"Even if there had been no Nazis, no concentration camps, no Dr. Glatschke, no NANY Inc., no anything else, at most his absence would accelerate the lightening of an error or a deviation from one's course.

"But for that, one must have died once already. Without that, one doesn't have a chance."

fourteen

This last sentence, to which the narrator, of course, attached no importance at the time and which he does not understand even today—although he writes it down as if he did—this sentence, which was left like a scarcely perceptible tremor, alluded to the frequently mentioned essay that was found among Lambert's papers after his death.

This essay, bearing the title "Complications," the narrator has placed at the end of this report. It is placed there because the narrator prefers to let Lambert have the last word, instead of presuming to form his own judgment. The title, however, is Edith's, although a passage occurs in the essay where the con-

284

cept of Complications is discussed in such a way as to suggest its use as the title. Edith and the narrator saw no need for pondering it at length.

First, let us turn once more to this sentence, "But for that, one must have died once already." It is now perfectly clear to the narrator that this sentence represents the utmost self-exposure of which Lambert was capable. And he said it for Edith's sake alone, to protect her from herself. Or, instead of "from herself," let us say from "unseemly curiosity," and this reproach of "unseemly curiosity" of course also applies to the narrator with his Security Police methods as Lambert called them.

With a sharp "That will do," Lambert indicated that this painful self-exposure was a unique event forced upon him by unusual circumstances.

For his part, the narrator wishes to emphasize that Lambert was never more Louis Lambert than at this instant. Perhaps this was the sole moment in his life that he achieved the identity of the name he had assumed. After this, only a heart attack was possible.

And this "That will do" did not even refer to Lambert personally, but marked the conclusion of the interrogation that led to d'Arthez's imprisonment. For Lambert had been explaining to the narrator that d'Arthez had not been imprisoned for performing an incriminating sketch, or because of a denunciation by his wife. By itself, the skit might have resulted in d'Arthez's being prohibited from ever again appearing on stage, but that was all.

As Lambert said, "As soon as I heard they'd picked him up, I called people I knew in the so-called Propaganda Ministry. Naturally, I had connections. I implored them not to make a mountain out of a molehill and to issue this Ernst Nasemann a reprimand and turn him loose. The people I knew were glad to oblige and rang up the Gestapo. But there was nothing to be done. My informant came back white as a sheet. They had let him read the minutes of that interrogation. After that, anyone who had come to the suspect's defense would immediately have been suspected himself of anti-Nazi agitation. My informant was still weak in the knees. You see, the Gestapo got interested in him for having taken an interest in the affair and grilled *him* as well. Today, of course, it is easy enough to call people cowards . . .

"That was a long time ago. And I did not read the minutes myself either, but I remember what my informant told me. But perhaps it was because he was so afraid that he read so carefully. For much of what he remembered was so typical even of the present d'Arthez that it simply had to be correct. And it will be interesting for you to note how little interrogations and the misunderstandings they beget have changed in the interval. The interrogator could have been our Dr. Glatschke. In your profession, isn't this referred to as 'getting at the truth'? Well? Congratulations.

"At this moment I can see only one truth, and that is that we spare a girl the sorrow of knowing what a stupid woman her mother is. Yes, stupid! Please note that. For to call her bad would be saying too much. And as far as you are concerned, just don't take one truth to be your truth when it can never be yours.

"But let's be done with the past, it's none of your business anyway. Why, not even our mistakes can serve as an apology for the mistakes that you're going to make.

"But to return to that interrogation . . . It must have gone something like this:

QUESTION: What did you think at the time, Herr Nasemann?
D'ARTHEZ: Think? I have learned that we must not think if we are to perform well.
QUESTION: So someone else conceived this distasteful skit?

D'ARTHEZ: No need for anyone to do that; it all just happens of its own accord when you walk on stage.

QUESTION: But all the scenery! Who thought up the scenery?

D'ARTHEZ: But scenery is just there. You don't need to think it up.

QUESTION: Are you aware of the situation you have gotten yourself into?

D'ARTHEZ: Oh yes, for quite some time now.

QUESTION: Quite some time? Since when?

D'ARTHEZ: Oh, I am no longer able to name the day.

QUESTION: Well, then, approximately.

D'ARTHEZ: I believe I must have been fourteen or fifteen. But please don't write that down!

QUESTION: Why shouldn't we write that down?

D'ARTHEZ: Because I might have been even younger.

QUESTION: How is that possible? In those days the Party did not yet exist.

D'ARTHEZ: Oh, it hadn't been named yet, but it has always existed. They should emphasize this point.

QUESTION: I believe that is something we can leave in the hands of the Ministry of Propaganda, Herr Nasemann. Who or what first gave you the idea?

D'ARTHEZ: Excuse me, but it is not an idea. It is reality.

QUESTION: Let us not argue about words. What cause did you have then or now to see what you term reality in this light?

D'ARTHEZ: One day you wake up. Unfortunately.

QUESTION: Unfortunately?

D'ARTHEZ: Yes. At first, things aren't so easy.

QUESTION: Is that why you became a comedian?

D'ARTHEZ: I am hurt when people call me that. I am dead serious, you see, as soon as I step on stage. But people will laugh, there's nothing I can do about it.

QUESTION: Let us return to your skit. Your wife implored you not to play this scene, is that correct?

D'ARTHEZ: My wife is big with child.

QUESTION: We are aware of that. You can depend on us to treat her with every consideration. All the more since we are of the opinion that your wife knows her duty to the State and the community better than you. Why didn't you listen to her?

D'ARTHEZ: But I did! She *is* bearing my child.

QUESTION: I think it would be more suitable, Herr Nasemann, if you stopped trying to play the comedian here. That won't work with us.

D'ARTHEZ: What did I tell you!

QUESTION: Please do not interrupt me. Your wife says, and we believe her, that she told you that your skit disparages the Führer. So don't try to play the innocent with us.

D'ARTHEZ: Disparagement? It can scarcely be disparaging to imitate a person's voice. And particularly the Führer's! On the contrary, one cannot hear it often enough. Only to imitate it badly would be unlawful. I, sir, destroyed every single disk which did not seem to me to capture that voice perfectly. In my wife's presence, and just to quiet her. Didn't she tell you of this? I exercised the most severe self-criticism. I practiced days on end in order to attain an imitation absolutely interchangeable with the original. That is difficult. If you were an actor, you would realize just how unbelievably difficult it is. And I rehearsed at home in my room and kept right on rehearsing—where else could I rehearse? No one could be permitted to overhear those imitations of the Führer that were imperfect. My wife alone heard all the attempts. We live in rather cramped quarters. She would come out of the kitchen and stand in the hall to hear me rehearse. There was no way to avoid this. But we can count on my wife's holding her tongue—I'd put my hand in the fire for that, as the saying goes. Yes, and finally . . . I joined my wife in the hall. I closed the door to produce the critical distance after putting the needle on the record. I was flabbergasted at how well my imitation succeeded. It sounded as though the Führer were paying us a visit and saying 'Providence!' there in my room. My wife will be able to vouch for what I said: 'What can we offer him? You know, he's a vegetarian.'

QUESTION: Do you really suppose we will swallow nonsense like that here?

D'ARTHEZ: But he *is* said to be a vegetarian! You see that everywhere.

QUESTION: And why did you salute with the German Greeting on stage?

D'ARTHEZ: You have a point there, that hadn't been rehearsed, it was pure improvisation. Suddenly, when I came up against the portrait of the Führer I thought, 'Do something to make your wife happy,' and raised my hand. Did I do something wrong?

QUESTION: And why did you use a Saxon accent for the words that accompany the salute?

D'ARTHEZ: That shouldn't have happened, something like that should not overtake an actor. But you see, I was born in Dresden, and in my excitement the inborn melody of our dialect asserted itself. There, that shows how sincere I was. And even if it was improper from the point of view of good acting, nevertheless it proves that the whole German people stand behind the Führer, even a Saxon.

QUESTION: Do you have any doubts about the way we stage elections?

D'ARTHEZ: There is no room for doubt, and by now everyone knows it.

QUESTION: Are you aware that you are playing for your own head now?

D'ARTHEZ: For my own head. That will be a new role for me. It will take a great deal of rehearsing.
QUESTION: That will do.

Lambert slapped his headless dressmaker's dummy on the shoulder and asked, "Isn't it true, love, that *will* do?"

That really will do. Anything else will be complications.

COMPLICATIONS

How did it happen that a man reported exactly twelve hours earlier than programmed for his negation? In order to avoid such occurrences in the future, which are quite unpleasant for all concerned, we deem it necessary, if not our duty, to report this case at some length.

First and foremost, we mean to demonstrate conclusively that the fault lies not with the man summoned, a man who had previously spoken of himself in the first person, if without much enthusiasm—simply because it is customary. On the contrary, he had often been aware of being on the point of slapping himself on the back and addressing himself in the second-person familiar. "There you are, old fellow," or whatever it is you say in the circumstances. Now that would have been an altogether imprudent gesture, easily interpreted as an admission of guilt. It was only after the event we are dealing with here that the first-person singular no longer seemed to him the appropriate costume. For this reason he provisionally started using the third person. "He," in other words. Provisionally.

The man summoned was neither a fool nor illiterate. He was registered with the police and paid his income tax punctually. He was in his prime, as the saying goes; somewhere in his early forties, as a guess. As everyone knows, once a man receives his summons, the years no longer count. Had he not a mere five or six months before sat at his dying wife's bedside?

She had taken an overdose of sleeping pills, yet not enough to prevent the medical profession, those incorrigible romantics, from employing all manner of efforts at resuscitation. And then he dozed off on the chair next to her bed. Admittedly, these are personal matters that can carry no weight in an objective investigation of this case. They are only brought up here to underline the fact that the man summoned was no village idiot.

That it was not an oversight on his part can be legally proven beyond the shadow of a doubt. Psychoanalysis, too, will endorse this verdict. This is emphasized so strongly because the opposite may appear to be the case, that he did in fact commit the oversight. Consider, for instance, that the regular printed notice was delivered to him today immediately after his afternoon nap.

Everyone knows that after his afternoon nap a man is not at the height of his intellectual powers and that this can lead to errors of judgment. Recent research has advised that one try to live with the fatigue rather than sleep after lunch. Whether this would prevent errors of judgment remains to be proven. Statisticians argue it both ways. In the meantime, everyone reacts the same when the doorbell rings immediately after he wakes up. One thinks, What son-of-a-bitch has the nerve at this hour of the day . . . Let the bastard ring till he's blue in the face! Nonetheless, one jumps up—and his stomach does a flip. Quite literally, and that's critical. One runs his fingers through his hair and stumbles through the room, bumping into the leg of a chair or the corner of a table, and curses life. When one has finally made it to the front door, one throws it open spoiling for trouble, ready to tell off whoever rang.

But then who should be standing there in the obscurity of the stairwell but a very courteous young man—perhaps a student working part-time for the post office or some messenger service for a little extra money. With an embarrassed smile, he hands one a letter. At the same time he presents a receipt and a ball-point pen to sign with. For it is a fact proven by experience that in such moments one never has a pen handy and much time is wasted in hunting for one. So one clears one's throat and says: Thank you very much. And pointing to the receipt, asks, Here? and signs on the dotted line, using the jamb for a writing surface. All the while, the young man observes one with large and rather frightened eyes. Yes, that's a fact! But do these illegible signatures that one scribbles standing have any legal validity whatsoever? What would happen if later one were to claim that this was not one's signature? In such a case, the young man would have to swear to the execution of the signature, and no one willingly swears to anything.

One doesn't even slam the door after the young man as one had planned. On the contrary, as soon as the lock catches, it strikes one that one should have had a tip handy. BY EXPRESS MESSENGER! MESSENGER PAID! Now, how much can he possibly be paid? So one opens the door again and steps out into the hall and leans over the banisters and shouts, Hey! Too late! Neither on the third floor nor on the stairs below is the young man to be seen or heard. He must wear tennis shoes and take the steps two or three at a time. The downstairs door did not even slam behind him. But then there's a pneumatic device to break the momentum. Too bad, one would have gladly given the young fellow something. Can he have wings? He must have to get away this fast. Well, after all, *express* messenger . . .

As for the letter, one tosses it unopened on the table and walks to the kitchen alcove first to put on water for some coffee. Then to the toilet. That is only routine. Even a letter delivered by express messenger can change nothing here. Such a letter is particularly incapable of doing so. For experience teaches that the writer alone imagines that his letter inspires haste; he counts on the red sticker next to the address to upset the receiver. And to top it off, the sender's name can be discovered only by opening the letter. What presumption! Why, that way anybody could get into the act . . . And PERSONAL! That's written diagonally across the left-hand corner in caps.

That is the way it happened this time too. Neither making coffee nor going to the toilet led to the oversight. At fault was the manner in which the time was indicated on the notice, and any doubt of this is out of the question.

Intrinsically, this was no different from any other summons anywhere that anyone can receive at any hour of the day or night—thus, nothing out of the ordinary or world-shaking. Formerly this was handled in a different manner; but this concerns us all the less, since the badly preserved texts that handle the subject describe it in such obscure poetic imagery that even scholars are no longer in a position to interpret them. In any event, the absence of system seems to have led to such imprecision that the whole world was on the verge of revolution. Anyone who is interested in this need only turn to the archives and read the letters that our outraged grandfathers and great-grandfathers wrote their newspapers.

Fortunately, the proper institution duly made up its mind to rationalize its operation in keeping with modern demands. Nonetheless, many improvements can still be imagined, simplifications that would do away with a certain amount of red tape. Take the wholly superfluous printing of PERSONAL with an exclamation mark; even if it should turn out to be nothing more than a joke hoary with custom, it might still be dispensed with in good conscience. The express-messenger service too, with the time-consuming receipt, one can only regard as prehistoric. Why not a simple announcement in the newspaper or on the radio? It is of consequence to us all that this business be carried out matter-of-factly and without a trace of sentimentality.

Would anyone dare imagine that a system obviously governed by the latest electronic devices could print the wrong time on its official notices? Or, not to be so childish as to reproach the system with mistakes, who nowadays could suspect programmers of such romanticism?

As already mentioned, the usual gray card with punches along the sides. Good durable paper, so the punches won't tear as the card runs through the system. Even the color gray must have some technical explanation. And the printed text runs, as usual:

> Receiver of this card will kindly report on the . . . at . . . to the branch of the WOWIPLIN indicated below for his negation.
> This card must be presented as identification.
> In order to avoid complications, the precise adherence to the above-mentioned summons is urgently requested.
> WOWIPLIN
——— Branch

Very well. The WorldWide Planning Institute requests your presence for negation. That's scarcely exciting. Some people react with a simple "Well, finally!"

The man who had just gotten up from his afternoon nap blew on his coffee and looked at his watch.

The date given was the next day. What date? October, November, December or even January? How quickly we forget dates! In short, he must report the next day. And the hour was 1:04. Why 1:04? Why not rounded off to one o'clock or at the least to 1:05? But as you wish, Lord System! I shall not be found wanting.

And as for the branch in question, it is well known. But what city was it? A few points bring Wiesbaden somewhat uncertainly to mind, the Wilhelmstrasse with the park across the street. But there must be hundreds of towns like that. A neighborhood's dogs and cats stick so firmly in the memory that we could easily pick up our conversations with them to this day, but what town the neighborhood belonged to has been swept from our minds. Nor is it the least bit important.

Of importance alone is the time of day: 1:04. The man summoned sips his hot coffee cautiously. To avoid coffee spots on his trousers. Otherwise, there they go to the cleaner's again.

1:04. That is still more than nine hours away. His watch is a trifle fast, it gains approximately five minutes a month. But as a known quantity, that can be taken into account. All the same, it is better to be on the early side than risk being late. One can wait awhile outside.

1:04. In other words, one hour and four minutes after midnight. The man who received this card grew up during the days when one still spoke of three o'clock, five o'clock in the afternoon, before the introduction of the twenty-four-hour method of reckoning time that has been in fashion on the Continent for decades now. In the beginning, purely acoustical similarities caused him a few embarrassing mistakes. He once mistook fifteen for five, and another time he appeared at a reception given at 17:00 two hours too late, at 7:00 in the evening, long after the reception was over, the buffet eaten up. Since then he has added or subtracted with pedantic precision, and nothing like that has happened since.

It would be ludicrous to suspect so modern, so exemplary an institution as WOWIPLIN of working with obsolete methods of indicating time when all schedules, programs, college catalogues, the hours of shops and religious services are announced according to the twenty-four-hour system. If the summons had been meant for the next afternoon, it would have read 13:04. This did not even require consideration.

Add to this a psychological factor. An hour and four minutes after midnight is a suitable hour at which to report for such an act. While a call for lunchtime compels the person affected to stand up from the table and apologize to the other diners:

Please don't let me disturb you. I have to put in an appearance across the way. Enjoy your meal! No, that would be absurd.

1:04 then. What does a man do with approximately nine hours on his hands? The rent for this more or less furnished room is paid up, and besides, the management company demands a deposit of two months' rent. Well, may they enjoy it. The cleaning woman who will come on Friday will find her regular pay on the table so that she won't have come all that way for nothing. She depends on this job, since she bought a TV set on installments. But isn't there some laundry to pick up? In which jacket pocket is the red-brown receipt hiding? Every time one has the same annoyance with the thing. Yes, and what does one wear on such an occasion? A dark suit is not exactly obligatory, but these unpressed flannels and the comfortable old tweed jacket . . . No, that won't do. On the other hand, one must avoid any semblance of solemnity. So let us have that dark gray suit which is never out of place, always proper and unobtrusive. It looks freshly ironed too.

Yes, what does one do? Naturally, one goes to the movies. And naturally the film is full of sex, that can be counted on. Rather boring in the long run, because this isn't the way things happen; yet, meanwhile, one can peacefully plot out his own more interesting film.

Well, there's the word "complications," for instance. That would do wonderfully as a title. In the summons, we read "to avoid complications," and so on! What sort of complications can they be? And for whom? For the institute, or for the man summoned? Yes, even the fact that the possibility of complications is reckoned with should be most instructive.

In the literature devoted to the subject, such cases do appear even in antiquity. People seem to have actually taken a certain pleasure, perhaps a malicious joy in the misfortunes of others, in recounting these cases over and over—and in listening to them. That individuals should have here and there revolted against the summons cannot be doubted, but we would like to know how the authorities of the time dealt with them. And it is precisely this that the similes, metaphors and adjectives conceal. For that they did deal with these heroes, as they were often termed, is proven by the course of history, which did not allow of any deviation by a few cries of protest. As far as we know.

But that is literature and an affair for linguists. Meanwhile, before the summoned man's eyes a highly artificial film, passed by the censor as Worthwhile, unwound its flashy sexual imagery, while the man played out his own realistic film entitled "Complications."

Perhaps it began this way: an ordinary modern man, scarcely a prominent personality, receives a summons, the usual gray card. Nothing could be further from this ordinary modern man's mind than revolt or similar exertions, but let us assume that he simply does not see any reason for changing his way of life just for the sake of this stupid card. That would be realistic. So he tears the card to pieces—SCRITCH–SCRATCH!—Sound, please!—and throws them in the trash. CUT TO: Scraps of paper flying into trash can. At the same time we hear the man say—but without emphasis, just his ordinary tone of voice, matter of factly: "They can kiss my . . ." Very realistic.

And then the man goes to his favorite bar. Change of scene. The owner behind the bar greets him with "Evening, Mr. X." And the waitress asks with a teasing wink, "The wife still out of town?" Realistic in the extreme, yes, one could say it's *contemporary*, for the ordinary modern man's wife happens to have gone to East Germany to visit relatives. The guys he plays poker with are already shuffling the cards.

CUT TO: A round of poker. Keep this short; what's there to see, really? The director should suppress any ideas about having our hero draw the ace of spades. That is corny. Contemporary audiences won't tolerate hackneyed symbols. They are only interested in the gamut of possibilities presented by the cards in his hand.

All this is just the overture. Naturally one can bring a few women into it, as many as one wants. For instance, the waitress can rub her breasts and her hips up against our poker player every time she brings someone at the table a beer. Admittedly this isn't sex and it needn't lead to complications, but it's realistic all the same and therefore belongs in the overture.

Yes, and finally we reach the complications, since that's what the film is about. Well, what happens really? What means would be chosen for dealing with an ordinary modern man who has thrown his card into a trash can and prefers to play poker? One can't bring in a nondescript fellow behind our poker player and have him tap him on the shoulder. Impossible. "Sir, would you mind stepping outside . . ." That would be the sort of film they made in grandpa's time. But how are such cases dealt with nowadays? Surely with the greatest tact, so as to avoid any stir. Above all, no hysteria! Could there be some sort of Security Police? And what authority is actually vested in this police? There is nothing about it in the constitution. Not a word about complications, and that's the point here.

The film could be organized in a totally different fashion, taking off from the scene in the film actually on the screen where the heroine tumbles around in bed so indefatigably with her boyfriend. How would it be if at this very moment the boyfriend were to receive that summons? You can't put that past the WorldWide Planning Institute! The doorbell rings, etc. In the meantime, the heroine sits on the edge of the bed. Give her time to slip on a negligee before she's caught by the merciless eye of the camera. We can assume that she takes a cigarette from the bedside table, lights it, and after the third drag thinks, Oh what's the use? I had better start looking for a new boyfriend. That would be realistic. Yet perhaps that is too realistic. Does everything we think between the lines, as it were, have to be photographed too?

Fortunately the lights go up at this moment, the film is over. There are still a couple of hours to kill, but that doesn't leave enough to work out the whole script. So he finds a little hash house and has a beer with a sausage sandwich. That can easily be stretched to last until almost 1:04. And then one goes home to change in peace and quiet.

What does one do in these hours in which one is waiting? Nothing any different from usual. Let's get down to business! At ten minutes to one, the summoned man leaves the house. Fourteen minutes gives him sufficient leeway. He crosses the main street against the light and walks casually through the Kurpark. Casually if only not to disturb the couples on their benches. On a delicate wooden bridge that spans the arm of a pond he even stopped a moment because a duck had quacked in the reeds. Was that in Wiesbaden, then? Is there a pond in a Kurpark in Wiesbaden, and ducks on that pond? What's the difference, all over the world ducks quack and no one knows why.

Nonetheless, he was a minute or two early and therefore waited a moment in the rim of darkness at the other side of the Kurpark observing the Institute's building. Lord, what a ritzy palace! During the day one didn't notice it, one passed by it a hundred times, but at night, when they have it all floodlit . . . In style a structure of the 1890s or a few years earlier. The driveway is even bordered with flowers, among which the floodlights are concealed. A tremendous terraced flight of at least six staircases covers half the façade. And over the main entrance an enormous portico having two great columns. Everything in readiness for the welcoming of princes. Whoever occupied this house had to be a millionaire.

How could the poor fellow have lived in such a place? Who

nowadays would be able to manage or even to heat these great rooms with their high ceilings? As a matter of fact, only the city can pay the bill. And even for the city it would be more economical to tear the monstrosity down and put up a building several stories higher.

What activity on the steps! From both sides of the drive, people stream uninterruptedly, hesitantly climb the steps, a card in their hands that they show the doorman, who motions them to the revolving door with a haughty nod of his head. The revolving door never stops, its glass partitions reflect the floodlights in repeated slices. Of course a fat doorman was standing there in his gray uniform as near as one could make out in such light. And a big gray hotel umbrella was leaning against one of the columns. They think of everything. Would one have thought it possible? Just at that moment a dark limousine pulled up, the chauffeur jumped out and ran across to open the door for an elderly lady and helped her out of the car. She thanked him with a nod of her head and tripped gracefully up the steps, felt in her handbag for the card that she showed with an imploring smile to the fat doorman. He almost stood at attention! He even helped her with the revolving door; by slightly braking it, he prevented the lady from being tossed into the room on the other side. Nothing can beat the old school and a true lady's smile.

Had the appointed time come? The man who had been summoned looked at his watch. At that moment a low friendly voice asked close beside him, "Can I be of any assistance?" A very young man, as young as the express messenger of the day before, had stepped noiselessly from the bushes to offer his assistance. What service!

"No, thank you. I can manage very well alone," the summoned man answered; taking the card from his breast pocket, he waved it at the young man, then headed for the Institute.

Obviously, the fat doorman did not snap to attention as he passed.

A gigantic reception room with paneling, marble floors and a coffered ceiling. Oh well, what would you expect? Reception was to the right, but of course there was a line, so naturally one took one's place and waited one's turn without any shoving. When our new arrival turned around to look, there was already someone behind him, and two persons ahead of him he recognized the lady who had come by limousine. She gently fanned herself with her card, but that was nothing more than a lady-like gesture, for the reception room enjoyed a pleasantly neutral temperature. Presumably, air-conditioned. And how hushed all noises seemed. Actually nothing was audible but a woman's voice repeating with listless regularity, "Next, please!" Or was it taped? For obviously the people standing in line would not be chatting with each other; they merely kept their eyes open so as to make no mistakes.

Not that anyone need be afraid that he might do something wrong. All one need do was what the person ahead had done, and everything worked like clockwork. One placed one's card on the table and when it was one's own turn shoved it to the young woman, who checked the date and time, stamped it and shoved it back. Then one moved on to the next official, who took the card and stuck it in a pneumatic dispatching tube in exchange for a number that she tore from a numbering machine. This second official was the one who kept things moving with her "Next, please!"

One could not help feeling sorry for those two girls. The first was a little brunette, a young thing; the second, a blonde with bags under her eyes and her mouth screwed up. Both of them wore rather becoming smocks, but what good was that when their work exhausted them so?

But the little brunette discovered the oversight immediately.

Our man shoved his card toward her just as the man ahead of him had done. She looked it over hurriedly and returned it unstamped. What's up? Why isn't it stamped? Are there several forms of clearance here? But the little brunette was already stamping the card of the man behind him and all he could do was allow himself to be pushed along by the line.

The second, the blonde, threw the card angrily in the out basket, punched a button and spoke into a microphone: "These eternal intellectuals!"

"Now wait a minute," our man wanted to protest, but she was already saying "Next, please!" Insulted and without a number, he was pushed along in line. And indeed almost as far as a railing, where a turnstile regulated the flow. There one turned in one's number and was allowed through. The turnstile made a slight click each time, which indicated that it too was counting as a further precaution. Still smiling in a ladylike manner, the limousine arrival had just passed through, to vanish into the endless corridors on the other side. And our man would have found it his turn if a nice-looking young man had not stepped up to him and said, "Would you be so good as to take a seat over there. Our chief of protocol will be here in a moment."

"That person over there . . ." the man began, and jerked his thumb over his shoulder at the blonde. But the young man pleaded: "Please be patient for a moment longer. The chief of protocol will certainly arrange matters suitably." And it was more his embarrassed look that silenced the man than his words.

Very well, very well. Let's wait for the chief of protocol. There was certainly space enough for waiting. Even overstuffed chairs and coffee tables. But the man chose to spend his time examining the pictures that hung on the walls. All of them beautiful posters mounted and framed, famous sites from all over the world, very artistic reproductions. Hun barrows surrounded by woods, so poetic. "Jutland" was printed below, aha. And next to that a shot of the three celebrated pyramids. Obviously, they could not be omitted. For all lovers of sun and southern countries. And then another swing to the north. Some sort of memorial cross, badly weathered but the ornamentation clearly Celtic. Nowhere but Ireland . . . Barren hills, an estuary, low fishing huts with roofs of thatch. A stormy region. But once again the air grows warmer. "Caecilia Metella" is printed below: a tomb. Something for the art historian. And following that, it's warmer still, and another woman's sepulcher. The Taj Mahal or something like that, a sort of mosque. An expensive affair. A king is said to have built it for his beloved. And to provide a little variety, and this time not just for the ladies, a hill with palms and exotic greenery. "Towers of Silence" reads the inscription. An agreeable designation, but due to all the greenery, one sees little of the towers; one sees swarms of vultures. Brrr. Fortunately, next to this hangs a winter landscape in Upper Bavaria well known from Christmas cards. The cemetery wall with its gate prettily arched, and behind it the church in Ramsau with its onion domes, deep snow everywhere, very soulful. All this gives one the urge to travel. One would really like to run to the reception desk and reserve a seat on the next plane. And what with those onion-domed towers, the next picture will doubtless be Lenin's tomb with the Kremlin in the background. Well, one can't see everything, and besides, there is no time for that now.

"Mr. X, if I am not mistaken?" this man avid for culture hears himself addressed. Now that is really the most astonishing thing of all. In spite of this summons, he is being addressed by the name that he left behind in his apartment once and for all. Aha, the fellow standing there behind him has the unstamped gray card in his hand. That's how he knows the name. Chief of protocol? Don't make me laugh! House detective and nothing more. Perhaps he has a revolver in his hip pocket or under his left armpit. It doesn't show. Double-breasted blue suit, perfect fit. Proper. So proper one feels like a factory hand just looking at him. And myopic of course, which explains the horn-rimmed glasses. "Aha, so there you are," says the man who was waiting for clearance. He doesn't really know what one ought to say to such a proper suit. "Pretty pictures you have here . . ."

The fellow doesn't bat an eyelash, the horn-rimmed glasses remain as proper as before. He speaks as though reciting from memory. Every dialectical objection dies in one's throat. One is in the wrong before one has even begun.

"I have been assigned the task of imploring you to pardon the regrettable incident that has come to the ears of the management. Our young ladies have received the strictest instructions to refrain from critical expressions. In our training program this is drummed into all of them. But in an undertaking of this magnitude and under conditions of overwork it can occasionally happen that a newcomer loses her self-control and allows purely personal reactions to crop up. Naturally I will relay your justified complaints if you feel strongly in the matter."

"Thank you very much, sir. We don't wish the poor girl any harm. A snippy answer more or less, what's the difference? So, what about my card and me?"

"We deeply regret to inform you, Mr. X, that you have answered our call twelve hours too soon."

"I . . . What have I done?"

"You were requested to report at 1:04."

"Well? I arrived right on time. My watch is correct, I set it by the radio. Here, see for yourself."

"No one doubts the accuracy of your watch, sir. But unfortunately you did not notice that you were scheduled for this coming afternoon."

"For this coming afternoon? But it says . . . Here, show me the card."

"The card reads 1:04 in the afternoon."

"Now will you tell me how one of us is supposed to figure *that* out?"

"If we mean *night*, the system prints NIGHT after the time."

"Why, it takes your breath away. Forgive me, sir. That is the purest romanticism. Then the occurrence of such oversights can scarcely astonish you."

"We do not reckon with the *possibility* of oversights. Why, our system . . ."

"Your system can . . . But why should we get excited? Twelve hours, you say? Very well, I'll take my card, please."

"Sorry, that is impossible."

"Oh, just you leave it to me! Twelve hours? That's a snap. Imagine, young man, some of us have held out for twelve long years, and they were hopeless years, I can assure you of that. So, my card, please, I shall not be found wanting. Shall we synchronize our watches?"

"That card is no longer valid, Mr. X, and it will have to be returned to Programming."

"What a lot of bother! Then you can give me another card. I will sit here or look at the pictures. I can even smoke if all those ashtrays are to be believed. And within twelve hours your organization will have been able to turn out a new card."

"If you will allow me to interrupt, I think you should know that you must be *re*programmed."

"Program me as much as you please. As you see, I'm not making a fuss. Between us, it's all the same to me. Very well, I wait here until noon, and that's that."

"Please, Mr. X, you still do not appear to grasp the situation. These chairs are meant for those who have arrived in too great a hurry and now must wait for their appointed times. We take this into our calculations. But in your case—that is to say, when there is absolutely no fixed time—you find us totally unprepared."

305

"Absolutely none? Can you call twelve hours an *absolutely* unfixed time?"

"All your data must be reprocessed. I am no technician, but I would assume that, after reprogramming, 1:04 in the afternoon will not come out a second time. No matter how regrettable we may find it, Mr. X, until you receive further notice, you are a free man."

"I am . . . What did you say I am?"

"Right this way, please!"

And as a matter of fact, the fellow was maneuvering this man who had to be reprogrammed toward the revolving door. What could he do?

"A free man, you say? How do you mean that?"

"Forgive me, sir, but that is of no concern to the Institute. But in case you need to reorient yourself to the condition, we have a guest house. One of our young men will show you in."

And in fact one of them was standing there. The information system that produces these young people out of thin air whenever they are needed must be far superior to any system of ours. For the fellow didn't lift a finger. Then he made a slight bow and said, "Au revoir, Mr. X." It was not ironical. What sort of protocol would they have if the chief of protocol allowed himself a hint of irony?

But he was still standing there to make sure that the man they had to reprogram did not try to sneak back in line with those waiting for clearance. The revolving door's regular flashes reflected in the round glasses he wore and the woman's voice called out in the same tempo, "Next, please!"

Yes, and if one no longer belonged among the next, what then?

"Left to the guest house, please," said the young man.

"Oho, the guest house, is it? I suppose one can sleep there."

"Our beds are good. They're clean."

"You sleep there too?"

"We receive our assignments. Mine is to accompany you to the guest house."

All right, my friend, if you're trained not to talk, then carry out your assignment. And there they were at the guest house already.

At least the place gave a more up-to-date impression. Bungalow-style. Windows close together. Probably very small rooms.

"Here you are, sir," said the young man, holding the door open. And he was gone. His assignment carried out. Should one have given him a tip? One always wonders about this too late. Not a very impressive entrance hall. Nothing more than a narrow corridor from the door to the stairs. So as not to waste an inch, probably. And tucked back under the stairs was the porter's lodge. Or was it a broom closet? Where did they hang their keys? Did no one lock his room here?

A gentleman was sitting there with his back to the door reading. He hadn't bothered to take off his hat, a dark homburg. He was so absorbed in his book that he did not notice the new arrival. When he turned a page, one heard a rustle.

Finally the newcomer cleared his throat. In any situation, clearing one's throat will serve to make an initial contact.

And the gentleman stood up at once and closed the book, using his index finger as a bookmark. And of course he took off his hat. He really was a gentleman. Scarcely to be believed. A black jacket, gray vest and good striped trousers. What was a diplomat doing in this guest house?

"Would you by any chance have a cigarette?" he asked. "Ah, thank you. I must have left mine lying in the dressing room, I was in such a hurry."

"You live here?" asked the newcomer.

"I? Do I look as though I am entitled to a pension?"

"Excuse me . . ."

"Oh, don't be taken in by my clothes. I'm only trying to give the press the slip. Those people always ask such impossible

307

questions. I see you do not smoke filter cigarettes either . . ."

"No, that would be cheating, wouldn't it? Either/or."

"Yes, you could call it cheating. That's why I made my escape direct from the stage to this place. Through the basement of the theater, past the furnace and all sorts of properties. You have to know the way, it's a bit different in each house. I do this in every town. No one thinks of looking for you here. That would never occur to the press. Naturally I rip off the mustache I wear on stage."

He pulled a clipped English mustache out of his vest pocket, looked at it and then let it fall into a bucket standing in the broom closet.

"The glue only lasts for one performance," the fine gentleman said as he rubbed his thumb and index finger together— some glue had stuck there. "My luggage is already at the station. I leave on an early train. That is another trick of mine. Yes, it's more pleasant waiting in such an establishment as this than in the waiting room. Someone must have left this book here. Do you know it?"

"Can anyone still read that?"

"*Illusions Perdues.* The title is a bit crude, I agree. But usually books are not left lying around here, believe me. I get around quite a bit, relatively speaking. Here today, gone tomorrow, as it always is when one goes on tour."

"Are you an intellectual?" the newcomer asked.

"Did they call you that?" the fine gentleman asked by way of reply.

"Yes, they threw me out." And the newcomer told his story: the oversight with the time, what the girl had said, the pictures in the entrance hall, the proper behavior of the chief of protocol; he did not even leave out the incident with the old lady who smiled, the one who had come by limousine. This lady seemed particularly to please this fine gentleman; he showed his approval with a nod of the head.

"So now I am free, they tell me," said the newcomer by way of a conclusion and sat down on the chair on which the fine gentleman had been sitting. "If you will permit me. I feel *empty*."

"Catch your breath then. It took me three months to get used to it," said the fine gentleman compassionately.

"Were you thrown out too?"

"You could say that. The methods then in use were different, not so proper as you describe. Maybe you won't believe it, but I was given a kick in the pants and stumbled out into freedom, as they call it. My feelings were terribly hurt. They wanted to shoot me or hang me, nothing unusual in itself. I said, 'Gentlemen, please,' and screwed my eyes shut tight, as one ought to do. Instead, the idiots began to laugh and one shouted, 'Oh, go to the devil!' To this day I don't know what I did wrong. Why, they even called me by my first name, if you can imagine that! And then that kick in the pants! I have worn this lovely costume ever since. I do have a time explaining to my tailor. You see, I can never admit to him that precisely this suit prevents anyone from ever calling me by my first name again. Not to mention being kicked in the pants. He had much rather see me go on stage in a uniform, as a colonel or even a general. But what sort of role would that be? Anyone would see through that in a second. Forgive me for speaking of my tailor. You bought that suit in a store, I can see."

"Yes, just a few alterations. Not at all expensive. If you will forgive my saying so, at the moment this strikes me as totally irrelevant."

"Marvelous! No wonder they threw you out. You look so unobtrusive. That is a difficult role to play. The most difficult role of all, congratulations. Wouldn't you enjoy transmitting information? No authorities and no computer could ever conclude that you transmitted messages. I know something about theater, the role is cut out for you."

309

This man who had been singled out to transmit information declined with a tired gesture.

"That may all be fine and dandy, thank you. But as you seem to know your way around here better than I, perhaps you could tell me if there isn't a register one must sign. Or at least a form to fill out for the police."

Now it was the fine gentleman's turn to show astonishment. "Don't tell me you still have a name to register!" he exclaimed.

"There, you're right again," the other sighed. "Isn't it miserable!"

"Not at all. There will be a name for you. Excuse me for not introducing myself at once. This suit counsels reticence, you understand. My style, if you please. My name is d'Arthez. I found it in that book there, but please do not be alarmed; the critics have long since grown accustomed to it. I took this name immediately after that kick in the pants, as it seemed to go with these clothes. The principal characters in the book have long since been forgotten: ministers, generals, writers and the like. All the celebrities have been programmed in advance by history and afterward we can do nothing with those names. But d'Arthez lives. He was not in on anything back then; he refused to play ball, he worked; he waited and kept silent, and that's why he is still alive. No one knows his whereabouts, just as in the old days. All anyone knew was that he existed and what his name was, but because he kept to the sidelines and didn't say anything, they couldn't get their teeth in him. A terrible nuisance. Just like today. But a name is necessary just to lead them astray. Yes, how would Lembke do for you? The name does not appear in that book, but no matter. Ludwig Lembke, for instance. But not for you to write it down *here*, for God's sake! No, just so you'll have one. The name suits the clothes you wear. No one would ever suspect a Ludwig Lembke of transmitting information."

"Lembke! Lembke?" The once-summoned man tried out his name.

"That is only a suggestion, Herr Lembke. Perhaps we will think of something better."

"On the contrary, the name strikes me as strangely familiar."

"You see? Naturally it will make people laugh, but that is a real advantage. And here and there at night someone will ask himself, Why does this Lembke let people laugh at him? Oh, forgive me, I must be getting to the station. Why don't you walk part of the way with me? We are going in the same direction. Oh yes, the book. Let us just leave it lying. That too is a sort of message."

So the two of them walked together back through the park. The benches were empty. The air had grown too chill for loving couples. But the duck was still quacking in the reeds as the two of them walked over the wooden bridge.

From the city—from what city, please?—one of the young express messengers came toward them. Clearly he had just completed one assignment and was eagerly rushing on to the next. But to the fine gentleman named d'Arthez it seemed a good joke to stretch out his left arm to block the young man from passing on this narrow bridge.

The messenger made no attempt to push the obstacle aside; he tried to smile, and that was scarcely bearable.

"No offense, Herr d'Arthez," he finally whispered.

Imagine this: a park late at night or early in the morning and one of these young messengers saying, "No offense." No, that cannot be imagined. It was simply unbearable.

"Another young man in a hurry," d'Arthez mumbled to himself.

"How did he know your name?"

"From the billboards, I'd guess. They haven't pasted over yesterday's posters yet."

For such a fine gentleman, his manner was rather diffident. So the two of them walked along together in silence, and leaving the park, they reached the main street. What main street, please? Yet, without a second's hesitation, they both turned left. Toward the station. Which way the station lies, everyone always knows, it's in our blood. And if this were Wiesbaden, then the next large cross street would be the Rheinstrasse. Wasn't there a museum on the other side? But what does that prove? In every town there is a museum, lions carved in colorful marble, and green sphinxes too. Those are symbols, we are told. On their way home, schoolchildren climb shouting over the backs of these symbols until the doorman chases them away. Herr d'Arthez stops and listens all around him. What does he listen for? "I am quite tired. Do excuse me. I will sleep in the train and that will do until my next performance. Very well, Herr Lembke. It was a great pleasure. You will soon get used to that name. And as for information . . ." Once again he listened all around him. "Oh yes, I am a bit melancholy. That does not suit the part I play, but we have no audience at the moment. These overly eager children make me melancholy. Not because they are in such a hurry, that is part of one's last year in school or one's first semesters at the university, it's no cause for melodramatic concern. But the way these young people are exploited and chased about with absurd assignments because they are so polite and tactful, and all this only because the stupid computers can't take care of people in a hurry, that . . . that . . . !"

D'Arthez shook his fist threateningly in the direction of the WorldWide Planning Institute, but in a moment he was in control once more.

"Forgive that pathetic gesture. And besides, a museum with sphinxes for a backdrop! The public would be shocked. A gentleman as finely dressed as this does not shake his fist at anyone. And who is he threatening, after all? Isn't he threatening

312

us? Most of them would laugh. Almost all of them would laugh. Only a few. Only one perhaps. We need transmitters of information who know how to hold their tongues. Au revoir, Herr Lembke. Ah, there it goes! Did you hear? I must run now . . ."

Noble and upright in bearing, he walked away in the direction of the station. And from three or four streets away, one could hear the noise of garbage collection. Like thunder the trash cans were hung on the great revolving drum, and like thunder the trash cans were set down empty on the paving.

And that demonstrates best of all that this did not have to be Wiesbaden. For in every town the day begins with the noise of garbage collection.